Daniel Ellis

Thrilling Adventures of Daniel Ellis

Daniel Ellis

Thrilling Adventures of Daniel Ellis

ISBN/EAN: 9783337341985

Printed in Europe, USA, Canada, Australia, Japan

Cover: Foto ©Andreas Hilbeck / pixelio.de

More available books at **www.hansebooks.com**

THRILLING ADVENTURES

OF

DANIEL ELLIS,

THE GREAT UNION GUIDE OF EAST TENNESSEE FOR A PERIOD
OF NEARLY FOUR YEARS DURING THE GREAT
SOUTHERN REBELLION.

WRITTEN BY HIMSELF.

Containing a Short Biography of the Author.

"How use doth breed a habit in a man!
This shadowy desert, unfrequented woods,
I better brook than flourishing peopled towns:
Here can I sit alone, unseen of any,
And to the nightingale's complaining notes
Tune my distresses and record my woes."
Two Gentlemen of Verona.

With Illustrations.

NEW YORK:

HARPER & BROTHERS, PUBLISHERS,

FRANKLIN SQUARE.

1867.

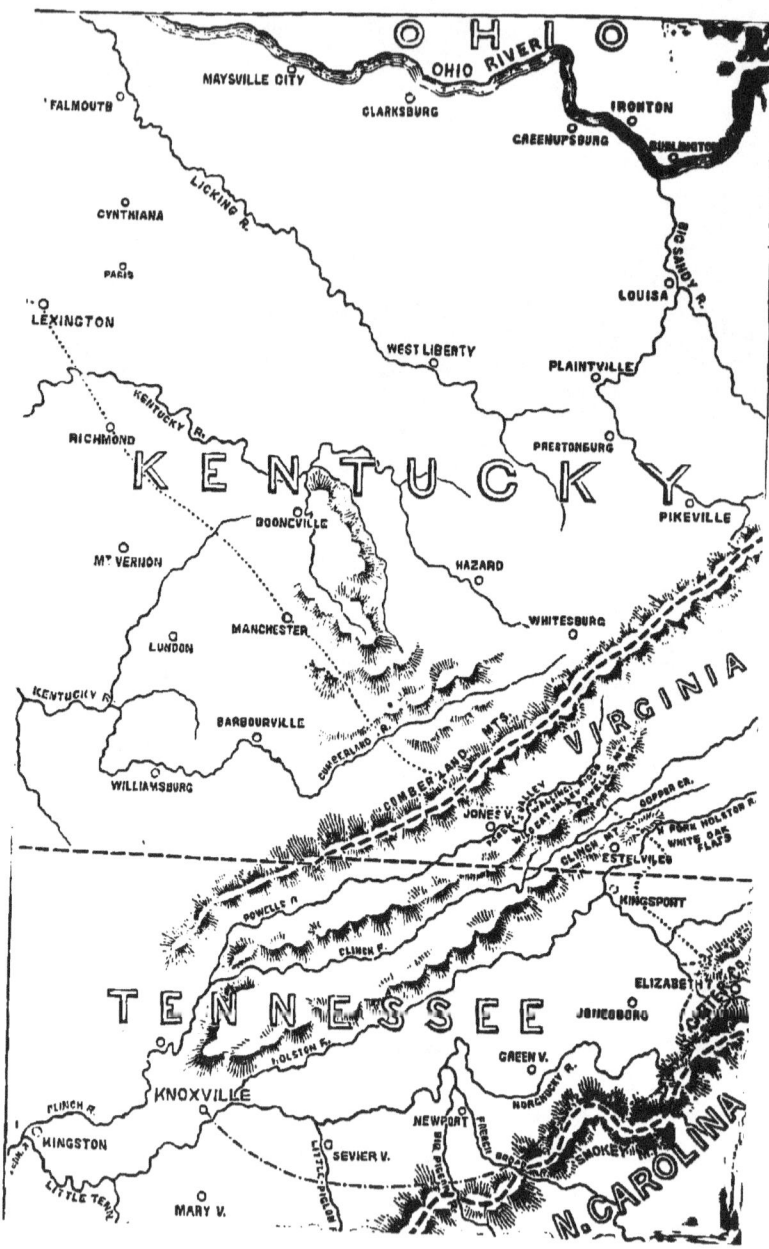

MAP OF TRAIL OVER THE MOUNTAINS

AUTOBIOGRAPHY.

In commencing this volume, I would remark that I feel very sensibly my inadequacy in appearing before the public in the capacity of an author, as I shall not presume to present any claim to those literary accomplishments which are usually boasted of by writers who are distinguished for elegance and refinement in composition. My education is not of that order which would justify such an assumption, and, therefore, I shall here lay no claim to profound acquisitions either in literature or natural science which I am conscious I do not possess. The only advantages in learning which I can boast of are those which are generally obtained in the "*old field school-house*," where it is well known by all who have been initiated into the first elements of education at that sacred retreat of boyhood, that the student is scarcely ever annoyed with the intricate problems of Euclid or Hutton, nor his mind enlightened with the rich versification of Homer, of Virgil, or of Horace, nor perplexed with the logical subtleties of Socrates, of Plato, or of Aristotle. Instead of rummaging into volumes of *black-letter lore*, the student is only required to seek for the attainment of proficiency in the ordinary branches of English education; and all the acquirements which I pretend to claim are based alone upon the common branches of English learning.

I have thought it necessary to make these prefatory remarks, so that those who may peruse the pages of this volume may not indulge the expectation of being feasted at all times upon the bright and beautiful scintillations of genius, but, on the contrary, I would urge them to expect nothing more than a faithful detail of my adventures for *a period of nearly four years*, written out in plain style, and unadorned with any unbecoming and fanciful flowers of rhetoric. And, what I consider very important, I will here assure all those who may give this volume a perusal, that they may rest certain they will find no incident herein contained, be it ever so thrilling and horrible, as to challenge the veracity of the writer or the unbelief of the reader, but what is strictly founded upon the eternal structure of *reality* and *truth!* I hope the reader will here indulge a short digression, while I give a very limited biography of myself, which I hope may be acceptable. I shall not annoy the reader with a recapitulation of any miraculous achievements on my part which would for a moment subject me to a charge of attempting *self-praise;* but believing that the public might probably be desirous of knowing something in regard to my previous life, has induced me to give a short history in allusion to it.

I was born on the 30th day of December, 1827, in Carter County, Tennessee, amid whose lofty and majestic mountains I have passed my life up to the present time. I was born to no proud titles or estates. The curse which was placed upon Adam, amid the delightful shades

and fragrant groves of Paradise, when he was told by his
Maker, that "in the sweat of thy face shalt thou eat
bread," I must here acknowledge has adhered to me,
as one of his degenerate offspring, with all the tenacity
of the fabled *shirt of Nessus!* I have been poor all my
life, but have struggled on and on, buffeting the waves
of adversity, endeavoring, as I passed along the dreary
vale of life, always to observe that true *honesty of purpose*,
which I always thought should be the great beacon light
of human ambition. I have the proud consolation of
knowing that I have never coveted any man's "gold,
silver, or apparel," but, having been blessed with reasonable good health, I have always caused my "hands to
minister to my necessities." I am aware that the possession of wealth is a convenience in this life, to some extent, but I can not now say that I have ever entertained
any extreme thirst for its possession beyond what would
supply my immediate necessities. The great code of
moral law informs us that "man that is born of woman
is of few days, and full of trouble," and also, that "naked
we came into the world, and naked we must go out of
it," and, therefore, I have always been unable to see any
real propriety or true philosophy in bending all the energies with which we have been so munificently endowed
by our Creator in the accumulation of the "sordid dust
of earth!" I think that there was sound philosophy in
the remark which Dr. Johnson made to David Garrick
on one occasion, when they were upon great terms of in-
timacy. Mr. Garrick, while Dr. Johnson was on a visit
at his splendid residence, was conducting him through his
magnificent parlors, which were furnished in the most

gorgeous elegance, which manifested in the extravagant proprietor the most extreme love of the world and its vanishing levities. Dr. Johnson stood for some time, and gazed around in silent meditation, surrounded with this profusion of wealth, and, at length, turning to his friend, he calmly and very truthfully remarked, "Ah! David, this is what makes a death-bed terrible!" I never have believed that wealth could confer upon its possessor any *true happiness*, for that can never be purchased. Indeed, it is my belief that *true happiness* alone resides in those distant realms beyond the stars, where mind and matter are totally disconnected, and where the soul, the essence of man's immortality, released from its tenement of clay, is permitted to feast forever upon the ambrosial fruits of heaven in the presence of the Infinite Eternal. The happiness of earth, which is purchased with wealth, is too often, when attained, found to be like the fabled fruit, which always presented a most beautiful exterior appearance, but, when presented to the lips of the enraptured admirer, it would dissolve at once into ashes; or it may be likened to the shade of Anchises embraced by Æneas, who, hastening to enfold the dear form of his loved relative, found that he was embracing a form as impalpable as the viewless air! But I must hasten on to a conclusion of this sketch.

After I had received the rudiments of a common English education I concluded to learn a trade, which I suspected would be the surest guarantee for supplying future wants. I therefore selected the trade of a wagonmaker, which occupation was most congenial to my taste when making choice of a handicraft. I therefore engaged with a workman in that employment, and remained in his service until I thought that I was proficient enough to obtain wages, or open a shop for my own personal emolument. I continued to work at this business for a number of years, until war was declared by the United States against Mexico. When a call for troops was first made in East Tennessee I at once volunteered in the service of my country, and marched onward beneath its cherished flag, to meet and to assist in chastising the enemy upon a foreign soil. The toils and hardships of the Mexican campaign were very severe, but I endured them as best I could, being urged forward by that steadfast love of country which has always animated my exertions while fighting against a foreign or an intestine foe. I found the climate of Mexico to be very unfavorable to my health, as it also proved to be to the health of most of the soldiers who had volunteered in the upper portion of East Tennessee. Many of the poor fellows who were taken sick in Mexico died in that distant southern clime, away from home and from friends, and a great many died as they were homeward bound, inspired to the last with the hope of once more being permitted to see their families; but, alas! that hope was vain and illusory, for they died often with the dear word of *home,* *wife,* or *children* lingering upon their quivering lips.

During the Mexican campaign I was made acquainted with the monstrous horrors of war. All that I knew previously was only from information which I had derived from history, which was only a theoretical knowledge, and which I found to be entirely different from person-

al observation; for one may read an account of the most
wretched and barbarous massacre, and yet will not appreciate it fully in all the terrors portrayed, as he would
if personally present and witnessing the occurrence. I
became convinced, during my stay in Mexico, that the
cruelties and the horrors of war were by far more terrible
and deplorable than I had ever formed any conception
of. I thought that it was no wonder that *war*, by common consent, had always been justly considered as occupying the foremost rank in the three greatest calamities
which has at various times scourged and desolated the
nations of the earth since the foundation of the world.
The three great national calamities referred to are war,
pestilence, and famine; and well may it be considered
that *war* has the more dreadful effects upon any nation
which is cursed by it than either of the preceding national afflictions. War unhinges society; it poisons the fountain of national happiness, and pours into its delicious
waters libations of wormwood and gall; it tears up the
sylvan shades of peace with its terrible engines, and plants
thorns and briers where the most lovely flowers were
wont to bloom, and scattered their fragrance upon the
air; it overturns the proud fabrics of civil jurisprudence, and discord, with all its attendant evils, runs riot
throughout the ill-fated nation which is cursed by its
awful presence; it severs the cord of human friendship;
man loses respect for his fellow-man, as his nature be-
comes changed to that of an incarnate devil, the goddess
of virtue is ostracized, and vice is worshiped in her absence. Indeed, I must confess that I am totally incapable
of employing language sufficient to describe the horrors

of war and its dreadful concomitants; blessed, and doubly blessed, is that nation which moves on in the even tenor of its way without engaging in direful conflicts of arms.

I remained in Mexico until the bright sunlight of peace had dispelled the dark and dismal cloud of war which had arisen over that distracted and unstable government, and immediately after the suspension of hostilities I returned to my native land, and, through the mercy of a kind Providence, I was again permitted to reach my home and family amid the mountains of my native county. For some time after my return I felt very seriously the disastrous effects upon my constitution, superinduced by the great exposure which I had endured during the terrible campaign which I had passed through, and, in fact, I have never since been able to recover the healthful energies of my system, which I lost during my stay in the malarious and sultry climate of Mexico. After I had witnessed the horrors of a dreadful war in my expedition into Mexico, I sincerely hoped that I should never again witness such terrible scenes of desolation and distress. Little did I then think that the next theatre in which I should be called upon to witness a repetition of the same awful tragedies which I had seen displayed would be in my own native and beloved country, in my own native State of Tennessee, and in my own dear native county. Little did I then imagine that the period was rapidly approaching when I, my neighbors, and my relatives, would be hunted and shot at like the wild beasts of the mountains, just because we were opposed to a mushroom "Southern Confederacy" supplanting and annihilating the best form of government which has ever been devised by the wisdom of man upon the whole face of the earth. Little did I then think that my own native hills would, in the course of a few years, be infested by gangs of murderous desperadoes, whom it were "base flattery to call villains," destitute of mercy, and without remorse of conscience, prowling through the country, insulting virtue and exalting vice by their lewd and infamous conduct, and seeking to bathe their hands in the blood of innocence. Little did I imagine then that in a few revolving years my own country would present the scene of an unholy, unjust, and internecine civil strife, for which ancient or modern history could furnish no parallel; where blood was to flow in torrents, and where the lives of hecatombs of human beings would be sacrificed at the shrine of the terrible Moloch which would be erected through the evil machinations of ambitious, base, and designing demagogues. "Ah! little did I then think that thousands upon thousands of my own countrymen and fellow-citizens would, in so short a period, be forced to engage in the awful conflict of arms, and fall upon the gory field and die beneath the raging storm of battle; be butchered in cold blood by heartless murderers, and starved to death in loathsome prisons, in order "to make a villain great." But it is even so; for it is well known that the infamous "Southern Rebellion" was conceived and matured by a set of vile and seditious politicians, and that thousands of their misguided followers rushed precipitately into the strife of arms, and fell as victims in the unholy cause of endeavoring to elevate an impulsive and ambitious individual, in the person of Jeff. Davis, to the chair of state

in the "Southern Confederacy." I shall not presume to
say what his dismal reflections have been since his imprisonment in the cells of Fortress Monroe; I should at
least think that his nightly dreams have been greatly
disturbed by visitations of the ghastly ghosts of his deluded followers, to whom he could not justly say,

> "Shake not your gory locks at me,
> Thou canst not say I did it,"

for they might abruptly deny his assertion, and more
promptly assail him with the "deep damnation of their
taking off," than did the pale ghosts which appeared
to old Richard III. the night preceding the battle of
Bosworth Field. They might in all truth say to him,
it was you that occasioned the winged messengers of
death to snatch away our lives, and hurry our unprepared souls into the presence of the great Eternal, with
"all our imperfections on our heads." It was you that
caused the early mildew to blanch and destroy the young
buds of our lives, and sent us to our final reckoning in
the very blossoms of our sins, "unhousel'd, disappointed,
and unaneled!" These, and more than these, have doubtless been the horrible controversies which have been experienced by Jeff. Davis amid the dismal hours of night,
while resting upon his couch, until the dreadful night-
mare was driven away and prevented from returning by
his waking meditations.

It is quite possible, notwithstanding, that Jeff. Davis, the great high-priest who filled the presidential
chair in the so-called "Southern Confederacy" during the
dark and gloomy period when our beloved country was
deluged with fraternal blood, may yet be acquitted of his

monstrous offenses against the laws, the peace, and happiness of the United States; for it is too true that

> "In the corrupted currents of this world,
> Offense's gilded hand may shove by justice;
> And oft 'tis seen, the wicked prize itself
> Buys out the law."

But he may truthfully say, in the language of the wretched King of Denmark, when he was deploring the foul and miserable crime of murdering his own brother,

> "But 'tis not so above;
> There is no shuffling; there the action lies
> In his true nature; and we ourselves compell'd,
> Even to the teeth and forehead of our faults,
> To give in evidence!"

He may also exclaim with truth, in the language of his ancient counterpart in sin and iniquity, the deformed and brutal King of England, Richard III., after he had been frightened in his midnight slumbers by the pale and ghastly apparitions of his innocent murdered victims,

> "My conscience hath a thousand several tongues,
> And every tongue brings in a several tale,
> And every tale condemns me for a villain!
> Perjury, perjury, in the high'st degree;
> Murder, stern murder, in the dir'st degree;
> All several sins, all used in each degree,
> Throng to the bar, crying all, Guilty! guilty!"

None of the reckless scoundrels who so earnestly labored to destroy our country, and to tear down the beautiful edifice of public freedom which had been erected by our forefathers, have been rewarded with that degree of punishment which the malignity of their crimes so justly merits. The government has been extremely lenient in extending pardons to the base and infamous rebels who, for several successive years, were industriously engaged in hurling their poisoned javelins of malice and hatred at the very vitals of the republic. It would probably be a safer guarantee for the future welfare of our country if a different line of policy had been pursued. I would have a solemn, inflexible will possessing the nation, to punish crime, whether little or gigantic, with a temperate vigor that should offer no hope of escape to the criminal, from the relentings of a false and selfish sentimentalism. Justice is sinned against by unseasonable and excessive lenity, almost as harmfully as by over-severity. Neither whimsical philanthropy nor devilish revenge should interfere with our award of retribution to the criminal. Even-handed justice, administered with obedient regard to the will of God, revealed in Scripture and in Providence, this is the solemn spirit in which public opinion should affirm the sentence of lawful punishment against crime. There is a painting by Raphael, whose profound genius is at all times exhibited in his numerous and inimitable artistic designs, which represents the Archangel Michael slaying that old serpent, which is the devil. The fiend under his feet turns his face upward toward the minister of doom, grinning with all the spiteful malevolence of hellish hate. Above him, soaring on heavenly pinions, floats the archangel, his countenance betokening neither compassion nor revenge, but placid in an ineffable expression of pure, passionless, peaceful sympathy with the divine behest, which he is obediently fulfilling. Such is the ideal of that retributive justice which should be unceremoniously meted out to all the despoil-

ers of our national happiness, for it is a duty which we
owe to ourselves as a people and a government, in order
to defend ourselves against a like future calamity as that
which the nation has providentially succeeded in defeating.   The unsuccessful attempt which was made by the
leaders and their cohorts in the late gigantic rebellion to
establish a government upon anarchy and independence,
upon the positive slavery of the poor and indigent classes
of its white, as well as its colored population, and glory
upon the most incredible shame, will most unquestionably be assigned to that infamy in history which it so
justly deserves, and henceforth will doubtless be associa-
ted most naturally in the thoughts of men with the nakedness of a crime which can but freeze the blood of humanity with the most profound indignation and horror
forever.

The defeat and overthrow of the rebellion has, I most
fondly hope, forever exploded the three great pernicious
theories which were urged with the most remarkable vehe-
mence by the advisers and the promoters of the civil strife
which at once arrayed the North and the South against
each other, and rushed them on to engage in the bloody
strife of battle.   The mischievous theories which I al-
lude to are nullification, secession, and the right of revolution in a republican form of government.   Nullification and secession are both most atrocious political here-
sies, differing, of course, to some extent from each other.
The doctrine of nullification, as expounded in 1831 and
1832, is, that a state has the right to nullify an act of
Congress, and yet remain in the Union; that a state is
its own judge of the constitutionality of the laws passed

by Congress, etc. The infamous and preposterous theory of secession recognizes the right of a state to withdraw from the general government, absolving itself from its allegiance thereto. The first of these outrageous theories did not reach the culminating point, owing to the compromise which was agreed upon in 1833. The last one had a most frightful culmination, as four years of a most desolating and bloody war sadly attests. Some of the Southern States, urged on by vile and mischievous politicians, concluded to try the experiment of secession, and the result is now seen by the nations of the earth. May we not now hope and believe that these two destructive theories are dead, beyond the possibility of future revival?

The remaining theory referred to is one which can never fail to have the most mischievous tendency, especially in a form of government like that of our own. The adherents of this spurious dogma falsely reasoned that, in certain contingencies, even in a republican government, the inalienable right of revolution exists, and should be exercised. Believing that one of these contingencies had occurred, some of our leading politicians in the State of Tennessee at once favored the practical assertion of the right of revolution. Among those who expounded the oracles given out by the hidden high-priests of secession to their deluded followers in Tennessee, I might mention the names of John Bell, Neil S. Brown, and others. They pretended to entertain great abhorrence for secession and its practical results, but seemed to glory in being revolutionists! They denied that the Constitution of the United States gives to a state the right to secede, but openly and boldly declared the right of revolution *above* the Constitution! One thing is quite plain to my mind, and, I think, should be just as self-evident to every person of a rational mind who can properly appreciate the ordinary deductions of plain and simple logical conclusions, and that is, that the right of revolution should never be exercised unless the revolution is known to be incontestibly *right*. The right does not nor can not otherwise possibly exist in any emergency whatever. The circumstances which make a revolution right and proper are entirely essential to the creation of the right of revolution. It requires no enthymemes or intricate logical syllogisms to establish this truth to the satisfaction of every one who will give the subject that just and proper reflection which its importance demands. I concede that under monarchical and aristocratic governments—that is to say, where the rights of the people are not properly recognized, and where oppressive burdens are imposed on them, the right of revolution does then exist, and should be exercised; for in its exercise resides the only hope of relief of the oppressed millions who have no voice or take no part in the affairs of government. But in a republican government I earnestly contend that the right of revolution does not exist. And why do I say so? Because it is the people's government; and if they wish at any time to change, alter, or amend the principles of government which they have established for their own benefit, they are fully at liberty to do so. If they do not desire a change, they can suffer it to remain as it already stands. There is no sense or reason in resorting to the very dangerous and destructive policy of revolution, if the majority at any time desire to amend their form of government, for they have the power to make such amendments as they may desire without resorting to revolution. The majority of the people in a republican form of government can never be under the disagreeable necessity of becoming revolutionists; for the undeniable fact that they are the true and correct source of all power, at once precludes the possibility of any such necessity existing. If this supposition be correct, what is the conclusion which must follow? Evidently, that if the right of revolution exists at all, that right resides in the minority. This is altogether absurd; for republican governments only recognize the right of the majority to govern, and there is a total disregard of this important right whenever the minority exhibit an unwillingness to yield to the wishes of the majority, and an attempt at revolution is plainly and palpably an attempt to annihilate one of the very fundamental principles of republicanism. If these premises are correct, it certainly follows that the right of revolution does not and can not exist in a republic. To allow its existence is at once equivalent to the very false and ruinous concession that the minority may rule in a republican government. This concession is repugnant to all human experience in the affairs of well-ordained government, and opposed to the best interests of organized society, and, in reality, constitutes an enormity in political science which I can never be induced to sanction.

I have extended this research into politics much farther than I intended at the outset; but I hope that my readers will pardon me, for the subject of the infamous rebellion, and the causes which urged it on the country, is a very prolific subject, and it is hard to restrain the utterance of sentiments of disgust and disapprobation which revolve in the mind whenever our most casual meditations are permitted to rest upon that subject.

Previous to the foregoing digression, I was indulging in an incidental narrative in regard to Jeff. Davis, of "Southern Confederacy" notoriety, whose infamy and moral turpitude I am altogether unable to employ language to describe. I doubt not that, since his downfall and capture, he has experienced a variety of times what one of the ancient poets terms "a dreadful *living death!*" If he could have a pyramid erected, composed of the bleached bones of his deluded followers who offered up their lives at the shrine of his unhallowed ambition, I doubt not but that he would then be thoroughly convinced of his own exalted wickedness, and he would then see and feel what it costs to endeavor to destroy a great and good government. If the ghastly skeletons could arrange themselves before him whose uncontrollable ambition consigned them to an untimely grave, he might then correctly appreciate the horrors of a civil commotion and a strife of arms which he assisted in promoting for his own personal aggrandizement, and for his own political exaltation.

But I must refrain from pursuing this subject any farther. If the government thinks it best to acquit him and turn him loose again, the people would probably be satisfied. It is true, the idea of vindictiveness being displayed by a great and magnanimous government is absurd as well as unpopular. It is true, his case has been

settled by the result of the rebellion; and I presume that
the time has already passed by when this great nation
should think of wreaking its vengeance upon a political
criminal. If he had been at once killed when he was
first captured, no fault whatever could have been attached to his slayer, for he deserved death in any form
in which it could have been inflicted upon him. But
the tocsin of war has ceased to reverberate through the
nation, and the white wings of peace again overspread
the land. While war's dread pinions waved over our
devoted country, murdering human beings seemed to be
a fashionable occupation, and life was estimated at a very
low rate. But, thanks to kind Providence, the reign of
terror has passed away with the suppression of the Southern rebellion, and I do sincerely hope that our government may never be again called upon to raise its strong
arm for the suppression of another vile and infamous internal strife; but I hope that it may be permitted to
move on in the accomplishment of the welfare and happiness of its citizens until the wings of time itself shall
become weary in its perpetual flight, and until the archangel shall place one foot upon the sea, and the other
upon the land, and proclaim that the affairs of earth must
be suspended;

> " When, wrapp'd in flames, the realms of ether glow,
> And Heaven's last trump shall shake the world below !"

During one of the campaigns of Alexander he met
with the philosopher Callisthenes, who was renowned for
his extensive erudition, and for his splendid rhetorical
accomplishments. At one of the convivial festivals furnished by Alexander the philosopher was present, and

was requested, when the cup was presented to him, to
pronounce a eulogium upon the Macedonians extem-
pore, which he did with so much eloquence that the
guests, beside their plaudits, rose up and covered him
with their garlands. Upon this Alexander said, in the
words of Euripides,

"When great the theme, 'tis easy to excel."

"But show us now," continued he, "the power of
your rhetoric in speaking against the Macedonians, that
they may see their faults and amend." The orator then
took the other side, and spoke with equal fluency against
the encroachments and other faults of the Macedonians,
as well as against the divisions among the Greeks, which
he showed to be the only cause of the great increase of
Philip's power, concluding with these truthful words:

" Amid sedition's waves
The worst of mortals may emerge to honor!"

This was quite a severe rebuke to extravagant ambition, which drew upon himself the implacable hatred of
the Macedonians, and the severe censure of Alexander
himself, for he doubtless very sensibly felt the exceeding
appositeness of the sentiment expressed by the philosopher.

The dark and boisterous waves of sedition ran high
during the Southern rebellion, but, even amid their terrible commotion, Jeff. Davis did not succeed in attaining
to any position which could be designated as a position
of honor; but, on the contrary, I think that the position
which he occupied will be looked upon in the future of
American history as a most infamous position, which he
obtained by the most scandalous and infamous agencies.

Then, I say, let the government deal with him as it may consider to be most consistent to the requirements of national magnanimity; and if it should be deemed most advisable, let him be treated as my Uncle Toby treated the fly which greatly annoyed him on one occasion. Let the government say to him, Go, poor devil, for the world is large enough for Jeff. Davis and the United States, and the extinction of your insignificant life could in no degree atone for your damning deeds, whose name is *Legion*, and are as black, ay, blacker than the raven wings of midnight, and for the perpetration of which you will receive your just reward in the unerring court of Heaven's exalted chancery!

I have extended this chapter much farther than I intended at the beginning, for which I must here crave the indulgence of my readers, to whom I will say, that if they should discover faults in this volume, as they advance in its perusal, they must not fail to remember that "'tis human to err, but divine to forgive!" I will just here remark, in conclusion of the short biography which I have given in regard to myself, that, after I returned from the campaign in Mexico, I have ever since resided in the upper portion of East Tennessee, engaging alternately in the occupation of farming, and in the business of wagon-making, until the culmination of the Southern rebellion, when I was driven from my home into the mountains by the base myrmidons of Jeff. Davis, at which time I came to the determination to make use of my best exertions in relieving my fellow-citizens from the wretched oppression of the so-called "Southern Confederacy," and in procuring soldiers for the Federal army. Consequent-

B

ly, I determined to act in the capacity of a pilot to conduct all good Union men safely through to the Federal lines who might desire to go there; and in this capacity I continued to act from the time I engaged in it regularly on during the prevalence of hostilities between the two sections of the country. I confidently believed that I could do more toward the advancement of my country's cause in suppressing the vile and iniquitous rebellion, by conducting men through by hundreds who desired to take up arms in the defense of the Union, than if I were to volunteer as a private soldier. And in this belief, I am now happy to say, I was not at all mistaken; for, during the time which I was thus engaged, I am proud to be able to state that I conducted thousands of men to the Union army, many of whom made brave and fearless soldiers, and continued in the service until the end of the war. This I can state without fear of contradiction, as hundreds of men could testify if they were called upon to do so.

During the period in which I was thus engaged I had many adventures, and made numerous hair-breadth escapes, which I shall now proceed to detail in regular order.

THRILLING ADVENTURES

OF

DANIEL ELLIS.

CHAPTER I.

IN the month of November, 1861, the troubles of the Union people in the upper portion of East Tennessee began in earn-est. Orders had been received from the government of the United States to burn all the bridges, and to destroy the rail-road from Chattanooga on up the country as far as it pos-sibly could be done. It was to be done at night, secretly; and every true-hearted Union man that was advised of this design readily engaged in a combination to assist in this contemplated work of destruction. It was generally be-lieved by all who had been advised of the project, that if this destruction could be accomplished, there would then be nothing in the way to prevent the Federal troops from com-ing to East Tennessee to stay; and, consequently, we all join-ed heart and hand in the business. Being a citizen of Carter County, I united with the company which had been selected to burn the bridge over the Holston River at the town of Union, in Sullivan County, Tennessee. The bridge over the Watauga River, at Carter Dépôt, six miles from Elizabeth-ton, Tennessee, escaped destruction, owing to the fact that a company of rebel soldiers were stationed there. The bridge at Union not being thus guarded, was destroyed without any trouble, as the few guards who were stationed there were suddenly captured, and their lives spared, as they avowed most solemnly that they would never reveal the names of any of the party concerned in burning the bridge. But their solemn asseverations soon proved to be "as false as dicers' oaths;" for so soon as they met with their partners in rebellion, they immediately disclosed the name of every man with whom they were acquainted, and guessed remarkably well in regard to those with whom they were not personally acquainted. This was not very hard for them to do, for up to this time there were not very many who had disclaimed their principles, but, on the contrary, openly declared themselves as firm and steadfast friends of the Union. The injury which was thus done so enraged the rebels, that the Union citizens, in order to insure their self-protection, assembled together in a body of some several hundred men, and armed themselves as best they could, believing all the time that the Federal forces would soon visit this portion of East Tennessee, and relieve them from the dangers which surrounded them. This assemblage of citizen soldiers were at this time stationed on the Watauga River, six miles from the Carter Dépôt, and the Union men coming in all the time, armed with such old guns as the mountain people could afford. Daniel Stover, a citizen of Carter County, and a son-in-law of President Johnson, was elected colonel, and forthwith consented to act as the leader of the Union force which had assembled together, assisted by Colonel James Grayson, of Johnson County, and several other strong and influential Union men. They were now meditating the policy of making an attack on the rebel force which was stationed at Carter Dépôt, and therefore a scout was sent out; they encountered a small lot of rebels, and drove them back with rapidity, killing several of the party in their retreat. Intelligence now arrived that the rebels were re-enforcing, and our band of Union soldiers moved their position, and marched out to the Big Spring, on Gap Creek, in Carter County, some three miles from Elizabethton, and on the same evening the whole force marched to Elizabethton. At this point they remained for three days, receiving information all the time that the rebels were constantly re-enforcing at Carter Dépôt, preparatory to making an advance, and killing every man whom they might find who had been concerned in the rebellion in Carter County. This was sad news indeed for our little party of undrilled mountaineers, who had been suddenly collected together to resist the tyranny of rebel desperadoes. It was therefore concluded that we should again change our position, whereupon all the guns, pistols, and other weapons of defense which could be obtained, were hastily collected, and the party then moved to the Doe River Cove, about six miles above Elizabethton, in the mountains of Carter County.

Colonel Ledbetter, than whom a more bloodthirsty and infamous scoundrel never set his foot upon the soil of East Tennessee, arrived at Johnson's Dépôt with a considerable force under his command, and, learning where our party were stationed, started in pursuit of us. Our pickets learning that the rebels were advancing upon us with a large force, came in and reported the news, and it was immediately advised that we should "break up camp," and every man take care of himself. This was late in the evening, and the next morning the rebel forces reached our late encampment, and captured several stragglers and quite a number of old flint-lock guns. They then robbed many of the Union families in that settlement, driving off their cattle and hogs, and destroyed nearly every thing in their houses which they could not carry away, and returned to Johnson's Dépôt,

some by the road which they had come, while some of them
traveled the road through the mountains which leads down
Doe River to Elizabethton.

I have now arrived at the juncture in which my own
eventful history begins. Colonel Stover desiring to form a
company of mounted men for a scout, I had visited my
home, in order to get my horse that I might join said company. I was not aware at this time that our forces had dispersed, until on my way back to the encampment I met
with some of our men who gave me the first intimation,
stating that some had fled to the mountains, while others
had returned to their homes to stand the threatened storm
of rebel vengeance, controlled and directed by old Ledbetter. I returned home, concealed my horse, and then took
refuge myself in a clump of cedar bushes on a hill which
overlooked the road, so that I might watch the movements
of the rebels as they passed along the road. I had not been
in this position long, when I saw a large body of men coming
down the road, and, as they approached nearer to me, I saw
that a number of our men were in the crowd; some were
mounted upon horses, but the greater number were walking. I thought at once that it was our own party, who had
partially reunited again, and, entertaining as I did this very
erroneous impression, I left my place of concealment, and
went down to them, when, to my utter surprise, I found
myself in the hands of the rebels. These were two companies of infantry and one company of cavalry, and the men
whom I knew had belonged to our own party were prisoners, whom the rebels had captured in the Doe River Cove.
They halted me at once and asked me my name, when some
one in the crowd that knew me (for there were a good
many rebel citizens with them) answered for me, telling
them that I was a bridge-burner without any sort of doubt.

At the very meution of *bridge-burner* their passions seemed to be greatly aroused, and I certainly would have been killed if I had not succeeded in making my escape, for, sure enough, I was the first bridge-burner who had the misfortune of being captured. The prisoners whom they had were boys and peaceable citizens, and the only charge which they had against them was that they had found them at our encampment. The moment that I was designated as a *bridge-burner* many of the rebel gang said, "Shoot him! shoot him!" At this juncture an officer stepped up to me and said, in a very angry manner, "You shall not live two minutes; I will kill you right here!" and placed me in the care of a sergeant, directing him to keep a strict watch over me until he could bring the two men who had told them that they would swear that I was a *bridge-burner.* That there were rebel citizens in that crowd who were mean enough to swear my life away, I could not for a moment doubt. We were now in a lane opposite to a house which stood some five steps from the fence. It was a double log-house, with an entry in the middle, and on the opposite side of this house there was a cleared hill-side some two hundred yards in extent, immediately beyond which a dense thicket of cedar bushes had grown up. As soon as the officer stepped away, I asked leave of the fellow who was guarding me to let me go into the house and get a drink of water, and walked off without awaiting his answer. I was halted in a very peremptory manner, but did not stop until I got to the house and in front of the entry, when, summoning all my energies for the trial, I leaped over the fence and ran between the houses, and started up the hill, aiming for the cedar thicket. Some bawled out at the top of their voices, "Shoot that man running!" but that only served to impart strength to my legs. The cavalry threw the fence down,

ESCAPE OF ELLIS.

and came after me on their horses like a storm, but the
ground being very soft from recent rains, they could not
make much speed, and I soon increased the distance between us. The cavalry seemed to be certain of recapturing
me, and the infantry could not shoot at me for fear of shooting the cavalry, but they found that I would make my escape, and commenced bursting caps at me; their guns failed
to fire, and one of them exclaimed, "My gun never failed
to fire before!" Surely at this time I was a special object
of the care of divine Providence, for not a single gun fired
which was aimed at me, and I reached the desired cedar
thicket in perfect safety, and there, crouching beneath the
low-spreading branches, I could see my angry pursuers gal-
loping around in search of me, and venting their rage by
the utterance of oaths which were enough to raise the hair
on a Christian man's head. I do not think that the army
which Sterne speaks of as swearing so "terribly in Flan-
ders" could in any degree furnish a parallel to the horrible swearing of these foul-mouthed rebel blackguards who
were thirsting for my blood. But I soon had the agreeable
pleasure of seeing them check their horses and return, vow-
ing and protesting vengeance against me if I should again
fall into their hands. That contingency, I thought, was in
the uncertain future, for the defeat of which I thought that
I might probably secure "a bond of fate."

I now considered myself free from rebel tyranny, which
I must confess was a most cheering reflection; so, emerging
from my place of concealment with the utmost caution, I
quickly hastened away, altogether destitute of either hat or
coat, having lost both in my precipitate flight. The coat
was a loose bear-skin over-coat, and I very easily dispensed
with it as I was running. As a general thing, I do not believe in dreams; but I must here acknowledge that the

dream which I had the night previous to my capture had a
decided agency in saving my life. I dreamed that I saw a
large company of armed men approaching, and that I went
to meet them, when I became frightened, and suddenly turned and ran away with all possible speed, and that when they
attempted to shoot me their guns would not fire. Consequently, as soon as I was captured I at once thought of my
dream, and resolved to endeavor to escape. I thought if I
had to die, I would prefer being killed while I was making
an effort to escape, rather than stand still and suffer myself
to be shot down like a dog. I did make an effort, and the
sequel I have already related. I have not, since my escape,
been such a total disbeliever in dreams; for I am convinced
that

"There are more things in heaven and earth, Horatio,
Than are dreamt of in your philosophy."

Before concluding this chapter, I must invoke a blessing
upon that "*dear old cedar thicket;*" for it most assuredly
saved one poor, unprepared soul from being suddenly expelled from its tenement of clay, and violently precipitated
upon the great ocean of eternity. Oh, woodman, let me
beseech you to spare that *cedar thicket ;* touch not a single
bush in its umbrageous pride; let it stand forever, and
flourish on amid the bright sunlight of day, or in the paler
effulgence of lunar light; for it will ever furnish to me a
cherished memento to awaken my recollection of one of the
most imminent perils which ever threatened my earthly existence as long as memory shall occupy a position in the
proud citadel of mind. Let me again say, Spare that *cedar
thicket,* for

"In danger it protected me,
Let me protect it now."

I never before in all my life so intensely appreciated the sentiment of the poet who says that

"Distance lends enchantment to the view;"

for I thought, in my desperate and rapid flight to that *old cedar thicket*, that it did really present a more enchanting prospect to my imagination than any forest scenery which I had ever before beheld, although I had often gazed with delight upon my native mountains, whose proud and lofty summits extend far up toward the azure blue of heaven. But the *old cedar thicket* deserves, and shall receive the highest meed of praise which I could possibly bestow upon it; for it saved my life from being extinguished by rebel bullets, and I therefore hope that the reader will pardon me for bestowing upon it, in the conclusion of this chapter, a parting blessing for a benefit it conferred upon me in an hour of great extremity between life and death which can never be forgotten.

CHAPTER II.

I NOW at once concluded that I would be compelled to
seek for safety in the mountains, to avoid being recaptured
by the desperate villains who were seeking to take my life.
Where my comrades were I could not tell, but I determined
to go in search of them.   However, I was totally unable to
commence an immediate search for them, for the terrible
race which I had been compelled to take to save my life had
so completely stiffened my limbs that I was almost incapable of standing erect.   I laid out all the night which followed the day of my escape without any covering whatever, save the blue and star-lit canopy of the sky.   The night
was very cold, and consequently sleep, the balmy restorer
of exhausted nature, did not often visit me upon my cold
and lonely bed.   As this was my first experience iu *scouting*,
the reader may correctly suppose that the night seemed very
tedious.   At times, as I lay upon my cold bed, and gazed up
through the blue ethereal at the bright and beautiful stars as
they twinkled in the celestial firmament on high, I thought
that my condition was melancholy indeed ; but I found some
consolation in the reflection that I was not the first man who
had been forced to the necessity of laying all night with the
cold earth for his bed and the heavens for his covering.   I
could but remember that I was only enduring what Crassus
once endured, who was considered to be the most affluent
personage in the whole Roman Empire.   History informs us
that Crassus, not being contented with his boundless wealth,
nor the exalted political distinction which it had procured

for him in the Roman government, proposed to place himself at the head of a large army, and march forth to chastise and subdue the Parthians, and desolate and plunder their nation.   But he totally failed in the object of his campaign, and a sad reverse of fortune overtook him amid the mountains of Syria; for, in a battle with the Parthians, his legions were cut to pieces and almost annihilated, and he and his son, who was assisting in the expedition of his father, were both slain.   The night before he was slaughtered, after his splendid army had been ruined, he covered his head, chose darkness for his companion, and stretched himself upon the ground, a sad example to the vulgar of the instability of fortune, and to men of deeper thought of the effects of rashness and ill-placed ambition.   Not contented with being the first and greatest among many millions of men, he had considered himself in a mean light, because there were *two men*, Pompey and Cæsar, in the whole Roman Empire, who he thought occupied a rank above him.

Immediately after Aurora, with roseate fingers, unlocked the golden portals of the morning, I arose from my cold bed, and started toward my once happy home, meditating, as I passed along, upon the beautiful verse of Byron, which says,

> " 'Tis sweet to hear the watch-dog's honest bark
> Bay deep-mouthed welcome as we draw near home;
> 'Tis sweet to know there is an eye will mark
> Our coming, and look brighter when we come!"

But, alas! I was not then approaching my loved home in that peaceful and happy state of mind in which I had often approached it before, but was now going to it cautiously and stealthily, watching on every side, for fear of being suddenly accosted by a rebel murderer; now the nightingale's melodious voice could have produced no music to my ear, for I was too intently engaged in listening and watching for my murderous pursuers. At length I arrived at my home, and hastily procuring a few articles of clothing, I immediately bade my little family an affectionate farewell, and started on a journey for the Pond Mountain, in Carter County, where I hoped I could again rejoin my friends, and obtain, for a while at least, a safe asylum from rebel scrutiny. When I arrived at the house of William Lewis, a good Union man, residing on the waters of Watauga River, in Carter County, I had the very agreeable pleasure of meeting with Colonel Stover, Jonas H. Keen, and others of our party who, like myself, had fled into the mountains in order to secure their personal safety. On my arrival there was a general rejoicing, as they had heard of my capture, and thought that I had already been consigned to the dreary and lonely sepulchre. Something now had to be done to secure our farther safety, for we still hoped and believed that the Northern troops would soon appear in this section of country and relieve us from our embarrassments. We concluded to go farther out into the mountains and build up a camp, for we well knew that the infernal rebels would use every exertion to discover our place of coverture, which we concluded to keep profoundly secret, even from our best friends, with the exception of Mr. Lewis and his son, who were to aid us in selecting a suitable hiding-place, and provide something for us to eat. Thereupon, with Mr. Lewis and his son for our guides, we shouldered a bushel of corn meal and a few pounds of bacon, and started for a more remote locality in the gorges of the mountains, leaving the busy world and the merciless rebels behind us, not, however, without deeply lamenting our deplorable condition should the Federal government fail to relieve us. Mr. Lewis conducted us far beyond the Pond Mountain, somewhere on the waters of Elk Creek, to an immense thicket of laurel and ivy bushes, which looked as if

they might have been growing there ever since the time
when "the morning stars sang together;" for they were of
such large dimensions, and their branches so completely in-
termixed and intervoven, that a bird could not fly through
them, and all the way that we could gain an entrance was by
crawling upon our hands and knees under the thick branches.
We were now, perhaps, where the foot of man had never before trod; and here in this dismal and lonely place we proceeded to build a camp to protect us against the inclemency
of the weather, for it was now late in the dreary month of
November, and the cold blasts of winter could already be
heard and felt as they rushed forth from the caves of old
Boreas. Our camp was not very comfortable, for we were
inexperienced in the business of camp-building, and also had
to build out of rough and unshapen materials. After we
finished it we covered the ground floor within plentifully
with leaves, which afforded us a tolerable good bed to sleep
on. Our fire was built at the door of our camp, which we
kept well supplied with fuel, for there was an abundance of
wood in close proximity. The weather, as I have already
remarked, was getting very cold, especially so in this remote
mountain region, and a good fire we found to be indispensable. We had not yet procured any cooking utensils, and
therefore had to bake our bread with the bran in it, by spread-
ing the dough upon a large chip and setting it up before the
fire. We did not prepare our bread after any style which I
have ever seen laid down in any of the fashionable "cook-
books" of the present day, but operated, in its preparation,
after the following fashion. We put our meal into a knead-
ing-trough, and poured the water into it with our hands,
which we procured from a small contiguous branch which
rippled along near our lonely encampment, and after working the dough sufficiently, we baked it as described above.

None of us being annoyed with dyspepsia, we generally ate with a most ravenous appetite. We cooked our meat upon the fire-coals, but we were shortly enabled to prepare our victuals in a more approved style, as our friend furnished us with a small oven to cook in, and some tin cups out of which to drink water. As for the luxury of coffee, we did not think of endeavoring to procure it, as the infamous rebellion had deprived the country of a supply of the genuine article, and we did not wish to substitute in its place the coffee which was used by the rebels, which was *wheat* and *rye*.

With the assistance of our friend, we laid in an abundant supply of bacon and flour, which we had to pack upon our backs some six miles through the valleys of the mountains. Some of our party proposed that we should pass a law that no man should stay in the camp unless he could pack fifty pounds of flour or bacon for the distance of *six miles* through the laurel thicket *on his back*. This, indeed, would have been a severer law than any which was ever instituted by that philosophic Spartan lawgiver, Lycurgus, and could not possibly have been obeyed with any thing like the same deference and respect which was awarded to the severe code of the eminent Spartan, even if the most distinguished and most beloved individual in our party had obtained a promise from all of us that implicit obedience would be given to the law until he should take a short journey and return, and then go into voluntary exile, in order to insure obedience to the law, which we are informed was the policy adopted by Lycurgus, in order to insure stability to his code of jurisprudence.

The law referred to above, as it may very well be suspected, received no general sanction, and was therefore never enforced; for some of our men had infirm constitutions, and of course did not wish to subject themselves to such a fatiguing manual exertion of their physical strength.

The men in our party all seemed to be afraid to venture far away from the camp, for fear of getting lost among the mountains. As for myself, I soon learned the road to the house of Mr. Lewis, and could pack my *fifty pounds* with comparative ease. We lived for some weeks in our camp, passing the lonesome hours away as best we could, with unshaven faces and dirty clothes, and looked a great deal more like savages than we did like civilized men. Time itself seemed to be shod with *leaden shoes*, so slowly and wearily it appeared to pass away. I could not be contented to remain in this " pent-up Utica" so long, and, after visiting the house of my old friend Lewis a few times, I concluded to venture back to my home, in order to see if I could hear any good news which would be calculated to cheer the drooping spirits of our party in their forlorn and lonely situation. None of the party would accompany me, and I determined to go alone; and after remaining in the woods a few days near my home, gathering all the information which could be obtained, I returned to my friends. Afterward, regularly once every week, I would visit my home, carrying with me numbers of letters from the men in our camp, which I had conveyed to their families, receive from them letters in reply, and all the news which I could hear, and then hasten back to the camp again. This was employment for me, and also enjoyment for the lonely and destitute party in the camp, whose spirits by this time were getting very low and desponding. During the first few weeks our hopes were buoyed up by the sincere belief that the "Yankees" would soon come to our relief; but as our hopes in this respect got " small by degrees and beautifully less," we became convinced that we must resort to some means of dispelling the gloomy cloud of despondency which was gathering in darkness around us.

Colonel Stover concluded to venture back home, and there endeavor to conceal himself from the industrious search of the rebel marauders, who were now prowling through the country. He was the first man that I ever engaged to pilot; for I had passed backward and forward so often that I was familiarly acquainted with every path which led from our camp to our homes, and he, having been so long confined, was not willing to undertake the journey alone. Therefore, after bidding his friends an affectionate adieu, and placing himself under my care, we started, and I succeeded in conducting him safely to his own home, and then I returned to the camp. The rebels were ransacking the country in every direction, and our little party at the camp were greatly troubled, fearing that our hiding-place would by some means be discovered, and no mercy could be expected from the ruthless enemy if they should succeed in capturing us, for we almost daily heard the terrible threats of vengeance which were made against us if we should be found. These threats we believed would be fulfilled to the letter; for it was just at this time that a young man by the name of Andrew J. Ward was foully and cruelly murdered, because he refused to take the oath to support the so-called "Southern Confederacy." He was a harmless, inoffensive, and a very pious young man, and was endeavoring to keep out of the way, in order to avoid being forced to take this infamous oath. He was murdered in Carter County by a squad of Colonel Vance's men from North Carolina, who, at this time, were in charge of a reckless scoundrel by the name of Landon Ellis, who was a citizen of Carter County. Young Ward did not try very hard to effect an escape when he saw the rebels, doubtless consoling himself with the reflection that, as he was a peaceable and quiet citizen, they would not probably molest him. But,

alas! little did he think that he was falling into the hands
of a set of obdurate devils, who were as destitute of mercy
as the lion or the tiger, when slaking their thirst in the life-
blood of their trembling victim. He told them that he was
a Union man, and did not wish to take the oath, neither did
he wish to fight on either side. Ellis then ordered him to
be shot, and his confederates in crime all agreed that it was
best to kill some Union man, as an example for the balance,
saying that that would urge them to come out of the mountains, cause them to take the oath of fealty, and join the
Southern army, rather than to encounter the hazard of shar-
ing a similar fate. It was therefore determined by this
sage body of rebel murderers to make young Ward the first
victim in Carter County to their hellish malice. He only
requested them to grant him a short time to pray; but this
request was instantly refused, and a miscreant by the name
of Joseph Murphy shot him in the left breast, the ball ranging through and coming out near the back-bone. He ran
about ten steps before he fell, when his murderers pounced
upon him like beasts of prey, stripping him of his clothing
even before the spark of life had entirely been extinguished.
This foul deed of rebel violence was perpetrated on the 14th
day of December, 1861.

After Colonel Stover left our camp I became quite restless, as there was now but very little *mail* for me to carry;
and as the number in our camp was constantly receiving
accessions by the arrival of more *bridge-burners*, I therefore left my friends in the camp and went to scouting among
the Union people of the country. I still continued to con-
sole myself with the reflection that, upon the return of
spring, the " Yankees" would surely come. But spring at
last returned, but no "Yankees" came with it. Summer
was now rapidly approaching, clothed in its rich garniture

of sunbeams and flowers, but I could not hear of any advance being made in this direction by the "Yankees." My friends still lingered in the mountains, and would not, like myself, venture out, and were constantly discussing the propriety of making an effort to get through the rebel lines. They unanimously agreed that if I would assist them, they could probably succeed in reaching the desired haven of repose. As for myself, I had no fears whatever in undertaking a journey to the Federal lines, and determined at once to engage in its prosecution.

Having a family who were dependent upon my exertions for a support, I knew that I could not remain here in idleness so long as a fugitive in the mountains, and knowing that if I was not permitted to work at home, I could go through the lines and find employment. A small party had prepared several times to go with me, and as often backed out, being too timid to face the danger which they imagined might lay before them. But I was determined to go at all hazard, and was requested by my friends to go and return again, so that I might be enabled to inform them if there were any hopes of an early deliverance for them. They thought that I would then be capable of rendering them greater assistance in accomplishing the journey with safety. I had no thought at this time of ever becoming a regular pilot, but I was willing, in order to befriend the suffering Union men as much as I possibly could, to do every thing which I thought might contribute to their advantage in alleviating their sad condition. I therefore promised that I would return in about three weeks, believing that if no unforeseen accident should prevent me, I could make the journey in that time, and then proceed to render them all the assistance in getting through to the Federal lines which I might think was most consistent and advisable.

CHAPTER III.

Upon the first day of August, 1862, I set out on my first trip through the lines. I was not entirely alone when I started, for a young man by the name of Dolan accompanied me as far as Bay's Mountain, in Sullivan County, Tennessee, his home being in that section of country. We started without provision for our journey, aiming to procure it on the road, and pass ourselves off as citizens in search of *saltpetre caves*. We had not traveled four miles before we met some soldiers; the reader may very well imagine that I felt somewhat alarmed, but as there was no chance to run, I resolved to meet them with a bold face. We spoke politely to them, as they did also to us, and asked us where they could buy some corn, saying that they were strangers in this part of the country. I told them where they could get corn, and they passed on, very much to my relief. After this adventure, we left the road and took to the woods, until I got out of my own neighborhood, when we again took an unfrequented road and continued to pass for *saltpetre diggers*, not failing to inquire of every person we met with if they knew of any saltpetre caves, and in this way we reached Bay's Mountain. Here my companion left me, and I prepared to pursue the remainder of my journey alone and unattended. I learned from my friend Dolan before parting with him the names of all the Union men in this region of country, and was therefore not at a loss to know where to go for assistance. I hired an old lady to furnish me with four days' provisions, which she cooked and put into a haversack for me, and for which I paid her five dollars. Shouldering my knapsack, I now started for Kentucky, but I had not traveled far down the mountain before I observed sixty rebel soldiers on horseback coming toward me. I had no chance to run, and immediately jumped behind a log which was well covered over with weeds, when I had the extreme satisfaction of seeing them pass on without observing me. I immediately resumed my journey, but took care not to travel in the road again.

In the evening I was informed by some Union people that there was a man in that neighborhood by the name of William M'Lane, who was quite familiar with the mountains, and would start that same night with a company of men for Kentucky. I pushed along, and luckily enough succeeded in getting into his company. He had quite a large company with him, and many of them I found to be my acquaintances from Carter County, who had traveled thus far alone. We were very much surprised, and highly rejoiced at this accidental meeting, and pursued the remainder of our journey together. Our pilot knew the mountains well, and we continued to travel during the night, crossing the north fork of Holston River, and getting far along in the gorges of Clinch Mountain against daylight, at which time we paused to take a short rest, and then started forward again. The weather was very hot and dry, and we suffered very much for water. We traveled as rapidly as we could during all of this day, and late in the evening, coming to some water, we stopped for the night. We were all very tired, and our feet were very sore, which we at once proceeded partially to relieve by applications of cold water, succeeded by a good greasing. Early the next morning we started upon our journey, traveling along upon the side of the mountain. The day was very hot, and against twelve o'clock our water was exhausted, and I was selected by the company to go in search of a supply. Taking two quart bottles, I started in the search for water, and in crossing over some large rocks I lost my equilibrium, and fell violently down among the rocks. As I started to fall, I was holding a bottle in each hand, and, in my endeavor to recover, I broke one of the bottles, by which means my hand and wrist were severely cut, pieces of the glass sinking deep among the leaders, occasioning the most excruciating pain. I went back to the company, and had the pieces of glass extracted from my hand and wrist as well as it could be done by a very *rough surgical operation*, and also had the gashes sewed up, which was done with a coarse needle, and still coarser thread, bound up my hand and wrist with a handkerchief, placed my arm in a sling, and for three dreadful weeks I had it suspended in that way.

The company now again resumed the laborious journey which lay before them, being compelled to travel until night without the cooling luxury of water to slake their parching thirst. At length, when we came to water, it was, unfortunately, nothing but a very small dirty drain, for the collection of which we had to dig holes in the mud, in order to accumulate it in even small quantities. We continued at this place all night, for we feared to leave our *little dirty mud-puddle*, as none of the company knew where there was any water to be found farther on, and therefore we unanimously concluded that it was wiser rather

> "To bear the ills we have,
> Than fly to others that we know not of!"

So soon as the first early tints of the morning appeared in the eastern sky, we started upon our journey again. The feet of some of the men were so sore that they could scarcely walk, but they hobbled along as best they could all that day. In the evening, after taking a short rest, we moved on, down Clinch Mountain, and crossed the valley below that night, and against daylight we found ourselves upon one of the lofty spurs of Powell's Mountain, and here we stopped to rest, and also to partake of our scanty morning meal, after which we concluded to advance higher up toward the summit of the mountain to seek a safe position, where we might enjoy the sweet luxury of sleep, which we all very much required. In the evening we arose from the soothing and gentle arms of Morpheus, and resumed our journey again. Some of the men, who were almost broken down with fatigue, begged hard to rest longer; but this could not be done, for we were getting scarce of something to eat, and thought it best to hurry on while we had strength to travel.

The mountainous declivities amid which we were now traveling were very rough, and yet we had not arrived at the roughest parts of them; for on every side nothing could be seen but steep and awful precipices and depressed hollows, and we all felt well assured of one thing, and that was that there was no danger of being pursued through this dreadful range of mountains by the rebel hordes, which, indeed, constituted one of Nature's safest pathways from the tyranny of the secessionists. We traveled slowly along that evening, and when the dark blanket of night was thrown o'er the face of nature, we halted and rested until morning, our sleep being disturbed with no noise save the harsh music of the whip-poor-will, as it reverberated through the hills and valleys around us. When morning dawned again, we partook of a hasty meal, and then went onward, slowly climbing the mountain all the day. Night coming on, we stopped and ate the last of our provisions, and pushed forward across a little valley during the night, pulling, as we passed along, some green corn, which we ate raw with a very good appetite. When morning came we were on the top of Walling's Ridge, which overlooks Powell's Valley, which was thickly settled, and which we found we were compelled to pass through, or else be forced to travel through the roughest sort of mountains if we chose to avoid it; we therefore determined to make an effort to go through the valley. We continued to travel all day on the lofty elevations of Walling's Ridge, and in the evening we supplied ourselves with some more green corn, which we procured from a field which had been planted on the side of the ridge. Having matches, we soon kindled up a fire, and, after roasting our corn and eating what we desired of it, we moved on slowly down to Powell's Valley. The night was dark and gloomy, and we succeeded in crossing it without any impediment whatever, not forgetting, however, to supply ourselves with corn as we passed through. By an hour by the sun upon the following morning, we found that we had arrived at the base of Cumberland Mountain, whose elevated chain separates the States of Tennessee and Virginia from Kentucky. We now considered that we were safe from the rebels, but still had a rough mountain to cross, whose high peaks rose up in magnificence and splendor into the blue welkin's vault. Before attempting to climb the side of this great natural barrier, we stopped to rest and take another repast upon our corn. Some of the men were almost dead from the great fatigue which they had endured, and presented truly a most pitiable aspect. Their shoes were gone, the rocks and snags having torn them from their feet, and as regarded our clothing, one had no reason to laugh at another, for we were all in tattered rags, the briers and brambles having completely divested us of pants from

C

the knees down. We succeeded in crossing the mountain that day, and when night came on apace, we prepared beds out of leaves, on which we slept quite soundly until morning. At this time we had nothing at all to eat, and were very weak and hungry; but we were compelled to travel all that day without eating, and in the evening we had the profound and inexpressible joy and happiness of arriving at the Federal camps at Cumberland Gap. Never did poor toilworn mariners upon the raging ocean, whose vessel had been driven with violence amid the darkness of night before the howling tempest's wrath, enjoy more real happiness and emotions of delight upon reaching a calm haven of repose, than did our tired and worn-out company of weary fugitives from rebel oppression, when they found themselves within the *Union lines*, and saw the dear old flag of their once happy country floating aloft in beautiful grandeur amid the bright rays of the setting sun.

This was, indeed, a happy hour for us when we found that we were in the company of our friends. The soldiers gave us a cordial greeting, and also plentiful supplies of provisions, and divided their blankets with us in order to insure us a good night's repose. The next morning we proceeded to General Carter's head-quarters. Having been born and raised in Carter County himself, General Carter appeared to be exceedingly glad to meet with so many persons from his old home, and asked us many questions in regard to the manner in which the rebels were demeaning themselves in the upper counties of East Tennessee. We related all our troubles to him. He said that he was very sorry that we were in so bad a condition, and said that he would use his best exertions to relieve us, and treated us with the utmost kindness. But, unfortunately, I was unable to see any prospect of immediate relief being extended to my oppressed and down-trodden fellow-citizens in Upper East Tennessee; and, in fact, I was a good deal more desponding than when I left my native mountains in Carter County. That the Union men could not stay there I was well convinced, and how they could ever make their way out through the dreadful mountain-barriers which intervened I could not surmise.

As I had promised my friends to return in the course of three weeks when I left them, I did not tarry long at Cumberland Gap; and as our pilot, William M'Lane, was going to return immediately, I thought it advisable to return in company with him, and thereby obtain all the information about the mountains and the surrounding country which I could, for I felt quite certain that I would have to travel through them again, probably alone, if no person should accompany me. General Carter gave me a large package of letters for his friends at Elizabethton, and also supplied me with provisions for my journey. Mr. M'Lane and myself now set out to travel that long and toilsome path through the mountains again. We were occupied for two days in crossing Cumberland Mountain, and on the night of the second day we crossed Powell's Valley, and also Powell's River, and reached the summit of Walling's Ridge. The rivers were now no very serious inconvenience in our way; for the weather was quite warm, and the waters were very low, the smaller branches being dry, which was some disadvantage to us in preventing us from obtaining water to cool our thirst. We now laid down under the thick branches of some bushes, and slept there very comfortably until late in the evening, when, arousing from our slumbers, we went on to the valley between Walling's Ridge and Powell's Mountain, which we crossed in the night, and got on to the spurs of Powell's Mountain just as daylight began to make its appearance. We continued to travel on until we came to water, and then we laid down and slept until the day had far advanced, when we arose and started on again, but did not travel but a few miles until we stopped for the night. Next morning we started very early, and traveled all day very industriously, and at night we crossed the valley between Powell's Mountain and Clinch Mountain. We waded Clinch River, and, pushing rapidly forward, we arrived at the base of Clinch Mountain just as the bright sunbeams began to sparkle in the silvery dew-drops of the early morning. Our provisions had been exhausted, and we now had nothing to eat but green corn, which we had procured in the valley which we crossed during the previous night. We kindled a fire, and, after roasting our corn, partook of it most heartily, and which, I doubt not, we enjoyed to as great an extent as the renowned and luxurious Lucullus ever enjoyed a meal in the magnificent eating-room which he termed the Apollo! I was now sixty miles from home, and this was the last meal which I ate until I arrived there.

My guide now left me, as his home was in a different direction from mine, and I had now to prosecute my journey alone, having some fears, as I passed through Sullivan County, which was one of the very *hot-beds of secession and rebellion*, and the few Union-men in that county were made the recipients of all the hellish malice and hatred which could be heaped upon them by their heartless rebel oppressors. At length I had the pleasure of seeing the tops of my native mountains, which presented to me a most cheering prospect, for they at once presented to my mind the joyful recollection of happier days, when sorrow pressed lightly upon the heart, and when I could go to my dear home with no fears of my path being intercepted, or waylaid by the cruel murderer. When I reached my native hills I sorely felt the dreadful effects of my toilsome journey, for I was almost starved, and nearly worn out with exhaustion. I can not possibly describe my sufferings during the three weeks which I had been absent; indeed my feet and legs seemed to be worn off to my knees. Just as soon as I partially recruited my exhausted system by eating and sleeping, I at once proceeded to hunt up my scouting friends, so that I might give them all the news which I had obtained. They were exceedingly delighted to see me; but, unfortunately, I had no *good news* to impart to them. They had either to remain in the mountains, or suffer all that I had suffered, and perhaps more, if they should undertake to go through the mountains to the Federal lines. At what time we should be relieved in Upper East Tennessee none could tell, and it seemed impossible to stay here, owing to the severity of rebel oppression.

The news soon spread among the Union people of Carter County that I had returned, and there was scarcely an hour passed that I was not applied to by some unfortunate Union man to conduct him to the Union forces in Kentucky. It was to no purpose when I told them about the terrible hardships which they would have to undergo in making the trip; in fact, I did not wish them to commence the journey without knowing as well as I could tell them about the almost impossible passage through the mountains. I directed their attention to my own stiffened limbs, and told them that I knew that I could endure much more than they could. But my expostulations had no effect whatever in deterring them from attempting the journey, for they said that they would rather try to *crawl* there, than to stay here and endure the monstrous oppression and insults of the rebel soldiery; and in this manner they continued their importunities, telling me that I must go through with them as a guide. I was too completely exhausted from the effects of my last trip to start on another one so soon, as I had not yet become accustomed to such a life of toil; and besides, all the men who wished to go were not now ready to start, and did not wish me to leave them, thinking that I might not probably return again. By this time quite a number of refugees from North Carolina had found their way into the mountains of Carter County; and as they were strangers in this section of country, they desired to move onward to the Union lines immediately. They proposed to pay me well if I would accompany them as far as Sullivan County, and there procure them a pilot if I could not go on myself. This I thought I could do, for by the time we could get into Sullivan County I had no doubt but that M'Lane would be ready to return to Kentucky, and would consent to act as a pilot for them. The greatest danger of annoyance by the rebel soldiery was, I conceived to be, from the place of starting in Carter County to a point in Sullivan County, making a distance of about thirty miles, and when we got to that point I knew that we could find a number of Union friends. From what I told them, they were willing to risk M'Lane, but rather preferred that I should go through with them; and if I had felt like making the journey so soon again without the most disastrous consequences to my already exhausted energies, I should certainly have agreed to guide them through. But I did not think that I could possibly undertake at this time to go with them farther than the point which I designated in Sullivan County, and therefore I told them to supply themselves with provisions for their journey, and appointed the night that we would start.

CHAPTER IV.

On the night of the 28th of August, 1862, I started with *seventy-five* men for the boat-yard in Sullivan County. Our starting-point was near Elizabethton, in Carter County, and the rout which I-projected was a direct line through the woods to the old·Pactolus Ferry, on the Holston River. The men were all provided with a small quantity of provisions, though not half enough for the trip; and as they could not procure a better supply before they started, they had to risk the chance of obtaining more when they arrived at the boat-yard, for I well knew that it would be almost impossible for them to get any thing to eat after they left the boat-yard without subjecting themselves to the danger of being discovered by bands of prowling rebel marauders. The men were all in high spirits at the thought of escaping from the rebels so nicely; as they were not yet guarding the roads for stampeding refugees, I felt quite certain that we could make the trip with safety did we not accidentally run upon the rebels in passing through the country, and of this there was not very much danger in the night, as they were not at that time apt to be stirring. They said that they did not mind the hardships of getting through if they could soon be permitted to return with our victorious troops, and repay the rebels for causing them to have to leave their homes. They had not yet learned the real horrors of war, and did not seem to think about the uncertainty of their return.

We had not advanced very far before every sign of an

approaching storm became quite visible. "The night put on her blackest robes," and we were at once involved "in Egyptian darkness." I could but think that the approaching storm was quite emblematic of the terrible storm of war which these poor men were doomed to encounter before they would again meet their families and friends in peace. And many of them never did return to their cherished and loved homes, but perished upon the gory battle-field, or languished and died in a loathsome Southern prison; for many of this company joined the 2d Tennessee Mounted Infantry, commanded by Colonel James Carter, and after serving as faithful soldiers for a long time, were at length captured by the rebels near Rogersville, Tennessee, and very few of them lived to tell the tale of their horrible sufferings. Some of my nearest neighbors that went through the lines with this company, and who were fine, promising young men, in the very noontide of life, and made as brave soldiers as ever shouldered a musket or carried a sword, were also captured at the time referred to, and fell the sad victims of rebel malice, being consigned as they were to a pestilential prison, where they were made to suffer all the miseries which starvation and haggard destitution could possibly impose upon them. But although they were thus ignominiously put to death, their friends have the proud consolation of knowing that they offered up their lives in the defense of their country, which is one of the highest virtues that can exalt and ennoble the human character. Although they were cut down in the very spring-time of their proud manhood by rebel tyranny, like young flowers which are nipped in their buds by some cold, untimely blast, yet the recollection of their noble deeds of patriotism will always occupy a green spot upon the panorama of memory, and their names, encircled with verdant chaplets, will be placed in the proud galaxy of fame, and suspended aloft in the glorious citadel of American freedom, which will furnish a lasting memento of their sacrifices and achievements in their country's cause as long as human liberty shall endure, and as long as exalted patriotism shall have an admiring votary upon the American continent.

We continued to travel on until about eleven o'clock, when the storm seemed to be approaching in all its fury. The clouds now rolled in volumes over the mountain tops. The rain began to patter down in broad and scattered drops; the wind murmured and howled through the branches of the trees; at length it seemed as if the bellowing clouds were torn open by the mountain tops, and complete torrents of rain came rattling down. The forked lightning leaped from cloud to cloud, and streamed quivering against the rocks in all its splendid and majestic undulations. The thunder burst in tremendous explosions; the peals were echoed from hill to hill, and, in the words of my Lord Byron,

> "From mountain peak to mountain peak
> Leaped the live thunder!"

There was a fearful gloom surrounding us, illumined still more fearfully by the streams of lightning which glittered among the rapidly-descending rain-drops. Never did I before witness such an absolute warring of the elements; it seemed as if the storm was tearing and rending its way through these mountain defiles, and had brought all the artillery of heaven into action. The wind blew in most tempestuous blasts, scattering the dead branches of trees all around us, and we were at last compelled to stop until the storm had somewhat abated; but, having no place to shelter ourselves, we had to stand like philosophers and endure

C 2

the "mad peltings of the pitiless storm!" The rain at
length ceased to fall in such perfect torrents, and as we
could do no better, we pushed onward. We were thoroughly wet to the very skin, and, sad to relate, our provisions were completely spoiled. It was still so dark that we
could scarcely see one another; some of the men ran against
trees, which were rendered imperceptible to them by the
black and impenetrable darkness, mashing their noses and
bruising their mouths in a horrid manner; while others fell
over old logs and stumps, wounding their legs and skinning
their shins to a most deplorable extent. They now began
to think more seriously of what I had told them. But they
considered before starting that the turmoils and hardships
which they would have to endure in making the journey to
the Union lines could not be compared to the threatening
dangers of rebel violence; and therefore they concluded,
that between the two desperate evils they would choose the
least, and endeavor to reach the Union army. As for myself, I managed to grope along tolerably well amid the darkness which environed me.

The men not being accustomed to traveling in the night,
could not get along very rapidly, and I went slowly forward in a direct course to the boat-yard. I was never lost
in the woods or mountains in my life; and although I was
now traveling in a direction which I had never traveled but
one time before, and that time being in the darkness of
night, yet I never for a moment lost my reckoning in the
direction which I had marked out, and went forward with
as unerring certainty as if I had been guided by a compass.
Daylight found us in a large corn-field, which was a good
hiding-place, but it was not the one which I intended to
reach, as we had been so long detained by the storm on the
preceding night. The clouds having dispersed, the sun

arose in the eastern sky in all his bright and effulgent majesty, and his warm and invigorating beams here shone down
upon as muddy, wet, and worn-out set of poor fellows as
were ever seen. We were muddy up to our waists, and
our clothes were dripping with water. I do not believe
that there was *one coat* in all the crowd which had not been
shorn of some of its proportions, which had been done by
the men catching hold of one another while they were stumbling along amid the darkness of the night. When we
stopped, some of the poor fellows fell down upon the wet
ground and declared that they could not go any farther,
even if they had to go in the Southern army, which was the
earthly hell they were now endeavoring to escape; but after resting a while and basking in the warm sunshine, they
changed their notion and concluded to press onward. We
passed the day in washing the mud off of our clothes and
drying them in the sun, and sewing on our coat-skirts; and
when night again clothed the face of nature in its garments
of sable blackness, we were so far recovered as to be able
to proceed on our journey. We made our way to the river
with some difficulty, and prepared to cross it below the old
Pactolus Ferry by stealing a ferry-boat. In this we crossed
the Holston River in grand style, and went on to a place
called the "White-oak Flats," which is in Sullivan County,
near the boat-yard, and was a very noted hiding-place for
the fugitives from rebel oppression, and was distant about
two good nights' travel from the mountains of Carter
County, being a distance of thirty miles. It is a large
body of land, covered with timber and thick undergrowth,
with immense thickets of green-briers matting and interlac-
ing among the bushes, until in some places you can not
crawl through them upon your hands and knees. This was
an excellent hiding-place for the company at this time, for

this was the place where they designed remaining until the services of another pilot could be procured, and also provisions for the remainder of their journey. The people in this settlement were generally for the Union; and after hiding the men securely, I went out among the people to get them something to eat, which was a very hard undertaking, as there were so many of them, and money was very scarce among them, especially among those from Carter County, they having but very little more than enough to take them through the lines, especially if any unforeseen accident should happen to them.

The citizens here were very kind, and I did not have much trouble in getting a supply for all. I now for the first time made the acquaintance of Mrs. Grills, a widow lady, who was a most excellent lady; and in my future trips to Kentucky she always assisted in feeding hundreds of poor stampeders. My sincere prayer is, that this kind and humane lady may always enjoy the most abundant peace and contentment in this world, and happiness in the world to come. On the present occasion she furnished me with all she had to spare herself, and then went out among the Union people and solicited donations of provisions, and carried it to her own house and cooked it. I found her to be truly a "friend in need," for I had not at this time any very extensive acquaintance with the Union people in this section of country.

Having, with the assistance of Mrs. Grills, obtained a supply of provisions for the men, I now went in search of William M'Lane, the pilot, who at once agreed to go and conduct the company through; but the men's feet were so sore, they wished to rest for a couple of days at least. They were all willing to go with M'Lane, but rather preferred that I should go with them. This I could not well do, as I had not yet sufficiently recovered from the fatigue of my last trip, and, besides, my friends at home were anxiously awaiting my return ; neither did I think that there was any reason for me to go, as I had engaged for them the services of a good pilot. I now commenced the task of getting provisions for their journey. The men from North Carolina and Virginia paid me for my services to them, but my own neighbors from Carter County, many of them not having a dollar in their pockets, and the balance of them not enough to pay their pilot, I therefore took the money which I had received and purchased a plentiful supply of bread and bacon, and divided it out among those who could not help themselves. Mr. M'Lane, their pilot, was a kind man, and was not severe upon them in his demands for his services. Their blistered feet and stiffened limbs were now much improved, and, after giving me a number of letters to take back to their friends, they started upon their journey in good spirits. This company M'Lane conducted safely through to Cumberland Gap.

I now turned my face homeward, and, as I was alone, I traveled in daylight, but I was not safe in so doing. I crossed the Holston River in a canoe, and went forward cautiously, watching for the rebel soldiers at every step; but I traveled along until evening without seeing any of them, and was thinking myself quite lucky, when, unfortunately, while I was passing through a farm in Washington County, some rebels saw me. I was some distance from the open fields, and was traveling in the woods, near the point where the Jonesboro' Road comes into the old Pactolus Road, which leads from Carter County to the boat-yard. At first I heard a clattering of horses' feet behind me, and, upon looking back, I observed a party of rebel soldiers coming toward me very rapidly. I felt sure that they were pursuing me; at any rate, I did not feel willing to meet them. The place where I was offered but few advantages for me to escape, as the near timber consisted of small scrubby oaks, with no undergrowth. I began to think that I "*was gone up*." Just before me there was a turn in the road. I walked on briskly until I got to a small hollow which concealed me from the rebel horsemen. In a moment I sprang out of the road, and up a steep acclivity, and at once lying down flat upon my back, I pulled a chinca-pin bush over me, holding it fast with both my hands until they passed me, at which time I heard one of them say, "*He has walked very fast*," and they immediately quickened their speed. I now sprang up and ran back to a large corn-field, and there remained until night. I did not, however, have to wait very long, for the sun was rapidly disappearing behind the western hills.

As soon as it was dark I took the road again. I had advanced but a short distance, when, to my surprise, I heard the rebels coming again. I stepped behind a tree, and they passed on, altogether unaware of their close proximity to that great object of rebel hatred, *a Union pilot*. I now started on again, and reached home without any farther adventure.

Upon my return, I found Colonel Grayson in the mountains with *one hundred men*, whom he had enlisted as recruits for the 4th Regiment of Tennessee Infantry, and desired very much to get them through the lines. I at once started to the boat-yard, in order to provide for their safety, and also to get a pilot by the name of Grills to assist me in conducting them through the lines, as I did not feel willing to venture alone for the first time with so large a company. At the same time David Stout came on with a large party of men, and engaged the services of Grills. Judging from the signs of the times, I felt sure that the rebel soldiers would be probably advised in regard to the movements of Stout and his party; and, sure enough, they were informed about the party moving toward Kentucky, and rushed forward in pursuit of them. The rebels killed and captured quite a number of this unfortunate party, who indeed met a worse fate than death, while a few of them made their escape.

I now concluded to conduct Grayson and his men myself, as I felt sure that I could go by a much safer route than the pilots were at this time traveling. The rebels were now aroused, and were vigilantly watching for stampeders, and several more parties were discovered, and at once dispersed by them. I was waiting for the times to become more auspicious for the Union men who were desirous of migrating to a "*better land*," but they daily grew worse, and I began to despair of being able to conduct this large party through to the Union lines before the chilling blasts of dreary winter would begin to howl amid the hills and valleys. I felt sure that I could conduct a small party of fifteen or twenty men safely through at any time; but the leaders, having collected these men for recruits, wished them all to go through at once. I now made several trips to the boat-yard to acquaint myself with the operations of the rebels, and also to learn a better route through the mountains. I now determined to try another trip through the lines with a small party of men, as I considered it best to test my abilities as a pilot before undertaking to conduct large parties so far as the Cumberland Gap. It was now November, and a large number of poor Union men still wandering through the mountains, hiding from the rebels, who had already killed and captured a number whom they found endeavoring to make their escape. Very few had succeeded in get-

ting through the lines, with the exception of the first company, which was taken through by M'Lane. Grayson was
now willing to go with only a part of the men whom he
had gathered, and, directing them to be certain and provide
themselves with a plentiful supply of provisions, I told them
on what night I would start with them.

CHAPTER V.

On the night of the 14th of November, 1862, I started on my first trip to Kentucky as a pilot with Colonel James Grayson, of Johnson County, Tennessee, and a number of men from the counties of Johnson and Carter. We met in the ridges near Elizabethton, and went straight forward toward Johnson's Dépôt, in Washington County. When we arrived at the railroad we stopped, and I went to the house of John Murray, who was a good Union man, and lived near the dépôt. I inquired of him if he thought there was any danger to be apprehended from the rebels. He told me that he did not believe that the rebel soldiers were stirring about any on that night. We had to cross the railroad within two miles of the dépôt, where there was a rebel company stationed. We crossed the railroad without being discovered, and by daylight we reached Holston River, two miles below the old Pactolus Ferry, a distance of thirty miles from the point we had started from, and which I considered was a good night's travel, for before it had taken me two nights to travel the same distance with a company of men. But, on this occasion, I told the men when we started that our success depended very much in getting the start of the rebels, and they exerted themselves during the night to move along as rapidly as possible. We crossed the river in a canoe which we stole, and then struck out for *White-oak Flats;* it was some time after daylight before we found a good hiding-place. We were now not far from the house of Mrs. Grills, to which I immediately went, to learn if there were any rebel soldiers in the neighborhood. She told me that there was no danger at this time, and promised to watch with vigilance, and if any thing occurred which she thought would endanger our safety, immediately to inform us of it. We here spent the day in the enjoyment of rest, of which our tired limbs were in great need after the hard night's travel which we had accomplished. When night came on we left the "*flats*," and soon reached the north fork of Holston River. Here there was no canoe to be had, and therefore we were compelled to wade. The water was very cold and deep, but we did not care for such trifles as that, and, taking off our clothes, we plunged into the stream. We all reached the opposite shore in safety, and, quickly dressing ourselves, we moved on at a *double-quick* rate of speed in order to get warm, for the night was quite chilly. That night we reached Clinch Mountain, and crossed over to the opposite side of it, where we could see over the Poor Valley, which lies between Clinch Mountain and Copper Ridge, and upon this elevation we remained all the day. We were not far from the road which leads to Sneedville, in Hancock County, Tennessee. All that day we could hear the rebels passing the road. We could hear the beat of their drums, and their loud cheering as they passed along. They were going in nearly the same direction that we were, but they traveled in the road, and we upon the mountain, doing the best we could to keep out of their way until night. While we were traveling along the mountain that day a company of scouters came to us; they had started to go through the lines before we did, but were pursued by the rebel soldiers and dispersed; and they were now hiding in order to save their lives, and being in a strange country, they did not know which way to go, and were afraid to venture back to their homes again. They were nearly destitute of clothing, and were in a starving condition, as they said they had ate nothing for two days and nights; besides, they had been chased by the rebel cavalry, and some of their party had been killed. They told us that they had seen their companions shot down without being able to afford them any assistance, while others were only wounded, and left to the mercy of the enemy, or to die in the mountains alone. They told us that we could never get through without being captured or killed. This, however, I did not believe, for I felt sure that bad management, occasioned probably by a bad pilot, had been the cause of all their troubles. We at once divided our provisions with them, and told them they could go along with us. We knew that we would all have to suffer when we divided our provisions before we could procure another supply, but we resolved to push on as fast as possible, and get through the sooner. We barely waited for darkness to come on before we started, and a very dark night it was, and extremely cold. We were now in the worst part of the mountain, with no sign of a path to guide us, climbing over fallen timber, going through brush, and often falling over rocks, wading the cold mountain streams when we came to them, which we had to encounter very frequently. Near daylight the rain began to fall; but having no means of protecting ourselves from its chilling effects, we pushed along until daylight, at which time snow began to fall, and the wind commenced blowing a terrible blast, and soon the rain and snow changed to sleet, which soon made it almost impossible for us to get through the brush on account of the ice which had there so suddenly congealed. But we could not stop until we could find a place where we could kindle up a fire with safety, and, therefore, we had to move on without finding such a place until we were exhausted and almost frozen.

We could go no farther. We now commenced making shelters, which was a hard task, as our hands were perfectly benumbed with cold. We cut small forks with knives, and drove them into the ground with rocks, and then, laying small poles across, we covered over the top with leaves. We kindled up a small fire out of dry bark, which would not smoke. We crawled under our shelters, and the men being so nearly frozen, just so soon as they began to get warm went to sleep. They did not sleep long, for the pangs of hunger and their aching limbs soon aroused them from their repose. We could not eat as much as we desired for fear of exhausting all our provisions, and the day was passed in resting and drying our clothes. Some of the men who came to us on Clinch Mountain suffered greatly for want of clothes, and, in fact, all the men that I started with seemed to be getting in very low spirits. We were now upon Powell's Mountain, and that night at two o'clock we stopped, as some of the men were nearly frozen. We were now in a safe place, and gathered all the old stumps and wood which was near at hand, and soon had a blazing fire, and raked away the snow to make as good a place as we could to sit down upon; we could not lay down, for when the fire melted the snow and the ice, the earth around the fire was completely saturated with water. The clouds now began to break away, but the wind continued to blow in dreadful gusts, which made it very uncomfortable for us to stay close to the fire, as it was blown upon us, and it was hard for us to keep our clothes from being badly burned. We staid here until eight o'clock, when we were compelled by hunger to move onward. We were doing wrong by traveling in daylight, and I well knew it; but in reality I thought that it was best for the men to move on while they had strength, and the nights were now so dark and cold that they could make but very little progress. We now had a small valley to cross called Wildcat, lying between Powell's Mountain and Walling's Ridge. We crossed this valley, and then commenced the ascent of the ridge beyond, which proved to be a very laborious task, as the leaves were frozen, and the bushes were bent to the earth with sleet; but we finally gained the summit, when we stopped to rest, and, looking some distance ahead of us, we saw a company of horsemen coming from Powell's Valley, which was the next valley that we had to cross. I thought in a moment that the citizens of Wildcat Valley had discovered us, and that some of them had taken a near route to Powell's Valley and reported us to a company of rebel soldiers who were stationed there. We were now in the very midst of rebels, being in Lee County, Virginia. The men now seemed to forget their hunger and weakness, and thought of nothing but making their escape. The brush and undergrowth was not thick upon this mountain, and, therefore, we could not hide very securely. I must confess that I was put to my studies for a minute, but there was no time for much thinking. We were on a high point, and could see the enemy plainly in the valley below. We started along the ridge in plain view of them, and they, seeing us, came on toward us. We moved on in this way for some time, when at length we got out of their sight, and started down the side of the ridge from them and took the *back track*, very hastily at that, until I thought that we were out of danger. I knew that they were waiting to intercept the company on one side of the ridge while they were on the other, and going in a different direction. Upon arriving at a dense thicket of bushes we crawled under them, and there remained until night. We were afraid to kindle a fire, and, consequently, suffered very greatly from the severe cold, and were also nearly perished for something to eat, as we had taken nothing to eat during the whole day. We shivered under these bushes with cold until dark, when we started again. Our clothes were frozen on us up to our waists, and knocked together as we walked like rocks, but walking revived and warmed us, and we all got along pretty well.

We now turned down the ridge toward Powell's Valley again, and had already come to the cleared land; it was now late in the night, and we traveled very cautiously along a cross-fence running in the direction of Powell's River. We finally reached the river, and were not long in divesting ourselves of our clothes and crossing the stream. There was a thicket on the opposite bank, where we stopped until we put on our clothes, and then went on toward Cumberland Mountain, which was just in sight, and we traveled rapidly until we reached it. The night was very dark and gloomy, but we began to ascend the mountain, which was very steep, pulling up by the grape-vines and bushes as we could see to get hold of them. At length we succeeded in gaining the summit, which we found to be covered over with laurel and ivy bushes to such an extent that it was hard to get through them at all, but I kept in a straight line for Kentucky, no matter what was in the way.

The brush was not now so thick, and we soon struck a blind path; and as it led on in the way we were going, we followed it for some time, and at length we came to an old deserted house, where we concluded to stop and rest. Upon going into it, we found that the floor was gone, and the hogs had a fine bed of leaves in it; *we drove them out, and took possession of their bed ourselves.* We were now out of danger, and would have kindled up a fire, but we had no matches; we were very much stiffened with cold, and almost starved, *as we had not tasted of any food for twenty-four hours!* It was now two o'clock in the night, and we rested until day-light, when we again went on. The rain was now falling rapidly, and the fog was so thick that we could scarcely see our way. We went on in the direction of Kentucky, travel-ing all day, wet, cold, and hungry, and in the evening we reached what is called Clover Fork, in the State of Kentucky. I never diverged from the route, which I projected in my mind before starting upon this trip, and traveled on through the mountains with as much certainty that I was pursuing the proper direction as if I had been traveling a public road. We now went to the house of a man by the name of Clark, who was a good Union man, and was very kind, supplying us with something to eat, and also furnished us with lodging for the night. We all now felt that we were free, and it is useless for me to attempt to describe the feelings of the men as exhibited by their expressions of gratitude and gladness; none but those who have suffered as they did in their pas-sage can form a proper conception of them. We remained here all night by a blazing and very comfortable fire, by which we dried our wet clothing; but by morning our feet and limbs were so badly swollen that we could not walk, and therefore we had to spend another day and night at this place, and were supplied with plenty to eat, and were treated with great kindness by our gentlemanly host. The next morning we all felt greatly refreshed, and were able to travel, and went on to a point on Cumberland River, where some home guards were stationed. We remained with them one night and a day. It was here that I separated from the company, which I had piloted through the lines with success, after the most cordial parting congratulations, which were mutually exchanged by all, they intending to go on farther into Ken-tucky, and I to return to the mountains of East Tennessee.

CHAPTER VI.

THE day that I left Cumberland River I went back to Mr. Clark's residence, where I remained that night, and bought a sufficiency of bread and dried beef for my journey. Next morning I started homeward again, to retrace that long rugged road all alone; but I did not care for that, as I thought that I could now travel to suit myself, and as fast as I pleased, having no one to wait for or hinder me, and during that day I crossed Cumberland Mountain, and went as far as Powell's Valley, where I stopped until night came on. It was two miles across the valley, and I slipped along a fence-row as far as I could, and then took the open fields. When I came to the river, I took off my clothes and went over in a hurry, and went on crossing the remainder of the cleared land, and reached the base of Walling's Ridge in safety without seeing or hearing a rebel. Here I rested a short time, and crossed the ridge, and also Wildcat Valley, and went on to the top of Powell's Mountain; and here, finding a good place to hide, and being very tired, I stopped. It was now some time until daylight; but I staid there until the next night, when I again resumed my lonely march, making my way as best I could through bushes and brush and over fallen timber, and wading the streams when I came to them. The night was very dark and cold, the sky was overcast with black and murky clouds, and every thing was so profoundly still in this lonely region that I could have heard the soft motion of a mountain ghost if it had flitted past me upon its gossamer wings. But I had no one to take care of or to guide

along in my dark pathway, and was in all probability the
only unfortunate human being who was wandering along at
this dark and unseasonable hour upon this wild and cheerless mountain. That night I crossed Copper Creek, Copper
Ridge, and little Poor Valley, and arrived at the top of
Clinch Mountain against daylight, where, owing to my excessive weariness, I was very willing to stop. I made a small
fire here, and rested until twelve o'clock, when, suffering very
much for water, I started down the side of the mountain in
search of some, which I did not find until getting near the
foot of it. That evening I traveled ten miles along the mountain toward Moccasin Gap, which is near the Holston Springs
in Scott County, Virginia. I could now hear the "rebel
drum" quite plain, and concluded to stop until night came
on; and a dark night it was, and also very cold. I now had
about one mile of cleared land to pass through and two public roads to cross, before I could reach the shoal in the north
fork of Holston River, where I desired to cross. The rebels
were thickly passing, but I went forward without being discovered. I suffered very much in crossing the river, as I had
to take off my clothes, and the water was deep, and icy cold.
By daylight I reached the White-oak Flats, and here found
that they were full of men, trying to get a pilot to take them
through to Kentucky. I was very much fatigued and worn
down with my journey, and therefore tried to excuse myself
from going back with them ; but they would not listen to a
refusal, nor even give me time to go home and return. I
could not disregard their importunities and turn away from
them in their distressing situation, knowing as I did that they
had been driven away from their homes by the worst tyranny which had ever been inaugurated in a free country, and
urged to wander forth like destitute pilgrims to a strange
land. I therefore determined to go with them, as they seem-

ed to be nearly all of them strangers in this region of country, and I did not believe that they could possibly make the
trip without a pilot who was acquainted with the long and
laborious journey which stretched out before them.   I immediately went to my old friend Mrs. Grills, who was ever
ready to assist me, and procured provisions for the journey.
I rested for two days, and the night before we started was
spent by the good Union people living near in preparing food
for the men to travel on.

CHAPTER VII.

On the night of the 10th of December, 1862, I left the *White-oak Flats* in Sullivan County, Tennessee, to pilot a large company of men through the rebel lines to the State of Kentucky. Bird Brown, of Washington County, Tennessee, and Lieutenant Luttrell, were the only two men in the company with whom I was personally acquainted. I did not much like the idea of starting with so large a company, as I knew that the danger of being discovered and intercepted was so much greater, but at this time I could not well do otherwise, as the men were strangers in a strange land, and surrounded by the merciless rebels. The night was dark and cold, and threatened a severe snow-storm. We went quite slow out of the "flats," stumbling along over logs and crawling through tree-tops, making, I thought, entirely too much noise for *fugitive stampeders.* At length we got out of the "flats," and began to ascend the little ridges, making our way to the north fork of Holston River, and before we could reach there we would have the main road to cross, leading from Moccasin Gap to the boat-yard. This caused me some uneasiness, owing to the fact of having so large a company with me. When we had advanced nearly to the road, I left my men in the brush, and went forward alone to look out for threatening danger. I could not hear or see any thing to give me any alarm, and at once gave a signal for the company to come on ; and I stood *on picket* until the last man had crossed the road, which they did with the greatest caution. I now went to the front, and led the way through the ridges until we came to the river, when I pro-

ceeded to select the best place I could for wading. We
took off our clothes, and tied them around our shoulders to
keep them dry. The water was very cold and deep, and
the river at this point was tolerably wide, which induced
the men to draw many *long breaths* before they reached the
shore; but after emerging from the cold water we soon put
on our clothes, and a brisk walk through some old fields,
where we expected every moment to encounter the rebel
foe, made us quite warm.

We now began to climb the spurs of Clinch Mountain,
and the rain and snow now falling very thick and fast, the
poor men became so weary, and their clothing so wet, that
it was very difficult for them to travel.   Some of them were
very poorly clad, and had neither blankets nor over-coats to
protect them from the cold and chilling wintry blasts, which
were now rushing and howling through the mountain defiles like mad giants : in fact, they were, in a manner, nearly
frozen, and we had to stop and build a fire to warm their
chilled and stiffened limbs.   We were now in a good place
of concealment, and staid there during the remainder of
the night, and also the next day.   A short time before daylight the rain ceased, and the snow began to fall with great
rapidity, which gave us the most indubitable premonition
that cold and dreary winter, in all its horrors, was about to
overtake us amid these rough and almost inaccessible mountain ranges.   The snow continued to fall until twelve o'clock,
when it was followed by incessant storms of rain and sleet,
which gave to the mountain upon which we were now lingering a most gloomy and desolate appearance, and caused
us frequently to contrast our present wretched situation to
the happy period when, around our own loved firesides, we
enjoyed the dear society of our families, before rebel tyranny
had severed, with its impious hand, the dearest ties which

bound us to earth. As soon as night came on and covered our pathway with its dreary darkness, we started again for the "promised land," which now constituted the bright cynosure upon which our hopes and expectations were fondly placed. We crossed Clinch Mountain, and now had little Poor Valley to cross, and also the main road leading to Rogersville and Bristol. I again went forward alone to see if there were any signs of danger ahead; but finding that there were none, I gave a signal for the men to advance, while I continued to watch with all diligence until they had passed the line of suspected danger, when I again took the lead, and conducted them on through as rough a country as ever a poor set of men were compelled to travel through during that dark and dreary night. Our pathway at times seemed to be completely hedged up, and we had to feel and grope our way along amid the terrible darkness, which seemed most vehemently to dispute our onward passage, and at times led us on through miry brakes and dreadful brambles, which, indeed, seemed to be a fit abode for "gorgons, hydras, and chimeras dire."

Toward daylight the sky became clear, and the glittering stars looked gently down from their distant *homes of blue* in all their bright and beautiful effulgence. The air was extremely cold, and our shoes were frozen upon our feet, and our wet clothing was freezing upon our bodies, and wrapping us in its cold and icy embrace. We were now compelled to stop and make a fire, and a portion of the men being so tired and worn down that they laid down upon the cold snow around it. We tried to eat, but some of the poor men were so nearly frozen that they could neither eat nor sleep. It was impossible to lay down by the fire with any degree of comfort, for the earth was covered deeply with its snowy garb, and, to make our condition more deplorable, we were now in a part of the rebel dominions where we were afraid to make up a very large fire for fear of being discovered. We were now in great danger of being seen if we traveled in daytime, for we had the Wildcat Valley next to cross. The day was miserably cold, and we were convinced that we must either march on or freeze to death. The men all wished to go on, choosing rather to run the risk of being seen by the rebels than to suffer the dreadful extremity of freezing.

I had never yet crossed the Wildcat Valley in daylight without being seen and pursued, and I must confess that I now felt some emotions of uneasiness in regard to the consequences which I was apprehensive might result from endeavoring to cross it at this time with so large a company of men. But on the present occasion I could do no better on account of the extreme cold weather, and therefore urged the men to advance forward as rapidly as possible, which order they complied with as well as their frozen limbs would allow them, and we all succeeded in crossing this hot-bed of rebellion in safety, and pushed forward to the top of Walling's Ridge, where we stopped to rest and to eat something, keeping a sharp look-out in the mean time to see if we had been discovered by the rebels in the valley. We could see no one stirring, and concluded that we had been quite lucky in escaping the vigilance of the rebels. . We remained here, watching and resting, until night came on ; we now had Powell's Valley to cross. After eating the last morsel of our provisions, we started down the ridge for the valley below, and on coming to the cleared land we halted, as I thought it advisable to wait until the citizens in the valley had retired to repose before we attempted to cross it. The night was gloomy enough, and the snow in the valley was at least *six inches* deep. This, I thought, was the place where we were to encounter the greatest danger of being discovered; but I knew that we must pass through the ordeal of danger at this point, or be compelled to travel a much longer journey through almost impassable mountains of snow. I do not think that I shall ever forget this place while my faculties of memory shall endure. For it appeared that right here the rebels, like incarnate devils that they were, were always on the alert, seeking the lives of the poor unfortunate Union refugees as they were endeavoring to escape from the oppression of the infamous rebel government.

By the time we reached the settlement in the valley the clouds had passed away, and the stars shone out in all their unclouded majesty, and the frost which the cold air had precipitated upon the white bosom of the snow reflected back their bright and lustrous beams with silvery beauty. We pushed forward, having about a mile to travel, through some fields; and as we went on we kept in the shadows of the fence-rows, which ran along in the direction that we were going, until we arrived very near Powell's River, at which time I again went forward by myself to see if our road was clear. I stood for some time intently listening, but I could not see or hear any thing to occasion alarm; all was still and quiet in the surrounding darkness, and no person seemed to be stirring. I went back to the men and requested them to move on toward the river. When we arrived at the river, we had to descend a bank some ten feet downward to get to the margin of the river. The men were taking off their shoes to cross, and I was already some five or six steps into the river, when a small dog commenced barking at a cabin which was near by. I stopped to see if the men were all ready, when, to my great astonishment, I saw a gang of rebel soldiers coming from the cabin and charging right on us. We had no time to lose; for by the time the men had all stepped into the water the rebels were firing on us, and being on the high bank above, the bullets fell around us like hail, sometimes throwing the water above our heads. It was a terrible time with us for a few minutes, but fortunately we all managed to get across without being touched by the rebel bullets. Five of the men had left their shoes and socks on the bank of the river in the hurry of the moment, and many more lost their coats and blankets in the river. Some stumbled and fell down in the river, and came near drowning before they could recover, and not one of us had a dry piece of clothing. Just as we emerged from the water we had to cross a high fence. The men charged the fence with the greatest precipitation, and I called to them to be more calm, and to stay with me; for, if they got scattered in the mountains, I told them they would never succeed in getting through, and would in all probability freeze to death. We now had a large brier-field to pass through, and very much fearing that the rebels would pursue us on horses, we stopped for no impediment which obstructed our pathway. I never saw such a perfect wilderness of briers as we here met with in all my life. I was leading the way, and the men followed closely behind me, when I came in contact with such a dense patch of large briers that I could not break them down fast enough with my *naked feet ;* and while I was trying to obtain a passage through them I stumbled down, and the men run over me before I could rise to my feet. I had been holding my hat and blanket in one hand, and my shoes and socks in the other; but before I could get through this terrible field of briers I was compelled to cast away my hat and blanket, which was done with the greatest reluctance. I held on to my shoes, and was soon in front of the company again.

This dreadful field of briers was at least three hundred yards wide, but we crossed it in a hurry, and were now in the woods upon the side of Cumberland Mountain. We hastened up the mountain for a quarter of a mile, and then stopped. Thanks to kind Providence, we were all yet alive and together, none of the men having been injured by the lead which had been so recently hurled at them by the rebels.

But we might as well have been killed as to be in the terrible plight which we found ourselves now to be in, as we would then have been relieved from our excruciating sufferings, which were almost now beyond the power of human endurance. My own feet were frozen so stiff that I could not feel that I was walking on them, and the balance of the men were in equally as bad a condition. Those who had not lost their shoes put them on; but a number of the men had none, and their clothing was wet, and frozen hard upon their bodies. To those who had been used to the comforts and even the luxuries of life, this was a bitter trial, but the thought that their lives had been spared made them quite thankful to get away upon any terms. We were all really objects of pity, and could our friends in the " *land of Dixie*" have now seen us, I have no doubt but that they would have been deterred from ever undertaking the same journey, even for the sake of liberty. We traveled on about three miles farther, when we got into a dense glade of laurel and ivy bushes, where we stopped and made up a fire, and thawed the ice off of our clothing; some of the men were badly frost-bitten. After making up a good fire, we began to make caps and moccasins out of our haversacks for the men who had lost their hats and shoes. We cut them to fit the head and feet as nearly as we could, and sewed them up in as good style as we could. Our profi-

D 2

ciency in the art of tailoring we did not suppose would have pleased the fastidious taste of a Beau Brummel or a Count D'Orsay; but we well know that it would suit the feelings of these poor bare-footed and hatless men, who were here amid the snow-clad mountains, and the wintry winds howling around them, entirely destitute of shoes for their frozen feet, and of hats to cover their heads. The cap which I made for myself was quite comfortable, and protected my ears and head quite well from the cold and chilling blasts of winter—indeed I thought it more comfortable than a hat, and continued to wear it until I returned home. But our moccasins did not so well supply our feet, in the absence of shoes, for our feet were full of briers, and were badly cut with rocks, besides being frozen. We were now near the end of our journey, and upon a very rugged mountain, where we knew that the rebels could not follow after us, where we could travel in daylight at our leisure; and if this had not been the case, I do not believe that many of these poor men could have ever arrived at the end of their long and laborious journey. We struggled on in pain and misery until twelve o'clock the next day, when we crossed the Kentucky line, and when night came on we had reached Clover Fork, and I immediately proceeded to the residence of my old friend Clark, where another forlorn party were fed and cared for by that estimable gentleman and his kind and obliging family.

Here we staid all night, which was now far advanced, during which time we were busily engaged in picking the briers out of our feet, which were very much swollen, and the thorns having forced themselves deep into the flesh, made this a very painful operation indeed. We continued thus to work with our feet until the pain became too severe to bear, when we would lay down and rest from our labor until the pain would partially cease, and would then rise up and begin the painful operation again. None but those who have experienced such severe trials can form any conception of our sufferings.

I could now enjoy the consoling reflection that these poor men who had for some time been the object of my care and solicitude were now safe from rebel oppression and rebel cruelty. I thought that they had paid dearly for the boon of liberty which was originally purchased for them by the blood of their forefathers, but was vilely and wickedly suspended by the uprising of the rebels, whose infamous leaders bragged and boasted that they constituted the *chivalry* of the Southern States; and they loudly proclaimed that when Greek should meet Greek in the "tug of war," that the aristocracy of the South would put the "Yankees" to flight, and also estimating that *one* of their white-handed gentry could whip *five* of the Northern men. But the battle-fields of the nation, where thousands fell, in the conflict of arms during the miserable rebellion, give at once the *lie* to this assertion. Oh! ye infamous and boasting demagogues and myrmidons of the Southern rebellion, where, oh! where is that *great government* which you aimed to establish upon the ruins of the proud fabric of government which was established by the good and wise men of America? Where is the proud *oligarchy* which you attempted to establish on the wreck of republican government? Where now is your "*Southern Confederacy*," that foulest "whelp of sin" which the nineteenth century has given birth to?

> "Gone, glimmering through the dream of things that were,
> A school-boy's tale—the wonder of an hour!"

The rebels have been awakened from their dreams of infatuation, and have been convinced that the idea which they conceived of destroying the American government was a monstrosity, born and nurtured in their excited imaginations, and much harder to accomplish than all the labors which were performed by Hercules himself. The proud and self-exalted *chivalry of South Carolina*,

> "Whose ancient but ignoble blood
> Has run through *scoundrels* ever since the flood,"

have retired to the *little one-horse city* which looms up at the junction of Ashley and Cooper Rivers, there to meditate upon their defeated hopes and ruined expectations of building up a great "*Southern monarchy.*" When that old rebel miscreant, Beauregard, was employed in this hot-bed of rebellion pointing his guns at Fort Sumter, and endeavoring to destroy the lives of the men who had been stationed there by the United States government, his bosom, no doubt, was inflated with all the reckless ambition which inspired the breasts of Cæsar, Alexander, or Bonaparte, who are distinguished by ancient and modern historians as the three greatest destroyers of nations and of national happiness that have ever participated in the active scenes of earth. And, in all probability, some of the "*chivalry*" referred to have retired quietly back into the swamps of the Pedee and the Santee, which were so thickly inhabited by their illustrious prototypes, the *old Tories of the first American Revolution*, who fought against *their own government* at that day, and their sons, as the faithful representatives of their *ancient Tory progenitors*, and, as "chips of the old blocks," fought against their own government in the dark days of the Southern rebellion, not forgetting that their *Tory ancestry* had fought in the cause of *tyranny* and *aristocracy* in the first struggle for American independence, when the true patriots of the country were led on to victory by George Washington, and, of course, they could not forget to engage in the cause of the Southern rebellion when they knew that the great object of its projectors was to establish an aristocratic government by abridging the political privileges of the poorer class of Southern citizens, and by enlarging those of the slaveholder and the landholder. Therefore, they rushed headlong into the rebellion, and used their best energies to subvert and utterly destroy the proud temple of American freedom. Their conduct in the infamous Southern rebellion was an exact counterpart of the base conduct of their *Tory forefathers*, and they will be inevitably assigned to that *infamy in history* which their foul crimes and their reckless depravity so loudly demand.

Next morning we left Mr. Clark's house, and went over to the place where the home guards were stationed on Cumberland River. There we rested for four days, endeavoring to alleviate the pains which we were suffering from our bruised and mangled limbs. The day for our parting now arrived, and I bade my friends a final adieu, and they started on toward Lexington or Louisville, or to whatever place they wished to go, for they were now free, and could go on unmolested wherever their inclination might lead them; and I made immediate preparations to go back and again *run the gauntlet* among my old tormentors, the rebels, who were now prowling amid my native hills like hellish demons, actively engaged in their missions of murder and rapine. I felt sure that my friends who were scouting among the mountains of Carter County thought that I had deserted them, or was dead; the latter supposition I thought they would think was far the most probable, as no news of the luck which I had met with, or what had become of me, could possibly have been communicated to them, no more than if I had gone to another world, as all the channels of information were thoroughly destroyed.   There was a man who told me that he wished to accompany me in my journey back to Tennessee, and I told him to get ready to start with me the next morning.

CHAPTER VIII.

The morning we started was clear, but very cold, and we traveled hard all day; we crossed the Cumberland Mountain, and reached Powell's Valley by the time it was dark. After resting a short time, we crossed the cleared land in the valley, and went on to Powell's River, which was the place where I encountered the rebel soldiers a few days before, when I was on my way to Kentucky. We crossed the river in safety, and went into a lane which led on in the direction that we were traveling, and continued to follow it until it led us out into the main road, which runs up and down the valley. I did not like to cross the road at this hour, but my companion seemed to think that there was no danger, there being only two of us, and, in fact, I preferred to travel on the most even ground, as my feet were yet very sore; but I felt rather uneasy, and listened and watched very steadily for the least approach of danger. I now thought that I heard some person approaching, as the ground was frozen very hard, and footsteps could be heard for some distance. We now leaped over the fence as lightly as possible, and, looking just ahead, we saw a company of rebels coming toward us; there was no chance for us to run, as the forest was at least half a mile distant, and, therefore, we quickly jumped behind two small stumps that were standing near the fence, and laid down behind them as flat as flying squirrels. The stars were shining very bright, and we counted eighteen rebels as they passed. They did not see us, although they were nearly close enough to us to bear the *pulsations of our hearts* if they had listened. They were walking very fast, and were carrying their arms trailing. Had we remained in the road one minute longer we should have met them, and would certainly have been killed or captured. This was another very narrow escape, which served to make me more watchful. My companion was now quite willing to leave the road, and I now traveled in the direction which I considered the safest. We went on without any farther adventure, and soon reached the top of Walling's Ridge, where we rested a short time, and went on, crossing Wildcat Valley, and ascending Powell's Mountain nearly to the top, when, thinking that we had done very well for one day and night, we stopped. It was now nearly daylight, and being in a dense thicket of bushes, where we could have a fire, and where there was good water to drink, we were promising ourselves a good day's rest, which we much needed, when, upon looking back in the direction we had come up the mountain, to our great surprise we saw a parcel of men with guns; but they seemed to be hunters, and I do not believe that they knew any thing about us. They passed near to our hiding-place, looking carefully into the bushes and brush, but they did not see us. We now slipped along through the bushes and watched them, but they did not appear to be in pursuit of us. We continued to watch for some time, without, however, seeing any thing to alarm us, and the sun shining out a little, we laid down without any fire, but the ground being so cold, we had to rise up and move about to keep ourselves warm. When night came on we started on our journey, being almost as tired as when we had stopped in the morning. That night we came down from Powell's Mountain, and waded a large creek at the foot of it, and then went on, crossing the intervening ridges between Powell and Clinch Mountains near twelve o'clock; we also waded Copper Creek, and about four o'clock we reached Little Poor Valley, at the foot of Clinch Mountain. We pushed on to the opposite side of this mountain until we came to water, in a small hollow, where we made up a fire, and rested there during the day. Late in the evening we started on again, and early in the night we reached the north fork of Holston River, which we found to be very difficult to wade, as the water came nearly up to our shoulders; but we succeeded in crossing, and pushed on rapidly, and at daylight we reached the "White-oak Flats," where we met with kind friends, who immediately furnished us with provisions.

I found that the "flats" were again full of men wishing to get through the lines, and I found it very hard to get away from them. I told them that my friends at home already thought that I was dead, owing to my long absence, and that many of them were anxiously awaiting my return, so that they might avail themselves of my services in escaping from the rebel tyranny, under whose *iron rod* they had long suffered. However, I promised them that I would return soon, and when darkness came on I started for my home, a distance of thirty miles. When I arrived at Holston River I had the good luck of finding a canoe, in which I crossed and proceeded rapidly on my journey without meeting with any difficulties, and reached my old scouting range in Carter County against daylight. My clothes were torn into tatters, and having my old haversack cap on yet, my appearance was so completely altered that my friends could hardly recognize me. Indeed, I did look more like a wild man of the woods than any thing else, for the sufferings which I had endured in the mountains had changed my natural appearance altogether. But when I put on better clothes, and received proper food regularly, I soon began to look like myself again. I had now become so perfectly accustomed to hardships that I did not much care for them, as I had to · spend all my time in the woods, whether at home or abroad. I was an outcast from the ordinary haunts of men, for myself and the rebels, like oil and water, could not be induced to mix together.

I found upon my return home that the rebel soldiers were still actively engaged in hunting the Union men, and, when they succeeded in capturing any of them, treated them with the greatest cruelty. It was now the first of January, and the face of nature in every direction was clothed in the dreary habiliments of winter. The mountains were full of men who were anxious to go through the lines. At times I would spend hours in giving them a history of my adventures, and detailing the terrible hardships which they would have to undergo, but it was all to no purpose. They said that the greatest toils which they could possibly have to encounter in getting through to Kentucky would be far preferable than to remain here, and be hunted and shot at like wild beasts of prey. The rebel citizens of Johnson County had now all joined the home guards in that county, and knowing every man in the country, and also being so well acquainted with all the paths through the mountains of Johnson and Carter Counties, that, in real truth, there was but very little chance for the poor Union scouters to escape their vigilance. And it was about this time that the rebel Colonel Fulk, who proved to be a most heartless and desperate villain, was sent with his regiment of ragamuffins into the counties of Johnson and Carter to catch "*conscripts*" who would not willingly join the "Southern army." I at once concluded to take another trip to Kentucky, in order to relieve the Union men, who were so anxious to go with me, from the impending danger of being captured by the rebel soldiery, which now seemed to threaten them in every direction.

CHAPTER IX.

On the night of the 9th of January, 1863, I again set out for Kentucky with Robert Lyles, James R. Boyd, Nicholas Carriger, and a number of others, entirely too numerous to mention. I must here state that Robert Lyles had, a short time previous to this, acted in the capacity of rebel marshal for Carter County, and a good marshal he was; for, during the time that he was invested with the rebel robes of office, the Union men of Carter County enjoyed quite a *saturnian period*, and his residence here as the rebel marshal ended in his becoming a good Union man. His disappearance created quite a sensation among the rebels of Carter County, but the "bird had flown," and they could not help themselves, only by denouncing him in the highest terms of abuse. He was always very kind to the Union people, and therefore I did not much fear him when he first made application to go through the lines with me, and more especially as my best and most intimate Union friends were assisting him in making arrangements to leave "the land of Dixie!" It had been arranged for him to meet me at Murray's, near Johnson's Dépôt, in Washington County, and I must confess that I had some misgivings when I was getting near the place of our meeting. I thought that probably I had taken a very rash step when I agreed to pilot him through the lines, and could not help fearing that, instead of meeting with Lyles at Murray's, I might possibly meet with a company of rebel soldiers. I resolved, however, to be prepared for any unexpected emergency, and went forward to the

place appointed for our meeting, where I found Lyles in
considerable trepidation, anxiously awaiting my arrival. He
seemed to be far more fearful of being discovered than I
was. My fears in regard to the probability of being betrayed by him into the hands of the rebels were now entirely removed, and we started forward on our journey, and
reached Holston River against daylight. We did not stop,
but crossed the river at once, and went on to the White-
oak Flats, where we remained during the day. Mrs. Grills
gave us a warm breakfast. The company was considerably
increased before we started by men wishing to go through
the lines. Just at dark we started on our wearisome journey; the rain was falling rapidly, and, after stumbling and
falling over the brush and briers for some time, we got out of
the flats, and I then moved on in a straight line for the north
fork of Holston River. When I got to the river, I found it
quite full, which made it very dangerous to wade; but there
was now no other alternative but to wade or turn back, and
that we did not wish to do; so, cutting a good stick apiece,
in we went. The water was very cold, and the current was
rapid, but, with the aid of our sticks, we soon reached the
opposite shore in safety. We put on our clothes, which we
had carried over on our heads to keep them dry, and pushed forward, and, after crossing some cleared fields and traveling through the woods for some time, groping our way in
the darkness which surrounded us, we reached the foot of
Clinch Mountain. It was now nearly daylight, and the rain
was still falling fast. We were cold, wet, and very tired,
and proceeded at once to make a fire to warm our chilled
bodies and to dry our clothes. We remained here until the
early dawn of morning, when we moved farther on up the
side of the mountain to obtain a position of greater security, where we could rest for the day. The rain continued to

fall, and the wind blew tempestuously. We propped ourselves against trees, and tried to shelter ourselves from the
peltings of the cold rain as well as we could, and here we
passed off the day in a weary and very disagreeable manner.

Mr. Lyles was all the time in a peck of trouble, fearing
that the rebels would follow after and capture us; and the
whole run of his conversation was about *hanging*, and the
terrible consequences "*he* might expect if *he* should be so
unfortunate as to fall into the hands of the rebels," etc.
And no doubt he would have been hung if our company
had been captured, just for being found with us, if for nothing else. I endeavored to keep him in good spirits, telling
him that he was not captured yet; and as long as we remained in such a rugged, mountainous region, I did not
think he would be in much danger of being captured; that
the rebels could not be every where, and that the place
where he now was offered no attraction whatever to the
rebels. I cheered him up by telling him that, if the rebels
should have the temerity to pursue us, we could kill them
by rolling rocks down upon them from the steep crags.
But the rebels did not follow us, and, when night came on,
we started on our journey. We crossed Clinch Mountain
and Little Poor Valley. The rain continued to fall, and it
was one of the darkest nights that I ever saw; but we
steadily pressed on, and crossed Copper Ridge, and waded
Copper Creek, which was quite a river in size, having been
much swollen by the incessant rain, which had been falling
for some time. We were now approaching Clinch River,
and the path in which we were now traveling stretched
along the river for some distance, and through the roughest
sort of cliffs. At times we were compelled to crawl on our
hands and knees between and under large rocks, in constant

danger of being crushed by loose falling stones; and sometimes we had to pull up over the crags by the hanging
grape-vines and bushes. We could plainly hear the roar-
ing of the river beneath, which served us. as a guide, as
we slowly pursued our way along this rugged and trackless
mountain, with no star to illuminate our dark path. At
length we reached the river, and I commenced searching for
the most practicable place to cross it. The river was full,
and, before venturing in with the men, I concluded to wade
in and try the depth of it myself. I therefore procured a
stout stick, and, taking off my clothes, I plunged into the
dark flood; but I did not advance far before I was thoroughly convinced that I could not cross at that point.
I turned back, and then tried to cross at several other
places, but all to no purpose. I found that it was impossible for the men to cross at this time, and therefore we
would be forced to go back upon the mountains and wait
until the next night, when I thought perhaps the water
would be lower. It was with sad hearts that we turned
back toward the rough mountain, which stood like a giant,
frowning amid the gloom of night; for we knew that we
should be compelled to suffer very much for want of fire.
We were now on a sharp ridge, and daylight was rapidly
approaching; consequently we could not go any farther, as
there were houses not very far off, and we were afraid to stir
for fear of being seen. We passed the day bad enough, as
our clothes were wet upon us, and we were afraid to make
up a fire to dry them; therefore we were compelled to lay
perfectly still all the day, for fear of having another company of rebels waiting for us at the river. We had to employ ourselves a good portion of the day in stamping and
rubbing our feet to keep them from freezing, and, as soon
as it was dark, we crept softly back to the river. I un-

dressed myself, and taking my stick, I tried the river again; the water was as cold as ice, and the wind was blowing so cold that it seemed as if it would chill the very blood itself. I tried the second time before I could make the trip through the deepest of the water, where the men would have to pass. I then returned to my comrades, and after they prepared for the cold embrace of the water, we all went into the river together. I never heard men catch their breath so fast as they did when the water struck them nearly up to their shoulders. I thought that some of them would be inevitably washed down by the wild and tumultuous waters, but, fortunately, we all succeeded in getting to the opposite shore. The river was wide, and it took us some considerable time to cross it, but, after a severe struggle, we all got safely over it; we then had to run some three hundred yards before we could put on our clothes, as we had to cross a public road, and were looking every moment for the rebels. When we got to the woods we were all nearly frozen, and as for myself, I was so perfectly chilled that I was compelled to get some assistance in putting on my clothes. We traveled on for the greater part of that night, until we arrived at a deep hollow on Powell's Mountain, where we stopped and built up a fire to warm our frozen limbs. So soon as we got warm, we laid down and went quietly to sleep, being so nearly exhausted with fatigue and cold that we could scarcely believe that we were *living* and *breathing* men. Lying around the fire in every fashion, we exhibited a spectacle in that wild mountain hollow, as it was dimly lighted by our fire, which I shall not undertake to describe, but shall leave it for the reader to imagine.

We remained in the hollow referred to until the next night, and, when evening came on, we prepared for another hard night's travel by washing the ashes and dirt off of our

faces, and partaking of a small portion of our provisions.
That night we crossed Powell's Mountain and Wildcat Valley, and got on to Walling's Ridge; we continued to travel
on the top of this ridge for about two miles, and then turned
off toward Powell's Valley, and soon reached the cleared land
next to the valley. The night was extremely dark, and a
fine mist was falling, which very much resembled snow; the
ground was quite soft, which made it very disagreeable and
tiresome to travel in the open fields. We at length reached the main valley. We made as little noise as possible,
and every thing seemed to be still, and quietly resting in the
dark and dismal night's embrace. I think that the dogs
were even wrapped in the arms of sleep, for we did not hear
one bark as we approached Powell's River. We did not
stop when getting to the river to take off our clothes, but
hastily plunged in and crossed over, for I had not forgotten
the sudden attack which the rebels had made upon me and
my companions when I was crossing this river a short time
before. It was now about a quarter of a mile to the spurs
of Cumberland Mountain, which distance we traveled in a
very short time; for I felt sure that when we got upon this
mountain we would be safe from the rebels if we should observe due precaution. But we could have no fire yet, for
fear of being seen, and therefore hurried on until we came
to water; we here took off our shoes and socks, and washed
the mud out of them, wringing the water out of our dripping garments. It was now about three o'clock in the night,
and so perfectly dark that we could go no farther, as the
mountain was very rough, and completely covered over with
dense thickets of laurel bushes. We were yet afraid to
build a fire, for fear of it being seen in the valley; for the
citizens who lived there were all rebels, and who, I felt very
well convinced, would at any time take as much delight in

pursuing and shooting at stampeders as they would in hunting and shooting at a pack of wolves in the mountains, and
at the same time think that they were doing a deed which
deserved great praise. This was in Lee County, Virginia,
where some of the most unmitigated and heartless scoundrels resided that ever disgraced the form of human beings.
They loudly boasted that they would take no prisoners; and
numbers of poor Union men who had the terrible misfortune
of being captured by them were at once most foully and in-
humanly murdered by them, just because they were endeavoring to escape from the dreadful oppression and tyranny
of the rebel government. But I have the consolation of
knowing that none of the men that I engaged to conduct
through the lines ever had the misfortune of falling into their
bloody hands, although I must confess that I made many
very narrow and almost miraculous escapes from being captured by them, and for which good fortune I shall ever tender
my perpetual thanks to Him alone who sees amid the darkness of night as in the noontide's splendor, and who rides
upon the whirlwind and directs the storm. The dark deeds
of blood which they have from time to time perpetrated
upon innocent and harmless men, have doubtless been regis-
tered against them in the great volume of the Eternal Judge
of the Universe; and if they are never punished in this world
for their monstrous crimes, they will meet with their just reward in the world to come.

Morning at length came, clothed in her beautiful robes of
Orient splendor. We were cold, wet, tired, and hungry, and,
the worst of all, we had nothing to eat. Notwithstanding
all these serious impediments, we pressed on through those
dreadful laurel thickets; and in the evening of this day we
crossed the Union lines—that goal upon which our bright-
est expectations were immovably fixed through all the days

E

and nights of our long and perilous journey. We now felt that we were free, which greatly revived our drooping spirits. We continued to travel on until night, when we came to a house about two miles within the lines, where we stopped and staid all night. The people were poor, but they treated us as well as they were able, and we had a good fire to rest by. Early the next morning we struck out for the home guards, and crossed a little mountain called Black Mountain, in Harlam County, Kentucky. The home guards were stationed on Cumberland River, and against night we reached their camps. It would be hard for me to describe the joy of the party when they arrived among the friends of the Union, where they could rehearse the sad tale of their toils and troubles beneath the dear old flag of their country, which in their native land they had seen torn and trodden down under the feet of rebel desperadoes. As for myself, I felt like a bird released from its cage; for it was a great relief to me when I succeeded in conducting the party through safely from a region of country where they were threatened with danger and death on every side to a land of freedom; and the bare thought that I had faithfully served my suffering fellow-men in escaping from the rebel despotism afforded me the most pleasurable emotions. After resting for three or four days, I prepared to start back home again. I went to the residence of my old friend Clark, where I remained all night, and procured a supply of provisions for my journey.

CHAPTER X.

On the 20th day of January, 1863, I started home. The weather was now very cold, and the tops of the mountains were covered with snow, which presented quite a dreary and desolate appearance to the eyes of a poor wanderer, who was just starting on his long and weary journey from the mountains of Kentucky, to revisit his native home amid the distant hills of Carter County, where still lingered the dear memories of early and brighter days, before the dark and dismal cloud of rebellion had spread out in all its hideous proportions over my beloved and happy country. The lofty summits of the surrounding mountains, dressed in their robes of snowy whiteness, gave me the most indubitable evidence that the season of cold and dreary winter was now in the ascendant, and its chilling blasts, which were now howling around me, furnished me with very satisfactory premonition that my meditated journey could not possibly be agreeable and pleasant. But I started on without hesitation,

> "With proud, elastic step,
>   To see my childhood's home ;
> How fondly do we think of it
>   Wherever we may roam !"

The first day I crossed Cumberland Mountain, and by dark I was ready to cross Powell's Valley, after resting and waiting until every thing was hushed and still in the silence of night. I started forward, crossing the river and cleared land in safety. I went on up Walling's Ridge, and, finding water, I sat down and rested for some time, when, finding that the air was too cold to remain long quiet, I started onward. A mist of rain had been falling, which now changed to sleet, and falling and congealing on the snow, made it very laborious and difficult for me to climb up the steep acclivities on the mountain side, as the low bushes were borne down with ice. After ascending to the top of the ridge, I got along tolerably well, and continued to travel along its top until I turned off toward Wildcat Valley. I then went on through fields and over fences, wading the mountain streams as I came to them, and at length I reached the foot of Powell's Mountain, which was at this time a serious obstacle in my way, for I knew it would require very laborious exertions on my part to ascend to its summit. However, I started up its side, scrambling forward, and at times slipping as far backward as I went forward; but after severe exertions I had nearly arrived at the top of the mountain, when I came to a large chestnut-tree, which was hollow near the root, in which I at once determined to take up quarters for the balance of the night and also next day, provided that I was not ousted. The sleet was falling fast, and this tree afforded me quite a comfortable shelter. I made up a small fire at the entrance, and felt that I was quite at home warming and drying my clothes, which were frozen on my back, and falling gently to sleep, I took a very fine nap until the return of daylight, when I awoke and renewed my fire.

I remained here all the day, not pretending to leave the bosom of the old tree only when I crawled out to rekindle my fire. Sometimes a severe gust of wind would blow the coals of fire and the sparks in upon me, burning my clothes very badly. This tree in the course of time had been burnt out, and the hollow of it was black, and I had turned and twisted about so much in it that my face and clothing were equally as black as the hollow of the tree was itself; and if the rebels had come upon me at this time, they might well have been frightened at my appearance, and might probably have imagined that I was one of old Vulcan's Cyclops, who had become tired of forging thunderbolts for Jupiter, and had left his smithery and taken up his abode in this dark and dreary mansion. When night came on, I bade my old tree farewell and started on again. It was a clear, cold night, and the ground was covered with snow; the bushes were bent down to the earth with the frozen sleet, but I pushed on down the mountain, and then crossed a number of ridges and creeks, all of which I had to wade, which proved to be a very disagreeable task, as the water was exceedingly cold. I crossed Copper Ridge and Little Poor Valley, and also the main road leading to Bristol and Sneedville, and then I began to climb up the steep side of Clinch Mountain, which was extremely difficult, as it was so completely covered with the frozen snow. When I got to the top of the mountain, I scraped the snow away and made up a fire, for by this time I was almost frozen. The fire soon melted the ice and snow around it, and I laid down upon the wet ground and endeavored to sleep, but this I was unable to do, for my bed was so cold and uncomfortable that I found it entirely impossible to court the gentle influence of sleep to rest upon my eyelids. I therefore arose from my cold bed and started down the mountain; but there was so much ice that I could scarcely stand up, and very often I slipped down over rocks and fell into the icy brush. At last, after many hard falls, I reached the foot of the mountain, nearly frozen to death. I gathered some dry wood and bark from off an old pine-tree, and having some tow in my pocket, I endeavored as well as I could with my frozen hands to kindle up a fire. Taking out my matches, I found that I only had *five* of them. I immediately struck one of them, and it failed to ignite; striking three more of them, they also failed as did the first. I now had but one more match, which to me at this time was of far more intrinsic value than all the gold of California or the silver of Peru. I held it in my hand for some time, fearing to strike it, as I thought that my life now depended on that last match, for my legs and arms were numb and chilled to my body, and there was no house near that I could go to. With trembling and fearful emotions I now tried my last match. The first time I struck it it failed, but I struck it again, and, to my great and inexpressible joy, it caught in a blaze. I was very careful of that little blaze, and touched it very tenderly to the tow, which caught at once, and I soon had a blazing fire, which I built near a large rock about three feet high, and laying down between the rock and the fire I soon got warm. Here I remained all the day, which was quite dreary, for the sky was overcast with dark and dismal clouds; snow began to fall, and the wind blew very cold. As soon as it got dark I started on my weary journey, and after toiling over a number of ridges and wading a few creeks, I reached the north fork of Holston River, which was full, and ice frozen upon its shore. I took off my clothes and tied them around my neck, so that if I should be washed down by the strong current of water, I thought that I could swim out without losing them. I now took my stick and broke the ice at the bank of the river, and started into the river. The water was very cold, and came nearly up to my shoulders; at times I thought I could not succeed in crossing, but I plunged forward amid the cold and angry flood until I at length got to the bank. My flesh was sorely cut in several places by the floating masses of ice that I came in contact with as I was crossing, and blood was flowing from the gashes. I was nearly frozen again; and how it was that I ever did survive

the sufferings of that awful day and night is a mystery to
me. If I had perished in that river, or upon the snowy
mountain which I had crossed, my friends could never have
been informed of my end, for I was entirely alone. As cold
as I was, after crossing the river I pushed on all night, and
just at daylight I reached the house of Mrs. Grills, in the
White-oak Flats. I knocked at the door, and she arose immediately and let me in; she made up a good fire to warm
me, for in fact I was nearly chilled to death. She gave me
a good breakfast, which revived me very much. I told her
that I would now go to the woods and stay there until night,
but she said there was no need of doing this, as there were
no rebel soldiers about, and thought if I would get under the
feather bed and be very still, so that no one passing could
see me, I could stay in the house very safely. I was so nearly dead with cold and exposure that I concluded to take her
advice, and after covering my boots to keep them from soil-
ing the bed (for I was afraid to pull them off), I got under
the feather bed as she directed. She now commenced ironing a lot of clothes, which she placed on the bed under which
I was lying, covering over my head very nicely with the
clothes that she was ironing. I had not been under the bed
long, when she came and told me that there were about thirty rebels coming toward the house, also telling me to be
very still, as they were nearly at the door. They came in
very quietly, and asked Mrs. Grills if " she had seen any conscripts lately ?"* She told them she had not, and continued
to iron her clothes. They searched under the floor and up
in the loft, and under the bedstead on which I was lying,
but they did not discover me. They then, to my very great
joy, left the house. This I thought was a marvelous escape
from being suddenly hurled into the jaws of death by these
blood-thirsty minions of Jeff. Davis and his compeers in
wickedness.

As soon as the rebels got out of sight, I left the house and went into the woods, where I passed off the day in a very disagreeable manner, for it was desperately cold, and I had to be constantly on the alert in looking out for rebel soldiers. I was afraid to make a fire, and consequently my sufferings during the day were very severe, which I endured with all the gravity of an anchorite. Just as soon as dark came on, I started on my journey, and when I arrived at Holston River I had the good fortune of finding a canoe, in which I crossed over, and pushing hastily on, by daylight I was among my own native hills again.

The news soon spread through the country that I had returned, and before I had half recovered from the terrible fatigue and exhaustion induced by my recent trip, I had many applications to start again. "Will you conduct me through the lines?" and "When will you start again?" were the interrogatories which were hourly propounded to me. Indeed, I could scarce obtain time to sleep only when I concealed myself from my friends. I now began to think that I would be compelled to become a regular pilot whether I desired it or not. The toil and danger were great in assuming this position, but I really felt delighted in being able to serve my suffering and oppressed fellow-men in these dark days of their troubles; and at the same time I managed to make enough to keep my family from want, and that was about all that I did do, for very many of the poor men were not able to pay me a dollar, and very often the small amount that I received for my services I had to divide with those that were destitute; and never, throughout all the cruel rebellion and war, did I ever see a man that was under my care and protection as his pilot suffer for any thing while I could command a dollar to supply his wants, which proud reflection now affords me more real pleasure than the money which I expended in this way possibly could afford me if I now had it in my pocket. I would freely have taken every poor Union man through the lines that I ever did take, "without money and without price," if my circumstances could have permitted it; but I had a support to make for a large family, and was therefore compelled to go and seek employment under the protection of the old Union flag, or to charge those a small amount who were able to pay me who desired me to conduct them through to the Union lines; and this I always thought was doing nothing more than simple justice to my family.

The signs of the times in Carter County now presaged nothing but danger for the Union men who had been driven into the mountains. A great deal of rain had fallen, which had raised the waters very high, rendering it useless now to start with a company to Kentucky, as I well knew that we could not cross the intermediate rivers. Day after day was spent by the anxious scouters patiently waiting for the waters to subside. The month of March, with its cold, bleak winds, had now arrived, and we had not been able to get off yet; and some of the men whom I had agreed to conduct through to Kentucky had the misfortune of being captured and cruelly murdered by the rebels. The infamous men who perpetrated these murders belonged to Folk's regiment, accompanied by some of the home guards of Johnson County, who had been ranging all over the country for conscripts, taking these home guards along with them for guides. The names of the poor fellows who were killed at the time referred to were James Taylor, Samuel Tatum, Alfred Kite, Alexander Dugger, and David Shuffield. They were all together when the rebels discovered them, they being on one side of the Watauga River and the rebels on the other. When they first observed these men, they at

E 2

once dashed across the river on their horses and surrounded them on a small ridge. Some of these men had arms,
which, however, were nothing more than a pistol or a knife,
which so enraged the rebel demons that they rushed forward like blood-thirsty tigers, and butchered these poor men
in cold blood, without pity and without mercy. And if
these black-hearted scoundrels had been unchained devils
from the infernal regions, they could not have imbrued their
hands in the blood of their innocent victims with more cool
determination than they did upon this occasion.

When the rebels first fired, poor Taylor surrendered;
they continued to shoot at him, while he begged them to
treat him as a prisoner, but, instead of this, one of these incarnate devils ran up and soon silenced him, by shooting
the top of his head off with a musket. Two of them then
caught him by his feet, and pitched him violently over a
large rock down a steep declivity, which bruised his body
and broke his limbs in a most shocking manner; and, not
yet content with this display of barbarity, they then threw
great rocks upon him. They then took from his mangled
person a very fine watch and a considerable sum of money.
Tatum was killed nearly at the same time that Taylor was, he
being first wounded in the shoulder, and then dispatched with
great cruelty. The other three men ran some distance, while
the rebels were shooting at them as fast as they could; at
length they surrendered, and commenced imploring for mercy; but they might as well have asked for mercy from a
gang of blood-thirsty tigers as to ask it at the hands of
these devils in human shape, for they were entirely heedless
of their piteous cries and lamentations. In vain these poor
supplicating prisoners told their reckless and infuriate captors that they had done nothing deserving death, and were
only trying to keep out of the Southern army. All their

asseverations could not save them from the dreadful doom to which their inflexible tormentors at once proceeded to assign them. Their hands were tied behind them, and they were taken to a bending sapling and hung. Some of the rebel soldiers took the ropes which they carried with them for the purpose of carrying forage on their horses, and tied them around the necks of their victims, while others would hold them up until the rope was tied to a limb, and then let them go. In this way all three of these poor men were hung up to torture, and suffer a thousand pangs of death; for they were hung so as not to break their necks, but rather to be choked to death by degrees, which was the refined and cruel mode of punishment which was resorted to by these inhuman murderers. Two of the poor fellows, before they were hung, begged hard for a short time to pray; but even this privilege was not allowed them. The other one had been severely wounded in the beginning of the bloody affray, and was not able to talk. While they were suspended by their necks, and before life was extinct, they were treated with the greatest brutality, by their reckless murderers beating them with their guns. Captain Roby Brown, a citizen of Johnson County, Tennessee, and one of the home guards in that county, enjoyed himself very much at this miserable feast of blood. He had a complete frolic around them while they were struggling in all the agonies of a terrible death. He knocked them with his gun, and would then dance up to them, and turn them around violently, telling them to "face their partner." He would say to them that "he did not like to dance with any person that would not face him;" while they, with tongues as black as ink protruding out of their mouths, and their eyes bursting from their sockets, exhibited a spectacle of horror which was enough to strike terror to the very soul of any person

CAPTAIN R. BROWN'S CRUELTIES.

who was not perfectly hardened in villainy and crime, and callous to the most wretched displays of human suffering, and steeped in the deepest depths of infamy. But I can not presume to say that this most desperate and incorrigible scoundrel, Roby Brown, was in the possession of a human heart; if he was, it was entirely impervious to human feeling and to human sympathy, and was as cold and hard as the glacier rock of Mount Jura's bleakest hill-top. He may rest assured that he will receive a just recompense of reward for his terrible crimes, both in this world and in the world to come, for an avenging Nemesis will pursue him with her terrible whip of scorpions around the whole orb of his earthly existence; and when the Dim Unknown shall unlock the casket which confines his guilty soul in its tenement of clay, and hurries it to appear before the great Omnipotent in all its naked deformity, there he will receive that just retribution which his iniquitous and wicked life richly deserves, in the " everlasting fire prepared for the devil and his angels."

The rebel soldiers remained where they hung these poor men until they thought that they were quite dead, and then left the place. Some kind citizens, who had been watching the conduct of the rebels not far off, immediately hurried to the place where they were hanging and cut them down, hoping to find that the spark of life had not fled from all of them; but they were all perfectly dead, and presented a sight too shocking to behold. Some of their ribs were broken, and their bodies were badly bruised, where the rebels had struck them with their guns. They were now taken up, and were taken a short distance from where they were hung, and buried quite secretly and in a very rough manner, as the Union citizens were afraid to make any noise or display when they were committing them to their last resting-place. Taylor was a gentleman. He had been a re-cruiting-officer in the Federal army, and was captured by the rebels and put in prison. He had escaped from the pris-on where he had been confined, and had come into Carter County, on his way back to his command, and was waiting when he was captured for the waters to fall, so that he might get through the lines. On many a dark night the poor fellow came to me to inquire "how long it would be until the rivers would get low enough to wade." The oth-er men who were killed were nice young men, belonging to our own mountains, and would have made good soldiers in the Federal army.

The massacre which I have detailed in the foregoing pages occurred on the 23d day of January, 1863.

CHAPTER XI.

ON the night of the 22d of March, 1863, I started to Kentucky with a large company. We had been waiting for the waters to fall, until we found that it was quite hazardous for us to wait any longer, as the rebels were in hot pursuit of us every day, and we began to think that it would be as well for us to run the risk of *being drowned* on our way to the Federal lines, as to remain here any longer and run the risk of being *captured and hung.* The night was clear, and the sky was decorated all over with bright and lustrous stars, which scattered their beams of loveliness down in rich profusion from their distant homes in the great silent night-heavens. The weather was not very cold, and my company was entirely composed of young men from the surrounding counties, who, under the despotic military laws of the so-called Southern Confederacy, were hunted and claimed as "conscripts." They were all in fine spirits, as they now expected soon to be free from rebel tyranny, and not for one moment thinking of the dangers and hardships they would have to undergo before they could obtain their freedom under the old flag of the republic. We did not travel more than twelve miles on the first night we started, as the men complained of fatigue very much; we therefore halted in a deep hollow, where we remained during the next day. We did not spend the day very pleasantly, as we could have no fire, for fear of being seen.

As soon as it was dark we started, having twenty miles to travel before we could reach our next hiding-place in the White-oak Flats. The men could not get along very fast, as their feet began to get sore at the commencement of the journey, and, consequently, it was nearly daylight when we reached Holston River. We had the good fortune to find a canoe, else we could not have crossed, as the river was full, and it was daylight before we all crossed over. We now had a mile to travel before we could get into the "flats." The kind Union people brought us plenty of provisions to eat, which enabled us to keep the provisions with which we had supplied ourselves before starting for any future emergency which might arise during our journey. At evening we were pretty well rested, but some of the men complained very much about the soreness of their feet. When night came on we started again, and got along very well until we arrived at the north fork of Holston River; and here we found ourselves in a very bad fix, as the river was so full that we could not wade it. After trying to cross at several places, we were on the eve of turning back to go into the ridges again, when, to my great joy, I accidentally discovered a canoe, which had been washed up in a pile of drift-wood. We quickly hauled it out, but had no paddle to steer it over with. One of the men went back to the drift and found a piece of plank, which served us for a paddle. Providence, I thought, had in this instance surely provided for us. I now felt sure that we would get through safe. The current was so rapid, that it was some considerable time before all of the men succeeded in getting across the river, and I thought that I would surely freeze before I was done paddling the canoe backward and forward across the river so often. But at length the toilsome task was accomplished, and we were all safely landed upon the opposite shore, and daylight was just making its appearance. I do not think that old Charon himself ever labored more sedulously in ferrying the ghosts, who had left their earthly tenements of clay, over the dark and turbid waters of the River Styx, than I did upon this ever-memorable night.

After crossing the north fork of Holston River, we yet had a mile to travel, and a public road to cross, before we could reach a position that was safe; and I must confess that I was somewhat uneasy, as we could now hear the rebel drum very distinctly. There was nothing that stimulated stampeders to active exertion in traveling like the idea of being in proximity to the rebel soldiers; and therefore, upon this occasion, the men at once forgot their sore feet, and marched on rapidly until we reached Clinch Mountain, where we found a good place of concealment, and remained until evening, at which time we started on and crossed the mountain. When we got to the foot of the mountain we stopped to rest until every thing was quiet and still, when we marched on and crossed Little Poor Valley, and went on and crossed Copper Ridge. We now arrived at Copper Creek, which was quite a river in size, owing to the recent hard rains; but there was no time to be lost, and we plunged in and waded across it, and went on at double-quick speed, and reached the foot of Powell's Mountain by daylight; we continued to move rapidly on, and reached Clinch River early in the night.

We approached Clinch River very cautiously, and found, as I had already anticipated, that it was too full for us to wade it. Something now had to be done, or I thought that we would yet be compelled to turn back. Every canoe and ferry-boat, where a poor scouter could cross, was vigilantly guarded. We had almost concluded that we were now completely blockaded in making any farther progress on our journey, when I happened to think of an old rebel

who lived not very far off, who always kept a canoe, but
kept it securely fastened. This was all the chance, and I at
once determined to take him by surprise, and so completely
circumvent him as to obtain his ready consent to ferry us
across the river in his canoe. We therefore went near the
house, and listened attentively for some time, but could hear
no one stirring. We proceeded a little farther, when a
large dog began to bark, which I was afraid might rouse
every person in the settlement, but I stepped up boldly to
the house and called. The old man came to the door. I
asked him to set us over the river. He replied that he
could not, as the river was too full to cross in the night, and
said that we must wait until morning. I told him that we
could not wait, and that we must cross now without one
minute's delay. He asked why we were in such a hurry?
I told him at once that we were going through the lines.
I also asked him if there were any soldiers near? He said,
"There is a company about a mile up the river, who are
stationed there to intercept and capture a man by the name
of Dan Ellis, who is engaged in piloting men through to
Kentucky." The old man continued, "I have never seen
this man Ellis, but I have seen the trail that he and his men
have made in passing through the mountains." The old man
went on to say, "Ellis is very hard to catch, as he travels
altogether after night; the soldiers were down here this
evening, and said that they were diligently watching for
him and his stampeders."

We now started him to the river, and bade him to set us
quietly over, or that he might meet with a fate that would
not be very agreeable to him. I thought we would never
get done crossing that river. The old man did not know
whom he was talking to, but I believe that he wished us to
stay there until morning, thinking that we would all then be

captured. We pushed ahead rapidly, for we had been delayed
so long at the river, as it was nearly midnight, before all of
us got across. The night was very dark, but we hastened
on through fields and woods until daylight, when we began
to climb the spurs of Walling's Ridge, upon which we stopped and rested, and ate our breakfast, keeping all the while
a sharp look-out for rebels, but none of them made their
appearance. We proceeded farther on toward the top of
this ridge, and stopped again, for the men were so completely worn out with fatigue that they could go no farther. We
were afraid to make any fire, fearing that the rebels would
see the smoke, and would thereby be enabled to find us.
Consequently, we were compelled to shiver all that day in
the cold and bleak winds, which are always characteristic
of the dreary month of March. The ground on which we
had to lay down was cold and wet, and the sky was overcast by dark and gloomy clouds, through which the warm
and cheering rays of the sun were totally unable to pene-
trate.

On the night of the 27th of March we started on our
journey again. The clouds looked heavy, and threatened
rain or snow, and the wind howled its melancholy dirges in
mournful cadences through the deep gorges of the mountains. We went on, falling over rocks or entangling ourselves in the bushes, wending our way out of the mountain
toward Powell's Valley. There were many little streams to
cross, which we waded through without removing our shoes
or socks. As we approached the valley, a universal fear of
the rebels seemed to pervade us all; for by this time the
clouds had passed away, and the moon was soaring along
through the blue vault of heaven in all her bright and lovely
majesty. A light snow had fallen, which gave considerable
brilliancy to the glittering moonbeams as they fell in radiant

showers upon its cold surface. Just at this time darkness would have been more preferable, not because our deeds were evil, but because we thought that the light of the moon would enable the rebels to see us at a greater distance than they could in the gloom of darkness. But we could not complain; for the hand of kind Providence had conducted us safe thus far, and, I had no doubt, would conduct us on to the end of our journey if we should observe proper care.

We were now in the cleared land, and the bright light of the moon rendered every thing quite visible for a considerable distance in every direction, and, the clothing of the men being dark, I was fearful that we might be seen. I must confess that I was at a loss to know what to do in the present emergency, when, just at this time, some dark flying clouds, like wandering spirits in the blue ethereal void above, rushed forward, and completely obscured the bright face of the moon. We now got by the side of an old fence-row, which was grown up with bushes and briers, and traveled on as fast as we could while the moon was thus obscured, stopping in the shade of the fence-row when the moon would at times flit out from behind the clouds. I thought, when I sometimes looked at the men by moonlight, that they were the largest set of men that I had ever beheld, and could but liken them to the fabled giants of other days. I thought that surely they could be seen for half a mile at least. I knew that the valley was full of rebel soldiers, and I can assure the reader that I did not draw many easy breaths until we all got out of it.

When we got to Powell's River, we went straight through it, without stopping to divest ourselves of our clothing. This river is not as wide or as deep as Clinch River. We now struck Cumberland Mountain, and I chose the most rugged route that I could find, as I had some apprehensions that the rebels might follow on our trail. We pushed on to the top, and some distance down the opposite side of the mountain, before we stopped, and none but men in the same forlorn condition that we were could ever travel again over the rough and rugged ground over which we traveled. We now collected all the dry wood that we could obtain, and made up a large fire. It was now daylight, and we were near the Kentucky line, and I considered that we were out of danger. But the ground was so cold, and the men were so perfectly worn out with fatigue and hunger, that they could neither sleep nor rest with any sort of comfort. I can not describe the terrible situation that we were in. It is true we were all delighted with the joyous thought that we were now free from the rebels, and that we would soon be in a land of plenty; but the poor men were so totally exhausted that they could not rightly appreciate the very agreeable change which they had now succeeded, with the assistance of a kind, overruling Providence, in making in their condition. It seemed as if they did not now care about moving, as they had no immediate danger to apprehend. They complained greatly about their sore feet and stiffened limbs, and I could not prevail upon them to move forward until I promised them a warm supper and a bed to sleep on if they would arouse from their stupor and travel on.

It was about eight o'clock in the morning before I got them all started on the road again, and traveling steadily on, we crossed the line into the State of Kentucky about three o'clock in the evening. We went on to the house of my old friend Clark, where we staid all night, and had plenty to eat and a good fire to sit by, and against morning the men appeared to be very much refreshed. Early in the morning we struck out for the camps of the home guards. The men who had come through the lines with me were now free to go wherever they pleased without molestation. We staid all night with the home guards, and, the next morning, all the men who had come with me through the lines started to go farther on into Kentucky, and I returned to Mr. Clark's, to make preparations for my return journey home, which I left, with the company of men from whom I had just separated, on the 22d of March. I quickly made the necessary arrangements for my trip back to Tennessee, for I was anxious to learn what farther enormities the infernal rebels had been perpetrating during my absence.

CHAPTER XII.

ON the 31st day of March, 1863, I started for home again. Knowing, as I did, the awful situation of the poor Union men who were scouting among my native mountains to keep out of the way of the rebel murderers, who were hunting them in every direction, I could not remain contented a single day, even to rest my weary limbs. During my journey back home I thought I should not ask the rebels any odds, for I should be entirely alone, and could travel as I pleased. The waters had fallen some, and when I came to Powell's River, I waded over it without any difficulty, and went on to the top of Walling's Ridge in safety. But when I got to Clinch River, I did not fare quite so well in crossing it, for it had fallen but very little, and was yet almost past crossing; but there was no other alternative but for me to go straight through it, as I did not like, on this occasion, to call on the "old rebel" to set me over, fearing that by this time the company of rebel soldiers, whom he told me were camped near his house, would be on the alert, and diligently watching for me at every available point. After I succeeded in crossing this river, which occasioned me some trouble, I traveled on into the roughest parts of the mountain.

When I was traveling along upon the very rugged elevations of this mountain, at times I felt quite lonely and melancholy, having no person with whom to exchange one word to pass away the tedious hours, as they winged their flight into the dim regions of the past. However, I passed the lonely hours as best I could in the solitary but romantic region where I was traveling. I would continue to walk until I was almost exhausted, and would then stop in some dark and secluded hollow and make up a fire, eat a small portion of cold meat and bread, and then lay down upon the cold ground and endeavor to court the refreshing influence of sleep for a short time. In this way I traveled steadily on both night and day, as I kept my pathway so high along the mountain elevations, that I feared but very little of being interrupted by the rebels. After many weary miles of very rough traveling through a remarkably rough and dreary country, I reached the north fork of Holston River. It was not quite so full as it was when I crossed it on my recent journey to Kentucky, but it was now rather too deep to wade with safety; but, having no time to tarry, I took off my clothes and tied them on my head to keep them dry, and, taking a stout stick in my hand, I plunged into the dark and angry flood. The water was full of mush ice, and seemed like it would chill me to my very heart; and when I got out it was with the utmost difficulty that I put my clothes on, and, when I attempted to walk, I found that it was almost impossible for me to move my legs; but, thinking how easily the rebels might now capture me, I continued to exert my suspended powers of locomotion until the blood again began to flow warmly through my veins.

It was daylight when I reached the White-oak Flats. I again called on Mrs. Grills, who always proved a constant and kind friend in the dark days of my adversity, who furnished me with a warm breakfast in the woods, where I remained during the day. The flats were again full of poor scouters, who desired to go through the lines, and tried hard to induce me to conduct them through. I could but sympathize with them in their distressing condition; but I could not consent to turn back at this time, for my friends at home I knew were in constant danger of being killed by the rebel marauding soldiery, and were anxiously awaiting my return. I therefore hastened on, and reached my native mountains before it was daylight. The poor Union men who were hiding in the mountains expressed the most unbounded joy when I returned, as a report had reached them that "I had been captured and killed." This report, I have no doubt, had been started by some designing person, who wished to engage in the business of piloting men through the mountains and selling them to the government. But these heartless speculators in human flesh and blood had but very little success, for I had now achieved the reputation of being such a safe and lucky pilot, that the Union men exhibited a total unwillingness to start to Kentucky with any other person. When I conducted men through the lines, they were at perfect liberty to go wherever their inclination might lead them. But it was not so with certain other persons who set themselves up as pilots, for when they engaged to pilot men through the lines, they required, as a prerequisite understanding, that when they arrived in Kentucky, they should agree to volunteer at once in some particular regiment. And the worst of all is, that these fellows who engaged in this outrageous system of brokerage in the liberty and rights of their fellow-men scarcely ever succeeded in making a safe trip through the lines, for they would not subject themselves to the fatigue of traveling through the rough parts of the mountains, but would lead the poor men who had been so foolish as to place themselves under their protection as their guide along the public highways and through the low valleys. These lazy and blind guides did not fancy the toil and trouble of traveling when their pathway was covered by the

F

darkness of night, and therefore led their men along in the light of day, while danger was threatening them at almost every step; and, owing to this sort of indiscretion, these pilots were very often captured and killed, while their men were scattered in every direction, and many of them captured and murdered in the most awful manner. All the pilots who pursued the line of policy in traveling which I have indicated, which was characterized by the most reckless incaution, were captured and killed, without, I believe, one solitary exception. The blood-thirsty lions, in the shape of rebel soldiers, who at all times threatened the pathway of the poor Union men in their migrations through the mountains to Kentucky, were never found to be confined with chains, as were the lions spoken of by John Bunyan in "The Pilgrim's Progress," but, on the contrary, they were at all times found to be unchained, and ready to pounce upon their innocent victims and butcher them at once, without the least check or remorse of conscience.

When I returned home, I found that the counties of Carter and Johnson were still full of rebel soldiers, hunting and searching in every direction for *conscripts*, and not a day passed but what some poor fellow was captured or killed while he was trying to keep out of the way. In four days after my arrival at home I had another company ready to start, and, from the signs of the times, I thought it was a very hazardous undertaking. But, knowing as I did that there was danger every hour of some of the men being killed or captured while they remained here wandering about through the woods and mountains, I thought that it was far better for them to make an effort to get away from the dangers which threatened them on every side. I thought that, after we started, if we should meet with the misfortune of getting captured or killed, we should be animated for a while at least with the delightful prospect of getting through safe.

CHAPTER XIII.

On the night of the 7th of April, 1863, quite a large company of men assembled in the ridges near the old O'Brien Forge on Doe River, some three miles south of Elizabethton, who had prepared to start with me to Kentucky. Among the number was William Gourley, who was subsequently Captain of Company A, in the 13th Regiment of Tennessee Cavalry, and who fell mortally wounded while gallantly fighting at the head of his company in an engagement which occurred at Marion, Virginia, when General Stoneman made his celebrated raid into that section of the Old Dominion. A man by the name of Hartly was in the company, who afterward rendered considerable service to the great cause of the Union. George Ryan was also in the company; he was a citizen of Carter County, and had been captured by the rebels at Wytheville, in the State of Virginia, where he was working at his trade as a blacksmith, and put into a dirty and loathsome prison, just because he was a devoted Union man. After remaining in prison for some time, he volunteered to work at his trade in the rebel army, and continued to work faithfully for some time. He applied at length for a furlough, so that he might go and visit his family, who were residing at Elizabethton, Tennessee, which request was granted him without hesitation. When his furlough was out, he was concealed by Mrs. William B. Carter, of Elizabethton, until he could meet with an opportunity of going through the lines, which opportunity he availed himself of at the time I have referred to at the commencement of this chapter.

The night was exceedingly dark, and one of those cold and disagreeable rains which often distinguish the early part of the month of April in this latitude was now falling rapidly, which made us shiver as it fell upon our houseless heads.

We were afraid to venture into houses or even barns; and as we were now far away from our mountain camps, we just had to take the rain as it came, without being able to defend ourselves from its cold embrace. We therefore resolved to make a beginning of our journey at any rate, hoping that we should be enabled to conclude it successfully. We had not advanced three miles on our road before many of the men expressed a desire to stop and wait until the next night, as the darkness was so intense that they could scarcely get along at all. I felt that our journey would not be as prosperous as I could wish for it to be, but hoped for the best. The rain continued to fall with such violence that we concluded to stop in the forest and wait until the next night.

The winged hours flew rapidly by into the invisible womb of the past centuries, the dark night wore away, and the bright beams of morning began to illuminate the eastern sky. We remained in the woods during the day, and, when the dark mantle of night was again spread out over the earth, I got my company in readiness to make another move on our weary journey. We traveled only about twelve miles during this night; crossing the railroad, we went on into a deep hollow, where we remained undiscovered until the next night. The clouds had cleared away, and the stars shone out in all their splendor. We started again, and for a while we got along quite well; but at length George Ryan's feet became so blistered that he could scarcely walk at all, his feet having become very tender from his long confinement. After traveling a short distance farther, more of the men began to complain of their sore feet, and went limping and stumbling along in a manner which was truly pitiable to behold. I had great trouble to get them along, and we had yet twenty-two miles to travel before we could reach the White-oak Flats, which I designed to make our next hiding-place. About midnight we all stopped and ate a small portion of our provisions, and rested for a short time, when we went on again through fields and woods, the men at times falling over logs, and at other times falling when there was nothing in their way, as they were journeying over strange ground, and were not accustomed to traveling in the night; it really seemed that some one of the company was falling down every minute. When we heard the first chicken crow for day, we were three miles below the old Pactolus Ferry in Sullivan County. I stopped at a cabin where I knew that a good Union man resided, and inquired about the rebels. He told me that there were six hundred rebel soldiers stationed about one mile below that place, and had hunted the flats all over the day before, and that he expected they would hunt them over again the next day. He advised me not to cross the river. I was now in a very sad predicament, and scarcely knew what to do. I was afraid to conduct the men any farther on, for daylight was making its appearance, and there was no good hiding-place that we could get to. Leaving the river a short distance, we concealed ourselves under some low cedar bushes in the open woods, where we could see all that was passing around.

We spent quite an awful day at this ever-memorable place; for we could see the rebels riding around all the time, hunting the poor conscripts, robbing houses, and whooping and yelling like savages. The day was cold and disagreeable,

and we should have suffered a great deal more than we did,
if it had not have been for our continual fears of being discovered by the rebel soldiers. Our fears at this time not
only made cowards of us all, but had the property of im-
parting an agreeable warmth to our bodies, for I do not believe that fire was once named during the day by any of the
company. The sight of the infamous rebels prowling all
through the country was quite enough to employ all our
thoughts, without studying any thing about fire. We could
neither eat nor drink; it was a day of fasting and trouble
to us, but I can not say that there was much praying on this
occasion. In fact, this was one of the most miserable days
that I ever experienced in all my life; but it was not on
account of my own personal safety which caused me to pass
such a miserable day, because I believed then, and still believe, that I could have made my escape even if the rebel
soldiers had discovered us; but it was on account of the poor
men who had placed themselves under my care, and I
thought that it would be impossible for them to escape, in
their crippled and exhausted condition, if we should be discovered. I determined, if the rebels should find us, not to
abandon my company, but to share their fate, or even a worse
one, if it should be assigned me by the rebel murderers.

There was not even a sufficiency of bushes nor brush in
the woods where we were concealed to prevent horsemen
from catching us, it being entirely an open wood. That day
seemed to be a week in length. But, to our very great joy,
it passed slowly away, and night—that much longed-for
night—again spread her sable wings over the earth, when
we once more felt comparatively safe. Being now relieved
from the troubles and fears of the day, we left our hiding-
place in a hurry, the lame men in the company seeming to
forget their sore feet, and, in fact, every thing else but the

desire of reaching a place of safety. We had not gone far, when we came to water, in a very secluded place, where we stopped, in order to give the men, who complained mostly of their sore feet, an opportunity to bathe their feet in the water, and also to eat a portion of our provisions, as none of us felt like eating during the day. After finishing a hasty meal, we started on toward the river, and upon our arrival there, had the extreme good fortune to find a canoe, in which we crossed over, and hurried on to the flats, through which we had to grope our way amid the darkness of night, which, in fact, would have been a serious labor even in day-light. When we got out of the flats, we went on through the open fields and woods, and after crossing several very rough ridges, we arrived at the north fork of Holston River.

We found that the river was low enough to wade, which was quite fortunate for us, and, quickly taking off our clothes, we passed through it to the opposite shore. It was now nearly daylight, and we yet had about a mile and a half to go and two public roads to cross, where I was apprehensive that we might run upon the rebels before we could reach Clinch Mountain. The night was dark and foggy, and we traveled along very cautiously, making as little noise as pos-sible, listening all the time for the least approach of danger. When we got in about fifty yards of the road, I heard some person cough, when I stopped very suddenly, and looking forward, I saw a small fire burning in a fence-corner near the road-side. I was in front, and the men were behind me marching in single file, with their boots and shoes in their hands, which they had taken off, so that they might travel without making much noise. I immediately turned about, and ordered the men to take the back track, designing as I did to cross the road at another point; but when we got there we had no better success, for we saw another fire just

ahead of us. We were now well convinced that it was
the rebel picket-guard. We made another attempt to cross
the road at another place, but here we again run on the.reb-
el picket. By this time we had ascended to the top of a
ridge, and could see their fires at different points all along
up and down the road. It was now near daylight; we
hastened back to the river and recrossed it, and fell back
on a ridge for safety. From this point we could see the
rebel camps scattered thickly all along the road, and also in
the valley. It was now the 11th day of April, which we
passed in a weary and lonely manner, as we were feverish
with anxiety, and could get no water to drink; here we remained perfectly quiet all the day, and when night came on
we went farther on down the river, and waded it the third
time. The road ran along the bank of the river, and, as
soon as we crossed, we started in a run to the woods, which
was some distance off, where we stopped and put on our
clothes. We then traveled on for a considerable time
through fields and woods, until we came near the road that
leads to Rogersville, and being now on a ridge, we could
see the rebel camp-fires for two miles or more. It was quite
dark, and a little rain falling, and I concluded to cross the
road at all hazards. When we got very near the road, we
could hear the rebels passing on horseback; we could distinctly hear them talking, and could even hear the rattle of
their sabres. We were now at the narrowest place in the
valley, and I knew that we would have to cross at this point
or turn back. There was a high fence that we had to climb
before we could cross the road, and we crept up to it cautiously in the darkest place we could find, but just at this
point we could not well get over, and continued to crawl
along farther up the fence. The rebels were constantly
passing; when we would see a party of them approaching,

we would lay perfectly still until they had passed by, and we would then advance slowly and cautiously forward. We at length arrived at the place where I designed to cross the road, where we had to stand quite still in the darkness for some time, in order to wait until a party of rebels had passed out of sight and hearing. I now charged the men to make no noise whatever upon the peril of their lives, and I then led the way over the fence, the men following immediately after me; but in their hurry they threw down the fence and broke some three or four rails, which made a considerable noise. I thought when the rails broke they could surely be heard for half a mile. We rushed now for the woods, which were near by, expecting every moment that the rebels would be after us, but, to our great joy, the rebels did not pursue us.

We had now arrived at Clinch Mountain, and after traveling on for several miles, we came to a deep and lonely hollow, where there was water, where we stopped about two o'clock in the night. We ate and drank, and then laid down to sleep and rest, for we had now done without sleep for two days and nights, which almost seemed like an age. On the first appearance of daylight I roused the men from their deep slumbers, and put them to washing and greasing their sore feet before starting on their journey. We now went farther into the mountain, and stopped to rest a short time again. Our provisions were now getting short, and we saw very plainly that we would be compelled to go on or starve in the mountain.

It was now the 12th day of April, and during this day we crossed over Clinch Mountain, and got near to Poor Valley against evening, at which time we stopped and waited for darkness to come on. We then crossed Poor Valley and Copper Ridge, and waded through Copper

Creek, which was quite deep, and then traveled on through open fields and woods, and after crossing several rough ridges, we arrived at Clinch River. We found the river very full, but we at once determined either to wade it or swim it. Each man in the company procured a good stick; we took off our clothes and tied them up, and in we went. The water was very cold, but it did not quite swim us; we soon reached the shore, and started on in a run for some distance, when we stopped and put on our clothes. We now pushed on, crossing ridges and wading branches, until we arrived at the foot of Powell's Mountain. We struggled on for some distance up the mountain, when, coming to some water in a hollow, we stopped, for the sun was now rising.

The men were very much worn out with fatigue and hunger, for our provisions were now exhausted, and we were yet many miles from Kentucky. We continued here all day, and as soon as night came on we started forward, crossing branches and climbing ridges until midnight, when we commenced the ascent of Walling's Ridge. After crossing this ridge, we came in sight of Powell's Valley, which at this time was not an agreeable sight to us, for it was illuminated all over with the camp-fires of the rebels. The night was very dark, and we resolved to try to *flank* them, and go through the valley at the darkest point we could find. We started on through some fields toward the valley, and, on getting near, we stopped to take off our shoes, to prevent making a noise in walking; but in passing a house, the dogs as usual began to bark, and they certainly must have scented us, for we made no noise at all in walking. Several men came to the door of the house and hissed the dogs, and hallooed several times, after which a number of horsemen rode up to them. We had not yet crossed the main road, or we might have been captured. We started back to the mountain with all possible speed, and the horsemen after us; but we made a short turn around a fence, and dodged into some bushes, and succeeded in making our escape from them. The darkness of the night was all that saved us, for they could not possibly see which way we had gone, and therefore they immediately turned back.

We went on up to the top of Walling's Ridge again, and by the time we got to the top of the ridge it was daylight. We had no time to lose; we saw that we were now compelled to go on in a hurry, or else be captured by the rebels. We therefore went on down to the foot of the ridge very rapidly, and after crossing Wildcat Valley, we got on to the spurs of Wildcat Mountain. The sun was now shining, and after going a short distance up the mountain, we stopped to rest, for the men were almost completely tired down, and could not travel any farther. While we were sitting here we heard a noise; and upon looking in the direction from whence it came, we saw the rebels following our trail across Walling's Ridge, for we made a tremendous trail wherever we went. They came on until they reached the mountain upon which we were now stationed. But we now had the extreme pleasure of seeing them turn back, seeming not to care about pursuing us any farther. We continued to watch their movements for some time, but I do not believe that they ever saw us. They were now out of our sight over the ridge, and we were again left to our reflections, which were not very pleasaut, and our feelings a great deal worse. We had eaten nothing for two nights and a day, and had traveled all the time, and had no prospect now of getting any thing to eat soon. About twelve hours' steady traveling from the place where we had to turn back

would have taken us across the Kentucky line; but we
were now on Wildcat Mountain, and the rebels traversing
the country which lay between us and the State of Kentucky. The men were tired down, and in a starving condition. This was another awful day which we experienced
on our journey. We commenced skinning bark off of the
elm-trees, which we ate with a good appetite, and chewed
little hickory sprouts, which relieved the cravings of hunger
but very little. I spent the day in studying what to do in
the present trying emergency. Food we must have, and
that very soon, or starvation would be inevitable.

At length I determined to go back about six miles, to the
residence of a very hot old rebel, and fix some plan to get
something to eat. When I made my determination known
to the men, they all agreed to it at once, and as soon as it
got dark, we started back, and reached the house about
nine o'clock. Taking two of the men with me, we advanced cautiously up to the house, and, when we got within about fifty yards of it, I called out. The dogs began to
bark in a most vociferous manner. There were *only* about
seven or eight hounds that were barking all at once, and I
do not think that any thing else could have been heard for
a mile around but the terrible yelling of these hounds.
Their loud and dreadful barking reverberated and re-ech-
oed through the contiguous mountains, and sounded most
awfully, as their deep and clamorous intonations fell upon
the deep silence of the dark night. One of the family at
the house ran out among them, but this only seemed to
" add fuel to the flame," for the whole pack now started fu-
riously toward us, and we had to climb to the top of a high
fence to avoid being torn to pieces. After a while they became settled and ceased their barking, when we left our position on the fence. The old man asked us to walk into the

house, and, regardless of danger, we walked into the house, and told him that we were very hungry, and wanted supper. He said that we could have it, and his wife commenced preparing it. I now told her that we were not all that wanted supper, that there were many more in the company who wished to get something to eat if they could get it. The old man, when he heard this, began to mutter and scratch his head; but the old lady spoke very pleasantly, saying we could all have supper if we would wait until she could have it cooked. I told her that we would wait. She then went into a room and brought out six bouncing girls, and I can assure you they made the pots and ovens fly around. A portion of the men stood around the house on picket while the old lady and her daughters were preparing our supper. I observed that the old man was very well fixed for shooting, as there were two or three muskets and three rifles in racks over the door.

The old man at length asked who we were. I told him that we were deserters from Colonel Slimp, who was then stationed in Powell's Valley. I told him that we had been trying for some time to get furloughs to go home, but could not get them, and that we had concluded to go without furloughs. He said "that was right; that he wished his own boys would do that way also." He said that he had two sons at Richmond, and had not heard from them for a long time, and supposed they were dead. He went on to abuse the Lincolnites at a dreadful rate, saying that "he would not give one of them a mouthful to eat if they were starving." The old fellow was not aware that he was now just about to feed a tolerably strong pack of them.

Supper was at length announced, and we proceeded at once to do ample justice to it. After we were all done eating, we paid the charge, which was twelve dollars in old state money. We bought a small quantity of bacon and some corn meal, and, after putting it in our haversacks, we left there pretty fast, and very much refreshed. The night was dark as pitch, and misting rain; we went about two miles into the woods and built us a fire near a little spring, intending to rest there until morning at any rate; but there was not much rest for us. The rain soon began to fall in torrents, putting out all our fire, and we had to stand up under the trees until morning. The rain did not cease until about ten o'clock in the day; the sun then came out, and we removed to a better place to bake our bread, and to try to sleep. I put a portion of the men to baking bread, and, taking some of them along with me, I went to watch near a road which was near by, to see if I could see any rebels passing about. The road was full of them all day driving cattle and sheep, but they made no attempt to drive our party out of the mountains. At night we returned. The bread was all baked and ready for supper, and I must here tell the reader how it was baked. Some of the men skinned the bark off of a small chestnut-tree, in which the meal was placed, and then, carrying water in their hands, poured it over the meal, and then worked it into dough. They heated some flat rocks, and then placing the dough upon them, baked it into bread.

We now divided out our meat and bread, and started on to try our luck again. After crossing a number of ridges, and crawling along through the brush, we again got on to the heights of Wildcat Ridge; every thing seeming to invite our advance on into the valley below, we pressed on. When we got to the foot of the ridge, we saw a light just before us toward the main part of the valley. Upon seeing this unfavorable indication, some of the men became

very much discouraged, and expressed a desire to turn back
home, saying, "we can never get through that valley."
The prospect before us, I must confess, looked very gloomy
and disheartening; but I could not think of turning back
after getting so far on our journey, and after we had encountered and overcome so many dangers and difficulties.
Therefore, leaving the men in the bushes, Jerry Miller and I
took off our shoes, coats, and hats, and crawled down toward the fire which had occasioned us so much fear, while
the men we had left behind in the bushes were listening for
the rebels to fire on us every minute. But the rebels did
not fire on us, and the fire which we had seen off the ridge
proved to be nothing but an old stump, which had been
fired by some person who had been plowing there the
day before. We returned, and after telling the men what
it was, they all now seemed very willing to go forward, and
we soon got to the top of Walling's Ridge again; we continued to travel along this ridge for some time, and then
turned off of it toward Powell's Valley. We now got in
sight of the camp-fires of the rebels again, when we stopped
and took off our shoes, and tied them up in our blankets,
intending to throw all away if we should be pressed very
closely. I now took the darkest route that I could find,
and when we got to Powell's River we went right straight
through it, without stopping to remove our clothes. We
pushed on, and reached Cumberland Mountain without being discovered, and soon getting to water, we stopped, and
washed the mud and sand out of our socks, and then pushed on until daylight.

We were now no longer afraid of being pursued by the
rebels, and at once built up several large fires to dry our wet
clothing and to warm our aching limbs. We lay around
the fire in every fashion of disorder. We were hungry, cold,

and wet, worn out with fatigue, and the sore feet of many of the men were bleeding from the severe gashes they had received in their passage through the rugged mountains. No person can imagine for a moment the miserable situation that we were now in, except it be some person who has also been compelled to travel this toilsome journey through the rough mountains to Kentucky.

It was about ten o'clock when we started on our journey, and by two o'clock we crossed the line into the State of Kentucky. We now stopped and sat down to rest, and I pointed out the line to the men. They now commenced bidding the land of Dixie a final adieu. Some began to sing songs suitable to the occasion, while others delivered farewell addresses to the Southern Confederacy. And a long farewell it was for some of these poor fellows, for they have long since gone to that bourne from whence no traveler returns, and will never again visit their native mountains to relate the story of their dreadful sufferings while they were journeying to a land of freedom. A large portion of the company, however, which I conducted through on this occasion joined the Union army, and made brave and intrepid soldiers, and fought gallantly on in the service of their country until the vile Southern rebellion was overthrown, and the rebel soldiery compelled to vanish away before the victorious armies of the federal Union like dew-drops before the bright rays of the morning sun.

After the men were done singing and speaking, we all went on, ballooing and shouting as we went, when we met with a man who told us that the rebels were thick in Kentucky and Powell's Valley. We were well convinced that they were in Powell's Valley, for we had already experienced enough of hardships in trying to pass through that valley to be acquainted with the fact. But the idea of the rebels being in Kentucky at once killed all our joy. This very disagreeable intelligence at once destroyed the young buds of hope which were blooming in our bright expectations, like an untimely frost when it falls upon the early flowers of spring. He told us that Humphrey Marshall had made a raid into Kentucky, had got badly whipped, and was now retiring.. I thought at once that a whipping and a defeat was no more than this Jack Falstaff of the so-called Southern Confederacy might have expected whenever he should have the temerity to make an advance against the Union forces; but we now began to look sharp for the rebels again; and as we were now compelled to have something to eat or starve, I went to the house of a Union man and hired his wife to bring us out something to eat. She brought us a plentiful supply for that night, and we again rested on the mountain, with our spirits very much depressed.

The next day we had to retire farther back into the mountains on account of the rebels, who were now prowling through the country in every direction, like wild animals of the mountains, taking every thing the people had to eat, together with their clothing, their horses, and their cattle. We remained all day upon a high elevation, and watched their destructive movements in the valleys, and I do not believe that one single fowl or bee-stand escaped these thieving and reckless scoundrels that happened to be in the line of their retreat. We were now suffering very much for provisions, and, in fact, we were in a fair way of starving again, which dreadful calamity did almost seem to be inevitable before we could get out of the mountains. When night came on, I went to another Union man's house and bought a bushel of corn, which I carried to the men, and divided it among them, which they at once ate without

cooking it.   I went around to all the near houses, and hired
the women to bring us corn to eat, and as much bread as
they could possibly spare.   Some of them told us how the
infernal rebels had shot their husbands and sons down in
their own houses or in their yards.   They would then search
their pockets for money, and if they failed to find any, they
would then knock their brains out with the end of their
guns; and, not yet being satisfied, they would then stab
their bayonets through their lifeless bodies some five or six
times, and then, to give the finishing touch to their already
sublimated villainy, they would then burn their houses and
every thing in them.   Very many families at this time were
living under clap-board scaffolds, with no other protection
from the inclemency of the weather, and in this way the
poor, wretched mothers, often with five or six little ragged
and destitute fatherless children, were thrown out of their
houses upon the cold charities of the world, to buffet and
battle against the dark waves of adversity, by these inhuman
monsters, who were thus permitted by their superior commander, Humphrey Marshall, *alias* Jack Falstaff, to devas-
tate and destroy the property of the innocent and unoffend-
ing citizens of his own native state, which has to bear the
eternal stigma of having to acknowledge him as one of her
degenerate offspring.

We continued to listen to the sad and heart-rending tales
of sorrow which these poor women related to us until it
was enough to make our hearts ache with pity, and, in fact,
we almost forgot our own troubles while listening to the
story of their dreadful woes; for we felt that we were much
more able to bear our hard fate than these poor women
were to bear up under the terrible calamities which had befallen them, and we thought that we had no reason to complain while we could get a single ear of corn to eat.   We

staid among these poor distressed people for three days and nights, and then removed to a place called Greasy Fork, about fifteen miles beyond Cumberland River, in the direction of Manchester, where we found great difficulty in procuring any thing to eat, as the rebels had so often passed themselves off in that section of country as Union men that the people seemed to be afraid to trust us, thinking that we were now trying to practice the same deception upon their credulity, which they were not willing to permit. Every person in this portion of the country was strange to me, for I had never gone so far into the State of Kentucky before. The citizens would not give us any thing to eat, nor would they give us any information, for fear of being betrayed by us. Again we thought that we should be compelled to starve, for we had partaken of nothing to eat for a day and a night, and had continued to travel all the time. Finally, I persuaded an old lady to believe us, and she then conducted us to a camp where her husband was staying, who, when he saw us approaching, precipitately fled away into the woods, and she had hard work to get him to return. After she talked to him for some time, she called me to them. I immediately went to them, and commenced talking to the frightened man like a brother. I told him that we were trying to get through the lines, and that we had been so long wandering about through the mountains that we were nearly perished with hunger, and that I wished him to aid us in procuring something to eat. He said that it would be very hard for us to get any thing to eat, as the rebels had robbed the country of every thing in the shape of meat and bread, with the exception of a very little which had been concealed out in the mountains by the citizens, and said that the rebels had even found some of that. But he now started off, and soon returned with only about half as much as we all could eat, which we hastily consumed, not even leaving a crumb for breakfast. We remained there all night, and, when morning came, we hired this man to go on with us to the next settlement, which was distant about ten miles across a mountain, and on a river which is called Red-bird. When we got in sight of the first house in the settlement, the rebels were just leaving it. We sent our pilot on into the settlement before us, as he was well acquainted with the people, and could more readily induce them to believe the story of our sufferings. We remained in this settlement all night and the next day, but did not get more than half enough to eat, and had our ears continually saluted with the most pitiful tales of distress from the poor women. We now had to scout our way to Manchester, which is about eighty miles from the point where we crossed over the Kentucky line, and was about fifty miles from the place we were now at.

We started on toward Manchester, and had to cross some of the steepest and roughest ridges that I ever saw in my life; we had to cross over ridges of this description every day, and were able to get but very little to eat. The day before we arrived at Manchester there had been a battle between the Union and the rebel forces; in which the rebels had been badly whipped, and were now running in every direction. We at length succeeded in getting to Manchester, with the flickering lamp of life burning feebly in our bosoms, and that was about all. We stopped at a house, which was called a tavern, but which, to our very great annoyance at this time, we found to be almost entirely destitute of all the characteristics of such an institution. We waited quite impatiently for supper to be announced, and at last the bell commenced ringing, and we all went and set down to the table. There were twenty of us together around that table, and six of the men could have very easily devoured every thing that was placed before us to eat. When we had consumed all there was to eat, we arose from the table almost as hungry as when we sat down to it. We passed off the night as well as we could, hoping for a more plentiful repast in the morning.

Morning at length came, and the bell rang for breakfast; but, oh! horrible to relate, when we again went to the table, we found that it was as scantily furnished as it had been the evening before. We quickly consumed all that was on the table to eat, and rose up, and asked the landlord how much our bill was. He replied that he would charge each one of us *two dollars in greenbacks*, as every thing to eat was hard to get. I thought that his table gave the most satisfactory evidence that what he was saying in regard to hard times was perfectly true. We therefore paid our bill, and struck out for Richmond, which was sixty-five miles farther on. We traveled all day on the main road, as we had now left the rebels behind us, which mode of traveling would have been quite a luxury to us if we had not been so annoyed with hunger. When evening came on, we stopped at every house and asked for something to eat, and endeavored to procure lodging for the night, but for some time we had no success in having either of our requests granted. It was now getting dark, when we came to another house, which we thought was our last chance. We made application to stay all night without much hope of success. The old man told us to come in, saying that he had but little to spare for us to eat, but said he would do the best he could for us. Feeling very much delighted with our good luck, we went in. He was a good Union man, and at once commenced relating to us the story of his troubles with the rebel hordes, who had on several occasions marched into Kentucky for purposes of spoliation, and, when they were met and overcome by the Union forces, would hastily retreat back, and would then, like the locusts of Egypt, destroy and take away every thing which man and beast could eat. He said they had robbed him four times of every thing he possessed, except a small supply of provisions which he had concealed away from his house. We fared very well here, and the old man only charged us one dollar each for the night's entertainment, which we paid him, together with our most profound thanks.

We started on our journey at an early hour with quite an exuberant flow of spirits, for this was our last day's travel to Richmond, which place we reached about sunset. We here met with a good many Union officers, who were very kind to us, and tried hard to get the men to enlist in their various companies, but this they failed to do. I went to a hotel and engaged entertainment for them all. We had an excellent supper, and were furnished with beds, which very much revived us all; and when morning came, if the poor ragged fellows could have had a clean suit of clothes to put on, each one of them might then have exclaimed, "Richard is himself again."

We arose quite early the next morning, and washed and combed, but I can not say that there was much laborious dressing done upon that occasion. The Federal officers treated the company of men very freely with all the brandy they would drink, and by the time the bell rang for breakfast they were all in a very genial mood. The dining-room was furnished with a number of small round tables, at which four men could set down at one of them at the same time. George Ryan, William Ryan, David Taylor, and William Gourley sat down together at one of these tables, and I must confess that I never saw such tremendous eating as these men displayed on that occasion in all my life. The biscuit were small, and one of them just made two bites for them; they kept their waiter very busy in bringing them bread, butter, and coffee. At length they continued on eating so long after every person else was done that the negro's patience was worn threadbare; and he exclaimed, " Well, massas, you do eat more bread and butter than any set of men I ever saw in my life. You have run us out of bread and butter this morning." The truth is, I do not doubt but that all four of them were half starved, and, being somewhat intoxicated, their appetites were consequently quite voracious, and therefore I did not much wonder that biscuit and beafsteak dissolved from before them like snow before the summer's sun. After paying our bill, which was one dollar and fifty cents, and which was quite reasonable, considering the amount of provisions which we had consumed for the landlord, we started on to Louisville. We were a ragged and dirty set of men to go into a city, for our clothes had nearly been torn off of us by the briers and brush through which we had been so long traveling, and our shoes had been completely torn to pieces by the rough rocks in the mountains over which we had passed. But I shall not attempt to describe the uncouth appearance which we now presented, and shall therefore leave the reader to imagine it.

We hired a coach to convey us to Lexington, at which place we arrived about twelve o'clock, and after dinner we took the train for Louisville, where we arrived some time after dark. The 4th Tennessee regiment of infantry, commanded by Colonel Daniel Stover, were stationed at that place, and as I had telegraphed to some of my acquaintances in this regiment that we were on our way to Louisville, we found them, upon our arrival, anxiously awaiting us. This was quite a joyful time for the soldiers of this regiment, as nearly all of them were citizens of East Tennessee, and were very anxious to hear from their homes. Nearly every man whom I had formerly conducted through the mountains to Kentucky I found in this regiment, and nearly every man in the company which I conducted through at this time also joined it. How these well-fed and well-dressed soldiers stared and laughed at our rags and dirt, but it was no wonder, for we formed quite a contrast to them, dressed as they were in their bright and shining blue regimentals.

The men who went through the lines with me were now relieved from their ragged and dirty garments, as the government furnished them all with good clothing. Colonel Stover took me under his immediate guardianship, and presented me with a handsome suit of citizen's clothing, and treated me with the greatest kindness and courtesy, and furnished me with recruiting-papers for his regiment. I remained at Louisville three days, and then made immediate preparations to return to the mountains of East Tennessee. Many of the soldiers gave me letters to take back to their families, as this was the first opportunity which had presented itself for them to send letters to their homes since they had left East Tennessee.

CHAPTER XIV.

On the 4th day of May, 1863, I started from Louisville, Kentucky, on my return trip home. I took passage in the train to Lexington, and from there to Richmond, Kentucky, I traveled in a coach. I staid in Richmond all night, and early the next morning I started on foot to Manchester, at which place I arrived after two days' hard traveling. A battalion of Union soldiers were stationed here, and I staid with them one day. The next morning I shouldered my knapsack, which was filled with letters, and started for Cumberland River, a distance of eighty miles, and, after two days of very hard walking, I arrived at the place on that river where my old friends, the home guards, had been stationed; but they had now "broken up camps," and had gone to work to raise something to eat, for the rebels had exhausted the country of provisions, in their late retreat through it. I staid all night at this place, and the next day I went on to the house of Mr. Clark, on Clover Fork, where I procured a supply of provisions for the remainder of my journey, for I knew when I left here that I would meet with no more kind friends until I arrived among my own native mountains. Leaving Clover Fork early in the morning, I traveled hard all day, and reached Powell's Valley by dark, which to me seemed now to be like the dark valley of the shadow of death; for at the bare mention of Powell's Valley thoughts of the danger which I had there so recently encountered, of meeting with a horrid death at the hands of the infamous rebels, arose unbidden in my mind. However,

G

I consoled myself with the reflection that Providence had again seemed to favor me, for it was now exceedingly dark, and the rain was falling in torrents; consequently, I did not think it possible that even the rebel soldiers would be stirring about in the rain, and amid the terrible darkness of the night. I therefore pushed forward, waded through Powell's River, and crossed over that hated valley, and commenced the ascent of Walling's Ridge; I crossed this ridge, and hastened on over the valleys until I reached the spurs of Powell's Mountain.

I was now very much fatigued and worn out, as wet as I could be, and the rain still falling. I therefore began to look around for a shelter, and by the red lightning's vivid flash I was enabled to discover a large hollow chestnut log near by, and at once crawled into that, which proved to be a very good retreat from the cold peltings of the rain. I searched about for some dry pieces of wood, and kindled up a fire at the entrance of the log, and after drying my wet clothes for some time, I folded up my wet blanket, laid down, and placed it under my head for a pillow; I was soon in a profound sleep. The fire dried the end of the old log in which I was sleeping, and it caught on fire, and the smoke which poured into the log awoke me from my dreams; and when I looked toward the end of the log, a very large blaze had covered the whole entrance, which seemed as if it might seriously dispute my escape from the "burning castle." I was almost suffocated with the heat and smoke, and quickly wrapping my head and hands in my wet blanket, I rolled out through the fire, getting pretty badly singed. I now removed the fire farther away from my mountain domicile, and thoroughly extinguished the fire, which was consuming the end of the log. I crawled back again within its capacious bosom, for the rain was still falling rapidly, which put out every spark of my fire ; but I was quite warm in the old log, and had a very pleasant night's rest, as my sleep was not disturbed any more after my hasty egress from the old log through the fire.

It was about nine o'clock in the morning when I awoke from sleep. The clouds had passed away, and the sun was shining brightly all around. It was really a beautiful May morning — calm and peaceful. The birds were chanting forth their melody, and in fact all nature seemed to acknowledge the potency of the beautiful queen of .the seasons. I built another fire, and spent the day here drying my clothing and my provisions. When night came on, I bid my old log adieu and went on, crossing ridges and valleys, and wading branches, until I reached Clinch Mountain, when I halted to rest again until the next night, at which time I started on, and crossed the north fork of Holston River, and by traveling hard all night, I reached the White-oak Flats by daylight. Here I remained all day with the scouters, and answered hundreds of questions which they propounded to me about the " Yankees." Early the next night I started on my journey, and traveling steadily forward, I reached my own home just about an hour before daylight, after an absence of about five weeks, as it was now about the 15th of May.

When I returned home I found my native county infested by a company of Indians, who had been sent there to hunt and catch the conscripts and Union men who were scouting in the mountains, and just the night before my return home, these red savages had been stationed by their officers within one hundred yards of my own dwelling to watch for me, and on the previous morning they had searched every hill and hollow near my home, hoping and expecting to find me; but on this occasion their search was

1ade a little too soon for me, and, consequently, I was not
und. The rebels always seemed to search about my own
remises for me just a little too soon or a little too late; and
etween these two very egregious mistakes, which of course
ere committed unwittingly by them, I always managed to
scape their vigilance.

When I opened my knapsack I found that all the letters
'hich had been intrusted to my care by the soldiers in the
th Regiment at Louisville, Kentucky, were safe and sound.
at once had each one of them conveyed to its proper des-
nation, and the arrival of these letters created a great deal
f talk and curiosity throughout the country, as they were
1e first letters which had been brought to East Tennessee
om Kentucky. I found a great many men in the mount-
ins hiding from the Indians, of whom they had the greatest
read, but were determined not to go into the rebel army
' they could possibly avoid it. I saw that there was no
ther alternative for me but to continue in the occupation
f a pilot, which I had undertaken more from motives of
eep sympathy for my oppressed fellow-citizens than from
1y other cause whatever, and I therefore concluded to act
1 that capacity until I was either killed or captured, and
1ere was constant employment at this time for a dozen pi-
ts, if their services could have been procured by the poor
en who had been driven into the mountains. There was
1t a day passed but that some of the poor Union men
ere either killed or captured by these infernal Indians, al-
1ough they were not half so cruel as the white rebel sol-
iers. In fact, they were *urged* to do whatever bad deeds
1ey did commit by their white officers. If I had been
ware of the fact at the time they were in Carter County
1at they desired to leave the rebel service, I would have
ied my powers of persuasion upon them to accompany me

through the lines, but I was not acquainted with their wishes in this respect. After they left Carter County, all of them deserted the first chance they had and went through to the "Yankees."

CHAPTER XV.

On the night of the 3d of June, 1863, I started for Kentucky with a company of twenty men, among whom were Jonas H. Keen, of Carter County, Dr. Locke, of Johnson County, and a son of Wilton Akinson, of Jonesborough, Tennessee. The starting-point was in the ridges near Elizabethton. The party all bid fair to stand the trip pretty well, with the exception of Keen, who had been so closely concealed for so long a time, hiding from the rebels, that I did not think he would be able to hold out during the tiresome journey which he was now about to undertake. The crime of which he was accused by the rebels was "bridge-burning," and he well knew that nothing but his neck would satisfy the rebels if he should be so unfortunate as to fall into their hands. He knew that if they ever succeeded in capturing him, they "would welcome him with bloody hands to a hospitable grave." He had deferred the much-dreaded trip to Kentucky from time to time, but had now made up his mind to go. When night came on, we shouldered our knapsacks of provisions and started on our journey toward the railroad, which I designed to cross somewhere near Carter Dépôt. When we arrived near that point, I halted the company and went to the railroad alone, to see if there was any threatening danger; but finding that there was none, I directed the company to cross the railroad with the greatest caution. I thought that the men were getting over the railroad finely, when one of them happened to step too low, and struck his heel against one of the iron rails, making it ring out loudly upon the gloomy silence of night. The rebels being close by, I now looked for them to take after us every moment, for I thought the noise could have been heard for a mile around, but the rebels did not pursue us. We only traveled about twelve miles the night we started, and the next morning we were in Washington County, where we staid all day, and passed it off as well as we could. Some of the company would sleep, while others would watch, which they continued to do until night came on. As soon as it was dark we pressed on again, and about eleven o'clock the party all seemed to be very tired, so much so, that we had to stop and rest every few miles we traveled. About two o'clock in the night Keen gave out, for his feet had already been so badly blistered, and were so extremely sore that it was a very serious labor for him to walk. I would have stopped until he could have walked better, but I knew that if we stopped where we now were we would all be in great danger of being killed or captured by the rebels. Some of the men carried his knapsack of provisions, and helped him along as well as they could. We did not go very far that night, and when daylight made its appearance we were in a very poor place of concealment.

We were yet several miles from Holston River, and in a place where a number of trees had been blown down by a storm, which now served us as a hiding-place. We crawled into the tree-tops, and some of the men got under the bodies and roots of these trees and laid down to rest. Keen was tired out, and several others of the men were in a not much better condition. As it regards myself, I was traveling along at my leisure, getting along extremely slow, I thought. We suffered very much for water, although there was a creek near by; but we were afraid to go to it, for fear of being seen by the rebel citizens, who were watching all the time for men who were aiming to get through the lines. When night came on, we hurried on, through fields and over fences, until we arrived at Holston River. I here left the men by a fence-row, under some bushes, and I proceeded to the house of a Union man that I was well acquainted with. I approached the house very cautiously, and when I knocked at the door it seemed to frighten the family very badly, for they said they thought it was the thieving rebels who had come again to rob them, as they had done not many nights before. The old man said that they had threatened to kill him if any more stampeders crossed the river, and said they would send all of his family through the lines for befriending the Union men who were scouting in the woods, for no such people, they said, should stay in the country.

The old man told me to take the canoe and cross the river in it, but to be careful and watch closely as I went to the river, for fear that the rebels might be watching for scouters. He said there had been no rebels about there that night. After I had examined the river carefully, I went back to the company and told them to move on to the river. After a long time, we all got across the river safely. The night was very dark, and we now had a rocky ridge to climb which was about three hundred feet high. We commenced the ascent, which was so steep that we could scarcely avoid falling backward at times, and it was so dark that we could hardly see each other. But finally, by holding to the rocks and pulling up by the grape-vines, we succeeded in reaching the top. I thought frequently, while endeavoring to climb this precipice, that if the fabled Tantalus had been doomed to roll his stone up such an acclivity as this, he could not, surely, have impelled it upward toward the top more than a few steps, before it would have returned to the foot of the hill again in spite of all his physical exertions.

We traveled on, through fields and woods, until we reached Reedy Creek, near the boat-yard, which we waded through, and then crossed the main road leading to Bristol, and pushed on, over ridges and through dense forests, in the direction of the north fork of Holston River. The night was so dark, and our pathway at times so completely blockaded with bushes and brush, that we made but very slow progress on our journey, but at length we reached the river. We were traveling down the stream, hunting for a convenient place to cross, when we observed a picket-fire on the opposite shore. The men at once became very much frightened, and away they dashed in every direction. I could not tell for some time what was the matter, and thought that the rebels had surely come on them in the rear; but, hearing the report of no guns, I knew that was not the case. I stopped, and on looking around a while I found there was nothing wrong, as the men had only taken the "stampeder's fright," which was very common for them to do. Some of them ran into brier-patches that a dog could not get through after a rabbit, while others tumbled about over old logs and over rocks. I called on them to stop, and told them there was nothing which I could see to occasion any alarm, and after a while I succeeded in getting them all together again. They said they were sure that the rebels were after them. I told them the rebels had not been after us yet, but that I very much feared that so much noise at this hour of the night would have a decided tendency to start them after us, and charged them now to be very quiet. We slipped on down the river, and at length we got to a good place to cross, and after taking off our clothes and tying them on our shoulders, we waded through with perfect safety. We now crossed the main road, and ran about one hundred yards to the top of a hill, where we stopped to dress ourselves again, and then pushed on toward Clinch Mountain, which we reached by daylight. Stopping at a branch which gurgled down a mountain hollow, we washed our faces and hands, and sat down to partake of our simple meal of bread and meat, and then laid our tired bodies down to rest. After sleeping until about twelve o'clock the next day, we arose and started on up the mountain. I thought we would be safe in traveling on the mountain in daylight, for a short time at least, until we should leave the mountain and get into Poor Valley, which was immediately below where we were now traveling. When we got near the valley we stopped and waited for night to come on, when we went on and crossed the valley, and also Copper Ridge.

I now had a great deal of trouble in urging the men to travel, for they were so completely exhausted, and the mountains were so steep and rugged, that it was really a hard labor for them to get along. I told them that they needed another small "awakening" from the rebels, which would at once give more elasticity to their movements. But they avowed that they would not run again until they knew that they were really threatened with danger. We continued to toil on in our rough pathway, sometimes crawling upon our hands and knees under the brush, and sometimes pulling up steep precipices by the overhanging vines and bushes. The patience of some of the men seemed to be almost entirely worn out, for they said that they would go and surrender themselves to the rebels rather than go any farther into the mountains in their wretched condition. I told them that they must not think of doing that; and by waiting on them, and encouraging them to use every exertion to pursue their journey to the end, I managed to keep them moving slowly onward. They were now too far from home to think about turning back, which also served to stimulate them to press onward in their journey.

When we arrived at Copper Creek we found it deep and wide. It was on this creek, but not at the point where we now were, that a pilot by the name of Gray had all his men captured a short time before this. We were sitting on the bank of the creek putting on our shoes, and were talking about the capture of Gray's company, while a portion of the men had crossed before us and gone on ahead for a short distance, when, to our surprise, we saw them running back toward the creek with great rapidity. When they came up close to us, they said, " Run, boys, the cavalry is after us." I immediately jumped into the creek and ran through, but not until some of the men had run over me. I never saw such a confusion so suddenly aroused in all my life. Some of the men fell flat in the water, and in fact we all got perfectly wet. One man, after he had succeeded in crossing the creek without getting wet, ran violently against a tree, which knocked him back into the water again. No one paid any attention to him as he floundered about in the water, but left him to get out if he could. At length we heard him calling on us to stop. I was high up on the mountain, and some of the men were still higher up than I was, who seemed determined to save themselves by hiding in old logs and brier-thickets. Not hearing any guns, I called to the men not to run any farther, and told them that I would go back to the creek and see if there was any danger ahead. When I returned to the creek, I listened and looked with all the ears and eyes I had, but could see nor hear nothing to occasion the least alarm. I returned back to gather up my scattered company, which I found to be quite a difficult task, for they had concealed themselves under the bushes and brush like a gang of frightened partridges, and did not like the idea of coming out where they could be seen. At length I got them all together, with one exception, and commenced

hunting and calling the man that was missing. He answered away off at some distance "Here I am. I thought I would
get where the rebels could not find me," and he crawled out
from between two old logs. Some of the men had crawled
so far into the brier-thickets that it was a serious labor for
them to get out again; and when they did get out, they
found that they had left a good portion of their clothing
hanging in strips upon the thorns and briers. Four of the
men lost their hats, and some of them lost their haversacks,
which contained all their provisions, which severe calamity
reduced them at once to a starving condition, for our supply of provisions was quite inadequate before any portion
of them had been lost.

The men were now convinced that they had again been
frightened at nothing, and appeared to hate it very much.
We now started on again, over logs and through bush, but
at length reached Clinch River, and, after some considerable
search, I found a place where I thought the men could wade
through it without serious inconvenience. The river was
deep and wide, but we succeeded in crossing to the opposite shore, when we all ran for about three hundred yards
to get into the woods, where we stopped to put on our
clothes, and then started on our journey, and by daylight
we arrived among the spurs of Powell's Mountain. We
now had nothing to eat but a little mouldy bread, which
we could not eat, and therefore had to pass off the day in
resting and trying to sleep, without eating any thing.
When night came on we prepared to start on our journey,
and all of us being very hungry, the mouldy bread was again
produced, but, finding it too unpalatable, it was again returned to our haversacks untouched. We started on, and
crossed Powell's Mountain and also Wildcat Valley, and arrived at the foot of Walling's Ridge. By this time the

men were more exhausted and worn out than any previous
company that I ever conducted through the lines before.
However, we pushed on up the ridge, and finally reached
the top of it, and then started down toward Powell's Valley. When we got to the cleared land we stopped to take
off our shoes. I sincerely hoped that we would meet with
no opposition in crossing the valley, for I thought if we did
some of the tired party would have to be left to the mercy
of the rebels. When we got near the houses in the valley
I thought that all the dogs had surely been watching for
us; there were two or three large dogs and one small one
at every house, and when one of them barked every dog in
the valley appeared to join in, which resulted in one loud,
spontaneous yell all over the valley. I felt sure that all the
citizens were awake and ready to assist in catching us, and,
to make the matter worse, just at this gloomy hour, when
the thoughts of all were vibrating between hope and despair, Keen became very much discouraged, and declared
he would not go another step in the valley, and began to
beg us all to turn back with him. I was willing to do any
thing for the best, and told the men that I believed the best
policy was for us to go on and endeavor to get through, for
if we turned back we should have a much farther route to
travel, and through the roughest sort of mountains, and, in
our present exhausted condition, I did not think that we
would ever be able to get through. I also told them that
Cumberland Mountain was now in sight, where we would
be safe from the "jaws of the lion," if we could succeed in
getting to it, and seek refuge upon its lofty elevations.
Some of the men wished to go on, and some of them expressed a desire to turn back. Keen declared we would all
be killed if we went on that night, and offered me five dollars if I would turn back, and Dr. Locke offered me five

dollars if I would go on. I did not regard the money which was offered me on this occasion, for I would have given any reasonable amount myself if they had all agreed to go forward without so much contention and endeavor to get through the lines. Keen and his company continued to insist on turning back, and at length we agreed to their proposition, but with heavy and aching hearts. We struggled on to the top of Walling's Ridge, and then went on down and crossed over Wildcat Valley, and by daylight we arrived at the foot of Powell's Mountain, and after climbing up its steep side for a short distance we stopped, being very much fatigued, and some of the men declared that they were unable to proceed another step.

We were now not only hungry, but were really nearly starved to death, and were compelled to eat a small portion of our stale and sour bread. We rested here until evening, when we started forward. Keen now began to notice the trail that we made in traveling, and declared that the rebels in the valley below would be sure to follow us, and said he would leave the company and make his way through alone, as one man, he said, could go where so many could not. I insisted on his staying with us, as it was more upon his account than any one else that the company had agreed to turn back. But he would not stay with us any longer. We therefore gave him a small portion of our badly-damaged bread, which was now so much spoiled that it had turned blue, having a few small pieces of the same kind left for ourselves. Keen having now left us, we pursued our journey on until night, when we crossed at the head of Powell's Valley, at a place called Big Stone Gap; and when we got to the spurs of Cumberland Mountain we built up a fire, and stopped for the remainder of the night. We had now been two days and nights without any thing to eat, and again taking out our damaged bread, we laid it on the fire-coals and burned the mould off of it, which singed and crackled as if we had been burning the hair off of a parcel of live rats or squirrels. We now made out to eat it, and thought it very good. After supper, some five or six of the men laid down in a small hole, piling together like hogs, for the night was tolerably cool. Some crawled under old logs, and every man selected a bed to suit himself. As for myself, I could not sleep for thinking about Keen, who had left us, I feared, to perish in the mountains, as his health was quite indifferent at this time.

Morning at length came, and the rain was falling, and the wind was blowing in a stormy manner, breaking great limbs off of the trees over our heads; we were in great danger of being killed by the falling timber, and the fog was so dense that we could not see one hundred yards ahead of us on the mountain. The wind was very cold, and after traveling until eight o'clock, we were compelled to stop and make up a fire to warm and dry ourselves as well as we could. We had consumed all of our spoiled bread, and were suffering greatly from hunger. After resting and warming our aching limbs, we pushed on through the falling rain, and through the bushes and brush, which were so thick that it was hard for us to get along at all. About ten o'clock we stopped again and built a fire, for we were completely chilled, and felt so weak from our terrible feelings of hunger that it was with great difficulty we could stand on our feet. After resting by the fire for a short time, we started on down the mountain, and when we reached its foot we were in Kentucky, where our fondest hopes had been centred during our long and weary journey. After traveling about one mile and a half we got in sight of Mr. Clark's house, which was the only house we had seen

since we left our native mountains in East Tennessee that
we could enter with safety. I knew that we could remain
at this place and procure refreshments until we felt able
to pursue our journey, and the sight that rejoiced us most
of any thing else at this time was seeing the old man and
his son carrying something from the still-house that looked
very much like a keg of brandy or whisky, and which,
when we got nearer to them, we found that we had judged
correctly. When we got to the house I gave a man one
dollar to make us a fire, for we were so weak and so nearly
frozen that we could not make it ourselves.

We now bought half a gallon of whisky, and, after drink-
ing it, felt very much revived, and soon afterward we all sat
down to a good and plentiful supper. We remained here
all night, and the next morning, after filling our canteens
with whisky and eating a hearty breakfast, the men whom
I had conducted safely through the mountains made immediate preparations to start on their journey to Louisville,
and I to return to East Tennessee again. We would have
parted in better spirits had it not been for the sad misgivings which we all entertained in regard to the probable
fate of our late companion, Jonas H. Keen.

CHAPTER XVI.

On the 10th day of June, 1863, I started for home again, to retrace, alone and unattended, the long and weary path through the mountains which I had so recently traveled. After a steady day's travel, I arrived at Powell's River just as night was setting in. Taking off my shoes, I waded through the river, and pushed forward across Powell's Valley, which was full of rebel soldiers. I walked as carefully and as cautiously through this hated and much-dreaded valley as if the ground had been scattered over with dragon's teeth, and I was momentarily expecting them to spring up in all the hideous proportions of armed rebel soldiers. I pushed on, and crossed over Walling's Ridge and Wildcat Valley. It was now three o'clock in the night, and I now stopped and rested until the next day about three o'clock in the evening, when I concluded to go on. But, as usual, whenever I pretended to travel in daylight something was sure to happen to me; for when I was now descending a long ridge, I saw a man before me with a gun, and he saw me about the same time. He raised his gun, and I dodged quickly behind a tree and presented a gun-barrel at him, which I was carrying home with me. It was, in fact, all the arms I had that could furnish any belief of my ability to shoot. It was now his turn to dodge behind a tree. I asked him who he was, and what he was doing in this lonely region of country? He replied that he was a scouter, and thought when he first saw me that I was one of Colonel Slimp's men, who was then stationed with his men in Powell's Valley. After questioning him a little farther, I found that he was a deserter from Colonel Slimp, and was under the impression that I was pursuing him. He vowed that he would kill the first man that attempted to capture him. We agreed to lay down our guns, and meet each other on the half-way ground. Seating ourselves upon an old log, we ate supper together. I found him to be a Union man; and after spending some time in conversation, we parted good friends, he to go on his scouting operations, and I to pursue my journey home. I crossed Clinch River and Copper Creek, and also Poor Valley, at the foot of Clinch Mountain, and reached the top of this mountain by daylight.

I now laid down and rested during the day. I felt quite lonesome upon the summit of this wild and lofty mountain alone, but, soon forgetting my melancholy feelings, I passed gently off into the land of dreams. When I awoke night had already thrown her dark shadow o'er the mountain's top, and I arose and started on toward the north fork of Holston River. When I arrived at the river I waded through, and hurried on to the big flats, near the boat-yard, where I staid the balance of the night, and also the next day. Early the next night I started on my journey, and some time before daylight reached my native mountains once more, worn out with fatigue, and almost destitute of clothing. I felt so perfectly exhausted that I wondered whether I would ever be able to take another trip to Kentucky. And it was a month before I felt able to undertake another journey, which I could not longer postpone, owing to the constant and pressing applications which I received from the poor men who were scouting in the mountains for my services in conducting them through the mountains to Kentucky. There was now a greater number of men laying out in the mountains of Carter County, wishing to go through the lines, than ever had been before, and the rebel soldiers were hunting and watching for them in every direction.

CHAPTER XVII.

On the night of the 9th of July, 1863, I started to Kentucky with a much larger company of men than I ever undertook to pilot through the mountain on any previous occasion. The most of this company consisted of men who had been employed in working for the so-called Southern Confederacy in the forges and saltpetre works, and, having no confidence in their exemption papers, they were expecting to be placed in the rebel army at any time; and in order to obtain a more sure exemption from the rebel service, they had determined to go to Kentucky. The times were not propitious for going into the mountains near their homes, as the rebels seemed to be every where, and, being well aware that numbers of men were running away to the Yankees nearly every day, they were constantly on the watch for stampeders. The starting-point which I had designated was near the old O'Brien Forge, some three miles south of Elizabethton. We traveled the first night we started about thirteen miles, and stopped in some large ridges on the Watauga River.

Our hiding-place during the next day was in a dense thicket, where we remained in safety until darkness again came on, and a dark night it was. We now had twenty miles to travel before we could reach the White-oak Flats, and the men fell and stumbled about at such a rate that we made but very slow progress. About midnight I stopped for the company to rest, as they seemed to be very tired, and some of their feet were already very sore. It was almost daylight before we got to the Holston River, opposite to the flats, and found the river so full that we could not wade it. I left the men in a secret place, and proceeded to the house of a good old Union man to inquire if the canoe was guarded. He told me if it was he did not know it, and while we were considering what was the best to be done, the men all came up, saying that they had heard some person whistle, and thought that it was me giving them the signal to advance. I told them that I had not whistled, and that it was quite likely the rebels were about, and sure enough they were. They were guarding the landing on the opposite side of the river, watching for stampeders. There was no guard on the side of the river where we were, and I determined to outwit them, if it could possibly be done.

I conducted the company farther on down the river, and told them to remain there, perfectly quiet, until I returned. I then proceeded to the ferry-landing and got into the canoe, and floated silently down the river to the place where I had stationed the company. I now began to carry them over the river in the canoe, and after a number of trips backward and forward across the river I succeeded in getting all of them safely across. The night was very dark, and we left the river without being discovered. We now had a piece of woods to go through, and a public road to cross, and I think the rebels must have been in the road, and heard us walking in the leaves, which we could not do without making some noise. We had left the woods, and were traveling in the road for a short distance, as in this way I thought we could get clear of danger a little sooner. The rebels now came very near running upon the rear of the company before they were discovered. I had been listening for them very intently, and at length heard them running to overtake us. In a second after I gave the alarm we were all flying up the road, which I continued to pursue for about three hundred yards, and then turned off into the woods about fifty yards, where we all immediately laid down behind some bushes, thinking by this means to evade our pursuers. We heard them coming on up the road, and when they came up opposite to where we were, they turned out of the road into the woods, and, to our very great surprise and terror, they came right on toward our hiding-place. We remained perfectly still until the rebels got within some twenty steps of us, when, seeing that they were coming directly on us, we all raised at once, and started through the woods like a herd of frightened buffaloes. The rebels commenced yelling like demons from the infernal regions, and the winged messengers of death, which they hurled after us from their guns, whistled around us in every direction, but, very fortunately, failed to inflict any injury upon the flying fugitives, who fled on through the woods as if they had been carried along upon the wings of the wind. The terrible explosions of the " villainous saltpetre," as it escaped from the rebel guns, only seemed to put us under good headway, and on we went, through tree-tops, and over old logs and stumps. Some of the men threw away their haversacks, and some lost their hats, but none of them stopped for the rebels to capture them. The rebels kept pretty close after us for some time, calling on us at every step to halt. But they might as well have undertaken to stop the course of the river at that time as to have endeavored to stop us in our wild and precipitate flight.

I was very well convinced that, if they should succeed in capturing me, they would not forget to bestow upon me a most ignominious death; and not wishing them to capture my men, I encouraged them all the time, telling them to follow on after me and we would get away. The men strained every nerve in their onward flight, and we soon got out of the hearing of our mad and vindictive pursuers. But we still went ahead in a sort of double-quick rate of speed, and by daylight we reached some lofty and densely-timbered ridges, which afforded us an admirable place of concealment.

When I came back on my return trip home through this section of country, where I and my company were chased so dreadfully by the rebels, I was told by a good Union friend that a company of rebel cavalry arrived there on the same evening that I and my company got to the Holston River. The rebels had been sent there for the purpose of watching for stampeders, and running upon our party as they did on that eventful night put them in fine spirits. My friend told me that the next evening, bright and early, the rebels dismounted from their horses and started on, shouting and cheering, to search the flats, saying they would be sure to capture the "old red fox" that day, as they were confident that no other person would have had the extreme audacity to cross the river in the very face of their pickets. They were sure that we were in the flats somewhere, and there they continued to hunt for us all the day, but they at length agreed to give up the search without finding any person, for the scouters who had been staying there, having heard of their arrival the evening before, had "taken time by the forelock" and made their escape. When the rebels started to search the flats, I was told that some of them loudly proclaimed that if they should succeed in capturing the "old red fox," they intended to give his hide a much deeper tinge of red from his own blood. I will here state for the information of the reader that the "old red fox" was the *sobriquet* by which I was known by the Union people, as well as the rebels, during the period that I acted in the capacity of a pilot. During the several memorable years that I was generally known under the name and style of the "old red fox," I must confess that I had many severe races and a number of very narrow escapes from the infamous rebel hounds who meditated and sought my destruction, but I always succeeded in defeating their best-arranged stratagems to accomplish my capture and ultimate death, and for which great mercy I shall ever render up my profound thanks and heartfelt praise to Him who can "take the wise in their own craftiness," and who, while on earth, "spake as never man spake;" who existed before "the morning stars sang together," and who will continue to exist throughout the ceaseless and incalculable ages of eternity.

I was told that when the rebels returned in the evening from their hunt through the flats, they did not cheer quite so loudly as they did when they started in the morning, but came back cursing and raving among the poor women, who they blamed for carrying news, saying that it was very strange that large companies of men could go through that section of country to the Yankees, having the river to cross, and escape without being caught. They did not think that "where there is a will there is always a way," and they did not know what tremendous barriers the oppressed Union men were capable of surmounting.

We remained all day near the north fork of Holston River, and just as soon as it was dark we started on, and crossed the river below the Holston Springs, in Scott County, Virginia. The river was tolerably deep, but with the aid of stout sticks we reached the opposite shore safely. We now struck out as rapidly as we could go for Clinch Mountain, as we considered that to be the haven for our present safety; when we got to the mountain we traveled along the side of it until we found a good place to build a fire, when we stopped, and dried our clothes, and rested there until daylight. When morning came we started on, and traveled all day, not believing it to be safe for us to remain long in one place. At twelve o'clock we stopped and rested a short time, and then pressed forward until evening, when we came to water, where we stopped, and sat down to eat our simple meal of bread and cold meat, not having even enough of that, as our stock of provisions was already running low, which was occasioned by a number of the party having to throw down their haversacks in their recent terrible flight from the rebels.

We now set out on our night's travel, and soon reached Poor Valley, which we crossed, and then crossed over Copper Ridge, and waded Copper Creek, at the foot of the ridge, and went on to Clinch River, which we knew we would have to wade, as every canoe and ferry landing was strongly guarded by the rebels. Upon reaching Clinch River, each one of us cut a stout stick to walk with, and started into the river. Some of the men could barely keep their heads above the water; but, after some considerable stumbling and plunging, we all got to the shore in safety, all of our clothing getting perfectly wet. We now took the ridges leading on toward Powell's Mountain, wading creeks, climbing knobs, and slipping through hill-side farms, until we reached the spurs of Powell's Mountain, and after finding a favorable hiding-place we stopped. The men had traveled remarkably well, but now seemed to be very much exhausted, and were also hungry, and, the worst of all, they had nothing to eat. Some of them had been so long concealed in holes in the ground, and in their little bark camps in the mountains, that they were entirely unable to purchase a supply of provisions for their journey to Kentucky, and therefore wholly depended on any fortuitous circumstances which might arise during their journey to supply themselves with provisions. We were now a good many miles from Kentucky, and the rebel soldiers at every house in the valleys through which we had to pass, and knowing, as we did, that there was great danger of the whole company falling into their hands if we ventured off of the mountain, all contributed to form a very gloomy prospect for us to obtain any thing more to eat.

We passed off the day upon the mountain, and at night we started again, weak and hungry, for another hard night's travel. How often did we think of the provisions that had been lost when we were running from the infernal rebels at Holston River, for the want of which we were now starving by degrees. The loss of our provisions made us think that our hatred for the rebel foe could never die, and the terrible sufferings which we were subjected to in consequence of losing our meat and bread can never be forgotten. We reached the foot of Walling's Ridge about twelve o'clock, and when we commenced going up the acclivitous ascent I wondered whether the poor tired and hungry men would ever be able to reach the distant summit. But after climbing and pulling up the steep places by the bushes and vines for a long time, we got to the top of the ridge, and then, traveling along on its top for about three miles, we turned down toward Powell's Valley, and when we got down to the cleared land we stopped, and after taking off our shoes we started on in our stocking feet, to prevent the dogs from hearing us walk, and thereby raise the alarm. We were not always successful, for sometimes they could tell that men were approaching from their scent alone. I thought that the poor men had already endured enough of trouble and vexation in their journey, and inwardly hoped

H

that we would be able to escape the dangers which always
surrounded the pathway of the poor Union scouters through
this despicable valley, and get on safely to the Cumberland
Mountain without meeting with any farther molestation.
My hope in this regard was eminently realized, for we passed through the valley without being discovered.

When we arrived at Powell's River we plunged into it,
without taking time to take off our clothes, and made our
way as rapidly as possible to the Cumberland Mountain.
When got to where there was water on the mountain
we stopped and washed our stockings and pants, and, after
wringing them as dry as we could, put them on again. By
this time it was daylight, and as the mountain was very
rugged, we went on until we could find a suitable place to
build up fires to dry our wet clothes. We were still in a
region of country where it was a matter of impossibility to
procure any thing to eat, for there were more or less rebel
soldiers at every house which was near to us, and therefore, after resting for a short time, we commenced preparing our feet for the remainder of the journey. Some of the
men's shoes were almost entirely gone, and ready to be
"numbered with the things that were," for they were now
compelled to tie them on their feet with rags. And some
of the men were destitute of hats, and were traveling with
no other covering for their heads than that which was furnished them by old mother Nature herself. I do not now
remember that I ever conducted a company of men through
the mountains to Kentucky but what quite a number of
them lost their hats and shoes before they got to the end
of their journey, and I am very sure that none ever reached
the Kentucky line with me without being perfectly ragged,
and I have no sort of doubt but that the rebels might have
often pursued us by the small pieces of the men's clothing
which were left hanging in the brush and briers.

It was about twelve o'clock before I could get all the company started, and when they did start I had very hard work to persuade them to move onward toward the end of their journey, and I could not blame them, for they were now so weak from the want of food that it was a serious labor for them to travel. In fact, quite a number of the poor men presented specimens of lean, gaunt, cadaverous human beings, who would have thrown Calvin Edson himself in the shade if he had been present to undergo a contrast with them. Famine, in its dismal habiliments of wretchedness, had conspicuous representatives in this company of forlorn, wayfaring, and hungry men. When we arrived at the Kentucky line we stopped to rest again. We soon started on, and I encouraged the men to press forward, and by dark we reached the residence of Mr. Clark. Here we got an abundance to eat, and a good fire to sleep by, and when morning came we all felt very much refreshed. After breakfast we set out for the station of the home guards on Cumberland River, where we remained all night with them. The next morning the men that I had conducted through the mountains started on to Louisville to join the 4th Regiment of Tennessee Infantry. I had done all that I could for them; they were now free from rebel tyranny, and could go wherever they pleased. I knew that my services were needed by the scouters in the mountains of Carter County, many of whom I had promised to assist in getting through the lines to Kentucky. After the company started I immediately returned to Clark's, where I staid all night, and bought a supply of provisions for my return trip to East Tennessee.

CHAPTER XVIII.

On the morning of the 16th day of July, 1863, I turned my face homeward again. When I got on the top of Cumberland Mountain I looked down into Powell's Valley, where I could see the rebel soldiers passing about in squads. After watching their movements for some time I went on down to the foot of the mountain, where I stopped to rest and to eat my supper. As soon as it got dark I pushed on to Powell's River, and, after taking off my clothes, waded through. Wishing to shun the valley as much as possible, I slipped along through some cleared fields to an immense thicket of papaw bushes, some of which had grown to be small saplings. There was an old fence running through the thicket, and a little blind path ran along the fence. I was walking in this path, and had walked in it for about four hundred yards, and was now almost out of the thicket, when I heard horses coming toward me. It was so dark that I could see no person, and turned and went back in the path some distance as fast as I could run, and turned out into the thicket some forty or fifty yards, and laid down behind an old log. I could now hear the horses approaching quite plain, and when coming opposite to where I was concealed, their riders turned off the path and came straight on to the log where I was hid. I laid perfectly still, and heard the riders dismount and begin to hitch their horses to the saplings. I thought that my time had now come sure enough, but remained still, meditating what was best to be done in the present emergency. I thought that there

would be no chance to effect my escape if I should run out
of the thicket, for there was nothing but cleared land all
around. I concluded that the best plan was to lay still.
One of the men came up to the log behind which I was lying, and, reaching over it, bent down a bush and tied his
horse to it. The horse, getting frightened, jumped back
and came near breaking his halter. The man now came up
to the log to see what was the matter, when, finding that I
would be discovered, I raised up, which frightened the man
as badly as he had frightened me, for he immediately turned
and ran away as fast as he could go. I called to him, when
he stopped and spoke to me. I found them to be negroes.
They told me that they were hiding their masters' horses
to keep the rebel soldiers from getting them. I asked them
how many soldiers were in the valley. They told me there
were some six or seven hundred. I now bid them good-
night and passed on.

I immediately got on to a high point, where I could see
the rebel camp-fires all over the valley, and began to think
that I would have to turn back. I studied for some time
whether to go back or not, and concluded to run the risk
of being captured rather than turn back. I selected the
darkest route I could find. I started forward into this
loathsome valley, which, if it had been covered all over its
surface with dead men's bones, I could not have detested
it any worse than I did. At one time I passed so near to
one of the rebel encampments that I could see them eating
and hear them talking. One of the rebels was playing
away on a fiddle, while others were engaged in "shaking
the light fantastic toe." The night was dark and cloudy,
and their fires gave a brilliant light; the houses in the valley were all lighted up, and the dogs were barking away in
a desperate manner. The rebels were singing and yelling

all around, but none of them seemed to be aware that there was "a looker-on in Venice" who was watching their frantic revelry. But I did not lose much time in watching their movements, for I was too anxious to get out of that rebel pandemonium, for which I entertained such profound abhorrence. I passed on through the valley unnoticed, without attracting the attention of any thing, with the exception of the rebels' horses, which would see me as I passed near to where they were hitched, when some of them would raise their heads high up and give a loud snort. I hastened on to the top of Walling's Ridge, where I rested a short time, and then, after traveling on the ridge for two or three miles, I turned down toward the valley, and by the time I got to the foot of the ridge the chickens were crowing for day. I had now to go at a rapid rate of speed in order to reach Powell's Mountain by daylight; and I did not quite make the reach, for before I got out of the valley it was quite light, and a parcel of rebel soldiers having seen me, they started after me like a gang of demons, yelling and loudly hallooing halt! halt!! halt!!! But in this peremptory order I did not obey them, but started on up the mountain as fast as I could go. They now commenced shooting at me, and, from the manner in which their bullets whistled around me, I was well convinced that they meant to do me serious injury. They were foot-soldiers, and I think they were armed with Colt's army pistols. Having not the smallest particle of love for these desperadoes, I soon got out of their reach. When I got on to a high point on the mountain, I looked back to see what had become of these fellows, who had desired to make my acquaintance so unceremoniously, when I observed them slowly returning to the valley.

I now pursued my way on top of the mountain until I

came to a good hiding-place, when I stopped to rest and to eat my breakfast. I remained here all day, sleeping finely during the greater portion of the day, and when night came on I started down the mountain, and, crossing over the intermediate valleys and mountain farms, I arrived at Clinch River, which I found to be tolerably full. I took off my clothes and tied them on my head, hoping to keep them dry, but in this I failed; for sometimes I was compelled to swim, and when I succeeded in getting over my clothes were perfectly wet. After wringing the water out of them as well as I could, I put them on and went on, crossing the little river knobs, wading creeks, and crossing valleys until I got to Clinch Mountain, and by the time I got over the mountain it was daylight.

I remained in the bushes at the foot of the mountain all day, and as soon as it was dark I pushed on to the north fork of Holston River. I again took off my clothes, but the river was so full I was compelled to swim, and again got them very wet. I put them on, wet as they were, and started on. I now had the road to cross leading from the boat-yard to Moccasin Gap in Clinch Mountain. The night was very dark, and when I got to the road I struck a match to see if there had been much traveling in it. The road had been badly cut up by horses and wagons, and I therefore began to look out for the rebels again, as the country was very good for them to forage in. When I got near to Reedy Creek I saw a good many lights burning, which at once convinced me that the rebels were encamped near the flats, and after advancing a little farther I perceived that their encampment was in an old field of about ten acres, which I would have to cross. I thought if I could only get through that field I could then easily dodge them in the brush, as there was a dense forest just beyond the old field. I resolved to try, as I knew that an effort in that direction was the only thing which could furnish a key to ultimate success. It was quite dark, and the light from their camp-fires was very brilliant, which rendered every object in the encampment quite visible, which was quite favorable on my side, for I was thereby enabled to watch all of their movements without their being able to see me. I now prepared to cross the field. I had recruiting papers for the Federal army in my pocket, besides a number of letters, which the men whom I had recently conducted through to Kentucky had sent back to their friends in East Tennessee, and also about two hundred dollars in Confederate and state money. Taking all these things, I wrapped them up carefully in my handkerchief, and placed them in the bosom of my hunting-shirt, a loose garment I always wore in the mountains, and then tied it tightly around my body, thinking that if I should be captured I could get hold of them conveniently to throw them away. Taking off my shoes, and fearing that I might be seen walking, I got down upon my hands and knees, and crawled along for some distance. When I got near the thickest part of the rebel encampment I thought I would have to get up and run. But I passed on undiscovered until I came to the fence which was near the woods, where I found horses tied to it as thick as they could stand. When I went up to climb the fence I passed between two of the horses, when they began to snort and paw the earth with their feet. I stopped until they became quiet, and then jumped over the fence and ran across the road. I now stopped in the woods to see if the rebels were pursuing me, as I had made some noise when I crossed the fence. I saw four of them come to the fence and examine their horses, and, finding them all right, they went back to their fires. I started on and traveled until I believed that I was out of danger, when I stopped to put on my shoes. I felt for my bundle of papers, and found that I had lost them. I felt quite certain that I had lost the bundle out of my bosom when I was crawling through the rebel encampment, as I was too busily engaged at that time in watching the rebels to know when the bundle fell out of my bosom. I knew that I had the bundle when I got down to crawl, and was quite sure that I had not dropped it after crossing the fence. But I never heard a single word about my recruiting papers or any of the letters afterward. If the rebels ever found them, I suppose they were ashamed to make it known, thinking that they might be too harshly reprimanded for permitting the "old red fox" to pass right through their encampment without being molested, for the papers indicated precisely who they belonged to, and what I was authorized by them to do. The letters, also, which I was bringing back from the men whom I had just conducted through the mountains, told very plainly who the bearer of dispatches was. If they did find my bundle of papers, I presume they thought that they were doing a slow business in catching stampeders. As I did not fancy the idea of returning to search for my missing bundle, I started on my journey, and when I got into a retired part of the country I stopped to rest until the next night.

I passed off the day with some of my scouting friends near the White-oak Flats, who warned me to observe a good deal of caution while I was traveling the remainder of my journey. They told me how the rebel soldiers had searched the flats the day after I had passed along with my company, and told me they were now constantly watching for my return. I did not enjoy myself very well during this day, for I was expecting every moment to see the rebels coming in hot pursuit after me, as I felt no sort of doubt but what they had found my papers, and would know at once from them that I was in the country.   But the day at last wore off, and no rebels came after me.

.As soon as it was dark I started on my journey.   When I arrived at Holston River I found that it was too full to wade, and I did not like the idea of swimming over it, as I did not now wish to get my clothes wet.   Knowing, as I did, where a canoe was kept, I thought I would steal it, and cross the river in it if it was not guarded.   When I got within ten steps of the canoe, to my very great surprise I was ordered very gruffly by some person to halt.   I turned in an instant, and, without bidding this stranger good-night, immediately took the back track, and that in a hurry.   He fired his pistol at me five times, and also bursted a cap, but none of the balls touched me, although they sung their direful music in close proximity to my listening ears.

It may very well be imagined that I did not attempt any more on that night to get a canoe.   I went to a shoal in the river to cross, where sometimes I could wade, and at other times had to swim.   When I got over I put on my wet clothes, which were very ragged and dirty; but, I must confess, the river on this occasion gave them a pretty good washing, which at this time did not feel very agreeable to my person.   I yet had thirty miles to travel in my wet and ragged clothes.   I reached the railroad about four o'clock, when I had seven miles farther to go; I traveled very slowly the last few miles of my journey, for I was very much fatigued and very weak from hunger, and my frequent cold baths in the rivers had done me no good.   I now thought that just one such trip as the one which I had now accomplished would have been enough to satisfy any person but myself with the business of piloting men to Kentucky.   But as soon as I changed my clothes, and rested for a few days, and recovered my strength by receiving enough to eat, I was ready " to run the gauntlet" among the rebels again, during the period which it required to make another long and wearisome journey from the mountains of Carter County. to the State of Kentucky, and which it sometimes required all my philosophy and courage to perform. However, I was always consoled in the reflection that I was contributing to the relief of my oppressed and suffering fellowmen, and at the same time serving my beloved country.

I reached home on the 20th day of July, 1863, and finding that the mountains were full of men anxiously awaiting my return, I immediately prepared to start upon another journey to Kentucky, after staying at home only three days.

CHAPTER XIX.

On the 24th of July, 1863, I started to Kentucky with as many of the poor scouting conscripts as I thought I could get safely through with. When I reached the boatyard I found that the rebels were still watching, but not so strictly as they were when I was there on my last trip. I here received an accession to my company of fifty-five men, who had assembled there from every direction, in order to avail themselves of my services in getting through the lines. Among them were J. J. James, from Fall Branch, near Bay's Mountain, Tennessee, and John Hunt, from the same place. There were many good sound Union men who lived at the boat-yard, and they watched and warned us of all approaching danger until we could get off.

We left the boat-yard on the night of the 24th of July, and made our way to the north fork of Holston River. Here we had the good fortune to find a canoe, in which we all crossed, and then set out for Clinch Mountain, which was two miles ahead. We soon arrived at the foot of the mountain, and traveled up it a long distance—at least the men must have thought it a long distance from the way that they complained of fatigue. When we arrived at a good situation upon the mountain we stopped and made up fires. It was now nearly daylight, and we laid down to endeavor to sleep. We remained here until twelve o'clock, when I thought that we ought not to remain any longer in one place for safety, so I urged the company to make a forward movement. We now went on across the mountain,

when, upon getting near to Little Poor Valley, we stopped
to wait until night came on, at which time we crossed over
the valley, and went on to Copper Ridge, making our way
to Powell's Mountain.   We now had steep and rough river
knobs to cross over all the time, so that our progress was
very slow and difficult; but we went steadily forward until
we reached Clinch River, when, taking off our clothes, we
waded through it and pushed on, and got to the spurs of
Powell's Mountain by daylight.

After we ascended the mountain some distance we came
to water, where we stopped to rest our aching limbs and
discuss the best way to cross over Powell's Valley.   We
had traveled thus far without any trouble with the rebels,
and we thought it would be a considerable achievement if
we should be able to pass this dangerous rebel rendezvous
without being discovered.   The sun shone out brightly,
and we rested finely in the warm leaves.   Early in the
night we started on, crossing hills and ridges until midnight, when we reached the foot of Walling's Ridge.   Some
of the men were now very much exhausted, J. J. James
particularly; he was now unable to travel without being
led, and he could not get up steep places at all without a
man under each one of his arms to assist him.   We got
over the ridge after about three hours' hard traveling, and
reached the cleared land next to Powell's Valley.   We now
pulled off our shoes and walked in our stocking-feet, in order to make as little noise as possible.   As good luck would
have it, we crossed the valley in safety, and hurried on to
Powell's River, and when we got to it we did not even
halt to take off our clothes; we marched straight through,
and pushed on to Cumberland Mountain, and soon arrived
at its foot.   We continued our journey up the mountain
until we came to water, when we stopped to wash the sand

and mud out of our pants and socks, and, after wringing them as dry as we could, we put them on, and then traveled on over one of the roughest mountains that a set of poor lame, tired, and worn-out men ever attempted to travel over before.

Some of the company now had to assist James all the time; they had to lead him and drag him together for more than ten miles while we were crossing the mountain. We got to the Kentucky line about two o'clock, when the company appeared to be greatly rejoiced that they had at last escaped from the geographical limits of the so-called Southern Confederacy. But I do not suppose that they were half as much rejoiced as I was myself, for I always had a very great dread on my mind from the time I would start with a company until I reached the Kentucky line, when a most perplexing load of responsibility would at once fall off of me, which was far more oppressive on me than the burden of Atlas was when he was supporting the world on his shoulders. The burden of Atlas was only created and imposed by some fanciful mythologist, while mine was a burden which oppressed and perplexed me in my daily meditations and in my nightly dreams.

We went on to the house of Mr. Clark on Clover Fork, where we got an abundance to eat and drink, and the next morning, there being no danger now in their way, the men, with gay and light hearts, all started on to Louisville with the exception of poor James, who could not walk a step, and was compelled to lay up until his limbs could recover their usual vigor and activity. His feet were very much swollen, and had turned entirely purple. I never saw a man suffer more than he did in performing the journey through the lines to Kentucky. I knew that I could do the men no more good by going with them any farther, and my services were too badly needed by the scouters in the mountains of Carter County for me to waste any more time than I could possibly avoid ; I therefore, after resting two days and nights, procured a small stock of provisions, and set out on my lonely and weary journey.

CHAPTER XX.

On the 1st day of August, 1863, I started on my return trip to East Tennessee. I traveled hard all day, and reached Powell's Valley just as night was setting in. After waiting until every thing was still and quiet in the valley, I went on across it, and got on to the heights of Walling's Ridge. Here I rested for a short time, and then pushed on, crossing Powell's Mountain, wading the mountain streams, and climbing the steep river knobs, until I reached Clinch River, which I waded through, after taking off my clothes. I do not think that I shall ever forget the depth and the breadth of this river, as I had it to wade so often. I now pushed on, crossing valleys, mountains, farms, and wading branches, until I arrived at Clinch Mountain; it was now daylight, and, finding a good place to conceal myself in, I concluded to remain here all day.

The morning was quite warm, and a hot day coming on, I laid down in the shade to sleep and rest during the day, of which I was very much in need after my severe traveling. I slept until about ten o'clock, when I awoke, suffering at the time very much for water. I well knew that I would be in great danger by going lower down upon the mountain, but my thirst was so aggravating that I resolved to risk it. I went along the side of the mountain for some distance, but could not see any sign of water. I now discovered at some distance below me a gap in the mountain, where I concluded there must be water. I went on until I came to a road leading on through the gap. I did not like to travel in roads even after night, much less in daylight. I hardly know how I had the extreme temerity to travel in this road as far as I did; but, notwithstanding the danger that I was constantly in of being seen by the rebel soldiers or citizens, I continued to follow this road until I came to a beautiful spring of water, where I drank as much as I desired, and then filled my canteen.

While I was engaged in filling my canteen from the crystal fountain my nose was saluted with a most horrible effluvium. I immediately began to look around for the cause of the noxious odor which had so suddenly visited my nostrils, expecting every moment to see the putrid and decaying carcass of a dead hog or some other animal, when, horrible to relate in a civilized country, I saw the fleshless skeletons of three human beings hanging to a stooping sapling. I went up nearer and examined them; there was no fragment of clothing to be seen, and the flesh had all decayed from their bones. Their hair had fallen off of their heads, and was lying beneath their feet upon the ground. The bones of two of them were still all united together, forming two whole skeletons of the former living men; and the backbone of the other one having separated just below his ribs, the leg and hip-bones had fallen to the ground. I presumed that he had been shot through the backbone, which had caused his frame to separate where it did.

They had been hung with hickory bark, which had been peeled off of some hickory sprouts growing near, for the hickory sprouts off which the murderers had peeled the bark were still there to be seen. I at once guessed that they were poor fugitives who had been captured while they were trying to get through the lines. I did not tarry long at this spring, for I well knew that the fate which had been

ELLIS VIEWING THE SKELETONS.

allotted to these poor men would most unquestionably be
meted out to me if I should fall into the hands of the rebels.
When I got a short distance from the spring I met with a
woman coming down the road, and, after the usual saluta-
tion, a short colloquy ensued between us as follows:

"How came these men to be hung upon that tree?"

She replied, "They were a parcel of Lincolnites that our
boys captured at that spring while they were getting water."

"That is a horrible sight, madam. Is that the way that
the Lincolnites are disposed of when they are so unfortunate as to be captured?"

"Yes; they receive no mercy whatever from our boys.
If you will go down the road about one hundred yards you
will find a parcel of them that were captured here a short
time ago, and were shot immediately, and were thrown behind an old log, and covered up with leaves and chunks."

"How does it happen that so many men are captured in
this neighborhood?"

"Why, there is a company of soldiers stationed on Clinch
River, and they have selected the best hunters in the country to watch the roads and mountain paths to catch men
who are making their way through the lines."

"Well, that is the most diabolical sight that I have ever
witnessed in all my life."

"Oh, that is not a strange sight to me, by any means. I
have seen the hat and shoes taken off of many Lincolnites,
and have seen them kneel to pray before being shot."

"And did it cause you no emotions of pity to witness
such a terrible spectacle?"

"No, none whatever. That is the very way that men
ought to be treated whenever they are caught running away
to Old Abe. All of them ought to be killed."

"But do you think that the poor men whom you have seen murdered so unceremoniously were really guilty of any crime for which they deserved to be killed ?"

"Yes, I have no sympathy for them whatever. I believe it is perfectly right to kill them whenever they are caught. I have a husband and two brothers in the Southern army, and every man who is unwilling to fight for the Southern Confederacy, who may be caught in the act of running off to Kentucky, ought to be hung or shot."

This pugnacious virago was quite talkative, and I do not think that she was more than twenty-five years of age. She was young in years, but old in wickedness. Scott says in one of his poems,

> "Oh woman! in our hours of ease,
>   Uncertain, coy, and hard to please,
>   But when affliction wrings the brow,
>   A ministering angel thou."

But I do not think that this vindictive amazon could in the smallest degree substantiate the truth of this poetic sentiment, for if she had descended from a race of anthropophagi, and had been fed upon human flesh and blood all her life, she could not have been more hardened to human woe or more dead to human sympathy.

I would have asked more questions about the murders which she had witnessed, and which she talked about with such perfect coolness, but I was afraid to remain any longer in this dismal valley, where the bones and skeletons of dead men seemed to give no terror whatever even to a woman. I therefore bid this loquacious female rebel good-day, and hastened on toward the rough mountain, for I was altogether out of my range. I must confess that I felt extremely melancholy after the terrible and shocking spectacle that I had seen near the spring, and, forgetting my weariness, I continued to travel on all day. Early in the night I reached the north fork of Holston River, which, after taking off my clothes, I waded through. I then traveled on, over fields and knobs, the remainder of the night, and by daylight I reached the flats, where my old friend, Mrs. Grills, gave me a warm breakfast.' I remained here all day, and when night came on I started on my journey, and reached the old hills of Carter County by daylight, being greatly fatigued, and with very sore feet, which had been occasioned by the severe journey which I had accomplished.

I found very many who had been anxiously awaiting my return, and was at once convinced that there was no rest for me, for the constant question was, "When will you start again?" And "Do not leave me this time," was the inevitable cry; and all of them being steadfast Union men, they could not think of being forced into the Southern army. The leading Union men were now all gone; and there being scarcely none to urge the common masses to hold on to their love for the Union, I thought that they deserved the utmost praise for adhering so steadfastly to their principles amid all the dangers and difficulties which surrounded them, and, therefore, I resolved to assist all that I possibly could in getting through the lines, regardless of the hardships of the journey, or the dangers which might threaten me in passing backward and forward. I also thought that I would thereby be contributing important service in furnishing soldiers for the Union army, and at the same time aid and assist in weakening the South. I thought that the wide expanse of the ocean was composed of drops of water; and natural philosophy teaches that, if one drop of water could be kept perfectly compact, it would be capable of poisoning the world. I therefore concluded that every single man that I could get safely through to the Union army would be at once subtracting that much of the bone and sinew from the South, and which, if it were suffered to remain in the country, might be employed in some way or other in the support of the miserable so-called "Southern Confederacy." I was also well convinced that the mountain-men would make the very best of soldiers, and would fight like demons when they would remember how they had been driven away from their families and homes by the rebel miscreants. These poor men knew that, when they started, they were leaving their loved families in the hands of a desperate and merciless foe, who, when they were convinced that they had gone to seek protection under the old flag of their country, would take pleasure in destroying every thing which they had left behind for their helpless wives and children to subsist upon.

I have seen many manly faces bathed in tears at the thought of the sad fate which awaited their helpless families when they were absent, and powerless to afford them any assistance; and a dark cloud would then overshadow their brows as the desire for future revenge would take possession of their hearts, when, with a silent farewell, they would turn their backs upon their now desolate mountain homes, while their poor wives and children were sobbing as if their hearts would break, as the husband and father would shoulder his knapsack of provisions for the journey, prepared by the hands of love, with the thought that even that was not enough to keep him from starving, if he should meet with any adverse circumstances to delay him in his journey. And this was very often the case; for the poor Union men were watched with as much scrutiny by the rebel soldiers as if they had been wild, ravenous beasts of the forest; and woe to the man who was caught while endeavoring to make his escape through the lines;

for he was not thought worthy of being consigned to the gloomy cells of a Southern prison, and was therefore murdered in a most brutal and barbarous manner.

The company which was now ready to start with me to Kentucky was very large, and all the men seemed to be inspired with the fond hope of soon being permitted to return again, if they should be able to endure the hardships which they would have to encounter in their journey. They had the most unbounded confidence in the United States government overthrowing the rebellion at an early day and freeing their homes from rebel tyranny; and when that day should come, they determined to pay the rebels up for all the insults and injuries which they had to receive and endure in silence with the most severe agony of mind. There were such constant accessions to the company which I was now about to start with, that I had some fears about being able to conduct them all through safely; but my heart and soul were now in the work, and I did not feel willing that one of the men who desired to go should be left to run the risk of falling a victim to rebel spite and malice. I therefore encouraged every one to go who came to me and signified a desire to do so; for I knew that I had conducted large companies of men through the rugged mountains when they were clothed in their cold, white robes of winter, and that I would now be much better enabled to elude and disappoint the vigilance of the rebels, when every tree and shrub was clothed in its summer livery of green foliage.

CHAPTER XXI.

On the night of the 17th of August, 1863, I started again for Kentucky with a large number of men, who had assembled with great trepidation to flee from rebel vengeance, as travelers would flee from the terrible simoom in the Desert of Sahara when it threatened to envelop them in its poisonous embrace. The starting-point was at the old forge, near Elizabethton. The night was clear and pleasant, and we traveled twelve miles, crossed the railroad, and stopped to spend the next day in a thick clump of bushes. As soon as it got dark, we shouldered our knapsacks and started on our journey. We had to travel twenty-two miles before we could reach my old hiding-place, the "White-oak Flats," and before we arrived there it was daylight, and we were told that there were numbers of rebel soldiers in the neighborhood. This was very disagreeable intelligence, for the men were very tired, and presented a most sorrowful appearance with their blistered, cut, and swelled feet; and all of them furnished decided proof that they had been greatly worsted by their hard and laborious march. We passed a very disagreeable day, being in constant expectation of hearing the tramp of the rebel soldiery in hot pursuit after us. We could neither eat nor sleep, and we were even afraid to take off our shoes in order to rest our tired feet; neither did we get any water during the whole long hot day to cool our parched tongues. Oh, with what anxiety we watched the sun until it attained its meridian height, and then start on in its path of declination down the western slope of the blue, ethereal vault of heaven. Surely Wellington was no more anxious for the approach of night, when he stood upon the bloody field of Waterloo, while the surges of battle were rolling around him with all their dreadful fury, with his watch in his hand, and exclaimed, "Oh for night or for Blucher," than we were during the wretched day which we passed in the "White-oak Flats."

But the tide of time rolled on, and the dark wings of night again overspread the earth, and we started on and traveled until we came to water, when we stopped to eat and drink. The men bathed their sore feet in the cool water, which appeared to afford them great relief, after which we went on, through woods, fields, and brier-thickets, sometimes tearing our clothes, and at other times our flesh; but knowing that there was no other alternative but to press onward, or run the risk of falling into the hands of the rebels, we rushed forward, despite of all the troubles and the dangers which environed our pathway. When we arrived at the north fork of Holston River, we took off our clothes and waded through, and after hastily putting on our clothes, we marched on. Some of the men had nearly put out their eyes with the brush, and some were so much worn out for sleep that they would almost fall asleep as they walked along; they would often fall down over stumps and logs, and bruise themselves very badly.

We arrived at Clinch Mountain just as the sun was rising, and continued on up the mountain until we found water, and a good place to sleep. We now stopped, took off our shoes, and bathed our hands, faces, and feet, and then tried to eat. But some of the men were so perfectly tired down that they went to sleep while they were eating. They could not keep their eyes open any more than if they

I

had been thoroughly drugged with opium. It was not
long until all of them were fast asleep, and the sun shone
down so warm that their faces and necks were severely
blistered. About two o'clock the men began to awake,
with their eyes swollen, and some of them very hoarse
from lying on the ground. It was late in the evening before I got them all roused up to make preparations for an
onward movement, for I knew that they had another hard
and fatiguing night's travel before them.

As soon as it got dark we started on across the mountain, and when we got near to Little Poor Valley, I left the
men in the woods, and went to the road to see if I could
observe any prospect of threatening danger. But I could
not see or hear any thing that gave me any cause for alarm,
and I went back and started the company on. We crossed
Copper Ridge and Copper Creek, and then went on, through
fields and over ridges, until we arrived at Clinch River.
We cut sticks to support us in the water, and then, after
taking off our clothes, we started into the river; we were
at a shoal, and the night was very dark, which made the
water, as it ran in deep channels or over rough rocks, look
very frightful. Some of the men got into deep channels,
and very narrowly escaped being drowned; but, as good
fortune would have it, we all reached the shore, and, after
adjusting our clothes, we went on, across fields, branches,
steep hills, and precipitous knobs, until daylight, when we
reached the spurs of Powell's Mountain. The sun was just
rising as we commenced the toilsome ascent of the mountain.

Beattie, in his beautiful poem of "The Minstrel," says,

"Ah! who can tell how hard it is to climb
    The steep, where Fame's proud temple shines afar?
Ah! who can tell how many a soul sublime,
    Has felt the influence of malignant star?"

I do not believe that, if "Fame's proud temple" had been standing upon the summit of this mountain, any one of these poor tired men would have made the least exertion to gain an entrance to its portals, in order to inscribe his name in any of its niches. But they had indeed felt the dreadful "influence of malignant star" when they were chased from their homes by the rebel murderers, and they were now compelled to toil, step by step, up the rugged heights of this mountain, to obtain farther security for their lives. The men were greatly exhausted, but they pressed on until we came to water, and a place of safety; for we had seen the sign of rebel cavalry in the last road which we crossed, and there was nothing that seemed to instill a spirit of endurance into stampeders like the sign of rebel soldiers. The sight of a rebel was enough to keep them traveling at any time. Hungry and weary though they might be, it appeared to invigorate them with a sort of new life.

We passed the day on the top of the mountain, and as soon as it got dark we started on. I had a great deal of difficulty in getting them along and keeping them together, for we would sometimes have to cross a ravine, crawling upon our hands and knees, and through the mud at that. We would sometimes get into immense thickets of laurel and ivy bushes, where some of the men would get lost; and when I would hear them hallooing and screaming in the awful darkness of the night, I would at once stop the company until I could again collect them all together. When we would emerge from such dismal places as this, we would look as though we had been incontinently dragged through a black mud-hole. We pushed on until we came to Wildcat Valley, where we had another public road to cross. Before getting to the road, I stopped the company, and went forward by myself to look out for any threatening danger; but seeing nor hearing nothing to cause alarm, I returned to the men, and started them on. We crossed the valley, and then got on to Walling's Ridge, where the bushes were so thick that it was with the greatest difficulty imaginable that we could get along at all in the extreme darkness of the night. After great labor and fatigue, we arrived at the top of the ridge, along which we traveled for some time, and then turned down toward Powell's Valley, which we now had to cross, although it was full of rebel soldiers, who were as mean and blood-thirsty as the devil himself could possibly wish them to be.

At every house in this valley there was a gang of dogs, and the dogs and men seemed to know very well when stampeders were passing. The little dogs would first give the alarm, and the larger dogs would then raise a most terrible yell, when all at once the rebel soldiers would rush out, hissing and hallooing, until the whole valley would be in a perfect uproar with the men and dogs. There were certainly more dogs in this valley than any other place I ever traveled through in all my life; and I have often thought that whenever the "Yankees" got into East Tennessee, I would get a company of them and go there, and have a general dog-killing frolic, for they occasioned me so much vexation of mind that I had become an enemy to the whole race of dogs. When we got near the valley, we stopped and pulled off our shoes, and I charged the men to be very careful, when they came to fences, not to throw down or break any of the rails. We started on like we were walking upon thorns, and arrived safely at Powell's River, which we crossed through without stopping to divest ourselves of our clothes. We had no time to lose, for the night was now far advanced; we therefore pushed on as rapidly as possible, and reached the foot of Cumberland Mountain just as the eastern sky began to exhibit the early morning's golden beams. We went up the side of the mountain some distance, when we stopped to rest. The sun was now shining brightly, and we had a fine prospective view of the valley below. We could see the rebel camps, and we could also see that we had made a very narrow escape, for we had passed along immediately between two of the rebel encampments, where we could now see the soldiers preparing their breakfast. I thought that, this time at least, I had succeeded most admirably in steering between Scylla and Charybdis.

We were now beyond the pursuit of the rebels, and could, for the balance of the journey, travel in daylight. We had exhausted all of our provisions, but we pushed forward upon empty stomachs, and by two o'clock we reached Harlan County, in the State of Kentucky, where we soon got something to eat. The men were entirely worn out, and they now pulled off their shoes, and after bathing their sore and blistered feet, they lay down on the ground to sleep in every fashion, some on their backs, some on their sides, and some on their faces, and very soon all of them were reveling in the land of dreams, snoring away at the rate of " ten knots an hour." Many of them slept the entire night just where they lay down, without even turning over. The sacred Psalmist says that "sleep is sweet to the laboring man, whether he eat little or much," and I thought that I had never seen the truth of this sentiment so clearly evinced as I did when I witnessed the profound and sweet sleep of these poor, tired, and worn-out fugitives. When at times I would look upon these poor men, sweetly resting in their quiet and deep repose, I realized to the fullest extent all the sentiment that is contained in the poetic lines of Dr. Young, where he says,

"Tired Nature's sweet restorer, balmy sleep!
He, like the world, his ready visit pays,
Where fortune smiles; the wretched he forsakes;
Swift on his downy pinion flies from woe,
And lights on lids unsullied with a tear."

We remained at this place during the day, and also the following night, when we started on again, for we could get nothing more to eat, for the people had been robbed of nearly every thing they had by the marauding rebel parties who had been for some time scouting through the country, obtaining thereby a precarious subsistence. They had taken all the mules, horses, cattle, and goods belonging to the people in this portion of Kentucky, and had conveyed them to Powell's Valley for safe keeping.

I concluded that I would not yet leave the men, but would go on with them as far as Manchester, a distance of eighty miles from the place we were now at. We went on, and crossed Cumberland River and Little Brushy Mountain, and arrived at a place called Greasy Fork, where we remained all night, and fared tolerably well in the way of getting provisions, but still had to lay on the cold ground. Early the next morning we started, and after traveling down Greasy Fork for several miles, we left it, and struck across the country toward a small river called Red-bird. Here we got some provisions, and set out for Manchester. We traveled hard all day, and at night we stopped at a cabin, where we applied for something to eat, and were told that we could have it. The place, I must confess, had quite a forbidding appearance, but the men were very tired and hungry, and said they were compelled to have rest. Every thing about the premises had the indelible mark of filthiness about it, and certainly nothing but hungry dogs, or half-starved men, could have had the stomach to partake of

any thing to eat at that dirty-looking place. But, owing to
the force of circumstances, we resolved to try one meal, at
any rate. When I entered the house, the first object which
attracted my observation was an old woman sitting in a
corner of the fire-place smoking a pipe. She was ragged
and barefooted; her feet were as scaly and black with dirt
as a toad's back; and her ankles (for her dress was too
short to conceal them) looked like a couple of old rusty
gun-barrels; and her hair had surely never been combed,
for it stood out in a thousand directions; in fact, she was
begrimed with dirt from head to foot. There were also
two girls, who seemed to be about eighteen years of age,
who ran into another room, and each one of them came out
habited in a calico dress, which was so thin, and their un-
der-dressing so scarce, if indeed there was any under-dress-
ing at all, that their forms were distinctly visible through
their scanty clothing. I did not believe that either one of
them would have exhibited a very agreeable picture to the
fancy of a Phidias or a Praxiteles, if he desired to chisel out
a chaste design in statuary; but I really thought that they
could have compared very favorably with Powers's Greek
Slave—in point of nudity.

They commenced making preparations for supper, and
one of the girls, accompanied by an old and very poor
hound-dog, started in pursuit of a chicken, which, after so
long a time, they succeeded in catching, and the girl pulled
its head off and laid it on a table, when a large cat jumped
up and dragged it off on to the floor, when two other cats
seized it by each wing, and the three then ran out of the
house with it, and attempted to get under the floor; but all
at once a hound puppy stopped them in their career, caught
hold of the chicken by the tail, and there they stood, each
one striving for the mastery with awful growls and snarls.
In order to end the dispute, one of the girls made a sudden

attack upon this squad of carnivorous animals with the fire-shovel and recaptured the prize, and at once proceeded to prepare it for our supper! We purchased a small hog that was standing in the yard, and had it cooked. We had plenty of corn bread, but it was baked out of meal which was badly spoiled, and was consequently not very palatable. And, to cap the climax of dainties, they cooked up a quanti-ty of green cabbage, which was full of worms, and not a particle of salt in the whole unsavory mess. We sat down to the table, and endeavored to eat as well as we could, and those of the men who partook of the cabbage would now and then rake a large worm to the side of their plates! But their appetites were too keen to back out at the sight of worms, and, after placing them to one side, they con-tinued to eat on. No person knows what they could be in-duced to eat until they suffer for several days and nights with the most excessive hunger. In that sort of an extrem-ity, the most fastidious and delicate taste very willingly ac-commodates itself to articles of food which otherwise would be most wretchedly abhorrent.

After supper we began to pile about upon the floor to sleep, for the beds looked so dirty and ragged that they afforded a most unpromising theatre whereupon to court the sweet influences of sleep, and I had no doubt, from every appearance, they were well supplied with vermin. We slept until morning, but did not stay for breakfast. We paid our bill, which was fifty cents each, and started for Manchester, and when we arrived there we learned that General Burnside, with a large force, was on his way to East Tennessee. Some of the men who had come through from Tennessee with me concluded to go on to Louisville to join the 4th Tennessee Infantry, while a number of them concluded to stay with me and go in pursuit of the Federal army, which was now marching to East Tennessee.

CHAPTER XXII.

I STARTED from Manchester with a number of the men who had come from Tennessee with me with the intention of overtaking the Union forces, who were now marching toward East Tennessee, under the command of General Burnside. I was in great hopes of being able to overtake the 2d Tennessee Mounted Infantry. We followed on in the rear of the army for several days, and at length arrived at Montgomery, which is near the Tennessee state line. At this place we overtook the 12th Kentucky Regiment, and were arrested by them as spies; but they treated us very well, and after examining my papers, they filled our haversacks with provisions and permitted us to go on after the Tennessee troops.

We now found it very difficult to procure any thing to eat, for the army had devoured almost every thing in the shape of provisions as it had passed along, and had left the mountain people in a deplorable situation, and very many of them were compelled to move where they could obtain supplies from the government. We went on to Kingston, and from thence to Lenoir's Station, which is twenty-four miles west of Knoxville, and from there we went to Knoxville, where we arrived on the 1st day of September, 1863. Here we came up with the 2d Tennessee Mounted Infantry, commanded by Colonel James Carter, and here I also got into company with many of my old friends. I remained two days at Knoxville, and left on the second train with the

I 2

100th Ohio Regiment for the upper portion of East Tennessee.

At every dépôt along the railroad there were large crowds of people gathered to welcome the "Yankees" with well-filled baskets of provisions, containing bread, pies, ham, and fowls of every description. Old men and women were busily engaged in making inquiries about their absent sons, about whom they seemed to manifest the greatest concern, while others were weeping and shouting for joy at the very sight of the "Yankees," and at the cherished idea of once more being freemen. They had been so long crushed down under the iron heel of despotism that I did not at all wonder at their joyful demonstrations. As the train moved on slowly up the road, I could see the roadside and the fences crowded with the admiring multitude of people who had assembled to welcome the Union soldiers to the eastern portion of Tennessee. Large numbers of ladies were present in every assemblage, who, with delicate hands, waved their white handkerchiefs aloft, with tears of joy sparkling in their eyes ; and those of the more humble class of females, having nothing more fashionable with which to express their sentiments of gratification, would wave their bonnets as tokens of their admiration ; and some of my friends declared to me that they observed one woman, in the extravagance of her joy, take her baby and whirl it around, while the child, seeming to enjoy the general happiness of the occasion, laughed aloud. Aged men could be seen all along the railroad leaning upon their staffs, whose locks had been whitened with the frosts of many years, uttering blessings upon the "starry banner," which was once more waving over their heads in all its proud and glorious majesty. Oh, with what extreme reverence did these old men seem to bow their heads beneath the folds of the dear old flag of their country! And their silent tears of joy chased one another down their furrowed cheeks, as they gazed with rapture upon this dear old emblem of their country's liberty. Never, until that time, did they know how much they prized and loved this cherished memento of American liberty, under which their country had arrived at the very pinnacle of national greatness. They now loved it the more, because they were convinced that an effort had been, and was still being made to supplant it, and hoist in its stead a striped thing—an ornamented bunting—to indicate the existence of the so-called Southern Confederacy. But this was their old flag, which had waved in triumph over their fathers, and which they desired to wave on in triumph over them and their posterity. Indeed, every smiling lineament of their furrowed faces seemed to say,

"The star-spangled banner, oh, long may it wave
O'er the land of the free and the home of the brave."

The demonstrations all along the road were of the most joyous character imaginable; men and boys waved their hats and coats, and shouted and cheered in the most extravagant manner. The years of dreadful oppression which they had suffered seemed now to be forgotten in the general jubilee, which they now engaged in so joyfully.

When the train arrived at Greenville the extreme joy of the Union people knew no bounds. Friends who had long been separated met. Husbands met with wives and children who had not seen them for years. And such a scene of rejoicing I never before witnessed in all my life. This reunion of friends, who had been long separated by circumstances growing out of the infamous Southern rebellion, will doubtless long be remembered by those who witnessed it, as well as by those who participated in it.

All were happy, extremely happy, but the rebels. The scene of general rejoicing afforded no happiness to them. Their doors and windows were closed, and none of them were to be seen, with the exception of their half-concealed faces, which could be seen occasionally peeping from behind a window-curtain. There was no welcome voice emanating from them, and the soldiers seemed to know every rebel house as they passed it. The train came on up to Limestone Dépôt, where it was compelled to stop, as the tressle-work across the creek had been destroyed. And it was at that point where General Alfred Jackson (familiarly known under the soubriquet of "Mudwall Jackson") met the advancing Union forces with a considerable force of rebels. I was sure that the "Yankees" would be at once demolished and captured, for the rebels outnumbered them at least four to one, and, if they had not behaved so cowardly, they certainly would have captured the small force of "Yankees," together with the train. But the rebels were too cowardly to go into a general engagement, and contented themselves with capturing a small body of the "Yankees" who had been left at a block-house at Limestone, and the main force of the Union soldiers returned with the train back toward Knoxville. Expecting as I did that the Yankee soldiers would all be captured, and not wishing to be found in the crowd of prisoners, I left them, and in the time of the prevailing excitement which followed upon this threatened concussion of arms, I made my way home without any difficulty, where I remained until Burnside came up to Carter Station, which was only a few days after the occurrence at Limestone Dépôt.

I met the Union forces at Johnson's Station, and remained with them during all the skirmishing which they had with the rebels from that point to Carter Station, giv-

ing them all the information I could in regard to the rebels
and the number of their forces in this section of the country. I think it was the 12th Michigan Regiment that drove
the rebels on before them to Carter Station. Colonel James
Carter afterward came on with the 2d Tennessee Regiment
to the bridge across the Watauga just below Carter Dépôt;
and being in a good position was ready for the fight, which
it was generally believed would occur the next morning.
But when the next morning came, to the great surprise of
all, there was not a single rebel to be seen. They had all
retreated during the night, and by so doing saved themselves from a good thrashing. General Burnside was now
ordered to return to Knoxville, and John K. Miller, a citizen of Carter County, obtained permission from the Federal
authorities to make up a regiment of Tennessee volunteers,
over which regiment he was to occupy the position of colonel. This was very easily done, for before the Yankees left
Carter Station I had one company ready to go into the new
regiment myself. This was Company " A," and it was the
beginning of the regiment which was afterward called the
13th Tennessee Cavalry. Company " A" was, therefore,
the *substratum* upon which was founded the 13th Tennessee Cavalry, that brave and magnanimous regiment whose
deeds of noble daring will live and shine upon the bright
historic page "to the last syllable of recorded time." A
Cæsar, an Alexander, or a Bonaparte, at the head of a large
army composed of such men as were those who filled the
ranks in our glorious old 13th Tennessee Cavalry, could
march on, " conquering and to conquer," and subdue and
ultimately fix the political destiny of any nation upon the
whole face of the earth. In order to accomplish great military events, there are three prerequisites which are entirely indispensable, which are these: brave soldiers, competent

subordinate officers, and a leading chieftain skilled and accomplished in all the tactics of military science. A large army which could boast of having these three necessary components would, like an avalanche, be altogether irresistible in its movements.

I could have been captain of Company "A," but declined it, as Colonel Miller wished me to remain in the upper counties of East Tennessee and recruit for the 13th Regiment. The Yankees now fell back, and I was again forced to go into the mountains to resume my old occupation of piloting companies of men through the lines. The Union men were in great hopes for some time that the Yankees would soon return, but they were doomed to be most sadly disappointed. The rebel General Longstreet was in a position east of Knoxville, with thirty thousand troops, and wintered all of this large force off of the upper counties. If the Union people were in trouble before this force made its appearance in East Tennessee, what can be imagined was their wretched condition now? Rebel gangs of soldiers were now prowling through the country in every direction, ransacking and plundering, and murdering many of the citizens. They took every wagon that they could find, and hauled off the small stock of provisions which the people had to live upon; and where the country was too mountainous for them to go with wagons, they would go on horseback and pack off the scanty provisions from the most humble cabin in the mountains. There was no other chance now for the few remaining Union men but to go through the lines and join the Union army, or be suddenly killed by the rebel thieves and murderers who now infested all parts of the country. Many poor and indigent families were now left without a protector, for the husband and father was compelled to leave his home in order to save his own life.   The distress which now prevailed among the Union people in Upper East Tennessee beggars all description. I will not attempt it any farther.   Cold, bleak winter was at hand, and it was almost impossible for men to scout and lay out in the mountains; for if by so doing they could succeed in hiding from the rebels, there was nothing which could be procured for themselves or their families to eat. Their only alternative was either to go through the lines or remain at home, and either starve or be killed.   My pathway through the mountains to the Union lines now led on toward Knoxville, and I made preparations to start on my first journey in that direction, an account of which the reader will find fully detailed in the next chapter.

CHAPTER XXIII.

On the 15th of January, 1864, I commenced my long and weary travels through the mountains to Knoxville, which was altogether a new route from the one which I had so frequently traveled in going to and returning from the Union lines. The company which had assembled to go with me on the present occasion numbered fifty men, among whom were Dr. Floyd Pettigru, from Virginia, John and Edward Johnson, from Johnson's Dépôt, and two sons of Dr. Young, of Carter County. The company assembled on Buffalo Creek, at Spencer Bowman's and James Martin's, about three o'clock in the night. We ate breakfast at Bowman's and Martin's; and just before daylight we started for the mouptain, and traveled along upon the top of it until night, at which time we came down off of the mountain to the Greasy Cove, in Washington County, and traveled on the east side of the cove for about ten miles or more, until we got to the red banks of Chucky River. We hired a man to set us across the river, and got into a road leading on to North Carolina, called the Flag-pond Road. This road is traveled but very little, and is quite solitary, as it winds along through narrow valleys, hedged in by dense thickets of laurel and ivy bushes, along the sides of steep mountains, and up and down lofty ridges. It is very seldom that wagons pass along this road, for at numerous places, if they should get out of the road by some accident, they would fall some three or four hundred feet. When we got to In-

dian Creek, we found that we would have to wade.   The
creek was full and wide, and ice was formed at each bank
about ten feet into the water.   After taking off our shoes
and stockings, we broke the ice and waded through ; the
main current was full of mush-ice, and by the time we got
to the opposite bank our feet were nearly frozen.   After
traveling about two miles farther, we stopped for the night
on the side of the mountain and built up fires, around which
we had to stand and sit, for the ground was too cold to lay
upon without freezing.   The night was cold and frosty, and
we had to pass it off in twisting and turning around the fire.

Morning at length came, and a cold and cheerless morning it was.   The sun was obscured by dark, intervening
clouds, and the wind was extremely cold.   It was about
eight o'clock when we started on over the high knobs,
crossing creeks and branches upon the ice, and after a hard
and toilsome day's travel, we passed out of Washington
County, Tennessee, and got into Madison County, North
Carolina.   About dark we reached Shelton Laurel, and
there, getting into a deep hollow, we built up fires ; but
the night was so excessively cold, that the men suffered
greatly from the terrible effects of it.   When morning
came, we started on, crossing branches and creeks, sometimes upon the ice, and at other times having to wade.   In
the evening the snow began to fall rapidly, and continued
to fall until about twelve o'clock at night, which proved to
be a very serious impediment to me, for I had never before
traveled through the range of mountains which now raised
their lofty summits around me on every side, and the snow
was falling so thick and fast that I could scarcely see my
way.   But I kept moving onward as best I could, and
urged the men to follow directly after me.   We at length
arrived at Paint-rock Mountain, and after crossing over it,

we came to the main road leading from Greenville, Tennessee, to the Warm Springs in North Carolina. We pushed on, across deep hollows and high ridges, until we got to Meadow-creek Mountain, and after crossing it, we arrived at Rhea Hennegar's, who was a good Union man, and who directed us to a safe place to camp for the night. We built up large fires, for some of the men were nearly frozen. When the fires melted the snow away, and warmed the atmosphere around them a little, the men began to fall asleep, for they were so much fatigued that they would lean up against trees and old logs, and go to sleep, regardless of the cold, which was so intense that it seriously threatened to suspend their earthly existence. It kept some of the men constantly busy to replenish the fires with wood, in order to keep the balance from freezing. It was about three o'clock in the night when we took up camps, and we rested there until the sun was about an hour high the next morning.

We started on, and traveled hard until evening, when we got near the French Broad River, which we had to cross. We went out in the mountain to the residence of an old Union man, who lived so remote from the habitations of his fellow-men that we thought he was surely never annoyed with the sight of human beings, unless they were stampeders like ourselves, in order to get his services in procuring a canoe for us to cross the river in. We had very hard work to persuade the old man that we were really Union men trying to make our way to the Yankees. After talking to him for some time, he told us that he could not walk a step, as he was badly crippled with the rheumatism. But I knew that the old fellow was pretending to be ill, thinking that we were rebels, and I also knew that he could assist us in finding a canoe if we could succeed in making him

believe that we were all right. After a good deal of cere-
mony, we got the old man to go with us, but he seemed to
doubt our sincerity still, for he would not go until he got his
old lady to accompany him. After he started to the river
with us, he told us that the rebels had frequently imposed
themselves upon the poor credulous Union men in that section of country, making them believe that they were stampeders trying to get to the Yankees; and after thus induc-
ing their unsuspecting victims to start with them to conduct
them out of the mountains, would, after getting them off a
short distance from their houses, murder them in the most
shocking manner.

The old man went to the canoe and got a negro boy to
set us across the river. This canoe belonged to Captain
Huff, who was then in the Federal army, and who had left
it at the river for the accommodation and rescue of stampeders. It was dark when we crossed, but we traveled on
in the direction of Greasy Fork and Big Pigeon Rivers.
The night was cold, and after traveling until about twelve
o'clock we stopped and built up fires, for the men were now
loudly complaining about their sore feet. The ground and
the air were so very cold that we could not rest with any
degree of comfort, which caused us to start on upon our
journey about daylight the next morning. We went on
over very rugged and steep ridges; sometimes having to
crawl through the thickets of laurel bushes which obstructed our path. When we got to Big Pigeon River we had
the good luck to find a canoe, in which we crossed, and
then steered our course toward Don's Creek, not forgetting
to inquire at every cabin we passed about the rebels, for
we were now in a section of country where the sentiments
of the people were in favor of the Union. They told us all
that they knew about the rebels, and where they were sta-

tioned, and by this means we managed very easily to evade them. We went on until we crossed Cosby Creek, twelve miles above Parrottsville. I thought it most advisable to postpone crossing the valley, which we had now arrived at, until the next night, and, consequently, we went into the ridges and built up fires, and laid down to endeavor to seek repose in the arms of sleep. Our provisions were now exhausted, and we had been living upon half rations for three days.

We resumed our journey weak with hunger and worn out with fatigue, and by three o'clock we arrived at Little Pigeon River, where we learned that the Yankees were at Sevierville, which was ten miles from where we were now. This was delightful news to us, for some of the men were almost broken down, and could scarcely walk at all upon their sore feet. The feet of some were swollen in a frightful manner. We therefore employed a man to take his ox-cart and haul some of the men who were worse crippled than others to Sevierville, while those who were able walked. We were not entirely certain that all of the rebels were out of the way, for it was reported that there were fifty of them on Little Pigeon River, some four miles below the point we were now at, and were stationed at a cross-road leading to Parrottsville. However, we concluded to go ahead, and trust to fortune to deliver us from falling into the hands of the rebels. The badly-crippled men now seated themselves in the ox-cart, and the driver, who was a negro boy, mounted one of the oxen and away we went. We had not advanced more than three miles until we got to the river, at which time we saw a company of men riding up the road immediately toward us. I feared that they were rebels, and some of the party declared they were. When this supposition was announced, the lame men all sprang out of the cart as quick as lightning and started up the side of the mountain as fast as they could run, which was much faster than those ran who did not possess such dreadful lameness. They ran with a good deal more agility than the balance of the company, for they kept far on ahead of all their competitors. If they had been running for a bag of gold, I do not believe that they could have displayed half such speed as they did upon this occasion. But this was not a strange sight to me, for, in all my travels through the mountains, I found it invariably to be the case that, whenever the rebels started in pursuit of a company of stampeders, the lame men always outstripped the sound ones. The very sight of the rebels appeared at once to render them oblivious to their lameness, and also to give new activity to their limbs.

We all continued running up the mountain until we concluded that we were out of danger, and then stopped to look behind. We expected every moment to see the rebels coming on after us, but we were disappointed, as well as very much delighted, when we heard the supposed rebels inviting us to return, and telling us not to be alarmed, that they were Yankees. After talking to them until we were satisfied that they were not trying to circumvent us, we went down to the road again. The lame men took possession of the ox-cart, and the driver remounted, and we went on about three miles farther, when we stopped for the night, which was very dark and cold. We purchased provisions enough for our supper and breakfast, which was quite an agreeable acquisition, for we were all very hungry, and felt keenly the demands of appetite.

Early the next morning we set out for Sevierville, and reached there early in the day, where we had the agreeable pleasure of finding that the Yankees were the "lords of the soil" in all that region of country. I had succeeded in getting my company through safely. I had conducted them from a land of tyranny and oppression to a land of freedom, where they could rest at ease, and dream no more that they had fallen into the hands of the rebel hangman. They could now walk forth amid the noonday's light, and meet their fellow-men as freemen meet freemen in a land of liberty. They may have felt some pangs of grief when their thoughts would wander back to their now-forsaken homes, but they consoled themselves with the reflection that the great Omnipotent, who governs the universe, was altogether able to bring order out of chaos, and would in a short time permit them to reunite with their loved families in the dear ties of friendship and love.

After bidding my friends adieu, I started back with the ox-cart, and staid all night at the gentleman's house to whom it belonged.

CHAPTER XXIV.

ON the 22d of January, 1864, I set out upon my return trip home. After traveling hard all day through the mountains, at night I came to a little cabin, where I got my supper, and the woman told me where I could find a camp in the mountains which would be a safe place for me to stay. I started in search of the camp, and found it as she had said, and remained there all night. I started early the next morning, and traveled until about eight o'clock, when I came to another cabin, at which I stopped and got my breakfast. The poor woman at this cabin gave me a most horrible detail about her troubles. The infernal rebels had murdered her husband in cold blood just three days before my arrival. She showed me his blood upon some stones which were lying in the yard. And the rail fence, which surrounded the house, at one place was completely covered with blood, and that was the place where she said they had dragged him over the fence by his feet. She said that, after they had shot him dead, several of the incarnate devils thrust their bayonets through his body. They then robbed her of her blankets and clothing, and left her with four little orphan children to buffet the dark waves of adversity in a friendless world. She said that her worldly means were already very limited, and that she and her little children would be doomed to suffering and want if she did not receive some assistance. Surely the vengeance of the Almighty will follow these murderers all along the journey of their infamous lives, and at last fully reward them for their iniquities in the dark regions of eternal despair. When I gazed in pity upon these poor little children, who were now thrown upon the cold charities of a heartless and unfeeling world by the brutal murder of their earthly protector, my heart seemed to melt within me, and tears of sorrow trickled down my cheeks. They stood before me as pictures of despair and distress; and as I looked upon their young faces, I thought that the tender blossoms of their existence were doomed to be nipped by an early frost; for, from what their poor mother had told me, I could see nothing awaiting them but penury, destitution, starvation, and death. I was utterly astonished to think that a parcel of men, possessed of human faculties, and made in the image of Him who says "Thou shalt not kill," could murder the father of these helpless children, and thereby robe them in the dismal habiliments of orphanage, and doom them to starvation and an early death.

Oh, it was sad to listen to that poor woman's tale of woe, and see the tears of sorrow flowing from her eyes, as she told how her best and only earthly friend was butchered by these inhuman monsters. What a stigma it is to this land of Bibles and civilization, that such demons should exist therein, capable of perpetrating deeds of crime which are calculated to shook and outrage the feelings of humanity! If these monsters are still living in the world, disgracing the upright form of human beings, if their pillows at night are not filled with thorns, and their dreams disturbed with visions of their innocent victim shaking his bloody locks before them, it is not because the dreadful enormity of their crime in murdering an innocent husband and father, and thereby making his wife a widow and his children helpless orphans, should not occasion it.

With a sad heart I left this desolate family, and traveled

all day along the side of a mountain, from which I could see the rebels in the valleys below robbing houses, hunting men, and doing every possible mischief which their wicked hearts could devise. After crossing Big Pigeon River, I went on to French Broad, which I reached early in the night, and crossed it in a canoe, and went on up the mountain. At length I came to a deep hollow, where I built up a fire, and passed the night disagreeably enough, for it was so cold that I could barely keep from freezing. I turned about the fire all night, for as fast as one side got warm the other side was freezing. When morning came I started, and after traveling some four or five miles, I came to a cabin and called for something to eat, which was readily furnished me. The poor woman who lived here commenced telling me her tale of trouble. Her husband was then in the Federal army, and had been there for some time. The rebels had been there and killed her eldest son, whom the father had left at home to take care of his helpless family, thinking that the rebels would not presume to disturb, much less murder, a young and innocent boy. They had taken nearly every thing that she had to eat, and left her with seven children to provide for in the best way she could, and, of course, not caring in the least if she and her children starved together.

I traveled on without meeting with any molestation whatever. The mountain upon which I was traveling ranged about east and west, and I considered myself safe from the rebels while I was traveling upon it. The greatest danger was in crossing the little valleys and the watercourses, which had carved out deep gullies in the mountain, and requiring considerable labor to ascend their steep banks; but I always succeeded in climbing up their banks with perfect safety. After traveling hard all day, at night

K

I arrived at Paint-rock Mountain, where I stopped at the house of James Hare. I was told that Hare and several other men were in a camp off in the mountain some distance, and I at once started to the camp, and found Hare and his companions safely lodged therein. I here passed the night very comfortably.

After partaking of an early breakfast, I set out for another hard day's travel in the direction of Chucky River. I was all day engaged in crossing over stupendous river-knobs, and when the gloom of night came on I was still in the knobs, and I continued to travel on until I could go no farther. I now stopped and built up a fire by the side of an old log, and passed the remainder of the night setting by it and meditating upon my lonely situation, and also upon the deeds of crime which the rebels were committing throughout the country. When daylight appeared I started forward, and, as I had partaken of nothing to eat after my hard travel on the previous day, I felt quite weak; but I pushed on until ten o'clock, when I came to a cabin, where I applied for breakfast. The woman gave me the best she had, and told me that the rebels had robbed her of nearly every thing she had, both to eat and to wear. I thought that surely I would never hear the last of these sorrowful and lamentable tales of distress.

I started on my journey, and after traveling steadily on all day, at night I arrived at the red banks of Chucky River; and after crossing over it in a canoe, I went to the residence of the Widow Bayless, where I got a good supper, a bed to sleep in during the night, and breakfast the next morning. When morning came I found that I had taken a severe cold, which I attributed to the luxury which I had indulged in of sleeping in a bed; for when I slept in the open air upon the ground, with nothing but my blanket, I was never annoyed with a bad cold. That was my usual mode of sleeping, and I thought that in this particular, at least, habit was a great promoter of health.

The sun was up when I left Chucky River, but I went on to the mountain again, and after another hard day's travel, I got into my own native hills, very tired, and much worn out with the fatigue of my hard journey. I supplied myself with a new suit of clothes, for my old suit was now ready to be shipped to the paper-mill, and after resting one week, I made immediate arrangements to start on my second journey through the lines.

CHAPTER XXV.

On the 2d of February, 1864, I started to Knoxville with my second company, consisting of Federal soldiers returning to their posts, Union citizens who could not stay at home, and a number of young men who were fleeing from the conscript law. We started from the old O'Brien Forge south of Elizabethton. The night was very dark, and it was raining and snowing. When we got into the woods the men could not see their way before them, and some of them were continually running up against the trees, mashing their noses and mouths in a fearful manner. This I thought was a bad beginning for them. When we came to water-courses it was so dark that we could not walk the crossings, and, therefore, we were compelled to wade them. The streams were all overflowing, which made it very difficult to cross many of them. About eleven o'clock the rain ceased, but the snow continued to fall; but we pushed on, and reached the Greasy Cove, ten miles south of Johnson's Dépôt, about two o'clock. We left the cove to the right of us, and went up on the spurs of Unaker Mountain, where I considered we would be safe.

We continued upon the top of the mountain until evening, when we received the intelligence that a lot of rebels had come over from North Carolina, and were stationed upon the road which I had designed traveling. This was quite unwelcome news to me, for I knew that I would now be forced to conduct the men over a much rougher and longer route. Some of the company talked seriously about turning back, and argued that it would be better for them to scout among the mountains where they were acquainted, than to run the risk of being captured while endeavoring to go through the lines. I told them that they need not indulge any fear of being captured, if they could travel where I would lead them, and not give out along the way. After I gave them this assurance they all concluded to go on, saying that they felt quite sure that they could stand the fatigues of the trip, if I would be sure to save them harmless from the rebels. I knew that it was impossible for the rebels to be every where, and, in order to elude them, I knew that I would only have to travel higher up on the mountain. It was now dark, and I at once told the men that there was no time for any farther parley, and all that wished to go on could follow me, and all those that did not could very easily find their way back. I started on, and every one of the men followed on. We pushed ahead, and soon reached Chucky River, which I now intended to cross much higher up than I did when I crossed it in my previous journey; the night was cold and disagreeable, and about two o'clock we stopped in a very remote recess in the mountain and built up fires, and rested until daylight.

After an early breakfast we started on our journey, and traveled all day from one spur of the mountain to another. We waded the branches, which were sometimes extensive, and constituted a serious impediment in our rugged pathway, and sometimes we had to crawl upon our hands and knees for at least half a mile through the dreadful thickets of laurel and ivy, while the bushes were bent down to the ground with snow and sleet. When night came on we stopped and made up fires as well as we could, which was a severe task, as we had no axe, and the wood was very wet. The men were suffering very much from cold, and the indifferent fires which we had afforded them very little relief. We spent the night in shivering and shaking around our small fires, and early the next morning we started upon our tiresome journey.

The path which we were now traveling through the mountains was exceedingly rugged, and, consequently, one of the men had the misfortune to become completely tired down, so that he was altogether unable to travel. The man who gave out upon this occasion was William G. Burrow, a citizen of Elizabethton, in Carter County. He was a tailor by trade, and, consequently, his uniform habits had been of a sedentary character, which almost totally disqualified him from supporting the terrible fatigue which he was now subjected to. We were delayed very much in our progress, as we were compelled to assist him in getting along. In the evening we started up Rich Mountain, and after traveling for some time we came to a hollow, which we crossed over, and then commenced the ascent of that tremendous acclivity known as the "big butte" of Rich Mountain. This is the highest and steepest part of this whole range of lofty mountains, and right here Burrow gave entirely out, and could not walk another step. I concluded to stop here for the night, hoping that he would partially recover his suspended energies against morning. Our encampment was on the steep mountain's side, where wood was very scarce, which prevented us from having good fires. The mountain had been thoroughly burnt over, and every chunk and log was perfectly black; and when we had succeeded in kindling up a few small fires, we found that we were all as black as negroes. Next morning the men presented a very laughable appearance; some of them had rather a frightful aspect, for they were so completely disguised with their covering of charcoal that it was quite

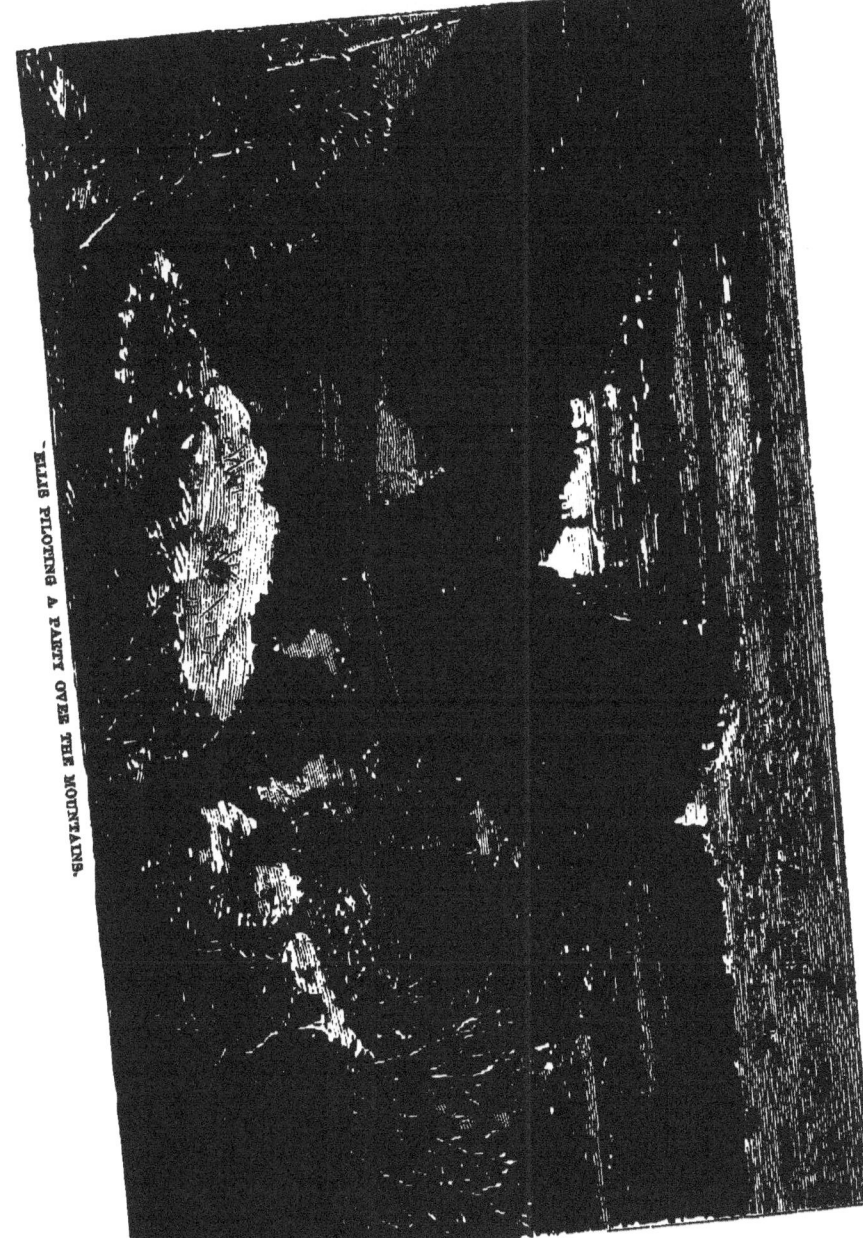

ELLIS PILOTING A PARTY OVER THE MOUNTAINS.

hard for them to recognize one another. We passed a very miserable night at this place, for the ground was so steep where the men laid, that when they would fall asleep they would frequently roll away several feet from the fire, and when they would awake from their slumber they would find themselves nearly frozen. The snow was at least six inches deep, and the wind blew hard enough almost to take a man's coat off of his back. I thought that this was the longest and the most disagreeable night that I ever experienced. We were six miles from the nearest house, and could not as much as hear a chicken crow when daylight was approaching to drive the dreary night away. Daylight came at last, and poor Burrow was still in a state of suspended animation, and could not walk a step. We were now in a very bad dilemma, for we were compelled to ascend to the top of that steep mountain and carry a large man all the way up its precipitous elevations.

As I could devise no other mode of carrying our heavy load of flesh and blood, I took my blanket and rolled him securely up in it. I then fastened leather straps around his head, body, and legs, and cut as large a pole as I could cut with my knife, passed the pole under the straps, and then a man took hold at each end of the pole, and carried him on in this manner. I thought that this was a slow and very tiresome way of going to the Yankees, for Burrow was a heavy man, and the mountain was so steep that we could scarcely stand upon its side. But we changed our load from one to another very often. A small accident happened to our passenger as some of the men were carrying him along, which occurred in this way: the men who were carrying him came to a very rugged place, and the foremost man had just stepped across a log when the pole accidentally broke, and Burrow was precipitated upon the log immediately upon his back.' I believe the fall came very near breaking his back, for he groaned loudly from the pain it had occasioned him. Another pole was quickly cut and run under the straps, and some of the men again shouldered him and started slowly forward. In this way we carried him the distance of four or five miles up the steepest mountain that I have ever seen. At length we reached the summit, where the wind now blew so hard and so cold that I thought sometimes it would cut us in two. We were now where there once had been a fine mountain-farm, but the buildings and fences had been all destroyed. In a pasture near by I observed that there were two colts feeding. I immediately went to them, caught hold of one of them, and tied a string around its head. I then led it up to where the men were waiting, and we then placed Burrow upon its back and led the colt along by the string. Just as it was getting dark we came to a cabin upon the mountain, where we left Burrow and the colt, for by this time he could not even ride. I do not believe that I ever saw a man who was in a worse condition in my life. Bloody water was running out of his eyes, and he exhibited every symptom of a man in the most excruciating misery.

We started forward again, and after traveling some distance we stopped for the night, made good fires, and rested finely, for the men were so tired they went to sleep almost as soon as they touched the ground. So soon as daylight came we started on without partaking of a very abundant breakfast, for our stock of provisions had now run down to a very low degree, and the worst of the bargain was, we yet had a long and tiresome road to travel before we could arrive at our journey's end. We traveled on all day through the roughest sort of mountains, not daring to go into a road or even a plain path, for at any time we would look we could see the rebels prowling about in the valleys below us. In the evening we got to Paint Creek, in Madison County, North Carolina, and continued to travel down its meanderings until late in the night, when, coming to a deep hollow, we stopped and made up fires, and passed the balance of the night pretty well.

When morning came we divided out the last of our provisions, which afforded a very small allowance to each man, whose appetite was keen enough to have devoured a much larger portion. But we thought of the old adage, that "a half loaf is better than no bread," and finished our humble meal and proceeded on our journey. About twelve o'clock we reached Paint-rock Mountain, and I went to the house of Mrs. Kelley to procure something for the men to eat, and before I had been in the house many minutes she commenced telling me how the infamous rebels had murdered her husband. I listened to her melancholy tale of woe, which excited the most profound sympathies of my heart. She furnished me with some provisions for the men, and I hastened to where I had left them. We now had the Warm Springs Road to cross; and as there were so many rebels in this section of the country, carrying on their daily business of stealing, robbing, and murdering, I concluded that it would be the safest for us to stop until night came on. When it got quite dark we started on, and, just as I had anticipated, when we got to the road I found that it was guarded, and, upon making some inquiry in the neighborhood, I found that the rebels were guarding the whole length of the road from Greenville to Paint Rock. I now had to seek for a chance for my company of men to get across the road irrespective of the vigilance of the rebels. We now approached near the road, where we could see their fires in different places along the road, and could hear them singing and talking. I selected as dark a place as I could find, and then telling the men to follow me, we all crossed the road with perfect safety just between two of their fires. The night was dark, and the wind was blowing severely, which was quite favorable for us when passing so near to the rebel camp-fires. The snow was falling very fast, which to us was another favorable circumstance, for it served most admirably to obliterate every vestige of the trail which we had made when crossing the road. We went rapidly on all night, and when morning came we were on the side of Meadow-creek Mountain, where we stopped and built up fires, for some of the men were nearly frozen. We had waded all the branches and creeks which came in our way, and our pants were stiff with ice up to our knees, and cracked together like rocks whenever our legs would strike against each other. Some of the men's feet were badly frostbitten, and their shoes were frozen on them, which occasioned them a great deal of suffering. I went to a Union man's house, which was near, and made arrangements to have something cooked for us to eat. The family exhibited a good deal of kindness, and commenced cooking directly after I told to what terrible extremities the men had been reduced for the want of something to eat. I returned to the men to wait until it was ready, and also to tell them of the good luck which had crowned my efforts to procure them something to eat.

We were all just about to start to the house to get our provisions, when, oh! horror of horrors! we saw the infernal rebels preceding us in our meditated journey to the house. They were following our trail, and the mountain was so rugged they had dismounted from their horses, and were now pursuing us on foot, while we could see the balance of their company down in the valley below leading on their horses. The reader may be well assured that we were not long in leaving that place behind us without even calling at the house to obtain our provisions, which, doubtless, were appropriated by the rebels. Although we were all very weak and hungry, we traveled on rapidly, and soon put several miles between ourselves and the despised rebels. We continued to travel upon the roughest parts of the mountain until night, when we got to French Board River, which we found to be entirely too full to wade. We traveled along its bank until we found a canoe, in which we crossed over and struck for the mountain again. When we got up to a high elevation on the mountain, we could see the rebel camp-fires at various places above the point where we had crossed over the river. The mountain was now so steep and rough, and so thickly overgrown with laurel bushes, that we had great difficulty in getting along upon it. We groped our way through the bushes, which were bent down with snow and ice, until about two o'clock, when some of the poor tired men declared they could go no farther. We therefore began to rake the snow away as well as we could in order to make up fires. With a good deal of difficulty we at length got our fires to burning, and then we all laid down upon the cold ground to sleep, and remained here until daylight.

The next morning we made an early start, and immediately after we had started some of the men happened to look back, and saw the rebels coming in hot pursuit after us. I at once concluded that they had found out by some means or other where we had crossed the river, and had thereby got upon our trail. It was a company of infantry who were now in pursuit of us. I therefore led the men on into the roughest parts of the mountain, and the rebels, just as I expected, soon got tired of following after us, and turned back to retrace their steps. The snow was about six inches deep upon the rugged mountain, and the weather was very cold, which doubtless urged the rebels to give up the chase, which, if they had continued, I have no doubt would have proved to them altogether fruitless. We traveled on at a slow rate until it got dark, when, perceiving that there was a house near by, we stopped, hoping that we might probably be able to get something to eat. After stopping the men, I went to the house and hallooed, and a woman immediately came out. I told her that I wished to get some provisions for a company of Union men, who were endeavoring to get through the lines, who had been so closely pursued by the rebels that they had had no opportunities of getting any thing to eat for several days and nights. To my speech she replied as follows:

"Oh, you need not tell that sort of a tale to me, for I know that it is impossible for any person now to go through the lines. The militia have come from North Carolina, and are now guarding every pathway through the mountains, and it is supposed that the rebels will take Knoxville in the course of a few days."

I told her that I did not care about the rebels, but wished to get something to eat for the men that were with me, for they were in a starving condition. But she was inexorable, and again replied as follows:

"I can not let you have any thing to eat. My husband is in Kirk's regiment at Knoxville, and the rebels have taken all that I had to live upon."

I went back to the company and told them about my ill success in getting any thing for them to eat, when two of them declared that they would go and see if they could not have better luck. They went on to the house, and soon returned with a bushel of corn in the ears, for which they paid her two dollars in greenbacks. We divided the corn, and then started on and traveled until two o'clock, when, coming to a deep and lonely hollow, we stopped, and, after raking off the snow in several places, made up fires, and laid down upon the cold ground to try to sleep. The ground was so cold and wet that many of the men could not rest upon it at all, but were compelled to rise up and lean their backs against trees and stumps, and in this position some of them remained during the night, trying to sleep upon their feet, which was a very disagreeable attitude in which to court the sweet embrace of sleep.

The next morning we started very early, not having a thing to eat. I began to fear that some of the men would lay down in the snow and die from pure hunger. About twelve o'clock we arrived at Don's Creek, where we stopped to rest, and upon looking down into the valley below, we saw the rebels moving about in every direction; they appeared to be foraging off of the farmers in the valley. We were at once convinced that it would be entirely impracticable for us to endeavor to get any thing to eat in that quarter of the country, and again took up the line of march with depressed and desponding hearts, when, to our very great surprise, we found two bushels of corn in the ears, which doubtless some person had concealed in the mountain for safe keeping. I thought that kind Providence had provided for us upon this occasion. We divided the corn, and after eating a portion of it, we then traveled on with renewed vigor. At night we stopped in a deep hollow, built up fires, shelled our corn, and, after roasting and eating heartily of it, we laid down upon the ground and slept soundly until morning. We made an early start, and after traveling until twelve o'clock, we came in sight of a house. I again left the men, to go and see what the prospect would be of getting something to eat. When I got up to the house I called out, and a woman came to the door. I told her our situation, and asked her if I could get something for the hungry men to eat. But she did not appear to believe a single word that I said to her, thinking, of course, that we were rebels. She said that the rebels had killed her son just three days before, and had taken every thing she had to eat, excepting a few bushels of corn which she had concealed. I at length prevailed upon her to let us have two bushels and a half of her corn, and for which we paid her four dollars. We put the corn into our haversacks, and went into the mountain and built up fires, and, after roasting a portion of our corn, we ate a hearty dinner, and then started on, and traveled the remainder of that day and a portion of the following night, and then stopped and rested until morning.

When daylight came we started on our journey, and during the whole day, whenever we looked down into the valleys below, we could see the rebels engaged in their plundering operations, and robbing the people of every thing which man or beast could eat. They were visiting every house, and packing off every thing that they could find to eat in wagons, and also upon horseback. Even the most humble cabin was visited and plundered by these rebel thieves and murderers.

About twelve o'clock we came in sight of Wier's Cove. We now sat down to rest, and one of the men said that he intended to go in search of something to eat, if he should be captured in the attempt. He started on down the mountain toward a house that stood out in an old field at least a quarter of a mile from the woods. We saw the young man go into the house, where he remained for some time. At length he came out of the house and started back toward the woods, at which juncture we saw seven rebel soldiers ride up to him and take him prisoner. This poor unfortunate young man has never been heard of from that day to this. He no doubt was immediately murdered by these inhuman devils, who did not regard torturing and killing their fellow-men any more than if they had been rattlesnakes. We continued to observe the movements of the rebels in the valley for a short time, and at length we saw a company of at least fifty of them coming directly toward the place where we were stationed upon the mountain. We at once suspected that the young man who went down to the house and was captured by them had betrayed us; and we therefore hastily fell back into the mountain gorges and went on our journey, without seeing or hearing any more from our pursuers. We continued to travel until eleven o'clock, when we stopped, kindled up fires, and rested until morning.

Just at early dawn we started on our journey again. We made our way around the head of Wier's Cove, and traveled over the roughest parts of the mountain until three o'clock in the evening, when I again went to a house upon the side of the mountain, to endeavor to procure something for the men to eat. But, as usual, the woman of the house commenced telling me a most doleful tale about the rebels, how they had robbed her house and taken nearly all that she had to eat. I told her we were starving, and she replied that she could not help it. Seeing some corn in an outhouse, we at once supplied ourselves with about two bushels of it, and started on our journey, eating it raw. During the night we came to a small river, which we traveled down for some distance, and had to wade through it some three or four times, which gave our clothes a thorough wetting, and caused them to freeze upon our bodies.

At length we arrived at the Chilhowee Mountain, and, it

being now about midnight, we stopped in a dense pine thicket, built up our fires, and rested until daylight. The men were so tired and weak from excessive hunger that they quickly fell down around the fires and went to sleep. Hard traveling, cold weather, and hungry stomachs, had been our incessant companions during the whole of this long and weary journey. When daylight came we went on across the mountain in the direction of Maryville, Tennessee, where we thought the Federal forces were stationed, and at which place we arrived early in the night. When we got there we heard that the Yankees and the rebels had been fighting near that place, and that the Yankees had removed their quarters to some other point which they thought to be more congenial to them. We found that it would not do for us to go toward Knoxville from this place, and that we would have to go on to Lenoir's Station, which is twenty-four miles below Knoxville. That night we got some tough beef, and also some flour, which we had to cook ourselves, and thought that we were faring well, to what we had been accustomed to for several days past.

Early the next morning we set out for Lenoir's Station. We made it a point to ask for something to eat at every house we passed during the day, and when night came on some of the men were pretty well supplied with provisions. That night we camped in a large thicket, where we had good fires, and rested finely all night. We started early the next morning on our last day's travel for Lenoir's Station, and arrived there against dark. We stopped here two days and nights, getting an abundance to eat, which we very much needed in order to recuperate our exhausted energies.

It was now the 20th of February when we left Lenoir's Station on the train to go to Nashville. We had very un-

comfortable quarters upon the train, for we had to get in
the box-cars, where we could have no fire, and the weather
was very cold. We had no place to sleep; it was very
hard for us to get any thing to eat, and even if we could,
we had no place where we could cook any thing at all.
We therefore experienced upon the train, in our journey to
Nashville, some of the annoyances with which we had been
rather too familiar for our own personal welfare during our
weary journey through the mountains. We were three
days in making the trip to Nashville, and the second day
after we started the train ran off the track, which came
very near killing several of our party. The poor fellows
had escaped the rebel bullets, and now, when they thought
that they were out of all danger, they came very near being
ushered into eternity by a sudden and unexpected calamity
upon the railroad, by which they were seriously crippled
and bruised.

We at last got to Nashville all alive; but I thought that
some of the men would not long remain in that condition,
for they seemed as if they would become self-murderers by
indulging their appetites to an unlimited extent. I often
heard men say, when they were attempting to go through
the lines, that they would much rather perish in the mountains than to fall into the hands of the rebels; and I thought
that the men who composed this company, who had made
this avowal, had uttered nothing but the truth, for I believe
that they would have infinitely preferred to perish in the
cold snow upon the mountains rather than to have been
captured by the barbarous rebels.

When we arrived at Nashville we met with a great many
of our acquaintances, neighbors, and friends. The 13th Tennessee Cavalry Regiment was stationed here, and I now
had the pleasure of meeting my old company, which I had

ELLIS DELIVERING LETTERS TO HIS REGIMENT.

made up in Carter County when I intended to go into the
army myself. All of the company were glad to see me,
as well as being very much surprised, for they said that
they could not imagine how I ever succeeded in conducting my company safely on, when such imminent danger
threatened us on every side. And now came the anxious
questions about home and absent friends. To some of the
poor soldiers I could say, that when I left home their families had not yet been molested by the rebels, while to the
greater number of them I had the disagreeable duty of
having to tell them that the infamous rebels had robbed
their families of almost every thing which they had to
subsist upon, and had even taken their bedclothes and
wearing apparel, and had not left them the common comforts of life, and, in some instances, not even a house to
shelter them, and that they were living upon the bounty
of friends who had but very little to spare for their support. This was sad intelligence for the poor soldiers to
hear, but it was too true.

I designated the day that I should leave Nashville, for
all the soldiers from the upper portion of East Tennessee
wished to transmit money and letters by me to their families. I told all of those whose families lived near together
to inclose the money and letters which they desired to
send home all in one packet, and then direct this packet
to some prominent and trustworthy Union man in the
neighborhood where their families resided, and by this
means the packages I thought could be more easily distributed.

I remained four days at Nashville, and after getting all
the packages of letters which the soldiers wished to send
by me to their families, I started back upon my long and
tiresome journey to the mountains of Carter County.

CHAPTER XXVI.

I LEFT Nashville on the train, and arrived safely at Knoxville, where I remained for two days waiting for the soldiers who were stationed there to write letters to their families in the eastern portion of the state. When I got the letters all packed up, I found that the bundle containing them weighed fifty pounds, which I thought would be quite an inconvenient load for me to pack upon my back through the rough mountains. When I left Knoxville, many of my friends bade me a final farewell, and some of them said that "this will be the last of Ellis; this trip will end his career, for he will never reach home with his load of money and letters."

I came on the train as far as the Strawberry Plains. Here I remained until dark, and then shouldering my sack of letters and as much provision as I could carry, I struck out for the ridges, and, against daylight, I arrived some distance above Mossy Creek, where I concealed myself among the hills until night came on again. So soon as it got dark I started on toward the French Broad River, and when I arrived there I luckily found a canoe, which I at once loosed from its moorings and crossed the river in it; and then pushing forward, by daylight I got into a range of lofty and rugged ridges, where I am confident no rebel ever thought about going in search of renegade Union men. I could now travel in daylight where there were no roads or valleys to cross. It took me seven days to perform the trip from Knoxville to Carter County, as I had to travel in such a terribly rough pathway, and carry such a heavy burden upon my shoulders. But when I was wending my way through the rough mountains, and bending with fatigue beneath my heavy load, I was constantly consoled with the reflection that the burden which I was bearing had been intrusted to my care by the noble patriots of Carter County, who had left their homes to risk their lives in defending their country against the evil and wicked machinations of the rebels; and that the reception of its contents would at once carry joy to the sad and sorrowful heart of many a poor and distressed wife who was mourning the absence of an affectionate and loved husband, whose presence they doubtless hoped would again be permitted to illuminate and enliven the household circle when the dreadful tocsin of war should be hushed, and peace be once more proclaimed throughout the length and breadth of the country.

After a very fatiguing journey, I arrived among the hills of my native county, and immediately delivered all the letters and money to the families of the soldiers who were living in my neighborhood. But when they received their letters with their valuable inclosures, that did not seem to satisfy them; for a great many of the fond wives, mothers, and sisters of the absent soldiers could not rest until they could see me in person and ask a multitude of questions about the dear husband, son, or brother. Many of them would come into my presence with the tears of joy sparkling in their eyes, and would exclaim, "Oh! your eyes have looked upon my husband, my son, or brother; tell me—oh, tell me every word that you heard them utter." And it afforded me the most delightful pleasure to talk with these poor, disconsolate women, and to impart to them every item of intelligence concerning the dear objects of their love. I now felt fully remunerated for the toil and fatigue which I had borne while conveying the messages of love and the memorials of fond regard to these poor, helpless women, whose husbands, brothers, and sons had fled from the wretched tyranny which oppressed their dear homes, and had cast their fortunes among the friends of the Union, who were striving to subdue the wicked rebellion and re-establish the proud standard of liberty in their beloved country.

When I came home on this occasion, by some means or other the belief became very prevalent among the rebels that I had brought with me a large amount of greenbacks, which at that time was a scarce commodity in the land of Dixie. A general search was now commenced by the rebel soldiers, and I do not believe that one single house in the whole country escaped them whose previous occupant was now absent as a soldier in the Union army. Every letter that fell into their hands was carefully read, and woe to the poor family where they found a letter whose contents disclosed the fact that it had contained money. For the money which they found therein spoken of had at once to be delivered to them, or the helpless family was subjected to that vengeance which was always the sure concomitant of their disappointed hopes and expectations. Every dollar which I brought to some families on this occasion fell into the hands of these rebel demons, who were at this time prowling all through the country like ravenous beasts of prey.

Oh, how it maddened me and vexed my very soul when I reflected how I had labored and toiled through the rough mountains to bring relief to the suffering families of my friends and neighbors who had been chased away from their homes by these rebel scoundrels, and then to learn that these poor, destitute, and perishing families had been robbed and deprived of that relief from want and starvation which I had hoped that my exertions in their behalf would be permitted to afford them! And while indulging in this train of reflection, a desire for revenge crept into my heart, and I determined to give to some of the thieving villains who were plundering the houses of destitute women a taste of lead from my trusty gun. I therefore proceeded to watch for them as they were returning from their expeditions of robbery, and at the sudden crack of my gun their loud and sportive laughing was often changed into melancholy mourning. I did not much desire to become a bushwhacker, but I thought that if the hated and despised rebels should ever again take by force any of the money which I might bring into the country for the benefit and relief of the famishing wives of the absent Union soldiers, that of itself would be a sufficient provocation for me to become one.

Nothing in the world caused me so much agony and perturbation of mind, than the reflection that a pernicious and ruffian set of scoundrels, who had assisted in destroying the peace of the country, and were now sporting over the miseries of helpless women and children, should derive the smallest benefit from any of my own exertions in behalf of the wives and children of Union soldiers. Instead of bestowing any benefits or favors upon the despicable miscreants who were constantly engaged in perpetrating deeds of crime sufficient in atrocity to excite the compassionate tears of angels, I would greatly have preferred to have been able to command some black and dismal storm-cloud to sweep them from the face of the earth, and consign them to the shades of everlasting forgetfulness, there to remain in the dark oblivion of night, until the loud trump of the Archangel should summon them to come forth to judgment!

I made immediate preparations to start upon my third trip to Knoxville, the attending incidents of which the reader will find in the following chapter.

CHAPTER XXVII.

On the 28th of March, 1864, I started with my third company to Knoxville. This company consisted of one hundred and twenty-five men, nearly all of whom I had recruited for the 13th Regiment of Tennessee Cavalry, as the rebels were still running their conscript law with a vengeance, which had a very decided tendency to make soldiers for "Old Abe." The starting-point was again near the Old Forge, three miles south of Elizabethton. The company commenced assembling in the evening, and against dark we were ready to "take up the line of march." This was a fine company, composed of stout, healthy, and athletic young men, who were anxious to go into the Union army, as they had been for some time hunted like wild beasts in the mountains by the rebel soldiers, who were now using every exertion to force the young men of the country to go into the Southern army, whose ranks now at every point were daily becoming "small by degrees, and beautifully less," owing to the constant desertion of men who had enlisted or been forced into the Southern army, and were now seeking an asylum from the horrors of the Southern service. I felt proud of this company, and thought that I was doing good service in the cause of my country by making such additions to its military prowess. I had three head of horses, which were the first that I had attempted to take through the lines.

We started on in the direction of the Greasy Cove, in Washington County, which place we reached about day-

L

light, and went up on the Unaker Mountain and built up
fires in order to dry our wet clothing, for we were all thoroughly drenched to the skin, as we had to wade through
every water-course which came in our way during the
night. We remained here until evening, at which time we
received the intelligence that the rebels had pursued us to
the cove. They had found our trail, which was not hard to
do, for the ground was wet and soft; and wherever we traveled the ground looked as if a large saw-log had been dragged over it. The rebels came to the foot of the mountain
upon which we were camped, and then turned back, probably thinking that we were prepared to defend ourselves
much better than we really were, for a few pistols which
some of the men carried were all the weapons of defense
that we had. I had not started with the intention of
fighting my way through, for the men were not yet soldiers; and I well knew that if I should lead this inexperienced company of men into an engagement with the rebels,
that while some of them might fight like veteran soldiers,
the greater portion of them would run away and leave the
field of strife. I always found that raw recruits were more
ready to run at the least appearance of danger, than they
were to exhibit any sort of desire to engage in the conflict
of battle. Therefore, in my peregrinations through the
mountains, I was never willing to engage with the rebels,
knowing as I did that a large number of the men would
run away, and thereby become an easy prey for the rebels
to capture. I must confess that, in all my travels through
the mountains while I was acting in the capacity of a pilot,
I was a great admirer of the true philosophy of the old ax-
iom which says that "peace hath her victories no less than
war."

As soon as it got dark we pressed on to Chucky River,

where we had the good luck to find a canoe, in which we
crossed, after a good many trips backward and forward
across the river. When we got across the river we had to
travel a short distance along a public road before we could
get to the point where I designed to ascend the mountain
again. The night was dark, and I was very intently engaged in looking out for any danger which might threaten
our pathway, when I observed just ahead of me a dim light
shining through the darkness. I at once halted the company,
and told the men not to follow on until they should hear me
whistle, which they might consider as the signal for them to
advance. I now went forward, in order to acquaint myself
with the cause of the light which I had observed; and after
advancing toward it for some distance, I found that it was
occasioned by a gap in the dark mountain through which
the feeble rays of light were gleaming from the western
horrizon. I then whistled for the men to advance, when
some of the company, unfortunately mistaking my whistle
for a signal of danger, started up the mountain as if they
had seen a thousand armed rebels rise up before them.
And the remaining portion of the company soon becoming
frightened at the precipitate flight of those who had already
started up the mountain, also started after their flying companions, and away they all went up the mountain like a hurricane which had started upon its desolating march through
the forest. This I thought was a very unfortunate occurrence, happening as it did just at the time when I wished
the company to proceed quietly and with as much rapidity
as possible. In their flight they threw away their haversacks, overcoats, hats, blankets, and every thing which constituted the least impediment to them in their rapid progress. At any other time I could have laughed heartily at
this sudden and unexpected movement; but at this junc-

ture I did not feel much in the humor of enjoying a laugh at their expense, for the hour I thought was "big with danger."

The whole company of men ran with such headlong fury that I could plainly hear the dry branches of the trees and the decayed saplings falling for several minutes after their rapid passage. I waited some time for the noise to subside which they had made, before I called on them to stop in their wild career, for the report of a cannon could scarcely have been heard immediately after they started. At length I commenced calling on them to stop, not caring now for any noise which I could make, as they had already raised such a rumpus that it could have been heard for a mile. After a short time they began to return, and, as I continued to call for them, they would answer from all the contiguous parts of the mountain, while some one of them would exclaim, "I should like to know who were so cowardly as first to start to run when there was no danger." They came on back, continuing loudly to attribute their discomfiture to the cowardice of one another, when I felt sure that one was to blame no more than another, for they had all ran away together, and all of them deserved to be equally rebuked for becoming so unnecessarily alarmed and disconcerted. There were three big negroes in the company; and one of them, while he was crawling up the side of the mountain with all possible speed and energy, ran his head between the legs of a boy, who was just ahead of him, and raised him up astride of his shoulders, where the boy continued to sit, holding on to the woolly head of the negro, who scrambled on perfectly heedless of his load; the boy got along finely upon his black steed until he ran violently against a stump, when his rider fell to the ground, and came very near breaking his neck. This circumstance caused the negro to halt for a moment, when he happened to hear me endeavoring to call the men together, and came back with them.

After I had succeeded in collecting the men all together, a general search was instituted for coats, hats, and haversacks, but they soon became convinced that it had been far more easy to discard these articles when they were running than it was now to find them, for some of the men never did find any of the articles which they threw away upon this occasion. At length I got them all started once more, and we went up Indian Creek until midnight, when we stopped and rested for the balance of the night. Just as daylight began to appear we started on our journey, and continued to travel up Indian Creek for ten miles, when I turned off toward Shelton Laurel, which I knew was the roughest, but much the safest route. After a hard day's travel we got to the house of William Shelton, and went out into a dense thicket of laurel bushes, where we built up fires and spent the night. Early the next morning we started on our journey, and traveled all day through a rough and very lonely mountain, having all the creeks and branches to wade which came in our way. Just at night we arrived at a gap near the Warm-springs Road, where we stopped to stay all night, and about ten o'clock the rain began to fall in torrents, which put out all our fires, and rendered our situation very disagreeable, as some of the men had to creep into old logs, but the greater portion of them had to sit and stand up under the trees until morning.

At the approach of morning the storm abated, and we again kindled up some fires to dry our clothing, and after warming, drying, and eating our breakfast, we advanced on our journey along the side of the mountain, crossing the Warm-springs Road, and making our way on to Meadowcreek Mountain. Here we were informed that the Yankees were at Russellville, and that the rebels had fallen back up the road. We continued to travel in the mountain-paths all day, and at night we crossed over Chucky River at the big bend near Warrensburg, and here we passed the night in a thick settlement, where we all found an abundance to eat.

When daylight made its appearance we started on again, and on that day we reached Russellville, where we found the Yankee troops stationed, and we here took the train for Knoxville. The 13th Regiment of Tennessee Cavalry was then at Nashville; and as the most of the men in the company which I had just piloted through were recruits for that regiment, they therefore continued their journey on to that place, and I stopped at Knoxville. When I parted with the men they were all in the most lively spirits, and some of them remarked that they could already see "the handwriting upon the wall," which plainly indicated in letters of fire that the rebels had been "weighed in the balance, and found wanting." The men all seemed to have an abiding hope that the war was drawing rapidly to a conclusion, and expressed the belief that the time was not far distant when, if their lives should be spared, they could again return to their loved families and homes, when the infamous rebel domination should be numbered with the things of the past. These poor men had endured a great deal of suffering, but hope, that sweet visitant of human wretchedness, had never forsaken them in all their trials and tribulations; and they believed that their manifold afflictions would yet secure for them a bright and glorious diadem of future happiness, when the rebel hordes should be scattered from the land like leaves before the autumnal winds. And while I listened to the expressions of their fond and cherished hopes, my inmost thoughts responded,

Hasten, on, my God, hasten the time when the power of the rebels shall be crushed, and when my country shall again stand up as a proud model for the nations of the earth, like a golden monument which has passed unscathed through the fiery ordeal of the infamous rebellion, which has only served to polish and brighten its magnificent proportions.

CHAPTER XXVIII.

I REMAINED at Knoxville three days, waiting for letters which a number of the soldiers desired to send by me to their families, and, so soon as I received them, I took the train and came up to Russellville. The Federal troops were now falling back to Mossy Creek. It was nearly night when I reached Russellville, which was as far as the train was now running up the railroad. I therefore shouldered my knapsack of letters and started through the woods again, and continued to travel on all night. Being now alone, I traveled both day and night, sometimes stopping at the little cabins which I came to in the mountains, in order to rest and to obtain something to eat. After a good many vicissitudes which I shall not here enumerate, I arrived among my native hills on the 10th day of April, 1864, weary and very much exhausted, where I found another company of men who desired to go through the lines, and were anxiously awaiting my return.

I had managed in my previous trip to succeed in getting three horses through the lines, and now there were at least a dozen individuals who wished to take horses with them. I thought that I could not be justly censured for taking a horse or two through the lines with me, for at this time they could be easily purchased in any of the upper counties for one fourth of their value, and when taken to Knoxville they could be sold to the Federal government for their full value. My expenses were pretty considerable, for the rebels kept my family destitute of both food and clothing, and a great many of the men who were now engaging me to conduct them through the lines were not able to feed themselves during the trip, much less to pay me any thing for my services; neither did I charge the government any thing for enlisting recruits for the Federal service, and never received one farthing from that source. The soldiers who were in the service sometimes paid me for carrying letters to their families, which constituted my greatest source of revenue which I had to rely upon to supply my immediate necessities, and which I must confess afforded me considerable assistance. The men were compelled to go through the lines or run the risk of being killed; and there being no other pilot, I was more than willing to conduct all away from the terrible oppression which the rebels had imposed upon those who desired to go. The Union men who were detailed to work for the so-called Confederate government were expecting every day to be placed in the Southern army; they were all good Union men, and had agreed to work for the mushroom rebel government in order that they might be permitted to stay at home, and they now began to suspect that this privilege would shortly be denied them, for the rebels were getting badly whipped whenever they encountered the Federal forces, and therefore they were in great need of soldiers. Consequently, I at once determined to clear the mountains and the rebel government-works in Carter County of all the Union men; and for the immediate accomplishment of that design I commenced making the necessary preparations, and in one week I was ready to start. I was well aware that the rebels were watching my movements with all possible vigilance, and were plotting in every conceivable manner to effect my capture. They even went so far as to offer a large reward for my head, which they threatened to hoist upon a pole, to serve as a warning to all others who might engage in the business of conducting Union men through the lines.   But, notwithstanding the awful threats of these blood-thirsty tyrants, I continued to pursue "the even tenor of my way," not forgetting, however, to observe all proper caution to prevent my head from being victimized upon the altar of rebel hatred and malice. I must confess that I had no sort of desire for my head to fall into the hands of the rebels, for I was very well convinced that, if they should obtain this much-coveted acquisition, they would have treated the palace of my soul with the utmost indignity; and if they could have secured that impalpable principle which animates and controls my earthly existence, they were fiendish enough to have chained it to the stake and invoked the fiery flames to destroy its immortal and indestructible essence.

The rebels were my inveterate enemies, and I must here acknowledge that I was no friend of theirs; they therefore used every exertion to procure my capture and consequent death, and I exerted all my energies to convey the Union men away from my native county, which was the most available method that I could devise to render their infamous conscript law ineffective.   They planned and plotted to secure my capture, and I used every exertion which I thought would contribute to the defeat and annihilation of their armies and the overthrow of the wicked rebellion. The reader will doubtless conclude that between the rebels and myself " honors were easy," and that there was not very much love lost upon either side.

I will now desist from pursuing this train of thought any farther, and proceed to give the reader an account of the events which occurred in my next journey through the lines.

CHAPTER XXIX.

On the 27th of April, 1864, the men who wished to bid farewell to the "land of Dixie" were engaged all day in assembling themselves together at the old starting-point near Elizabethton, which I have mentioned in several of the preceding chapters; and by the time it was dark a large company of men had collected together, and a great many of them were mounted upon horses. I told them before starting that we would be compelled to make a good night's travel, as the trail which the company would make would be so plain that the rebels would have no difficulty in pursuing us. In fact, I knew that the public road would be no plainer than the track which we would leave behind us. We started, and after traveling until some time after midnight, we came to a public road, at which time one of the company bawled out at the top of his voice, "The rebels are after us!" This, as it may well be expected, furnished the signal for another general stampede. I knew that it would be perfect folly in me to attempt to stop the men in their sudden flight by exclaiming that there was no danger threatening them until they had finished their race. The laurel bushes were now parted at every point to admit the passage of the frightened men; men jumped off of their horses, and away they went through the woods, while in many instances these faithful and sensible animals followed in a brisk trot after their retreating masters. I at once knew that this was another false alarm, for there was no sign of the presence of rebels in any direction. After quiet was somewhat again restored, I called upon them to come back, and told them that their alarm was altogether imaginary. So soon as they heard my voice they came back, stumbling through the brush, with bleeding noses, skinned shins, and bruised legs, while some of them were imprecating the most awful curses upon the man who gave the false alarm about the rebels. Some of the men who became so dreadfully terrified upon this occasion never did return to the company any more, and it was at least two hours before I got all who did return to start on their journey. I told them that, if they were wicked men, they had certainly established the truth of that line in Holy Writ which says, "The wicked flee when no man pursueth!"

At length I succeeded in getting them started again, and, as we traveled at a rapid rate of speed, we reached the Greasy Cove by daylight, where we concealed ourselves, in order to rest in security during the day. I enjoyed a good many hearty laughs and jokes on some of the men about their terrible race through the woods on the previous night; while some of them had no joke or laugh to exchange with any one, for they were too deeply engaged in meditating about their deserted homes and their helpless families, whom they had been forced to leave to the unpitying sympathy of a vile and altogether merciless foe. They well knew that their now destitute wives and children would be stripped of every thing that they had to eat, and would be even deprived of their few articles of clothing by the rebel thieves; for the rebel soldiers, who were at this time prowling through Carter County like devils "seeking whom they might devour," were entirely oblivious to human woe or to human suffering, and were destitute of all the fine sympathies of the heart which are calculated to ennoble and dignify the human character. The sorrowful grief and lamentation of the widow whose earthly protector had been savagely murdered, occasioned no emotion of pity to enter into their hardened and fiendish hearts; and the mournful wail of the orphan only afforded to these wicked wretches food for merriment and laughter!

When the dark shades of night again covered the earth with their black canopy we struck out on our journey, and after traveling a short time, we arrived at Chucky River, crossing it in a canoe, which was very slow work, and caused us to delay a good deal of our precious time. After crossing the river, we went far into the deep gorges of the roughest mountains; and when daylight began to make its appearance we went up on a steep mountain spur, where we could rest during the day in safety, and where we could obtain water for our horses. Every man who had a horse was provided with a sack of corn or oats, which served as a very good substitute for a saddle. We rested here until evening, when we started on, making our way through immense beds of laurel and ivy bushes, through which we had very great difficulty to get our horses along; and very often we had to climb steep spurs of the mountain, where we had to pack our sacks of corn and oats upon our own shoulders, as the mountain was so steep that a sack would not stay on a horse's back. When I got to the top of a lofty spur on the mountain, I stopped to look back at the long company of men and horses as they slowly toiled along up the side of the steep mountain; and when I saw the company stretch out its long length so far away down toward the foot of the mountain, I was surprised at the extent of it, and thought that surely a good many more men had fallen into our ranks as we were passing along. As I gazed back upon this large body of men, I became very deeply concerned about their welfare, and seriously wondered whether I should ever be able to get them all through the lines without any of them being captured by the rebels, who were now watching for the poor fugitive Union men with the most perpetual vigilance. History informs us that upon one occasion when Xerxes was prosecuting a most terrible march of invasion, that he stood upon a lofty eminence from which he could overlook his whole tremendous army; and while he was thus engaged in looking over the multiplied thousands of men who were stretched out for miles before his vision like a boundless sea of human beings, he was seen to wipe away the unbidden tears from his eyes. And upon being asked the reason for the tears, which were flowing from his eyes, by one of his intimate attendants, he replied that he could not refrain from shedding tears, when he looked abroad over his vast army, to think that, one hundred years hence, all of that great host of living men would be numbered with the pale nations of the dead. I can not say that I shed any tears after the manner of the proud despot of Persia, but I must confess that I felt some emotions of deep concern when I contemplated the dark problem of doubt and uncertainty which presented itself to my mind while reflecting whether or not I should be able to conduct my large company of men and horses safely through the rough mountains to the Federal lines.

I waited until the men reached the summit of the elevation upon which I had been for some time standing, observing them toiling along up the precipitous ascent of the steep mountain's side, and then, after waiting for them to enjoy a few hours of rest, we started on, and traveled steadily onward until we arrived at Carter's Bridge, across the Chucky River. I knew that we would now have to observe a good deal of caution in the prosecution of our journey, as the whole country was full of rebels. We reached the cleared land just at dark, and advanced noiselessly on toward the bridge. The men seemed to be very much frightened at the idea of so suddenly descending off of the rough mountains on to the level cultivated farms. Just before we got to the bridge the road made a very short turn, where some of the foremost men, who were ready to become frightened at a shadow, observed the rear of the company coming around the turn in the road, and at once thought that the rebels were close after them. Away they went, like a gang of frightened deer. I was afraid to call loudly for them to halt in their unnecessary flight, but by the immediate exercise of great exertions I succeeded in collecting them all together again, and we then crossed the bridge without meeting with any farther disturbance. I thought that the rebels could not have been watching very closely on this occasion, or else we would most certainly have been discovered. But Providence surely favored us at this time in escaping the observation of the rebels, and we pushed on rapidly, and arrived at Russellville that night.

When we got to Russellville, to our infinite gratification, we found the Federal troops stationed there, to whom the men immediately sold their horses, after which we all took the train and proceeded on to Nashville. The 13th Regiment was then stationed at Gallatin, and we therefore continued our journey to that place. I now had an entire company to add to that regiment; besides, there were many others that had come through the lines with me, who were now ready to engage in any other occupation at which they could make wages. I had a good many letters for the soldiers in the 13th Regiment from their families in the upper counties of East Tennessee. It was late in the night when we reached Gallatin, and the soldiers were sleeping in their camps; but the news soon spread in the camps that we had arrived, which immediately caused the soldiers to arouse

ELLIS RELATING HIS ADVENTURES.

and shake off their drowsiness, and, as they rushed to me, I could not observe a sleepy eye among all the men whose families and homes were in the upper portion of East Tennessee.

The constant inquiry which now saluted my ear was, "Ellis, have you got a letter for me?" And to this inquiry I had the exceeding gratification of frequently answering affirmatively, which answer always seemed to afford to the anxious soldier the most rapturous sensations of delight. But the most of them had to wait until morning for their letters, as I had placed them in the hands of the captains of the different companies, so that no mistake would be made in distributing them.

The soldiers all had money, and all of them who were from the upper part of East Tennessee wished to send some presents and money to their friends and families, many of whom were suffering greatly for the common necessaries of life. Contrary to my wishes, I was now compelled again to agree to pack my knapsack with money, letters, and presents for the soldiers' families. I did not like to pack money and goods through the mountains, knowing as I did that my pathway almost at every step was environed by rebel bayonets; and if I should be so unfortunate as to be captured in my passage *in transitu*, the rebels would then have the pleasure of enjoying the treasure which I was bearing to the destitute wives of the soldiers and their starving children.

The soldiers continued to insist on my carrying letters and bundles for them, and I at length consented, as I knew that the families of many were actually suffering; and I thought that if I did not carry the money which they were proposing to send home, that probably they would spend it foolishly, and knowing as I did that the soldiers generally made way with their money in the most negligent and reckless manner.

Captain Northington, of Johnson County, himself made up a package worth five hundred dollars, consisting of money and goods for his family. As I did on the former occasion, I directed the soldiers to put all their letters, money, etc., in packages, and then direct said packages to some good and reliable Union man living in the neighborhood where their families resided, and requesting him to attend to the distribution of the various articles. This time my load weighed sixty pounds, which I had to pack on my back through the rough mountains.

CHAPTER XXX.

AFTER enjoying myself remarkably well for several days among the soldiers at Gallatin, I made all necessary arrangements for my return trip. I came on to Nashville, and there took the train and came on to the Strawberry Plains, and upon my arrival at that place, I then started on foot through the woods toward my old path through the rugged mountains, there to endure again the same fatigue and hunger which I had recently experienced in my former trip back to Carter County, bending beneath my tiresome load. The casual reader may pass lightly over the words fatigue, exhaustion, and hunger; but to me these words had the utmost significance and weight, for I was constantly enduring all the bodily infirmities which each one of these distressing sensations could impose.

I traveled on with my heavy burden, up the steep mountains and then down their craggy sides, and at times, when getting in sight of the humble cabins which frequently occurred in my pathway, I would lay down my knapsack and advance cautiously to them, and get a small portion of provision, which was generally very coarse; but I knew that it was as good as the poor, disconsolate women could afford, for there was not one of them whose humble cottage had not been robbed by the rebels of nearly every thing it contained, and frequently the husband or the father had been killed by the heartless robbers. In spite of every obstacle which occurred in my rough pathway, I made my way across Rich Mountain to Indian Creek, where I left

one of the packages which I had brought from Gallatin at
the house of a stanch Union man who was one of my
warm personal friends, so that he might properly distribute
the letters and other articles which it contained to the soldiers' wives who resided in his neighborhood. I then came
on to the Greasy Cove, where I left another package, and
then hastened on toward my native hills; and after a very
tiresome journey I arrived at home, and immediately sent
the letters and other articles which I had brought with me
to their proper destination. Oh, how many sad hearts
were now gladdened and cheered by the precious memen-
tos of love which had been sent by the absent husband to
his loved and affectionate wife! Oh, how she would gaze
upon the photograph or the daguerreotype likeness which
she had received in that letter from her loved husband, who
had gone to defend his country against the wicked designs
of the rebel minions and desperadoes! There was the dear,
absent face, betokening love in every lineage; and there
were the little presents, which were cherished as dear memorials of the fond regard which still occupied an exalted
position in the bosom of the absent husband for the dear
partner whom he had chosen to share with him the joys
and the sorrows which he might alternately meet while
traveling along the dreary pathway of life. Oh, how that
fond wife prized that little picture which presented the dear
image of her husband, who had gone forth as a patriotic soldier in the service of his country, and, in all probability,
would never more return to listen to the sweet voices of his
prattling children, nor to enliven the heart of his melancholy wife in her now dark and desolate home! I know of
many affectionate husbands and fathers who were compelled to leave their families and homes by the tyranny of the
fiendish rebels, who went forth to obtain relief from insult

and oppression beneath the old starry banner of their country in all the strength of vigorous manhood, who often expressed their hopes to me that the dismal storm-cloud
which then overshadowed the nation would soon pass
away, and that they would then return to their homes and
families, and unite again in the dear ties of friendship and
love which had been violently severed by the infamous rebellion.   But, alas, many of these poor men never returned
any more ; for they met the enemy in the terrible conflict
of arms, and sacrificed their lives in the defense of their
country upon the gory battle-field, where the angel of
death often flapped his dismal wings o'er scenes of carnage
and human butchery which were enough to excite the tears
of pitying angels.

> "The breezy call of incense-breathing morn,
>   The swallow twittering from the straw-built shed.
> The cock's shrill clarion, or the echoing horn,
>   No more shall rouse them from their lowly bed.

> "For them no more the blazing hearth shall burn,
>   Or busy housewife ply her evening care ;
> No children run to lisp the sire's return.
>   Or climb his knees the envied kiss to share."

I now went on to Johnson County with the remainder
of the letters and goods which I had brought with me, as I
did not wish to trust the letters and other articles into the
hands of any person else, for fear that the persons to whom
they had been sent might fail to get them.   When I arrived in Johnson County I found that the home guards
were prowling about in every direction, which prevented
me from going to Taylorsville.   I therefore concluded to
leave the package which had been intrusted to my care by
Captain Northington with Richard C. White, Esq., who
was a steadfast friend of Northington, and also a reliable

Union man. The balance of the letters and money which I now had I sent to their rightful owners by persons in whose integrity I had the most exalted confidence.

I must confess that I now felt very much relieved. I knew that the rebels would not be apprised of any money or letters having been sent into Johnson County, if the people to whom the packages had been sent would only be smart enough to keep every thing properly concealed. But, alas, the secrecy which I had hoped would involve my visit to Johnson County was doomed to have but a short duration, which visit was elucidated and exposed immediately after my return from that county in the following manner: When White received the package which I had consigned to his care to be forwarded to the wife of Captain Northington, he unfortunately addressed a note to Mrs. Northington, requesting her to come to his house, where she would receive intelligence concerning her husband. This note was dispatched to Mrs. Northington by a small boy, who was stopped on the road by the rebel guard, and an immediate search being instituted, the note was found and read. The rebels at once proceeded to White's residence and commenced searching his house. As may reasonably be expected, they soon found the doomed package, and seized like hungry wolves all its valuable contents. White was forthwith arrested and hurried off to prison. This affair was conducted by the leading rebel citizens of Johnson County, who were urged on in the perpetration of their reckless deeds of infamy and villainy by Bill Waugh and Sam M'Queen, two of the wealthiest citizens of Johnson County, who were generally the leaders or advisers in all the dreadful acts of crime which were committed in that county during the memorable reign of the miserable rebellion.

The rebels having thus learned that I had been on a visit to Johnson County, induced them at once to give the whole county a general overhauling. The delightful thought of finding greenback money sent them raging through the county in search of it like a pack of famished wolves after a flock of unprotected sheep. And, most unfortunately, I am compelled to acknowledge that the infernal rebels succeeded in obtaining nearly every dollar which I had carried into Johnson County on this occasion. They would get ten, twenty, and sometimes as much as fifty dollars at a house. Wherever the poor women offered any resistance to the wholesale robbery which these cormorants were perpetrating they were wretchedly abused, and, in many instances, their clothes were torn off of them because they refused to produce the money which their persecutors suspected them of having.

I now became thoroughly aroused at the inhuman treatment of these helpless women, and determined to have this money back, or the worth of it. I considered that the poor soldiers should not lose so much of their hard-earned wages without an effort being made on my part to recover it back again, or at least a portion of it. The mountains were at this time full of men whose feelings had been so perfectly outraged by the rebels, that they were willing and ready to join in an expedition to inflict punishment upon them. Consequently, I soon had a company of men ready to make a raid upon the rebels of Johnson County, among whom was Captain Lafayette Jones, who had been upon a previous occasion captured by the same rebel home guard, and at which time he had been robbed of a large sum of gold by this same Bill Waugh, whom I have already referred to, and sent off to prison, from which he effected his escape by joining the rebel army.

At the time Jones was captured, Waugh promised him faithfully that the money which had been taken from him should be given to his parents, who were then living near Waugh's residence in Johnson County. But this promise was never fulfilled, as Waugh képt the money, and appropriated it to his own use. When Jones became acquainted with Waugh's duplicity in this matter he vowed that he would kill him the first opportunity that presented itself. At the time I was meditating this trip to Johnson County to recover the money which I had distributed among the soldiers' wives in that county, and of which they had been most villainously robbed by the rebels, I was altogether ignorant of the treatment which Jones had received from Waugh, and for which injury he had solemnly protested he would have revenge by taking the life of Waugh.

After I collected my company together, we proceeded at once to Waugh's house, which Jones boldly entered, and shot him down, killing him instantly. This circumstance threw the whole company into a panic for a moment, but, after reflecting for a short time how their homes had been devastated, and how they had been robbed of every thing valuable which they possessed, the current changed, and they were ready for action again. The house was then thoroughly searched, but no part of the missing goods or money could be found. We then went to the residence of Sam M'Queen, who was one of the most violent and outrageous rebels that belonged to that wicked and infamous conclave known under the name and style of the Home Guards of Johnson County. When he was taken prisoner, he trembled like Belshazzar when he saw his destiny defined by the handwriting upon the wall. Doubtless he expected to be killed without any mercy being shown to him; and if the monstrous crimes which he had committed against the laws of the country, and the total disregard which he had paid to the dictates of common humanity itself, had been placed in the balances and permitted to determine his fate, his guilty soul would have been at once hurried into the awful presence of the great Eternal. But he implored for mercy—for that mercy which he had so totally disregarded when he and his coadjutors in wickedness were hunting and murdering the Union men of his county, and persecuting and robbing their destitute families. When he was hunting up Union men like the wild beasts of the forest he forgot that mercy is an attribute of God himself, and he therefore extended it to his helpless and prostrate victims with a sparing hand. But on this occasion mercy was extended to him, for his life was spared when he solemnly swore that he would never interrupt another Union man or his family. There was no other man killed by any of the company during this expedition into Johnson County, although every principle of justice sternly demanded the life of Sam M'Queen, for he had perpetrated a multitude of crimes sufficient in atrocity to have shocked the sensibilities of any person that was not perfectly hardened to human sympathy and destitute of manly feeling, and for which his life should have been made to atone. If M'Queen had been killed on this occasion, as he richly deserved to be, the life of very many innocent Union men would thereby have been saved; for he did not long observe the solemn protestations which he made in regard to his future conduct toward the Union people when he saw death staring him in the face. However, he at last met with his reward; for when the Federal forces came into the upper counties of East Tennessee in the spring of 1865, he was captured and shot by some of the very men whom he had so foully wronged.

We searched M'Queen's house, together with several

hers, some of which were garrisoned by rebel soldiers, who
mediately fled as if they were carried upon the wings of
e wind when they heard us approaching. But we failed
find any of the lost treasure for which we were searching,
ith the exception of two pairs of ladies' shoes. As we had
iled to recover the money and property which had been
rcibly taken from the wives of the soldiers, we concluded to
pair the loss by taking the rebels' horses, the greater number
which belonged to the rebel soldiers, and the remainder
the home guards. After taking enough of the said horses
pay the soldiers back the money which the rebels had
ken from their wives, the balance of them were left in the
nds of the capturers, and we then left Johnson County,
d made immediate arrangements to go through the lines.
I do not think that the oppression of the people in the
per counties of East Tennessee would have been any
eater than it had been for a long time, if it had not been
r Sam M'Queen, and an outrageous rebel guerrilla by
e name of William Parker, who was generally known by
e cognomen of "Old Bill Parker," and was a bell-wether
nong the home guards. This fiend in human shape had
ready driven many families from their homes, hauled off
eir property, and burned their houses to the ground. In
ct, there was scarcely a dwelling-house in Johnson Coun-
which belonged to a Union soldier but that was burned
ashes by this old scoundrel. It is said that Erostratus
rned the magnificent Temple of Ephesus in order to per-
tuate his memory, wishing that his name might occupy a
ace upon the page of his country's history, even if his de-
e should be accomplished by the commission of a base
d sacrilegious crime which was entirely calculated to
ing upon him the deep and lasting curses of his fellow-
en and the everlasting frowns of the gods. And if "Old

M

Bill Parker" entertained a desire to be remembered by future generations, the magnitude of his crimes and the enormity of his flagitious villainies are eminently sufficient to
give him that unenviable notoriety upon the page of his
country's history which serves to distinguish the most brutal murderers and black-hearted cut-throats which the world
in its prodigality has ever produced.

It is really astonishing to think how man, made in the image of the great Omnipotent Architect of the universe, can
so suddenly change his human nature to that of an incarnate devil. But it is even so; and " Old Bill Parker," during
the last year of his iniquitous life, furnished one of the most
indubitable illustrations of this remarkable transformation
that has ever come under my observation. It afforded him
the utmost delight to subject the wives and children of the
Union men (who left their homes to save their lives) to the
most terrible suffering which could possibly be inflicted
upon them. He would stand and laugh when the devouring flames were wrapping their houses in their destructive
embrace. If he had been a devil, fresh from the infernal regions, he could not surely have exhibited any less respect
for the sorrows and sufferings of helpless women and their
innocent children. When he would be engaged in holding
the fiery torch to the houses of Union men with an un-
flinching hand, if a poor woman should approach him to
implore him to desist in his hellish work of destruction, he
would instantly knock her down with his gun, and bestow
upon her the most foul and terrible curses which his wicked
heart could originate. He burned a number of poor and
destitute women's houses with the utmost degree of reck-
lessness, when he was well aware that they had no other
protection to shield themselves and their poor little barefooted and starving children from the cold and stormy.

blasts of winter. He would stand, with a devilish smile
playing upon his fiendish countenance, and look with delight upon the horrible scene which was presented, when
the poor women, with tears streaming from their eyes,
would turn away from the smouldering ruins of their humble habitations, followed by their little children, whose naked feet would leave their impressions upon the cold, white
bosom of the snow, to wander forth amid the dreary mountains, without a home and without a shelter to protect them
from the chilling winds of a dreary winter.

Many innocent Union men had already fallen victims to
this old scoundrel's devilish malice, and now, with Sam
M'Queen (regardless of the solemn oath which he had taken
to cease in his persecution of the Union men) to assist him
in his fiendish work, they progressed most admirably in the
work of devastation and murder. Old Bill Parker had no
respect or sympathy for gray hairs, if they were found upon
the head of a Union man. Old age afforded no sort of protection from the assaults of this brutal miscreant, for he
shot down old and decrepit men, who were unable to leave
their fireside without leaning upon a staff to support them
in their faltering steps, just because they happened to have
a son in the Union army, or were friendly to the Union
cause themselves.

I will close this chapter with the short address which
Gratiano made to the relentless and implacable Shylock
when he saw him whetting his knife to cut the pound of
flesh off of Antonio's breast, as it fully and poetically illus-
trates my sentiments in regard to Old Bill Parker:

> "O, be thou damn'd, inexorable dog!
> And for thy life let justice be accus'd.
> Thou almost mak'st me waver in my faith,
> To hold opinion with Pythagoras,

That souls of animals infuse themselves
Into the trunks of men : thy currish spirit
Govern'd a wolf, who, hang'd for human slanghter,
Even from the gallows did his fell sonl fleet,
And, whilst thou lay'st in thy unhallow'd dam,
Infused itself in thee ; for thy desires
Are wolfish, bloody, starv'd, and ravenous."

CHAPTER XXXI.

On the 15th of June, 1864, we met on Gap Creek, in Carter County, as the rebels were watching for us at the old starting-point, and had been watching for us ever since we made the raid into Johnson County, which occurred on the 10th of June.

Some of the company were armed, but we did not think about engaging in any conflict of arms, as many of the company were already frightened out of their wits at the mischief we had accomplished during our raid, and declared that if we should now be captured there was no telling what sort of a death we would have to die. I determined to go through the lines as secretly as possible, where the men could learn to be soldiers before they were led into an engagement with the rebels. Small squads of men and horses continued to arrive all day, and some two or three men had brought their wives and children with them. While some were leading horses packed with blankets, food, and clothing for the journey, others had nothing, not even decent clothes to wear, for some of the men were recently-escaped prisoners, and some had been scouting so long they had become perfectly destitute of every thing.

When night came on we were ready to start upon our journey. I was quite apprehensive with regard to the trail which I knew the company would now leave behind them, for I was certain that the public road would be no plainer; but I consoled myself with the reflection that our pathway would lead through such a rough and uneven country, that the rebels would not be likely to travel it in pursuit of us. In fact, the trail which a large company of men and horses would always leave behind them had a very strange appearance, running as it did through such rough portions of the mountains. The Union people living in the country through which we passed always knew the road which we had made when they saw it, and sometimes the rebel soldiers would also observe it when it happened to pass along over a level section of country; and whenever they would see it, some of them would be sure to exclaim, "There is Ellis's trail again. Can't he be stopped from stealing our men and taking them through the lines every month?" And this question would be answered by some one of the party as follows: "Not while these everlasting hills and mountains stand to protect him and his bands."

Indeed, I never knew until after the rebellion occurred the real use of such rough mountains, which only appeared to be a suitable abode for wild beasts. But now, how eagerly the Union men sought their protection from a merciless and blood-thirsty enemy! When safely lodged within their silent and dismal recesses, we could laugh their threats to scorn, and dream of the revenge we would yet live to have for our days of dreadful suffering.

We continued to travel hard all night, and by daylight we reached the spurs of Unaker Mountain, near the Greasy Cove; and after we traveled up the side of it until we arrived at a position which we considered to be safe, we stopped and spent the day there without any interruption from the rebels. As soon as darkness came on, we started on along the side of the mountain toward Chucky River. We now had twelve miles to travel before we could get to a safe place to cross, and I directed my course to a shoal in the river where I knew the men who had no horses could easily wade, as there was no time to be lost in waiting for them to cross in a canoe. When we got to the river we crossed it in a hurry, and went on into a long range of rugged mountains, whose lofty elevations stretched out before us to a great distance, and, after a hard night's travel, when daylight came we were in a secure place upon the mountain, where we rested at ease without any fear of being molested by the rebels. I knew that they would be certain to discover our trail where we had crossed the river, but I had no idea that they would presume to risk their precious lives in a journey upon the rough mountain over which we were then traveling.

We rested until twelve o'clock, and then started on across Rich Mountain, through deep hollows and over steep spurs, where we had to pack our horse-feed upon our backs, and had great difficulty in getting our horses along. Some of the men were now greatly fatigued, and as soon as it got dark we stopped for the night, as the whole company expressed a desire to rest until morning. The men washed and rubbed their stiffened limbs, and, after a good night's rest, all appeared to be very much refreshed the next morning.

We set out quite early for another hard day's travel. Some of the men were very stiff and sore, which caused them to go limping and stumbling along at an awful rate; but, notwithstanding, we pushed on as rapidly as we possibly could, and at length got across the mountain, and stopped to spend the night on the head-waters of Horse Creek. Some of the men rested and slept very well, while others were groaning and complaining all night long with pains in their limbs. There were some of the poor fellows who seemed to be in great distress about their homes and families they had left behind, and this was by far the greatest source of trouble to them, for perhaps they had not a single dollar in their pockets, and their poor, destitute families left without any visible means of procuring the common necessities of life. This I thought was indeed a sufficient cause for sorrow and trouble; for, oh, what a terrible devil creeps into that man's soul who sees poverty and starvation standing at his door! These men had been waiting for a long time for the Federal forces to take possession of the upper portion of East Tennessee, and at last were compelled to go through the lines, or be captured and forced to go into the rebel army.

When morning came we started on our journey, over rough ridges and through immense laurel thickets, which usually occurred in the deep hollows, and also through large patches of green briers, which tore our clothes in a wretched manner. At night we stopped near Shell's Cove, in the lower part of Green County. That night I thought it best to push on across Chucky River, and therefore, after eating supper and feeding our horses, we started on, and reached Allen's Bridge about ten o'clock, where we crossed the river without any trouble, and then traveled on all night, and when daylight appeared, we were about ten miles south of Bull's Gap, and safely ensconced in a position high up on Bay's Mountain.

The men were all very tired, and some of them were so completely exhausted that they would doubtless have fallen out by the wayside, had it not been for the horses which were in the company, the owners of which rendered every assistance to the worn-out men who were walking, in permitting them to ride their horses; and this sort of interchange greatly facilitated our progress. We had done some very hard marching; but, as may well be supposed, men whose lives were in constant jeopardy did not stop long at any time to discuss the dreadful fatigue to which we were subjected by our tiresome journey through the rough mountains. I very well knew that, if this company should be captured by the rebels, every single man of them would at once be murdered in a most shocking manner; for the raid which we had so recently made into Johnson County had instilled into the rebel soldiers a desperate thirst for revenge, and, therefore, I was convinced that the innocent portion of the company would have been made to suffer with the guilty, and, consequently, I was determined to make use of all my energies to avoid such a dreadful calamity. I was very well acquainted with the country through which we would have to pass, and I was also well aware of the severe fatigues which we should be compelled to undergo, if we succeeded in making a safe migration through the mountains to the Federal lines. I always experienced a good deal of trouble in getting the men along who were badly tired down, for they would generally think that they could hide successfully from the rebels in any small patch of woods they came to; and this is the very reason why so many pilots, together with their companies, were captured while they were endeavoring to make their way through the lines; for they would unfortunately listen to the suggestions of the tired and lame men in their companies, which were always made to secure their own personal ease and comfort, irrespective of the welfare of the balance of the company, and would thereby be induced to stop at places where every principle of vigilant precaution ought to have urged them not to tarry for a moment.

After another hard night's travel we reached Morristown, at which place we had the very agreeable pleasure of finding a number of the Federal forces stationed, to whom we disposed of our horses, and then took the train for Knoxville. We remained at Knoxville one day, and

M 2

then started on the train for Nashville; and upon our arrival there we learned that the 13th Tennessee Cavalry Regiment was still stationed at Gallatin, and continued our journey on to that place.   On this occasion I had many recruits to add to the 13th Regiment, and I also had a great many letters for the soldiers who had families in East Tennessee.   Many of the soldiers commenced fixing up packages for me to carry to their families.   I related to them the misfortune which had attended the greater portion of the goods and money which they had sent home by me before, and I then paid the principal losers for all they had lost out of the proceeds which I had received for the horses which I had taken from the rebels, and told them that I would not again be responsible for any thing which might be lost in future.   But this avowal on my part did no good whatever, for my knapsack was soon filled with packages of letters and other articles, and weighed on this occasion at least sixty pounds.   All of the letters contained more or less greenback money, together with penknives, needles, pins, photographs, and a variety of other articles.   The various articles which filled my knapsack at this time amounted to at least three thousand dollars, which I thought was entirely too rich a burden for me to carry upon my shoulders while running the gauntlet among the starved and ragged rebels.

CHAPTER XXXII.

I BADE the soldiers from East Tennessee farewell, and shouldered my heavy knapsack. I came back to Nashville, and there took the train for Knoxville. When I arrived, at Knoxville, my friends ascertaining that I had such a heavy burden to carry, procured a horse for me to lead through the mountains, and upon which they said I could frequently ride, and thereby get along more agreeably with my heavy load. This I was afraid would be a very difficult task, but I agreed to undertake it, and thereupon I had eight thousand dollars more added to the amount of money and other property which I already had in my care.

I now set out upon my journey home again, but not alone, as some of my neighbors, who had visited Knoxville, concluded to return home with me. We took the train at Knoxville, and came on to the Strawberry Plains, where we had to begin our journey through the woods and mountains, as the train was not at this time running any farther up the road.

On the night we left Strawberry Plains we got on our journey some distance above Mossy Creek, where we rested during the day, and the next night we reached Russellville. Here we concealed ourselves all day, and as soon as night came on we made our way into the Chucky Mountains. Now our toilsome journey had to be begun in earnest. My horse was already overloaded, and, consequently, I had to shoulder my heavy knapsack, for I could not confine it on the horse's back while he was tugging and climbing up the sides of the steep mountains. And the worst of all was, we found that there was a scout of rebel soldiers, who were searching through the range of mountains where we were now traveling, and we had not advanced very far until we found that they were pursuing our track. I immediately changed the direction we had been traveling in order to give them the dodge. We crossed Chucky River, which we had to wade, and at once made our way into the roughest parts of the mountain just as daylight made its appearance. I now considered that we were in a safe position, but, unfortunately, we had nothing to eat, and I was very hungry and weak, as I had packed my heavy load a distance of twenty-three miles the previous night. I tried to sleep, but I was so thoroughly exhausted that I made but very poor progress in the land of dreams; and, as a crowning misfortune on that day, I had a severe attack of bleeding at the lungs. I thought that I had undertaken on this occasion more than I was about to get through with, for sometimes I believed that I was about to end my troubles upon this lonely mountain. But when night came on I felt able to pursue my journey, and we started on, while my companions assisted me in carrying my heavy burden, which was a great inconvenience to them, for they all had about as much to carry as they were able to get along with in our rough mountain pathway.

We traveled on without being able to procure any thing to eat until about midnight, at which time we stopped at a house, where we got some bread and bacon. The man who lived at this house told us to get away from there with all possible speed, for the rebels, he said, had been at his house since dark. We went on two miles farther in the mountains, where we stopped to rest, and to eat our bread and meat.

We were now on Rich Mountain, which we crossed during the day, and oh, what a hard day's travel it was! When I suffer my meditations to dwell upon that hard day's travel now, I wonder how I ever succeeded in getting over that stupendous mountain in my frail and weakly condition, for I had not yet recovered from the hemorrhage of my lungs, which had weakened me very much, and I was also weak from the excessive hunger which I had endured for some time. I often thought, as I toiled along over that rugged mountain, that this would most inevitably be the last trip that I would ever be able to make through the mountains, and I frequently despaired of ever reaching my home; for as I traveled up the side of the mountain, I could not walk a hundred yards at a time without stopping to rest, and, when I started to descend the mountain, I would very often sink down on my knees.

On that evening we got to a place where we obtained something to eat, and remained all night with some men who were staying out on the mountain in a camp, and it was twelve o'clock in the day before we left the camp. We went on to Chucky River, and crossed it in a canoe, and about midnight we arrived at the house of John M'Inturff, in the Greasy Cove, in Washington County. We remained in the woods until daylight, at which time I went near the house, and seeing the old man going to his barn, I called to him, and he came to me. I told him that we were very hungry, and he at once returned to the house, and soon had a very plentiful breakfast brought to us. I gave him the letters which his three sons had given me to take to him, who were in the 8th Tennessee Cavalry Regiment, and also the packages which had been sent by me to be distributed among the soldiers' wives who were living in that settlement. We rested until we got dinner, after which we started on our journey, and got as near to our homes as it was safe for us to go that night.

My horse-load of goods all belonged to the soldiers' wives who were living in Elizabethton, and I had them conveyed secretly by night to the proper owners. Oh, what a happy time it was now for these women! Many of them were now placed in possession of a nice new dress and shoes. Calico, and all the finer qualities of ladies' dress goods, were denominated as "Yankee clothing," in the refined nomenclature of the land of Dixie at this period of time. A piece of new calico, or, in fact, any other article in the dry-goods line, was a perfect curiosity to the rebels for some two years or more before the suppression of the infamous rebellion. Indeed, if one of the fire-eating rebel women could have secured the possession of a pound of coffee, a spool of thread, or a paper of pins about this time, she would have thought herself remarkably well off, and would doubtless have at once imagined that "a good time was coming." A cup of genuine coffee during the last years of the rebellion was about as scarce among the rebels as good money; and if they could have been permitted to sip a good cup of Mocha, Java, or Rio, they would have considered it equally as delightful as the nectar or the ambrosia which was used at the splendid banquets of the fabled gods!

I soon succeeded in distributing the entire cargo which I had brought with me into Carter County, but not without an occurrence of bad luck happening somehow or other in the said distribution, which, in a pecuniary point of view, proved to be the most embarrassing circumstance that had ever previously befallen me. Every person for whom I had letters and money on this occasion could not come and receive the letters from my own hand, for fear of being known; and, consequently, I had to intrust several of the packages of letters containing money to persons in whom I confided to convey the said letters to their proper owners; and in doing this, a small package of letters, containing seven hundred dollars in money, altogether failed to arrive at its proper destination. And, strange to say, the individuals whom I had selected to distribute the said letters could not give any account of them at all. This was another source of trouble and vexation for me, for I at once determined to replace the amount of the missing sum of money out of my own pocket. It is true, I told the soldiers very specifically before I received this money into my care, that I would not be responsible for any money which might be sent to East Tennessee by me, for I well knew that some unforeseen accident, over which I could have no control, might prevent the safe delivery of it. But, notwithstanding this avowal which I made, and reiterated to the soldiers time and again, as I could not ascertain who had lost or improperly appropriated this money, I was apprehensive that some persons might entertain the very erroneous impression that I had made use of it myself. Therefore, rather than to become liable to such suspicion, I determined to pay the last dollar of the lost money out of my own pocket. This left me penniless, with a broken and shattered constitution.

I now again concluded in my own mind that I would never carry any more letters; but this I need not have done, for my health was now in such a precarious condition that I could not do it, even if I had any desire to continue it. I thought that it was quite enough for me to have the disagreeable reflection that I had very nearly sacrificed my life in packing heavy loads of letters, goods, and money through the rough mountains, and then have to take the last dollar of my own money to render as an equivalent for money which had been accidentally lost, and of which I had no knowledge whatever. I was now even with the world. Out of all the soldiers which I had added to the Federal army, and all the men whom I had conducted through the lines, I was now totally unable to buy myself a suit of clothes! This, I thought, was poor encouragement for all the dreadful fatigues to which I had so long been subjected, both mentally and physically; but I consoled myself with the reflection that I had done important services for my country, even if I had been so inadequately remunerated for them.

CHAPTER XXXIII.

It was now the 1st of August, 1864, and at this time there was a company of rebel soldiers stationed on the Watauga River, two miles from my home, under the command of a one-armed rebel scoundrel by the name of Teener. This company was composed of a most graceless set of villains, whose daily and nightly business it was to prowl about the country, and rob and plunder the houses of Union men to a degree that was perfectly heart-rending. They were certainly the worst and most unfeeling set of scoundrels that had ever before been sent into Carter County, and the vile infamy of their conduct toward the Union people will be long remembered by those who had to endure the terrible oppression, and suffer in silence the insults which were constantly imposed upon them by these miserable thieves and blackguards.

My health at this time was so extremely delicate that I did not feel willing to undertake another journey through the lines, and therefore I and two or three of my scouting companions determined to unite ourselves together as a band of brothers for the purpose of mutual protection, and also for the purpose of defending our homes from being plundered by these rebel vandals, whose monstrous enormities had become proverbial throughout the whole county. We were well armed with eight-shooting Spencer rifles, and we also had an abundant supply of ammunition, and we determined to stay together as much as we possibly could.

It was not very long before our courage was put to the

test; for on the very next day after we had entered into the agreement referred to, while myself and Elbert Tread-away were sitting on a hill that overlooked, and not fifty yards from my house, we observed three of these house robbers approaching. I was engaged in conversation with several females, who had come to hear from their friends, and the Yankees in general; and as I never went into my own house, they of course had to come to me, and this is the reason why we had left the forest and were in an open field. Robert Treadaway was sitting in the porch in front of my house, when his brother Elbert exclaimed, "Yonder come three rebels, and Bob is at the house." An effort was at once made to let Bob know that they were coming, and they discovered us. Instantly they leveled their pistols and fired at us. This was the immediate signal for an attack from us, and in a moment our rifles were belching forth their leaden messengers of death, and the surrounding hills were made to reverberate the echo of one explosion after another until the last load was exhausted. The rebels were riding, and, when we began to fire on them, they at once leaned down in a bending posture upon the necks of their horses, and left the field like a flash of lightning. Our guns worked like a charm. I had always thought before that mine was too hard on trigger, but at this time I found nothing wrong, and I thought that nothing had been want-ing but the sight of rebels to make me pull the trigger hard enough, for upon this occasion I was unable to find the least objection to its performance. The rebels succeeded in getting away without receiving any serious injury; how-ever, they left a large lock of hair behind them, which at once testified that a ball from one of our guns had saluted the head of one of them very abruptly. We received no injury whatever, but the rapid firing which occurred on this

occasion frightened the ladies very much with whom I hac
been conversing, and Bob was suddenly scared out of th
pensive reverie in which he had been indulging while sittin;
in the porch.

We confidently expected that the whole company oi
rebels would come in pursuit of us the next morning, anc
on that night myself, Elbert, and Bob Treadaway lay side
by side in the forest near my house, with our rifles graspec
in our hands. If we had remained together, we should have
been ready for action when the rebels made their appear
ance; but just as daylight began to dawn, having heard
nothing of them as yet, I left my companions, and went to
a spring which was some distance beyond the house; and
when I was returning, the rebels discovered me about the
same moment that I observed them, and immediately opened
a heavy fire on me, and one of them seemed to be so inten·
upon hitting me that he went to the corn-crib, and there
resting his gun upon the end of a log, he took as deliberate
aim at me as if he had been going to shoot at a panther oi
some other ravenous beast; but, notwithstanding the desire
which he manifested to make sure of hitting his mark, hif
ball whistled along past me without effecting any injury.]
had left my gun with my companions, and hastened on to
take possession of it. When I got back to our coverture
I found that Bob was missing. Myself and Elbert Tread
away being now alone, we immediately concealed ourselvef
behind trees, and then for some time we made good use of
our guns. The rebels would not come into the woods after
us, and the position that we occupied was a very bad place
for us to engage in an open-field fight against such greaf
odds; we therefore watched them for about half an hour.
waiting for an opportunity to present itself when we could
attack them without incurring so much risk.

The rebel force was composed of fourteen infantry, and twenty cavalry or more; and while part of the force were engaged with myself and Treadaway, the balance of the rebels were engaged in plundering and robbing my house. They stripped my family of all their clothing, and also of all their bed-clothing, and carried away all they possibly could; and what few articles they could not carry away were so perfectly destroyed that they were fit for no farther use whatever. The cavalry now started from the house along the main road, and the infantry started through the fields, in order to rob some houses in the neighborhood. When they started they seemed to be in fine spirits, as they made several loud huzzas, and some of them exclaimed that "they had routed the bushwhackers, and had got all their goods." We now thought a propitious time had arrived for us to make an attack upon them. The fields through which they were now going extended on to their encampment, which was about two miles distant, and were flanked all the way by woods; and I can here assure the reader that we did not give them time to rob another house. The cavalry had moved on ahead, and we now had only the fourteen infantry to fight. We fell behind trees, and began to fire on them slowly. They returned our first fire. We now opened a brisk fire upon them, and the hills and valleys reverberated with the turbulent intonations which emanated from our rifles. The rebels, not fancying the way that our balls were singing around them, jumped behind some old saw-logs that lay in their way. We now had the advantage of them, for, when one of them would raise his head, one of us would immediately fire at it; our balls, however, failed to hit any of them, but filled their eyes with particles of old wood and dirt.

We continued to fire at them, and at length they arose

and started off as rapidly as they could, while we continued firing on them at every step. Treadaway, who had a remarkably strong voice, would sometimes mount upon a fence and yell out at the top of his voice, "Head them, boys; flank them, boys;" and I do not doubt but that the rapidly-retreating rebels imagined that there were at least forty or fifty men in pursuit of them. In this way we ran them at least a mile, when, upon getting to a cabin, they stopped to get water, but we did not give them time to drink, for we opened a heavy fire upon them. One of them was just raising the cup to his lips when a Spencer ball whistled past his ear; he immediately dropped the cup, and all of them started again on a run, and we after them, shooting and yelling in a most terrible manner. In this way we ran them to their camps. We then returned to get breakfast, which we ate in a small thicket of bushes near my own door. And now Bob returned. He had not been idle; for when he observed the cavalry occupying a position in the road, waiting for the infantry to run us out of the woods, he placed himself in a position of safety and commenced firing upon them with his eight-shooter, and wounded one of them in one of his thighs so badly that he died soon afterward. We soon learned from reliable authority that we had inflicted severe wounds upon several of these brave rebels, and so completely frightened the balance of the party that some of them returned to their camps with their eyes bathed in tears.

They now reported that there was a bushwhacker behind every tree and bush in the settlement where I lived, and they also reported that they had been engaged with at least forty or fifty of them, and said that, while a portion of the bushwhackers were fighting with their infantry, the others were engaged with their cavalry. Owing to this terrible report about bushwhackers, which was loudly proclaimed by these cowardly thieves and robbers, a company of one hundred men, belonging to John Morgan's command, were immediately sent into Carter County to clear the country of bushwhackers.   But they never had the luck of finding any of the great host of bushwhackers, which had only been conceived in the imaginations of the scoundrel. Teener and his base and reckless myrmidons, for I, not having yet recovered from my recent indisposition enough to undertake a trip through the lines, had gone to assist Treadaway in conducting through the most dangerous parts of the mountains a company of men whom he had undertaken to pilot through the lines.

The rebel soldiers who were now sent into Carter County had orders to burn my house, and which orders they would have doubtless executed, had it not been for the interference of the rebel citizens of the county.   They told these soldiers that they would prefer having their own houses burned, for, said they, "If you burn Ellis's house you will kindle a flame that can not very soon be extinguished."   The rebel citizens, with but few exceptions, were my personal friends, and they would willingly have made up the losses that I had sustained by the rebel soldiers, if they could have done it without being detected.   But I concluded to make an attempt to recover back my property which the rebels had recently taken from me, and which attempt was shortly made, and successfully accomplished, in the following manner: The rebels were now engaged every day in hauling forage, such as hay, oats, and green corn, which they were unceremoniously taking from the fields and the farms of the citizens, and I concluded to relieve them of one of their teams at least.   I made my intention known to Elbert and Bob Treadaway, and also to two other friends, who at once agreed to assist me. We therefore took a position on the side of a road, and it was not long until we observed a wagon approaching, to which was attached four very fine mules, and the forage-master, who accompanied the wagon, was riding a very fine horse just behind the wagon. We stopped the team in the road and took out the mules, and also captured the forage-master, and told him to get down off of his horse. He and the wagon-driver were frightened dreadfully at being so suddenly and unexpectedly surprised in the public road, and began to haul out their Confederate money and their pocket-knives to offer us as a ransom. I told them that we had no use for their Confederate money, without it was to kindle fires with, nor for them either. I told them that they could go on; that we only wanted the mules and the horse for the Federal government. They left in a hurry, and so did we.

We hastened with the prize which we had thus captured to a neighboring forest, where we stopped to await the pursuit of the rebels. We did not have to tarry very long until we saw a large squad of rebels coming on the track of the mules, which was very easy to be seen, as the ground was wet, and the tracks of the mules and the horse were plainly exhibited. Each one of us had taken a position behind a tree, having a well-loaded navy pistol and an eight-shooting Spencer rifle apiece. We were very anxious for the rebels to continue their pursuit on this occasion, for we wished to pay them for the outrageous villainies which they had been recently practicing upon the Union people; but when they got to the edge of the woods they very wisely checked up and took the back track, doubtless feeling unwilling to risk the dangers which they thought might suddenly environ them beneath the umbrageous foliage of the forest trees.

They now went on to Carter Station, and reported that
the Yankees had come in above them, and had captured a
portion of their men and horses; and another report was
started that John Morgan's wagon-train had been captured
by the Yankees in the mountains of Carter County.   But
the rebels made no more efforts to recover their lost mules;
and although a company of them were constantly searching
the country for me, yet I ranged through my native hills
at pleasure, where my health soon returned, and I was
again making preparations to start with a company of men
through the lines, when the news came to me that the Yankees were again marching up the country, and I determined
to wait a short time for them.

CHAPTER XXXIV.

THE month of September, 1864, had now arrived, and the times were yet bad for the Union people in Carter County, but were much worse in Johnson County, for the rebel home guards in that county had assembled, and entered into the horrid agreement to kill every Union man they might find in the county, burn their houses, and drive their families through the lines! Sam M'Queen, Green Moore, B. O. Johnson, John K. Hughes, William Shown, Jacob Wagner, and other influential citizens of Johnson County had voluntarily entered into this miserable conspiracy. They selected old Bill Parker as their leader in all their hellish works of mischief, and a more suitable person to act as the leader of this combination of blood-thirsty scoundrels could not have been found.

The work of death and destruction now commenced anew in all their horrible aspects, and three old gray-headed men were murdered by Parker in one day. The first of these old men who was murdered was John Hawkins, who was eighty years old. He was taken from his own house to Pleasant Grove Meeting-house, in Johnson County. Parker ordered some of his men to shoot him; but they could not summon the fortitude to quench the flickering flame of life which was now burning feebly in this innocent old man, and which accumulated years were momentarily threatening to extinguish. When he found that none of his men would agree to shoot him, he said that he

N

would shoot him, and at once ordered the old man to turn his back toward him, which he did, and at the same time meekly folded his hands on the head of his staff, which he leaned on for support. His head was uncovered, and his gray locks fluttered in the passing breeze. There stood old Bill Parker behind his back, aiming his pistol with as steady a hand as if he had possessed no soul which would be inevitably summoned before the bar of the infinite Eternal to answer for the terrible crime of shedding innocent blood! The sight was too horrible for even rebel soldiers, for they all left the place, and Parker proceeded to immolate his aged and innocent victim alone and unattended. He burst two caps, and the third one accomplished the work of death! The ball went into the old man's back and came out at the lower part of his breast, lodging itself in his wrist. There was no charge preferred against him, only that he was a Union man. He did not even have a son in the Federal army.

The next victim who fell into the hands of these inhuman scoundrels was John H. Vaught. He was a good citizen of Johnson County, and was also a very pious man. He did not take either side in the war. He said that he was old and in feeble health, and was willing to abide by the laws of which ever side might be in the ascendant. But, alas, old Bill Parker happened to find him away from his home on one occasion, which was a sufficient cause, in his estimation, to murder him. Parker at once accused him of carrying news to scouters, and of knowing where they were camped in the mountains, and told him if he did not direct him and his men to their camps they would kill him. This of course he could not do, as he did not know where their camps were. Some of old Parker's gang of demons then began to beat him over the head with the but-ends of their pistols, calling him an old liar and a traitor; and at length Parker stepped up and, with the utmost coolness, shot him in the breast, holding his pistol so close to his body that his clothes were considerably burned. He lay a whole day and night at the place where he was shot, as his friends were positively afraid to go and bury his dead body. He was sixty-five years of age.

This company of inhuman murderers left their gray-haired victim weltering in his blood, and started forward, to bathe their hands in some other poor Union man's blood. They had not proceeded far from the place where they had exhibited their last tragedy, until they met with an old man by the name of David Oaks, who they immediately shot down as if he had been a wild beast, without exchanging a word with him.

A portion of the home guards of Johnson County, commanded by old Bill Parker, went to the house of Levi Guy. He was seventy years old, and scarcely knew what either side of the contending parties was fighting about. The only charge they had against him was that he had two sons in the Federal army, and one scouting in the mountains, his fourth son having died in prison at Richmond. The old man was sitting at the table eating his breakfast, when these fiends rode up to his door and told him that they had come to take him off. He arose from the table and went out to them, when they tied his hands behind his back and started him on in the road before them. His daughter, being deeply concerned about the probable fate of her aged father, started to follow them, when some of these reckless demons rode back and caught hold of her very roughly, and whipped her until the blood ran from her arms and back profusely, and then drove her back to the house! They drove this old man on before them, like

"BRAVE BILL PARKER."

a dumb animal doomed to the slaughter-pen, for a·distance of half a mile, when they stopped and twisted a hickory withe, and hung him up to the limb of a tree, some of them holding him up while others tied the withe. The withe was too stiff to close tightly around his neck, and, consequently, his toes touched the ground, and in this situation he suffered all the indescribable agonies of a horrible death! In the evening the daughter who had received such a severe flagellation at the hands of these ruffians started again to see if she could discover any thing in regard to her father. She followed the trail of the horses until she arrived at the spot where her father was hanging by the neck. The ground immediately under him was worn perfectly smooth where he had moved his toes backward and forward while he was struggling in the fearful agonies of death. She let him down, and then returned to the house, and got her aged mother and some children, and went back and carried her dead father to the house, and buried him the next day. Oh, what a dreadful act of cruelty to be perpetrated by civilized men in a Christian land, where the light of the glorious gospel of the Son of God brightly illuminates the pathway to Heaven, wherein all may walk without stumbling who desire to shun the broad road that leads to hell!

Enoch Guy, a son of Levi Guy, and who was a Federal soldier, was captured and shot at the house of George Campbell. The first ball that was shot at him wounded him in the side of his head. He was then taken off about a quarter of a mile, and shot with three more balls, one of them striking him in his head, and the other two in his breast. His murderers then stripped him of his clothing, and threw his lifeless body off of a cliff, which was at least forty feet in height, among the sharp rocks that covered the ground below, which mangled his body in a horrible manner. He belonged to the 8th Tennessee Cavalry, and was recruiting for that regiment when he was captured. His recruiting-papers were found in his pocket. Campbell's house was immediately burned, because Guy had been found there.

The next man that was murdered by these brutal fiends was David Guy, a son of Levi Guy, who was also a Federal soldier. He had come home on a short visit to his family, and was in his house when the home guard rode up to his door. He walked out and surrendered, when one of these inhuman murderers drew out his pistol and shot him in the shoulder. He now begged them not to kill him, telling them that he was a Federal soldier, and was then their pris-oner. His poor wife now came out, and stood like a statue of distress between her husband and his murderers, and begged them with tearful eyes to spare his life, and his lit-tle children, who were weeping most piteously, implored them, with all their childish eloquence, not to kill their fa-ther. But the sorrowful wail of the wife and the mournful cries of her children altogether failed to awaken any feeling of human pity in these inhuman monsters, for one of them proceeded to shoot him in the back, and then others of the party sprang off of their horses and pushed his wife vio-lently away, and kicked some of the children down. They then robbed him of his money, and stripped him of his coat, pants, and hat, and then mounted their horses and rode off, while one of them proclaimed with a loud voice, "That is the way to treat all the Yankee soldiers who left the South to fight for Abe Lincoln."

These men were killed in August and September, 1864. Another son of Levi Guy was killed in the month of Feb-ruary, 1865. He was captured at his home, together with a young man who had been scouting in the mountains with him for some time. They were taken off about fifteen miles to an old house, where the rebels tied their hands behind them and hung them up to a joist. The blood-thirsty wretches then beat these men with their guns, and broke their arms and several of their ribs while they were struggling in the agonies of death. These two men were hung about dark, and the next morning some women who were going to feed their cattle discovered their dead bodies hanging in the old house. They were hung on the edge of North Carolina, on the main road leading from Jefferson to Taylorsville.

A man by the name of John Tilly also fell a victim to Bill Parker's vengeance, and was savagely murdered in the following manner: Tilly had been scouting for some time, and one of his twin children was taken violently ill, and was not expected to live; he had come to the house to see his sick child, and was nursing it in his lap when Parker and his gang of murderers rode up to his house. He laid his child down, and went out in the yard and surrendered, when Parker drew out his pistol and shot at him, giving him a severe wound in the head. He was now convinced that they intended to kill him, and asked them only to allow him a few minutes to pray. But they returned him no answer, and continued to shoot at him. The poor fellow now turned to run, but he soon fell to the ground, his body having been pierced through with ten balls. His wife now ran toward her murdered husband, screaming and crying with wild and frantic agony, when one of these incarnate devils seized hold of his gun and knocked her down by the side of her dead husband. His little children cried and begged for their father all the time, but as well might they have raised their tiny hands and feeble voices to calm the raging storm in its mad career, as to endeavor to stop this gang, of rebel demons in their bloody work of murder. After waiting until their victim had breathed his last, these man-slayers went on their way laughing at the terrible misery they had left behind them, and looking forward in search of more human blood.

They next met with three men, who were entire strangers to them, on the Laurel Creek, some six miles from Taylors-ville. They at once captured these men, and, after tying their hands behind their backs, they then tied them all three together. They then marched them on for a short distance, and stopped and shot them down in the woods, and rode carelessly on, leaving the bodies of their murdered victims to be consumed by the buzzards and hogs. The bodies of these men were found, several days after they were killed, by some men who were scouting in the mount-ains. When they approached the place where their bodies were lying, a gang of hogs were devouring them, and they did not know that the hogs were eating human flesh until they went up to the place where they were fighting over the remains of these poor murdered men. The men who found their bodies proceeded to search in their pockets, thinking that they might find something by which they would be enabled to identify them; but they found nothing but a small Bible in one of their pockets, in which the name of its former owner was written. The man's name that was found written in the Bible was Lafter. He was a Methodist preacher from North Carolina, and he and his companions were endeavoring to get through the lines when they were unfortunately captured by the rebels in Johnson County. The men who accidentally found their remains buried the parts of their bodies that had not been devoured by the hogs. They will rest quietly, in the profound stillness of their lonely graves, until the loud trump of the Archangel shall sound, when they will rise to meet their infamous murderers at the bar of the great Judge of the universe, "who seeth not as man seeth, and who can not look upon sin with the least degree of allowance."

In the month of November, 1864, the home guards of Johnson County captured a man by the name of William Church, who was a conscript, and was scouting in the mountains at the time he was caught. They made him run before their horses for about a mile, through the creeks, branches, and mud-holes, when they halted, and told him they were going to kill him. He commenced begging them to spare his life, and told them that he would immediately go into the service of the Southern army if they would not kill him. But as well might he have attempted to stay the earthquake in its desolating march, as to have attempted, by any sort of piteous importunity, to dissuade his murderers from taking his life. One of his merciful captors replied to him, "I do not wish to guard you, and, therefore, I think it would be the best policy to kill you." Another one of them said to him, "You shall be killed, for I want your clothes. I should consider myself at any time to be well paid for killing a Lincolnite by getting his hat and boots." This poor supplicating prisoner was now convinced of the hardened and reckless character of the ruffians into whose hands he had fallen; he knew that they intended to kill him, and he fell upon his knees and commenced praying. One of the rebels then raised his gun and shot him while he was on his knees. The gun was held so close to his body that his clothes were badly burned where the bullet struck him; and when he was found, the buttons that had been on his shirt and vest were lying loose upon his breast just where they had been burned off of his clothes. The

N 2

fiend who shot him took his hat, coat, and boots as a fee for killing him.

The foregoing are but a few out of very many similar cases of horrible murders which were perpetrated upon innocent men by the rebel home guards of Johnson County. I could extend this chapter much farther by relating the sickening details of a number of other foul and horrid murders, where men were unfortunately captured and shockingly massacred by the base and vile rebel monsters who styled themselves "the home guards of Johnson County." But I presume the reader is already tired of perusing the history of such monstrous human depravity as was displayed by the base and infamous rebels who participated in the terrible murders which I have alluded to in the present chapter. I will therefore refrain from pursuing the disagreeable subject any farther.

CHAPTER XXXV.

DURING the summer and fall of 1864, not less than one hundred dwelling-houses were burned, belonging to the Union people of Carter and Johnson Counties, and the most of them were occupied by the families of men who were serving as soldiers in the Federal army at the time their houses were burned, who had not seen their homes for a number of months. Old Bill Parker was at the head of all this dreadful mischief. The lower part of Carter and Johnson Counties were thronged with women and children who had been driven away from their homes, and all their property destroyed by this old miscreant. Many of these poor women made their way through the lines, as they had been rendered perfectly destitute by the destruction of their houses and all their household property, while many others wandered about the country, enduring all the privations and intense suffering which starvation and nakedness could impose, without a home to go to; and, indeed, these poor women were afraid to go near their old places of abode, for they seemed to be in as great a dread of Parker as if he had been a ravenous tiger that had been let loose in the country for the purpose of destroying men, women, and children. They had not a bed to lie down on, for every thing which they could call their own had been destroyed when they were driven away from their homes, and their houses burned to ashes. They would often say, while the tears were streaming from their eyes, "If Bill

Parker was away, we could go back to our friends." His end was now drawing near; in fact, it now amounted to an absurdity for the Union men in the country to think about permitting him to live any longer than could possibly be avoided, for there was not a day passed but what some poor Union man was killed by himself or some of his men. He was now frequently heard to boast that he had killed twelve old Union men himself, and said that he would kill twelve more if he could find them! He called himself "Brave Bill Parker!" But no real and genuine bravery ever took up its abode in the black heart of this despicable wretch. He was nothing more than a base and cowardly assassin, who at all times shrank back from danger when he thought that his own personal safety was in jeopardy.

Old Parker was always well guarded by a set of vile, mercenary scoundrels, who followed after him as the jackal follows the lion, for the purpose of participating with him in his feasts of blood, for he was now in constant expectation of being killed, on account of the many horrid crimes of which he had been guilty. It was very hard to get a chance to kill him, on account of the heavy guard which he always kept about him, and the men who were scouting in the mountains, being too weak to attack him openly, resolved to bushwhack him, as the safest plan of ridding the country of such a terrible scoundrel; and a number of men took their positions on several occasions for the purpose of completing this design, but when an opportunity would offer for them to shoot him their hearts would fail them. At length, in their extremity, they came to me, and requested me to aid them in seeking the destruction of their dreadful foe. How many Union citizens I have heard exclaim, "I would freely give all I possess in this world if this monster was killed!" And the women would also say, " Our husbands are far away, engaged in the service of their country as soldiers in the Federal army, and we are driven away from our homes, and our houses burned down, and all our property destroyed. If Bill Parker was killed, the balance of his adherents would not be so bad!"

All the old and feeble men who entertained Union sentiments, and who had not already been murdered, had left the section of country which was most constantly cursed by his presence. I at once determined to assist the men who were scouting in the mountains to get rid of this old blood-thirsty tyrant; but, the worst of all, there were but few guns and very little ammunition in the country. However, in spite of every difficulty, I concluded to take him alive, and convey him through the lines and deliver him up to the Federal authorities. This I knew would be hard to do ; but I disliked the idea of killing him secretly, without letting him know who it was that was assaulting him and why it was done. There were ten men in the company who formed the conspiracy to take old Parker's life. We armed ourselves as well as we could, and went forth upon our mission to rid the world of one of the vilest and most reckless scoundrels that ever walked upon the face of the earth in the upright form of man.

When we arrived in the section of country where he lived, we proceeded to waylay the road along which he usually traveled for five days and nights before we got to see him. Two of the men who belonged to our party pretended to know him well, while I knew nothing about him only from description, and, in consequence of this, I thought that I might be deceived; for I had frequently been informed that he made it a point to change his clothes every day, and also to ride a different horse, the reason of which was, that he no doubt expected to be bushwhacked, and wished to guard against it as much as he possibly could.

Rebel soldiers and home guards passed the place every day where we were concealed, but none of them answered to the description of Parker. On the fourth day a buggy, containing a lady and gentleman, passed along, and some of the men declared that it was Parker who was in the buggy, and wished very much to fire at the lump, and kill the man and woman both. But this I would not allow to be done. Directly after the buggy passed on, a parcel of soldiers came riding along the road, and a single man on horseback was riding some distance behind them. Some of our party now declared that this man who was riding by himself behind the soldiers was Parker without any doubt, and that the soldiers who were riding before him were his men. This I could not believe, for this man did not at all fill the description that had been given to me in regard to his personal appearance. When this man rode up I would not allow any of the men to interrupt him, and he passed on. Some of the men now became angry and discouraged, and saying that I would not permit them to capture Parker if he should come along, they took their guns, and forthwith left the company. This caused our little company to be reduced down considerably; but I did not regard that, for I had come to capture Parker, and therefore I did not want any person else in his place.

At length, on the fifth day, just about twelve o'clock, a small company of soldiers passed along, and some distance behind them we observed a man riding along by himself. As he approached a little nearer, I concluded at once that this was Parker without any doubt whatever. I now stationed the men at several different stands along the side of the road, and, taking one of the men with me, we advanced very near the road where I designed waiting until he rode up, when I intended to jump into the road just ahead of him, and seize his horse by the bridle in true robber style when he calls on the traveler to "stand and deliver." I felt quite sure that he would at once surrender, for I never knew a cruel man to be a brave man. Cruelty and cowardice are inseparable concomitants, for they always go hand in hand. Parker came on, and passed by the first lot of men whom I had stationed near the road, and was approaching the second sentinels, when the first and second guards fired at him simultaneously, hitting his horse, when, instead of coming on towai _ __e, he wheeled about, and started on the back track. Every gun was immediately let loose after him, and he was seen once to lean forward in his saddle, which we viewed as a plain indication that some of our balls had struck him. The horse bore Parker on for several hundred yards, when all at once the animal fell down in the road, and, when we went up to him, he was lying dead in the road, but Parker was gone. But when we started toward a thicket near by, we found his coat, which had several bullet-holes in it, but we could find no trace of Parker.

We could not hunt for him long, for his men soon came hurrying back, and at once commenced searching through every thicket for their missing leader, but he was nowhere to be found. His followers continued to search for him for several days, but their efforts to find him proved entirely fruitless. As no trace of him could be found, the rebels came to the conclusion that those who had killed him must have carried off his dead body, or that they had captured him alive and had conducted him away. If they had known it, we were just as ignorant in regard to his fate as they were. His ultimate fate being involved in such doubt and uncertainty, I thought that some of his rebel friends had found him and concealed him, to prevent any farther assault from being made on him.

A period of two months had elapsed before his fate was fully known, and then it was disclosed in the following manner: The skeleton of a man was found about three miles from the place where we made the attack upon him. When he was found he was lying with his face on the ground, and the most of his clothes were still entirely whole. The pockets in his pants being searched, it was immediately found to be Parker, without any farther doubt. A quantity of chewed bark was found upon the ground where his stomach had lain and rotted, and the knees of his pants were entirely worn through, plainly indicating that he had crawled upon his knees for a considerable distance. From every appearance, he must have lived some four or five days after he had been shot. He was found about a mile from the house of Jacob Wagner, who was a stanch old rebel. Some of Wagner's family said, after old Parker's skeleton was found, that they remembered very distinctly of having heard the voice of some person calling and hallooing on several occasions in the direction where his skeleton was found just about the time when he was first missing, which they were unable to account for, but they now felt assured that it was Parker whom they heard hallooing and calling at the time referred to. It is quite probable that in his last agonies he called for his old friend and fellow-rebel, Jake Wagner, to his assistance, knowing that

"A fellow-feeling makes us wondrous kind."

That he died a most miserable death no person has ever presumed to doubt, which was a just reward for his monstrous crimes. After old Parker was killed, the times were not so bad for the old men and the helpless women of Johnson County, for his followers in crime either must have looked upon the fate of Parker as a warning to them, or else they were not so thoroughly dead to the feelings of humanity as to perpetrate the awful deeds of crime which had rendered their leader so notorious.

CHAPTER XXXVI.

It was in the month of September, 1864, when the loyal people of East Tennessee, who had suffered long and patiently under the dreadful yoke of rebel tyranny, hailed with delight the arrival of General Gillem's brigade of Tennessee Cavalry, whose object was to rid the upper counties of rebel soldiers. But this was not effected as easily as it had been expected it could be done, as the rebels did not intend to abandon a section of country which yielded such immense supplies to their resources without a struggle.

Gillem's brigade, composed of the 8th, 9th, and 13th Regiments of Tennessee Cavalry, in their advance through East Tennessee, found a force opposed to them equal in number and sometimes greatly superior to their own; and many of the brave sons of East Tennessee were destined to be offered as a sacrifice upon the altar of their country before the old starry banner could again be permitted to wave in triumph over her mountains and valleys, and proclaim liberty to her oppressed citizens.

Many scenes were enacted in East Tennessee, which, in a less exciting and critical period of the war, would have created more sensation; but they were now almost lost sight of in the more dazzling and exciting engagements of grand armies in different parts of the country. I hope, however, that the reader will indulge me in noticing a few of the movements of this little brigade of cavalry commanded by General Gillem.

JOHN MORGAN'S RAIDERS.

On the 30th of September, 1864, we find the soldiers in this brigade quietly in camp at Bull's Gap, little suspecting that the renowned General Morgan, with a force superior to their own, was advancing toward them, confident of obtaining a certain and easy victory. A dark and rainy night approaches. The vigilant commander of the Union forces ascertained that Morgan's command had arrived at Greenville, eighteen miles distant from a portion of his force that occupied a position in the direction of Bull's Gap, and had gone into camp. The 13th Regiment of Tennessee Cavalry, commanded by Colonel Ingerton, received orders at eleven o'clock on the night of the 3d of September to get in rear of Morgan's advance, which order was successfully accomplished by daylight on the morning of the 4th of September. Ten companies were formed in ambush about one mile from Greenville, to await the attack of the remaining part of the brigade, which was moving up the main road. The rebel dispatch-bearer was now captured, and it was thereby ascertained that Morgan and his staff were in Greenville, at the house of Mrs. Williams, some distance from and in the rear of his main force. Captain Wilcox (who was afterward promoted to major) was at once directed to take charge of the remaining two companies of the 13th Regiment, and go into Greenville and endeavor to effect the capture of Morgan and his staff.

A few random shots which were fired at the rebels in the streets warned Morgan of approaching danger, and also aroused his slumbering troops, but it was too late to save their chieftain from his impending fate. Regardless of the shot and shell which were thrown from the rebel batteries, the daring Captain Wilcox surrounded the house and lot of Mrs. Williams and captured Morgan's staff. Morgan, perceiving the imminent peril which now threatened him in every direction, fled to the garden, and concealed himself among the thick clusters of vines which overspread the summer-house, but he was soon discovered and shot by private Andrew Campbell (who was afterward promoted to lieutenant), of Company G, 13th Tennessee Cavalry. When Morgan's staff officers were all captured, a man came in who said that a man had been killed in the garden. One of the staff officers desired to see who it was, and requested the guard to go with him. When he approached the body tears commenced flowing down his cheeks, and he exclaimed, "That is John Morgan."

Being violently assailed by a superior force of Morgan's command, Captain Wilcox withdrew in good order, carrying with him the body of Morgan and forty prisoners, including his staff officers. In the mean time the main rebel forces were attacked some distance below Greenville by General Gillem, who succeeded most admirably in routing and driving them back in the utmost confusion, while their advance, coming upon the part of the 13th Regiment in ambush, received a most terrible and galling fire, which killed and wounded quite a number of the rebels as they ran. The main column now turned suddenly, and in great confusion, into the woods on the left side of the main road, the companies of the 13th Regiment who were in ambush being on the right side of the road. Colonel Ingerton, hearing the firing in the direction of Greenville, and entertaining fears in regard to the safety of Wilcox, allowed the rebels to escape while he hastened with the main part of the regiment to the assistance of the small force which had been sent into Greenville under Wilcox.

The entire brigade had now moved up, and when General Gillem saw the body of Morgan, he waved his hat around and cheered the 13th Tennessee Cavalry with the greatest

enthusiasm, while the soldiers, as they passed along, seemed to be perfectly wild with delight, as one after another would exclaim, "Morgan is killed;" and "Charge the
rebels," was the constant cry of the soldiers. Morgan's
force now made a stand on College Hill, a short distance
east of Greenville. The Federal forces under General Gillem moved on up the road, and a sharp fight occurred,
which resulted in the complete rout of the rebels and the
capture of their artillery-wagons, together with upward of
two hundred prisoners. This was the end of the romantic
career of John Morgan, who had, perhaps, done as much
real injury to the Union cause as any one man in the Confederate service.

The Federal troops now moved on up as far as Carter
Station, in Carter County, when it was ascertained that
General Vaughn had reorganized Morgan's old command,
to which had also been added the rebel force under the
command of Colonel Palmer, of North Carolina; consequently, General Gillem fell back to Bull's Gap, and then
to New Market, leaving Vaughn in full possession of the
upper counties, and as far on down the country as Morristown, at which place he established his head-quarters.
Scouting parties of the rebels would now attack the Federal pickets every night, and annoy them all they possibly
could. This operation was continued until the 27th day of
October, 1864. General Gillem, having learned the strength
and position of the enemy, and believing, moreover, notwithstanding the superiority in numbers of the enemy, that,
by making the attack, he could succeed in vanquishing
them, he accordingly moved his forces in the direction of
Morristown, where the rebels were reported to be in position. He soon met a small reconnoitering party of the rebels, who stubbornly opposed his advance. But steadily

driving them back, he encamped on the night of the 27th of October within a few miles of Morristown.

Early on the morning of the 28th of October his column was in motion; the enemy was now in considerable force in front, but they could not stop the advance of Gillem's brigade until they came in sight of Vaughn's entire command, drawn up in line of battle immediately on the opposite side of the town. The 13th Regiment was drawn up in column of companies, and ordered to charge with drawn sabres, which they did in splendid style, the 8th and 9th Regiments being held in reserve. The shock of the sabre-charge of the 13th at once disconcerted the rebels and broke their lines, and the 8th and 9th being now ordered to move forward, rushed onward with a loud yell and with drawn sabres. The rebels, now confused and panic-stricken, broke their ranks and fled in every direction. They were closely pursued as far as Bull's Gap, when the brigade discontinued the chase, and returned to Morristown, having captured the artillery and wagons belonging to the rebels, together with some two hundred prisoners.

General Vaughn and his men had been for a long time saying that they would take Knoxville, and their prediction was now accomplished, for Gillem sent their wagons and teams, together with their drivers, who were made to continue at their posts, and the prisoners, all on to Knoxville together. The Union soldiers would say to them, " You are now going to take Knoxville sure enough." The rebels would answer that they believed it, but they would take Knoxville on this occasion in quite a different way to what they had expected.

The brigade returned to Morristown, and went into camp. The loss on the Federal side was very slight. The ambulance was sent out to bring in the dead who had fallen

FIGHT WITH VAUGHN'S REBELS.

pon the field of battle, and fifty rebels who had been killed
rere brought in on that day. The next day the search was
ontinued, and thirty more were brought in, besides many
rho were badly wounded.

When the Federal troops fell back from Carter Station
n the 1st of November, 1864, I was with them; and al-
hough I did not then belong to the service, I engaged in
he Morristown fight as though I had been a regular soldier.
After the battle I again returned to the counties of Carter
nd Johnson, to enlist recruits for the 13th Regiment. I had
njoyed myself finely while I was assisting to defeat and
un the rebels at Morristown, and now, unfortunately, the
ext race was to be one in which I had to work in the lead,
nd which I can assure the reader I did not enjoy half so well.

After my arrival among my native hills, having, as usual,
large number of letters to circulate, I proceeded at once on
ıy mission to distribute the letters, and also to enlist recruits
or the 13th Regiment. My first place of destination was
he Doe River Cove, in Carter County, as I had a large pack-
ge for the widow Campbell, who had two sons in the 13th
Regiment. I felt very much troubled in my mind as I went
long, for which I was altogether unable satisfactorily to
ccount. But I have since often thought that it was an
ıstinctive melancholy foreboding of my approaching trouble
rhen my life was to be placed in imminent peril. At one
ime I almost concluded to turn back; but having generally
ıade it a rule never to begin any thing without accomplish-
ıg it, and nothing urging me to turn back except my mel-
ncholy feelings, I went on, and soon overtook two of my
couting friends, who were *en route* for the same place that
was. My depressed spirits were now somewhat dispersed,
nd we soon arrived near the house where I designed
topping.

O

I told my companious that I would call Mrs. Campbell up on a ridge which was close to her house, and give her the package that I had for her, where I could watch for any rebel soldiers that might be prowling about. To this proposition my friends objected, saying that they were going to the house, and that I must go along with them, as they did not think there would be any danger in so doing, for there had been no rebels in the cove for three weeks. But I still protested against the proposition of going to the house, and they started on, leaving me alone. I sat on the hill for some time, looking up and down the road for rebels, but I could not see any person stirring about. Having torn a rent in my pants, I now concluded to go down to the house and have it mended, and hasten away, as I had many places yet to go to. After taking another observation up and down the road for rebel soldiers, and seeing none, I proceeded to the house. There was a clump of spruce, pine, and laurel bushes standing between the house and the road, and not fifty yards from the house, which completely obscured the part of the road running immediately behind it from my view. This thicket was full of rebel soldiers, who had doubtless therein concealed themselves for the purpose of watching my movements. But having failed to discover them, I went into the house, where I found my companions. I at once called for a needle and thread, and while one of the family was getting it for me, I went to the door to look out for danger, as I was altogether out of my true element whenever I was in a house, and I now felt restless and uneasy. When I looked out at the door, oh, horror of horrors! I saw a number of rebel soldiers not forty yards from the house coming as hard as their horses could carry them, with their guns and pistols drawn. Some of the family said, "Get in the cellar, and we can hide you." But on this occasion I did not approve of the suggestion, and jumped out at the door in an instant, and started as rapidly as my legs could carry me for the woods. The rebels now commenced firing their guns and pistols in good earnest. When I sprang over the fence surrounding the house, the bullets were singing an awful dirge all around me. One ball struck the top rail on the fence, and scattered the splinters in my face. By this time my two companions were with me, running as eagerly and as desperately as if there was to be a valuable prize awarded at the end of the race to the successful competitor in the terrible contest. We had about three hundred yards to run before we could get to the woods, and the worst of it was, there was no undergrowth in the woods that we could hide in, even if we should succeed in getting there. On came the rebels, hallooing, " Halt, halt, halt!" and shooting at us all the time. We had not run very far until both my companions were captured. One of them was captured immediately before me, and the other one just behind me, and how I ever did escape will always be a source of astonishment to me, for their horses were all around me.

When I started from the house I had dropped my pistols and belt, but I held on to my sixteen-shooting rifle. The odds against me were so great that I immediately saw it would be perfectly simple for me to endeavor to defend myself by fighting, and therefore I determined, if possible, to save myself by flight. I knew that they would murder me in a most shameful and ignominious manner if they should succeed in capturing me. I therefore resolved that I would much rather be killed while endeavoring to make my escape, than to be taken alive by these infamous scoundrels, who, I had no doubt, would take the greatest delight in putting me to the utmost torture. I therefore strained every nerve to save myself, for I thought that, while I had

life, I had a hope of saving it. I could not entertain the
idea for a moment of being caught and shot in that mountain by these brutal soldiers, who had no more mercy for a
Union man than they had for a sheep-killing dog, and I
well knew that they would rather kill me than kill a rat-
tlesnake. Summoning all my strength, I sprang out of the
crowd which surrounded me on every side, and ran up
a steep bank, while they were firing at me continually.
One of them exclaimed, "Knock him down with your
gun!" and another one hallooed, "Run your horses over
him!" But I got away from that crowd, and ran on up
the ridge, where I was met by another squad of soldiers
that I had not before seen. I was now almost exhausted.
They began to charge on me with their horses, and shooting at every jump. I still thought that my life was too
dear to be surrendered to these ruffians, and I determined
to die rather than surrender! Making another desperate
effort, I suddenly turned from them, and ran on up the
ridge. But I saw that I would be taken if I continued on
in that direction, for they were now so close on me that
they frequently tried to knock me down with their guns,
and I could feel the air pass my back as it was driven
against me by the motion of their guns when they would
strike at me so violently, but, as good luck would have it,
none of them hit me. A bullet now passed through my
clothes across my back, cutting the skin a little, but it did
not hurt me; and now several other bullets passed through
my clothes without touching my body. I now changed
my course, and dodged past the men and horses, and ran
down a steep declivity into a hollow, where their horses
could not follow me very well. The rebels immediately
dismounted and opened another fire on me, and at the
same time some of them ran around to head me as I endeavored to get out of the hollow.

They now made the third charge on me. I was now so perfectly tired down that I could scarcely move one foot after the other; but I could not think of falling into the hands of my blood-thirsty enemies while I had any breath left in my body. I started on up the hollow, running with all the strength that I had left, and the rebels after me, crying as loud as they could, "Shoot him! shoot him! Halt! halt!" But I thought that they had already told me to halt often enough to know that I had no idea of obeying them while life continued to animate my body; and their incessant shooting so far had availed them nothing, for a kind and beneficent Providence had protected me from injury by their bullets. And, while life shall last, I shall always thank and adore my heavenly Father for His protective care which was thrown around me in that awful hour, and shielded and saved my life.

As I struggled on up the hill, I caught hold of every bush, log, and stump that came in my way, to assist me in getting along in my devious pathway. The rebels were now pursuing me on foot, and, by exerting all my remaining energies, I soon outstripped them. They began to think, I presume, that I would get away in spite of them, and all of them fired another volley at me. The bullets fell around me like hail-stones, cutting the saplings, and tearing the dirt up at my feet, and making the leaves fly as if a hurricane had been passing through the forest; but I hurried on as rapidly as I could get along upon my weary limbs, while the rebels were yelling and shooting after me like a wild and infuriate gang of Indians. They continued shooting and hallooing at me until I got about three hundred yards up the mountain. I was now so completely tired down that I did not believe that I could go much farther. This was the first opportunity that I had during the race to shoot at them, and I turned twice round to fire at them. Throughout the whole fearful race I held on to my sixteen-shooter, thinking that when I could run no farther, if my enemies should continue to pursue me, that I would then stop and sell my life out to them as dearly as possible. But when I made the attempt to shoot, I found that I was so nearly dead that I could not hold my gun up. I now got behind some rocks that I thought would serve me for a defense, and just at this time the rebels fired their last volley at me, and one of their bullets struck and passed through the leg of one of my boots, and stopped when it struck against the flesh on my leg. If this ball had not been so far spent when it passed through the leg of my boot, it would certainly have broken my leg.

I do not believe that I could now have run any farther if the rebels had continued to pursue me. I now looked back, and the glorious sight at once met my observation of seeing the rebels returning down the mountain, having finally given up the chase in despair. I immediately laid down on the ground, not able to breathe; my heart was beating as if it would burst out of my bosom, from the terrible excitement and exertion which I endured while endeavoring to make my escape, and my throat and lungs were entirely dry. I still had my canteen around my neck, in which I generally carried water or brandy, and at this time there was nearly a gill of brandy, which I happened to think about. I had barely enough of strength left to raise the canteen to my mouth. I swallowed enough of the brandy to wet my throat, and I really believe that it saved my life. I was yet unable to breathe, and with another effort I turned up the canteen again and swallowed a small portion of brandy. I pulled off my vest and shirt, and fell down behind the rock again. I thought that I would die upon that mountain alone, where no kind friend could wipe the cold sweat from my brow in my last expiring moments, but I thought that would be far better than to have been horribly massacred by the vile desperadoes who had been so long and so anxiously thirsting for my blood.

I laid my head upon a rock, being almost entirely unable to breathe, believing that the few remaining sands in my hour-glass of life were rapidly running out. I waited for some minutes, in constant expectation that the shaft of death would soon put out the quivering light of my earthly existence, and precipitate my soul upon the great ocean of eternity. But the summons did not come, and I still lived. I did not think that a man could be so near the door of death and recover his physical energies. It seemed that my work was not yet done. It is true there were very many poor Union men who were still scouting through the mountains, anxiously waiting for me to conduct them through the lines, and for this purpose I thought that my life had been miraculously spared.

After lying behind the rock for several hours, I got up and put on my shirt and vest, and it being late in the evening, I crawled into a large hollow log, where I endeavored to compose myself to rest as well as I could. Late in the night a hard storm of wind and rain came on, and the rain leaked in upon me so badly that I crawled out of the log and sat down by the side of a tree until morning. I now started down the mountain toward the house from which I had been chased by the rebels on the previous day, and when I got near the foot of the ridge I called out, and one of the girls who lived there immediately came to me. I told her where I had dropped my pistols, and she at once went to the place where I had thrown them down when I was running, where she found them and brought them to me, together with my breakfast. Some one of the family had also found my coat, and had taken care of it, and presented it to me. I had lost nothing in the race that the rebels succeeded in getting. I paid the girl seven dollars for her trouble in bringing my breakfast to me, and returned home through the woods, being very well satisfied with my adventures for one day and night. It was a long time before I recovered from the terrible effects of the race which I was forced to take on this occasion by the base and infamous rebels who labored so ardently to take my life. If I should live to be an old man, the terrible scene which I passed through on this day can never be effaced from my memory; for my remarkable escape on this ever-memorable occasion will always serve to afford to my own mind the most incontestable evidence that "truth is stranger than fiction."

The rebels who gave me this dreadful race were the home guards, and some other soldiers from Johnson County.

CHAPTER XXXVII.

In the month of December, 1864, a most infamous scoundrel by the name of B. H. Duvall, who took his first lessons in rebellion in the city of Louisville, Kentucky, was sent into Carter and Johnson Counties with a company of reckless soldiers, and it was the 1st of January, 1865, before I could get my company ready to start through the lines. The last of November and all of the month of December was very cold, and the mountains were full of snow and ice, which made it an awful task for men to scout in the mountains; for they could not come within three miles of their homes, without running the risk of being captured and killed by some of the villains who were controlled and counseled by Duvall. This gang of thieves did nothing but rob houses and search the country for Union men, to kill them in the most barbarous manner. So perfect had they become in the business of house-robbing that nothing scarcely could be concealed from them. The poor women in the country had to take their few articles of wearing apparel, and all other articles that they wished to hide from these rebel thieves, out of their houses, and conceal them in stumps and hollow logs. But these scoundrels soon became acquainted with this mode of operation, and every stump, old log, or bank of leaves which they found near a house was thoroughly searched, and not always without success. They would take women's dresses, and have shirts made out of them for their own use. They would also go to the Union men's houses and haul off their household property to Eliz-

O 2

abethton, and sell off the various articles to the highest bidder.

There is a place on Indian Creek, near the line between Carter and Sullivan Counties, which, in the polite phraseology of the rebels, was denominated "the bone-yard." This was the place where the rebels carried many of their prisoners to murder them. It is a lonely spot, surrounded by lofty hills, on the side of a ridge, where a small flat place had been formed by the fall of a large tree. Here they would conduct their prisoners and shoot them down, and would then go on to the first house and tell the Union people, "if they would take a wagon and go to the bone-yard, they would find another dead dog ready to be hauled off." The Union citizens would often see them conducting prisoners to this spot, without having the least power to render them any assistance, hallooing and uttering rude jokes, as if they had been going to one of their drunken frolics. Their victim, with downcast head, and with his hands tied behind him, would walk dejectedly on before them, while his wife, and probably a few other female friends, would follow on behind, exhibiting the greatest distress imaginable.

This was exactly the manner in which they treated a man by the name of Henry Archer, who was an innocent man, and all his neighbors united in giving him the character of a "good man." He was afflicted with fits at times, which prevented him from going through the lines, and, consequently, he endeavored to save himself by hiding in a camp in the mountains. He was betrayed by some person, and his camp was pointed out to Duvall's men, who at once proceeded to capture him; they said they had hard work to get to his camp, having to crawl on their hands and knees through a very dense laurel thicket, where his camp was situated, and he not expecting that his camp would be discovered, was captured without any difficulty. He was then conveyed to Elizabeton, where he was confined in jail for several days. His distressed wife, with a young child in her arms, followed him on to Elizabethton to intercede for his life; but, alas, her interposition proved to be altogether unavailing, for her tears and sorrowful entreaties totally failed to excite any feeling of sympathy in the wicked heart of Duvall. He was at length taken out of jail and handcuffed, and the rebels drove him on before them to the bone-yard as if he had been a dumb brute. Just before starting he took leave of his wife and child, bidding them farewell with the utmost tenderness, asking his wife at the same time not to follow him. He kissed his little child, and the company started with him, while his poor wife followed on after them with suppressed cries and doleful lamentations. One of the brutal soldiers said to her, "That is beautiful music for our march," and then they all commenced cawing like buzzards, which intimated that the buzzards would soon be picking the prisoner's bones.

When they got near the place of slaughter they ordered his wife not to advance any farther, and told her if she did they would shoot her. She stopped, and directly afterward she heard the report of the gun that was fired at her husband, after which she got several other women to go with her to the place where he had been murdered.

When these ruffians got to the place where they designed killing their victim he asked them to give him a little time to pray, which request they allowed. He knelt down and offered up a most fervent prayer. He first prayed to the Lord to take care of his wife and helpless child, and assist her in supporting the burden of grief to which she had been subjected. He then prayed for his murderers, that they

DUVALL MURDERING UNION MEN.

might be forgiven for what they were about to do. His prayer was so affecting that all of the rebel murderers, with the exception of one, were melted to tears, and turned away, saying they could not kill him after hearing him pray for them as he did. They permitted him to pray as long as he desired, and when he arose, a hardened wretch by the name of Foster shot him twice, and then stripped his coat and boots off of him. They all then left his body lying where it had fallen. His wife and two or three female friends now went to the place where he was lying, and her demonstrations of grief were perfectly heart-rending. She took off her skirt, and after tearing it open, wrapped him in it; that night he was hauled to a barn, where he was left until the next morning, the people being afraid to suffer his body to lay in their houses. The next day a few friends removed his body, and consigned it to its last resting-place.

John Smith, of Carter County, was captured by some of Duvall's men on the 1st of January, 1865. He was captured in the road, in what is called "the Lyon Settlement," in Carter County, by Jacob Nave and a few other rebel soldiers. Nave was a citizen of Carter County, and had lived a neighbor to Smith all his life; and although Smith had never done him any harm, he assisted in taking him to the jail in Elizabethton, and abused him shamefully on the road. After detaining him in jail a short time, he was handcuffed and taken to the bone-yard, guarded by four of the most outrageous villains that belonged to Duvall's command; they were as destitute of pity as if they had no souls to be saved or a hell to shun. In fact, they seemed to rejoice at the sight of human suffering, and one of the party, whose name was Motte, said that he would much rather shoot a Union man than a squirrel, that he loved to see them jump when the ball struck them. What mercy could Smith have expected at the hands of such men? In vain he implored them to permit him to see his wife and children before they murdered him. His request was abruptly denied, and he was ordered at once to kneel and receive the ball if he did not wish to be shot standing up. He then got down upon •his knees, begging them not to shoot him but one time. This request was granted, but they took particular care to make one shot answer their purpose, for the ball passed very near or through his heart, and he fell upon his face, and died instantly.

They turned him over on his back, and seeing a small gutta-percha ring on one of his fingers, attempted to take it off; but his finger was so much swollen the ring could not be gotten off, when Motte deliberately took his knife out of his pocket and cut off the finger, took the ring, and placed it on his own finger, where he continued to wear it during the time that he remained in Carter County. They now left him, and the Union people removed his body at night and buried it. Smith was a good citizen, and no charge had been preferred against him, only that he was a Union man, and had been scouting to keep out of the rebel army. At the time he was captured he was engaged in getting up a small company to go with him through the lines.

A short time before Smith was murdered by Duvall's men, a company of rebels from Johnson County, under the command of a notorious scoundrel by the name of Clifton Blevins, made a trip into Carter County. They murdered several men in a most brutal manner before they arrived at Elizabethton, where they tarried all night, and started back the next morning toward Johnson County by the way of Stony Creek. Before starting, however, they secured the services of old Ike Nave, a violent rebel who lived a short distance from Elizabethton, to go with them and point out the Union men's houses, as he was well acquainted all through the country where these rebel thieves and murderers desired to go. When they got near the house of William Blevins, he happened to see them approaching, and immediately ran and concealed himself in the bushes under the steep bank of the creek. When they arrived at the house they searched it from garret to cellar. At length Blevins was found by old Ike Nave, and dragged from his hiding-place by his savage and vindictive enemies. Nave ordered him to turn his back around to receive the deadly bullet, and then placed his finger upon the spot where he wished Blevius to be shot. One of the fiendish gang of desperadoes then raised his gun and fired, and another poor Union man's soul suddenly winged its flight into the dim regions of the eternal world.

These murderers then started on in their desolating march, shooting at Union men as if they had been wild beasts, and robbing their houses in a most shameful manner. When they got a few hundred yards from Blevins's house, several men saw them, and plunged into a pond of water in order to effect their escape. The rebels fired at them, and one of their balls struck one of the men while he was swimming in the water, giving him a severe wound, but he finally recovered from it.

CHAPTER XXXVIII.

On the 19th of November, 1863, a most notorious and miserable scoundrel by the name of Witcher landed in Carter County from the State of Virginia, having under his command four hundred men, who were as mean and reckless as the devil himself could have desired them to be. I think that their leader's name was either James or Samuel Witcher, but I do not know which was his correct name. I wish his name to be correctly known, and justly execrated, for a more blood-thirsty and desperate villain never disgraced the world's history! They camped the first night they came into Carter County near the Carter Station, and the next day-they moved on up Buffalo Creek to the Greasy Cove, and camped near the residence of Benjamin Swingle the next night. Witcher said that he and his men had come to give Carter and Johnson Counties a general overhauling. They were led on by a parcel of very bad rebel citizens living on Buffalo Creek, and also in the Greasy Cove, among whom I will mention Nathaniel Brown, Alfred Leslie, William Peoples, and his son, Madison Tennessee Peoples, whose infamous conduct inflicted a foul stigma upon the state whose name he bore. These men reported the people in the country as being all Lincolnites. The evening they reached the Greasy Cove, and the night following, several men were killed, and the next morning, still being conducted by these rebel citizens, this regiment of murderers set out for the Limestone Cove. They arrived first at the house of James and David Bell, who were strong Union men; and, to add fuel to the already furious flame that was burning so violently in the hearts of these rebels, a man by the name of John Bryant, from Wilkes County, North Carolina, had just stopped at Bell's house with fifty-seven men, whom he had enlisted as recruits, and was endeavoring to pilot them into my neighborhood in order to engage me to conduct them through the lines to the Federal army.

These men had traveled all the night before, and had stopped at Bell's house for the purpose of enjoying an hour's rest, obtain something to eat, and also to get information how to proceed in their journey, as they were all from North Carolina, and were strangers in East Tennessee. They were sitting under some trees in Bell's yard, not dreaming of any danger, while the family were preparing breakfast for them. The rebels, commanded by the aforesaid Witcher, suddenly came in sight, and the alarm was instantly given. The poor fellows tried to save themselves by flight, being closely pursued by the rebels, who were shooting at them and charging on them with their horses at a terrible rate.

There is a small valley leading from Bell's house to the mountain, and the fugitives ran into this valley, and would doubtless have succeeded in getting away in a piece of woods near the valley, if the rebels had not cut them off from it. The chase lasted about three quarters of a mile, and all of the men got away with the exception of eleven, ten of whom were killed, and one wounded, as they ran up the valley.

The first man who I shall mention as being killed was Calvin Cartrel. He was shot in the breast; and as he lay upon the ground, writhing in terrible agony of pain, he begged them not to kill him; but seeing that they were determined to take his life, he requested them to allow him a little time to pray. They abruptly denied his request, and at once commenced beating him with the butts of their guns until they knocked his brains out, and then thrust their bayonets through his lifeless body.

John Sparks was shot in the head with a musket ball, which completely tore the top of his head off, leaving his brains perfectly exposed.

Wiley Royal was shot in the shoulder and back, and when he fell to the ground, one of the rebel demons took a fence-stake and beat his head into the earth, breaking his arms and bruising his body in a shocking manner, while he continued to beg as long as he could speak for them to spare his life.

Elijah Gentry was shot in the breast, which killed him instantly. He had no time to implore for mercy at the hands of his murderers, which, of course, they would not have listened to, in their hot pursuit after his blood.

Jacob Lyons was shot in the breast, which immediately extinguished the flaming light of life. He fell into a creek, where he soon breathed his last, and his murderers left his body lying in the water.

B. Blackburn was shot in the shoulder, and, being badly wounded, he fell to the ground. The rebels then beat his brains out with clubs, broke his arms, and bruised his body in a terrible manner.

Preston Pruett was shot through the breast, which wounded him severely. He begged them to permit him to pray, and requested them to send word to his wife and children, and inform them in regard to his death. But he might as well have talked to the winds, for while he was speaking to them they knocked his brains out with the butts of their guns.

The rebel murderers now went back to the house, taking James Bell, who was an old bachelor, and considerably over the conscript age, away from the house about one hundred yards, where one of the rebels prepared to shoot him. When the old man perceived that the villain was going to shoot him, he ran up to the monster and placed his arm around his neck, which prevented him from shooting; but soon another rebel murderer ran up and shot him. The old man fell upon the ground, and his murderers caught hold of him and laid his head upon a rock. They then took another rock and beat his brains out with it; and not being yet content, they got rocks and threw them upon his body.

Mrs. Bell, the wife of David Bell, seeing they were going to murder her brother-in-law, went out and commenced interceding for him. Two of the ruffians approached her, and began to punch her with their guns, drove her back to the house, threatening to shoot her if she offered to speak again in his behalf.

William Sparks also belonged to the company of stampeders; but being sick, he was in the house when the excitement occurred in the yard, and asked Mrs. Bell to conceal him. She immediately raised a plank from the kitchen floor, and he crept under the kitchen, where he remained until the rebels had finished their bloody work, and returned to burn the house, which they first commenced by piling up clothes in the centre of the floor, and setting them on fire just over the cellar where the sick man had been concealed. The clothes not burning well enough, they procured a straw bed, and placing it on the floor, they put a chunk of fire into it; the smoke began to ascend in clouds, when they were compelled to go out into the front yard to obtain fresh air. There were two doors to the

MASSACRE OF UNION MEN.

kitchen, and the wind passing through, closed the door next to the rebels, which gave Sparks an opportunity to make his escape from the house. He crept out from the cellar through the smoke, and went through the back yard about ten steps from the house, and concealed himself under some dry weeds and vines in the garden, where he remained until the buildings were consumed, suffering intensely from the terrible heat of the fire.

The rebels now went up the valley among their murdered victims for the purpose of stripping them of their clothing. Miss Elizabeth Morrison, who lived in the neighborhood, and was at Bell's house during the whole time of the dreadful excitement, procured a lady's dress, took it to the garden where Sparks was concealed, and told him to put it on. She then gave him her own bonnet, which he put on, and thereby most admirably disguised his sex. She then told him to walk along slowly across the fields and go to her father's house, and she said to him, "When you get to the house, my father will conduct you to a place of safety. All of the family will at once know my bonnet, and that will furnish them sufficient evidence that you are not a traitor." Sparks went on as the kind young lady directed him, and was concealed and saved; but he had been so terribly frightened that he did not recover his proper faculties of mind for several days. The horrid scenes he witnessed on that dreadful day surely can never be erased from his memory until death shall have closed his earthly existence.

A man by the name of Madison had been badly wounded in the beginning of the affray, and the rebels, thinking he was dead, left him lying in the yard; and when the house was burning, some clothes were thrown on him, and saved him from any farther notice. When the rebels went off to rob the dead bodies of the men whom they had slaughtered,

Miss Morrison, Mrs. Bell, and one of her little boys, and a small girl, carried the wounded man off about one hundred and fifty yards. When they saw the rebels returning they laid him down, and started back to the house, stopping on their way back at a mill-branch to wash the blood off of their hands, which had got on them while they were carrying the wounded man.

The rebels came along, meeting them, and asked them where they had taken that man. Miss Morrison told them, and started on with Colonel Witcher toward the place where they had laid Madison down, begging eloquently for his life all the way. Witcher asked her if the wounded man wanted water. She told him he did. Witcher then told his men not to kill him, as he would soon be in hell any how.

The rebels now left him, and when they left the neighborhood Madison was carried to Thomas Green's house, which was close by, where he remained for four months until he recovered from his wound. He was then captured by the North Carolina Home Guards, his hat, boots, and coat were taken from him, and he was then made to walk barefooted through the snow to the town of Asheville, in North Carolina, where he was detained for four months, when he was released by the Yankees, and returned home.

A man by the name of Harris was wounded in the thigh of one of his legs, and in the knee of his other leg. He crawled to a log, and burrowed under the leaves, pulling some brush and a large "poke-bush" over him. Here he remained until the neighbors collected in the evening to look upon the scene of the dreadful slaughter and house-burning, when he called to them. They immediately went to him, assisted him in leaving his dreary abode, and kindly took care of him.

After the horrid massacre, the rebels returned to the smoking ruins of Bell's house, and exhibited the butts of their guns to the women, which were covered with the blood and the brains of their slaughtered victims up to the gun-locks. They also displayed their bloody bayonets, saying, "We are the fellows to kill Lincolnites and Yankees." They boasted amazingly, and seemed to be in the finest sort of spirits at the idea of having murdered a parcel of innocent and helpless men. After they had completed their work of murder and house-burning, they held a council with the rebel citizens, who told them that they were in a strong Union country; and for fifteen miles to the Watauga River, where the rebels were then going, these citizens told them they would pass through a section of country altogether inhabited by Union people.

The rebels determined to take no prisoners, but to kill all they captured, and this determination they strenuously adhered to; for when they arrived at the house of a man by the name of Commodore Slone, who was fifty-six years of age, they shot him down in his own yard. They shot him twice, and then run their bayonets through his body. Some of these fiends then struck him on the head with the butts of their guns until they mashed his head in a horrible manner. They went on to the house of William M'Kinney, where they found a man by the name of William Bird. They took him out of the house into the yard, and shot him twice in the breast. When Bird fell, they beat out his brains, and then went on in their bloody march, killing every man, old and young, that had the misfortune of falling into their hands, just because they had been represented as Lincolnites by a parcel of vile rebel citizens. Many men were badly wounded, but succeeded in making their escape by getting into the woods. When Witcher arrived at Elizabethton, like an accomplished and brutal murderer as he was, he boasted of the infamous exploit that he and his ruffian followers had killed twenty-one Union men in the course of one day and night.

Witcher and his gang of thieves and murderers left Carter County shortly after they perpetrated the outrages to which I have alluded, and I suppose they returned to their rebel associates in Virginia, to charm them with their eloquent details about the massacre of Union men in Carter County. The rebels in the State of Virginia, throughout the whole period of the rebellion, entertained the most malignant feelings of animosity toward the people of East Tennessee; and these feelings were practically exemplified by the infamous scoundrels who from time to time came into East Tennessee from that famous hot-bed of rebellion for the purpose of murdering Union men, burning their houses, and robbing their families. Carter County was the theatre wherein these vile and restless scoundrels enacted many of their bloody tragedies, which should ever brand them with an indelible mark of infamy. When Witcher left Carter County, he was soon succeeded by a base and despicable villain by the name of R. C. Bozen, who proved to be an exact counterpart to his black-hearted predecessor in every species of iniquity wherein the nature of man seems precisely to conform with that of an infuriate demon, counseled and tutored by the invisible monarch of the infernal regions. I will make a cursory reference in the following chapter to a few out of the many enormities which were perpetrated by Bozen and his band of murderers during their stay in Carter County. Let it be remembered that this scoundrel and his associates in crime were also from the State of Virginia.

CHAPTER XXXIX.

THE pugnacious and redoubtable Captain R. C. Bozen being a citizen of Grayson County, Virginia, at the commencement of the rebellion jumped headlong into it, and used all his energies to promote its ultimate success. The company he commanded was composed of men whom he had collected together in Grayson County, and who, as well as their leader, seemed to be entirely destitute of human feeling. When they came to Carter County, they said that they had been sent to the counties of Sullivan, Carter, and Johnson to catch conscripts; but while they remained in Carter County they appeared to have no desire whatever to engage in any other business but that of murdering Union men, and plundering their houses and robbing their families of what little provision they might have to keep them from starving. The following verse of a song, which was composed by a scouter in the mountains of Carter County, serves pretty well to describe Bozen and his thieves:

"Bozen's rogues prowl about in dark nights;
Killing and stealing they call Southern rights:
They rob our houses, they plunder and press,
And frequently take a lady's fine dress,
And it's hard times."

This gang of cut-throats and robbers came into Carter County about the 1st of December, 1863, and about the first thing they did after their arrival in the county was to murder a man named William Thompson. After Witcher and his followers left the county, there being no other soldiers

P

about, some of the men, who had been scouting for some time concluded to go to their homes and work a while. Thompson was one of the men who concluded to leave the mountains, for a short time at least. He was gathering corn, and had already brought one load of it to his barn, when he saw Bozen and his men approaching, and, before he could make his escape, he was unfortunately captured by them and taken to Elizabethton, where he was confined in jail for two or three days. He was at length taken out, placed on a small mule, with his feet tied under it, and a rope around his neck. One of the rebels led the mule, while another held to the rope, and in this condition he was conducted back to his home in the Greasy Cove, a distance of seventeen miles, where he was closely guarded for three days, with the rope still around his neck. During the time these rebel fiends remained at his house on this occasion, they robbed his family of all they possessed.

The idea of taking Thompson to his own house to punish and torture him, proves at once the base and degraded character of the villains who participated in murdering him. This was a refinement of cruelty which Bozen and his mercenary scullions were quite capable of devising. Before they killed him, he was punished and abused in every possible manner. They would make him sit down in a chair, and then knock him out of it with their guns. They hung him two or three times until he was nearly dead, and would then cut him down. This merciless and inhuman treatment was exhibited toward him in the presence of his wife and children, who were begging these ruffians all the time to have mercy, and to desist from inflicting such intolerable punishment upon him who was so near and dear to them. But, alas, the petitions of his wife and children failed to touch any cord of sympathy in the hearts of these implacable demons, for they continued to torture him in every way which their wicked hearts could suggest, until at last they got tired of inflicting punishment on him in the presence of his family, and determined to take him away from the house and murder him.

They mounted their horses, and, taking hold of the rope which was around his neck, they drove him on before them, through creeks and mud-holes, and over a very rough road, until they arrived at the residence of old Thaun Brown, who was one of the infamous scoundrels that directed Witcher and his gang of murderers to Bell's house. He was taken on a short distance farther toward the back part of Brown's farm, where his murderers shot five holes through him, and then left their victim weltering in his blood; and when his disconsolate wife, followed by her little fatherless children, went to get his body to consign it to its last abode, it surely must have been an awful spectacle for them to see the inanimate form of him, who was dearer to them than any one else in all the wide world besides, mangled and torn with bullets, and to see that loved familiar face covered over and disfigured with his own blood, which had been so wickedly shed by the foul hand of rebel violence.

I was now busily engaged in recruiting for the 13th Regiment, and had to observe a good deal of caution in order to avoid Bozen's men, who were ransacking the country in every direction, while the Union men were endeavoring to hide from them as well as they could. I had no sort of difficulty in obtaining recruits, as the men were very anxious to get away, but my fear of being unable to conceal them until I could get ready to start gave me great uneasiness of mind. And, at this particular juncture, it appeared as if the fates were working against me, for I had enlisted forty-five men to go into the Federal service, and had them concealed in a camp far out in the mountains, where I knew there would be no danger of the rebels discovering them by any fair means.   Just at this time the rebels captured two very imprudent men, who belonged to the 13th Regiment, who were lurking about their homes when they ought to have been at their posts in the regiment.   The two men referred to were brothers, and were citizens of Carter County; their names were William and Alexander Matherly.   They both knew where the men were, for they had been at the camp themselves, and both of them designed going through the lines with me, and, therefore, I did not feel afraid to trust them.   After they were captured, Bozen said to them, "If you know where there are any camps in the mountains where the scouters are staying, and will direct me to them, you shall be immediately released."   This proposition at once met the decided approbation of these two vile traitors, for they straightway conducted Bozen and his men to the place where the men were stationed in their remote and solitary encampment.

It was about midnight when Bozen and his men surrounded the camp, and most of the poor men were wrapped in profound slumber, not dreaming for a moment of the fearful destiny which was now confronting them.   The rebels commenced firing and charging on the camp, and succeeded in wounding several and capturing twenty-one of the unsuspecting Union men.   One of the men was so badly wounded that he died in a few days.   He was a Federal soldier, who had been captured by the rebels and imprisoned, but had made his escape into the mountains, and no doubt was now indulging the fond hope of soon being permitted to meet his friends again, from whom he had been for some time separated by the fortunes of war.   But, alas, the evil machinations of two vile traitors unexpectedly caused his bright hopes to be suddenly blasted, and doomed him to meet with an early death. He died among strangers, in a strange land, far away from home and from friends. His body was consigned to the grave, where it will remain until the trump of the Archangel shall sound, to summon the pale nations of the dead to arise and come forth from the dark and dismal sleep of death, to appear at the bar of the great and all-wise Judge of the universe!

The men who were captured by the rebels on this occasion were taken to Elizabethton and put in jail, where they were detained for several days. In the mean time, however, one of the prisoners was taken out of jail and shot. His name was Thomas Heatherly, and was nothing but a boy, being only seventeen years of age. And the worst of all was, he was exceedingly stupid and simple; indeed, his general ignorance at all times indicated that he was not far removed from perfect idiocy. He had never fired a gun in his life.

The reason why the rebels determined to kill him was principally on account of the terrible malice they entertained toward two of his brothers, who had, from the beginning of the rebellion, done every thing which they possibly could to obstruct and defeat the rebel cause, which, of course, did not fail to secure for them the extreme hatred of the rebels. Consequently, when the Indians were sent into Carter County, and assigned to the control and management of Robert Tipton (who was a son of Isaac P. Tipton, a citizen of Carter County), Tipton, in the plenitude of his "brief authority," conducted the Indians to the house of Thomas Heatherly, the father of the young men at whom the rebels were so enraged, and destroyed his property in a shameful manner. Old Thomas Heatherly and his

wife were then taken and hung for a short time, in order
to make them tell where their sons were; but this they
could not do, for doubtless they were as ignorant in regard
to the whereabouts of their sons as the rebels were themselves.   Two of Heatherly's daughters were then forced to
go with the company into the mountains to hunt for their
camps; but they entirely failed to ascertain any thing in
regard to the young men for whose blood they were so ardently thirsting.

When Heatherly's two oldest sons heard about the treatment of their father and mother, and also about the monstrous abuse of their sisters, they declared they would kill
Tipton whenever they could get an opportunity; and in
this respect their design was shortly afterward accomplished.   They collected together some of their scouting friends,
and went one night to his father's residence, where Robert
Tipton was staying while he was engaged in his military
operations in Carter County.   When they arrived at the
house, one of the party called Bob Tipton to the window,
and by relating a very plausible story to him he induced
him to come out into the road immediately opposite to the
house; and just so soon as he got into the road he was
firmly seized by several men, and taken out on the back
part of his father's farm, where he was killed by being shot
with two balls, one of which passed through his breast, and
the other one struck him about the centre of his forehead,
killing him instantly.

When Bozen and his men got young Heatherly into their
clutches, they doubtless considered it a splendid opportunity to avenge the death of Bob Tipton by taking the life of
an innocent boy, just because he happened to be a brother
of the two Heatherlys who were concerned in the killing
of Tipton.

DOZEN'S ATROCITIES.

The men who escaped from the camp had a very serious time of it, for it was raining and sleeting, and the weather was extremely cold. Many of them left their hats, shoes, and pants, and went some six or seven miles before they pretended to stop; and quite a number of them were badly frostbitten.

There were four Federal soldiers in jail when these men were captured in their camp, and on the very night of the capture we had been planning a scheme to release them from their imprisonment, and we had fixed on the next night to undertake our project for the release of these soldiers; but Bozen and his men defeated our arrangements, and spoiled our anticipated sport.

The men who were captured on this occasion by the rebels were confined in jail for a few days. They were then taken out, their hands tied together, and marched off in a row of two and two, the whole company being joined together with one rope, which passed along between them. In this way they were marched to Bristol, a distance of twenty-five miles. Some of these men were thinly clothed, and the weather being very cold, and they having to wade the creeks and branches, they came very near freezing to death while they were on their march.

But the whole number that the rebels started with did not arrive at Bristol; for when they got to the place which they called "the bone-yard," they untied one of the prisoners by the name of John H. Blevins, and conducted him up the lonely hollow to murder him. He implored them not to kill him, as he was guilty of no crime which should deserve such a fate. They then said,

"We are going to kill you because you are a bushwhacker."

To which false accusation he replied immediately, saying,

"I have never shot at a man in all my life, and I have never knowingly wronged any person; therefore, if you kill me, you will kill an innocent man."

One of his murderers then. very coolly said to him, "Well, then, if you have told us the truth, you need not be afraid to die!" They then shot him three times in the breast. And after untying his hands, taking off his boots, and placing his hat over his face, they started on after the balance of the prisoners. Some citizens covered his body over slightly, and after remaining where he had been killed for ten days, his friends went and removed his body, and gave it a more decent sepulture. He was said to be a good man and a good citizen; but he had been reported by some rebel citizens who were prejudiced against him, and that was entirely sufficient, in Bozen's estimation, to have him put to death.

Bozen's murderers next captured a man by the name of Pritchard. He was a young man, and had been scouting for some time, endeavoring to keep out of the way of the rebel soldiers. The two Naves, who lived on the Watauga River, both being violent rebels, used all their influence against him, as they did against every Union man who had the misfortune of being captured by these desperadoes. Pritchard was confined in jail for several days, and was then taken out and drove about a mile from Elizabethton before three of Bozen's ruffians, who rode along behind him on their horses. They took him into a small thicket of bushes about one hundred yards off of the main road, and shot him through the head, breast, and bowels. One of these fiends then took up a large club and struck him across the forehead, crushing his head perfectly flat. They then left him, and rode on up the road, laughing and talking as if the bloody tragedy in which they had just been participating had afforded them the most pleasant and agreeable diversion. He was killed about twelve o'clock in the day, and his mangled body remained where he had been killed until about twelve o'clock on the next day, when his aged mother, accompanied by a few friends, removed the body of her murdered son, in order to bestow upon it the last sad rites of parental affection.

CHAPTER XL.

ON the 2d day of January, 1864, Bozen and his men captured Isaac Yonce at his own house near the Walnut
Mountain, in Carter County. He had been a citizen of
North Carolina, and had but very recently moved into Tennessee, and had been residing at the place where he was
captured but a very short time. He and his little son, who
was about fourteen years of age, were forced by the rebels
to go along with them to the Walnut Mountain, for the
purpose of hunting for scouters. When they arrived at the
mountain, the rebels ordered their prisoner to show them
the camps of the scouters; but this the old man could not
do, for he was as ignorant in that respect as the rebels were
themselves. They took a halter-strap and hung him up,
thinking that they could make him tell them in this way;
but when they let him down, he could tell them no more
than he did before they hung him. They hung him up three
times until he was nearly dead, and would then let him
down. They then procured hickory withes, and lashed his
back in a shocking manner, and then, to cap the climax of
their villainy, they shot him four times: once in the head,
twice in the breast, and once in the bowels. After stripping
him of his clothes, they commenced whipping the poor little
innocent boy; they whipped him until they thought he
was dead, and went away, leaving him on the side of the
mountain. The boy at length recovered from the unmerci-
ful whipping which he received at the hands of these unfeeling monsters, and, when he got back home, he related,

with tearful eyes, how his father had been punished and murdered. This old man was altogether innocent, and perfectly harmless. The rebels thought that just because his residence was contiguous to the mountain, therefore he must have been acquainted with the movements of the men who were scouting in it.

Bozen and his men would not have gone to the part of the Walnut Mountain where the scouters were in the habit of staying, nor would they have gone to Yonce's house, had it not been for the information they received in regard to the country from two simple-minded Union men whom they urged to accompany them. And in regard to these two men one of the scouters composed the following verse:

> "When Bozen and his men to the mountains did go,
> For pilots they pressed Harris Whaley and Joe;
> They killed Isaac Yonce, and threatened his wife,
> And whipped his little boy for carrying a knife,
> And it's hard times."

In the month of March, 1864, Bozen and his men made another trip to the Limestone Cove, on which occasion they captured Robert Dowdel at his own house. He was then taken to the residence of James Bell, where the rebels hung him up three times to make him tell where James Bell and Samuel Smith were concealed. Being altogether ignorant in regard to these two men, he was of course entirely unable to impart to his capturers the required information. They retained him in custody all night, and before daylight on the next morning three more men were captured and brought in by a party of these murderers, who had been prowling about the neighborhood, actively hunting for more victims to sacrifice upon the altar of their unhallowed ambition. The names of the poor men who unluckily fell into their hands on this occasion were John Campbell, John Fry, and Eli Fry.

This gang of murderers proceeded to tie their prisoners together, and made them run before their horses, through creeks and mud-holes, for a distance of two miles, and then, halting them deliberately, shot three of them, who were tied together at the time. And while they were engaged in shooting these three men the fourth one broke loose, and ran with all the energy which an inherent desire to save his life from being crushed out by the hand of violence could possibly urge him to exert. But the poor fellow was soon overtaken by the rebel messengers of death, who at once commenced beating him as if he had been an inanimate statue of wood, instead of a human being possessing immortal faculties of mind, created and bestowed by the great omnipotent Architect of the universe, and destined to exist throughout the endless ages of eternity. His hands were then tied behind his back, and he was placed in a standing position against a tree, when one of the infernal miscreants stuck his bayonet through his neck and pinioned him to the tree, and thus held him fast until one of the other wretches shot him. They then stabbed the dead bodies of all four of their murdered victims full of holes with their bayonets, and beat one of them on his head until his brains run out on the ground. These men were murdered in the evening, and remained where they had been killed during the whole of the following night; and when a few citizens of the neighborhood assembled on the next day to consign their bodies to the grave, they found that the hogs had mangled, torn, and disfigured them to such an extent that it was a very hard task to distinguish them apart. Their bodies had frozen very hard during the night, which probably prevented the hogs from destroying them entirely.

This was the way that the Union men of East Tennessee were slaughtered by the rebel murderers, who came from

the State of Virginia to take the lives of their fellow-men,
just because they would not agree to aid and assist them
in accomplishing their hellish design of destroying the best
fabric of national government that was ever established by
the profound ingenuity of man in the whole world, in order
to erect upon its mighty ruins a vile and miserable oligarchy, which was baptized with the euphonical soubriquet
of "the Southern Confederacy," to captivate the affections
and insure the allegiance of the unsuspecting people.
When these infamous murderers from the rebel State of
Virginia would come into East Tennessee vengeance was
depicted in their countenances; and when they came into
the county of Carter, where they knew that public sentiment for the success of the Union cause was in the ascendant among a large majority of the people, they went forth
in the pursuit of blood with the same deliberation which so
eminently characterizes the ravenous wild beasts of the forest when they engage in the chase after their hapless victims.   The deeds of crime which the rebel fiends from Virginia perpetrated upon the innocent Union men of Carter
County are eminently sufficient to fix upon them the curse
of the Almighty while they live upon the earth, and forever
blast their hopes of future happiness in the world to come.
If the black-hearted scoundrels, Witcher, Bozen, and Duvall,
ever suffer their mind's eye to gaze through the telescope of
fancy down through the dim vista of the future, they surely
can not fail to see a terrible death-bed awaiting them,
where, in all probability, their disordered imaginations will
cause the pale and ghastly ghosts of their murdered victims
to rise up before them and point them to the bar of retributive justice, where the foul and damning crime of murdering their innocent fellow-men will rise in trumpet-tones
and plead for their guilty souls to be hurled into the fiery

billows in that dark and dismal region " where their worm
dieth not, and where the fire is not quenched." A day of
reckoning is rapidly hastening on, and a terrible day it will
be to all the vindictive scoundrels who disregarded and so
totally disobeyed the holy mandate of God himself, which
expressly says, "Thou shalt not kill;" and although they
may have viewed this injunction as possessing very little
importance when they were bathing their hands in the
blood of their fellow-men, they will doubtless appreciate
all of its weighty significance when they hear the awful
sentence pronounced against them, "Depart, ye cursed, into
everlasting fire, prepared for the devil and his angels."

CHAPTER XLI.

On the night of the 8th of January, 1865, I started with a company through the lines, which was composed of Federal soldiers returning to their posts, of Union men escaping from the rebel tyranny by which they were surrounded, and also a number of prisoners who had escaped from the rebel prison at Salisbury, in North Carolina, who had, by cautious management, made their way through a rebel country for a distance of nearly two hundred miles, and came to me just as I was about starting with my company, to engage me to conduct them through the lines.

Albert D. Richardson, who had been captured by the reb-

PORTRAIT OF RICHARDSON.

els while he was engaged in acting as an army correspond-
ent for the "New York *Tribune*," was also in the company.
Mr. Richardson had, by a "lucky freak of good-fortune,"
made his escape from the miserable rebel prison at Salisbury, North Carolina, where he had been suffering in "dur-
ance vile" for a long time the dreadful tortures which were
usually imposed upon the unfortunate Union prisoners who
had the wretched misfortune of being assigned to quarters
within the gloomy walls of any of the horrible Southern
prisons. When I first made the acquaintance of Richardson, I was at once convinced that he possessed the accomplishments of a gentleman, and my continued association
with him for several memorable days and nights, only
served to confirm me in the impression which I had at first
formed in regard to him. Although the "dust of travel"
had somewhat soiled the original neatness of his apparel,
yet his refined manners and the strict propriety of his conversation were peculiarly captivating, and, I must confess,
that he attracted my highest regard with a sort of magnetic
enchantment which was entirely irresistible. Whenever I
gazed into his intelligent face, the bright beam of intellect
which sparkled in his eyes seemed to say, "I once dwelt in
Arcadia." During the whole period of time in which I
acted in the capacity of a pilot, I never met with any man
for whom I entertained any greater concern, in regard to
his personal welfare, than I did for Richardson, owing to
the fact that I found him to be an agreeable associate, as
well as a gentleman of fine intelligence; and I was really
glad when he succeeded in once more getting within the
Federal lines, where, beneath the proud folds of the old and
cherished banner of his country, he could again walk forth
and mingle with his fellow-men, and once more enjoy the
inestimable immunities of a freeman.

Since the suppression of the Southern rebellion, Richardson has published a very interesting volume, entitled "The Field, the Dungeon, and the Escape," in which he gives a very vivid account in regard to the inception and the progress of the great rebellion; he also gives a full history of his own capture by the rebels, and of his imprisonment in the rebel prisons at Richmond and Salisbury. The book which he has published eminently deserves, as I have no doubt it has already received, a wide circulation; for it is written in a style which can not fail to please the taste of the most fastidious reader. His descriptions of the great battles which occurred during the war, and, in fact, all his descriptive narratives, are elegantly portrayed, and will doubtless receive the profound admiration of all who may desire to read an eloquent and faithful detail of the terrible scenes which transpired during the memorable Southern rebellion.

The escaped prisoners were all in a very bad condition for traveling, but, having three horses of my own, I soon had them mounted, a sack of corn on each horse serving them for a saddle. We traveled all night, and at daylight we reached the red banks of Chucky River, which we crossed in a canoe, or, at least, all who were walking did, while those who were riding swam their horses over. We traveled on four miles farther, when we went into camps for the day. And now, for the first time, I missed Richardson out of the company. Elbert Treadaway and myself immediately started back in search of him, and we had not proceeded very far until I had the agreeable pleasure of seeing him coming on toward us. We went on to the encampment, and passed the day and the night there. The weather was extremely cold, and the snow on the ground was at least six inches deep. The water-courses were all up, and we had the most of them to wade. Some of the men had started with old shoes and boots on their feet, which by this time were nearly torn off, and, in fact, some of them were entirely barefooted, with the exception of their socks, which afforded very indifferent protection to their feet against the inclemency of the bleak wintry weather; while others had on old shoes which they had tied on their feet with bark and strings. Their feet were as wet as if they had been altogether destitute of covering.

When morning came, on the 10th of January we started on our journey. To-day we had the big "butte" of Rich Mountain to cross, and shortly after we started we commenced the ascent of its steep spurs. We were now compelled very often to walk, and pack our sacks of horse-feed on our backs, which was not a very agreeable task by any means, especially for the weaker portion of the men, and, consequently, our progress was very slow. When I got on a lofty peak, I looked back and saw the men and horses on the peak behind me slowly and tediously toiling onward; and when I looked back at the long row of men and horses, I could not refrain from saying to myself, "Shall I ever be able to get them all through safely or not?" And the thought of having to leave any of them behind to fall into the hands of the rebels made me redouble my diligence in studying out every plan which I could possibly think about, in order to secure their safe deliverance from the power of their blood-thirsty enemies.

After a long, hard travel (for I do not think I ever crossed this mountain when the travel was harder), we reached the top, and then commenced descending its steep declivity on the opposite side. The road had been washed into a deep gully by the heavy rains, which made it very difficult to travel in it without continually stumbling from one side of it to the other. Night was hastening on, and I was aiming to get to an old deserted house, which was near the foot of the mountain, where I thought we could obtain shelter for the night, as the rain and snow were now falling rapidly. But, alas, when we at length reached the coveted haven of repose we found that the house had been blown down. Some of the men propped up the roof, which had partially held together, while others built up little camps out of the boards and timbers, which served to keep the rain and snow off of their heads, and that was about all the protection which their rough shelters afforded them. We passed a very disagreeable night at this place, for our little shelters were constantly tumbling down during the night, and at one time a very boisterous wind blew down the old roof under which some of the men were lying, which caused them to cry out loudly for assistance. They were soon extricated from their uncomfortable quarters, and after elevating the roof again, they crawled under it, and passed the balance of the night.

During the night we received information that the rebels were thick in the valley below, and that we would have to employ the utmost vigilance if we wished to avoid being captured. This intelligence greatly discouraged some of our party, and they immediately concluded to turn back, choosing to risk themselves where they were better acquainted. They also advised the balance of the company to turn back with them, declaring that none who should have the temerity to go forward would ever reach the Federal lines. But I thought that I could manage to escape the enemy, and, consequently, I started on in a back pathway which led on deeper into the recesses of the mountain.

We had not proceeded very far until we discovered where the rebels had come into the road, and had gone on

ahead of us. Having some armed Federal soldiers with
me on this occasion, I selected the most active of them, and
started rapidly forward in pursuit of the rebels, leaving the
company under the care of Treadaway for the day. We
soon caught up with them, and came very near capturing a
portion of the party, who only saved themselves by a precipitate flight. We continued to chase them for about six
miles, when we returned to the company again. The men
kept up remarkably well during the whole day, for they
were all anxious to be in front for fear of being surprised
by the rebels. Just about dark, on the night of the 11th
of January, we arrived at Kelly's Gap, in the Chucky
Mountains, where I had intended to stay all night. Treadaway and myself went to the house of Mr. Stephens, who
was a good Union man, to learn something in regard to the
whereabouts of the rebels. We found at once that we
were in great danger, for we were told that there were seventy-five rebels stationed at an old furnace about two miles
below, and that the party which I and the Federal soldiers
had been pursuing belonged to that company, and that they
were making preparations to follow us the next morning.
I at once determined to divide the company, and start the
horsemen on in one direction and the footmen in another,
under the care and management of Treadaway, who had
frequently traveled the same route with me, and was a
good pilot. By separating the company in this manner, I
hoped to lead the rebels on the trail of the horses, which I
knew they would be very likely to follow first. I determined to cross Chucky River at Carter's Bridge, which was
seven miles distant, and the fear of meeting with the rebel
pickets at the bridge was all that occasioned me any uneasiness. But this difficulty was nicely obviated as follows:

Miss Melvina Stephens, a true heroine, volunteered to go

with us to the bridge, cross over it, and then return and inform us if there were any rebel pickets at the bridge. It was midnight when she mounted a horse and proceeded with us to the encampment, where the men were all wrapped in the arms of sleep. I soon aroused them; and immediately after the horsemen were mounted we started forward, leaving Treadaway to guide the footmen in a different route, which he succeeded in doing without any difficulty. We arrived at the bridge in a short time, and Miss Stephens crossed over it, while we remained concealed some distance behind. She returned directly, and told us there was no impediment in our way, and then left us to pursue her lonely journey back home, amid the dismal gloom of a dark night, entirely alone and unattended. Oh, that angels may watch over her pathway through life; and when her magnanimous soul shall have been released from its earthly habitation, that she may forever find a peaceful abode in the kingdom of everlasting happiness, is my humble and devout prayer!

We pressed forward, and crossed over the bridge, and I now felt that we were out of danger. We now left the public road, and turned off to pursue our journey through the woods and open fields. We traveled at a sort of breakneck speed during the balance of the night, and at length we arrived at Lick Creek, some distance below Bull's Gap. The creek was too full to cross, and, consequently, we had to go several miles out of our way in order to cross it at a bridge which is on the main road leading on to Bull's Gap. After crossing the bridge we again struck for the woods, and traveling on about a mile farther, we stopped to rest our tired horses and to warm our frozen limbs.

After we had warmed and fed our horses, we started on, and, after another hard day's travel, we arrived near the

PORTRAIT OF MISS STEPHENS.

town of Russellville, where we stopped in a pine thicket
and built up a large fire out of fence-rails. The men and
horses were very much exhausted, and our provisions having been consumed, we had to forage among the people.
Some of the men succeeded in getting something to eat,
while others were unable to get any thing. We passed the
night very disagreeably, and when morning came we started on along the back roads, that were not usually traveled,
being very particular to watch in every direction for rebels.
In the evening we procured some corn and fed our horses,
and then traveled on until dark, when we stopped for the
night.

The men went out among the people, and had the good
luck of obtaining an abundance to eat. We passed the
night very well around our fires, some of the men sleeping
finely, while others were groaning and mourning most awfully all night. When daylight made its appearance we arose
and fed our horses, and prepared for an early start. We
traveled on rapidly, and in the evening we arrived at the
Strawberry Plains. Oh, what a joyful time it was now for
the escaped prisoners when they beheld the dear old flag
of their country floating aloft in majestic grandeur, amid
the bright and lovely beams of the declining sun, cheered
with the proud reflection that they were now safe from
the rebel tyranny! They could now walk forth and mingle
with their fellow-men as free men, and lay down to enjoy
the sweet repose of sleep without their dreams being disturbed with horrible visions of rebel murderers, with bloody
hands, claiming them for their victims.

I now went to the 13th Regiment, and at the earnest
request of my friends I joined the regiment. Company
A being then without a captain, I consented to act in
that position. As I have before stated, this company was

raised by my own exertions, and was composed almost entirely of my old friends and neighbors from Carter County. I did not wish to be in the army, for I had lived all the time free and independent since the war had been progressing, and did not fancy the idea of being subject to orders, or in that confinement which I knew a position in the army would necessarily impose; and, in fact, I well knew that I was doing more for the government in acting as a pilot for the Union men than I could possibly accomplish in any other capacity in which I could act; besides, the stirring and active life which I had followed for a long time in the mountains now had a fascination for me, and I did not care about discontinuing it; and my frequent encounters with the rebels had become to be more a source of enjoyment than any thing else. It is true I suffered a great deal, but I had now become accustomed to suffering, and it did not go very hard with me.

The principal officers in the regiment were very well aware of the important services I had rendered to the Federal army ever since I concluded to act as conductor for the Union men who desired to go through the lines, and were now unwilling for me to discontinue my operations in the mountains. Consequently, I received immediate orders to return to the counties of Carter and Johnson, to collect all the men I could for the 13th Regiment. The mountains in the upper counties were full of soldiers belonging to the Federal army, who had been left when the Yankees had last advanced up the railroad. These soldiers had gone home to see their friends and families when they were in close proximity to them, and were now almost considered as deserters; but a pardon was offered them if they would at once return.

Q

I started on my return trip, but not without being encumbered with a considerable load of letters, although I had determined never to carry another. My promise in this particular was not adhered to, for the soldiers would receive no denial.

CHAPTER XLII.

I STARTED from the Strawberry Plains, on my return journey, on foot, and came on to Vale Springs, where the 4th Tennessee Infantry Regiment was then stationed, where I remained all night, and the next morning several young men who desired to visit their homes started with me. We started early, and traveled hard all day, and passed the night at a small cabin in the knobs. The next day we traveled twenty-five miles, and at night we arrived at the Meadow-creek Mountain. We laid out in the mountain all night, and the next morning we started early; but my feet were so badly bruised from the effects of a new pair of boots which I was wearing that my powers of easy locomotion were greatly obstructed. We arrived at a good Union man's house about eight o'clock, where we got breakfast. He told us to look out for a gang of rebels who were some distance ahead of us, watching for Union men who were returning home from the Federal lines. He said that they had already captured and killed several men who were returning loaded with goods. He thought they would consider me an excellent prize, as I had a heavy load of goods which the soldiers had sent to their families. We did not tarry at this house long, but immediately went up higher on the mountain, and then traveled on without difficulty until we came to Shell's Cove, which we had to cross, and we had serious fears that the rebels would get after us before we could arrive at a place of security. But as the majority of us were armed, we pushed ahead, and had almost succeeded in getting across the cove, when we saw five horses hitched at the door of a little cabin at the foot of the mountain. I was convinced, from every appearance of the horses, that part of them, at least, belonged to rebel soldiers, and I told my companions that we would take possession of them, as we needed them very badly. I thought that our party could surely whip five rebels; but when I made the proposition to go and capture the horses, to my very great surprise, I found but one man in the company who could be prevailed on to go, and that man was Peter Shelton. The balance were too fearful that mamma's darling boys would either get crippled or killed; indeed, they were very careful of their dear lives, and at once begged leave to be excused from participating in the excursion.

Shelton and myself laid down our knapsacks, and made all necessary preparations for our premeditated visit to the cabin, while the balance of our comrades retired to a safe position on the side of the mountain, where they could watch the progress of events as they transpired, or perhaps to see us killed. The snow was about four inches deep, and the wind was blowing extremely cold; consequently, the occupants of the cabin, as well as their visitors, seemed to be keeping very close doors, for there was no person to be seen moving about the premises. We pursued our way toward the cabin along a fence-row, to prevent the dogs or any person in the cabin from seeing us until we got to the house, when Shelton immediately ran to one door and I to the other; but the door that I went to seemed not to be in use, as it stubbornly resisted all my efforts to burst it open. I rushed around to the other door, where I found Shelton standing, with the muzzle of his pistol presented toward a crack in the door. I pushed the door open instantly, and both of us rushed into the cabin together, when we found ourselves in the presence of two rebel soldiers and the family, which consisted of an old man, an old lady, and some small children.

I had my sixteen-shooter Henry rifle in my hand, with the hammer drawn ready for shooting if the rebel soldiers pretended to offer any resistance; but one of them surrendered to Shelton, and the other one to me, without a word of disapprobation in regard to the sudden and unexpected proceeding. I never saw men so badly frightened in all my life, and the uproar which proceeded from the family circle was somewhat amusing, for it was a good deal worse than a "tempest in a tea-pot."

The old man fell down upon his knees and offered up a very devout prayer, asking the Lord to have mercy on them all, especially himself and family, and not suffer them to be killed. And the old lady fell down upon the floor, and commenced crying and praying at a terrible rate, while the children, four or five in number, ran under the bed, and commenced yelling equal to a gang of young panthers. After a few minutes of turbulent excitement quiet was again restored, and "order reigned in Warsaw." The old man informed me that two of the horses belonged to him, and that the other three belonged to the rebel soldiers. We then took possession of the three horses, together with the navy pistols belonging to the rebels; and, ordering our prisoners to start before us, we decamped to the mountain.

When we got up on the side of the mountain, we saw a company of sixty rebels in the valley below just about the time they observed us; but when they saw the balance of our party, who were on another spur of the mountain, they immediately turned and started away, and so did we. They could have captured us very easily if they had exerted themselves to do so, for the mountain we were on could have been traveled over with horses at almost any portion of it. I thought we had succeeded in playing them a bold trick; indeed, I thought it was far more bold than wise, for I could not refrain from viewing our adventure as a hair-breadth escape. Two more days' travel brought me to my home, or, at least, to the hills which surrounded it. For three long years I had not staid about my own house, and but very little about any other. The trite old adage says, that "a man can go home when he can go nowhere else;" but I must confess that this was not true in regard to my own case, for my home was the very place of all others that I could not go to. I had learned to build my fire in some lonely hollow, and, wrapping myself in my blanket, lay down to sleep, regardless of snow, rain, or sleet, and very often, when I would awake, find myself buried in a bank of snow, or my blanket a sheet of ice, and my fire to-tally extinguished. This was my usual way of faring during the winter months; but I was not the only individual that had to endure this hard fate, for it was precisely what every poor Union man was compelled to suffer who was forced to leave his home to seek an asylum from the rebel tyranny amid the mountains of Carter and Johnson Counties.

I was now again where I had already experienced so many adventures with the rebels, and I soon found that they had been waiting with great anxiety for my return; for by this time they had become pretty well acquainted with my coming and going, and it afforded them the utmost pleasure to seize and appropriate the Yankee goods and the greenbacks which I brought into the county for the fam-ilies of the Federal soldiers. I did not believe that they expected to get any thing from me, for I had always suc-cessfully defeated all their arrangements, so far as I was personally concerned. Their only hope of obtaining these articles was by robbing the houses of absent Federal soldiers after their families had received the money and goods which had been sent to them by me, for the rebel scoundrels were always very particular about searching the houses of the absent soldiers, and even the person of their wives, whenever they were apprised of my return to the county. One lady living in Carter County, who was the wife of a Federal soldier, had her clothes torn off of her entirely, and the belt containing her money and jewels taken from around her waist. But even this was not as bad as the treatment which was received by Mrs. Elbert Treadaway at the hands of two of the scoundrels who belonged to the command of the infamous Duvall. They went to her house at the hour of midnight, where she was alone with three small children, and the house of her nearest neighbor being half a mile distant; they called her up, and forced their way into her house, and compelled her to remove her clothing to an extent which was at once shocking to a lady who entertained exalted notions in regard to decency, in order to search her person for money; and she only escaped farther outrage by telling these brutal villains where she had concealed some of her clothing near the house, and, while they were gone in search of it, she took her babe in her arms and went forth amid the dreary darkness of a cold night, followed by her other two little children, to seek for refuge in a cedar thicket which was close to her house. It was a cold night in the month of January, and she and her little children suffered greatly from the chilling temperature of the air, as they were all nearly naked; for she had been compelled to leave her house without taking time to procure clothing for herself and children.

After she had concealed her children in the thicket, she

ran to the nearest house to obtain the assistance of a lone woman, who was the wife of an absent soldier, in taking care of her children. They returned to the thicket, and conveyed the children to a place of security. The two heroes continued to watch her house until daylight, returned to their camps, carrying off with them all of her property which they thought would be of any service to them. Mrs. Treadaway went to Elizabethton in order to report the base conduct of these two robbers to Duvall, entertaining the hope that he would at least have the magnanimity to urge them to restore her property back to her. But Duvall, who was totally destitute of all the attributes of a gentleman, and equally as mean and despicable as any of his infamous desperadoes, treated her supplications with the most perfect disregard, and very abruptly said to her, "My soldiers shall not be punished for any thing they may do to the Lincoln-ite women, and, if they do not wish to be abused, they must go through the lines to their Yankee friends."

This was the kind of consolation which this poor helpless woman received from this Kentucky scoundrel, whose black heart was entirely impervious to any feeling of human sympathy for all, both male and female, who entertained a desire for the success of the Union cause. And these were the kind of men from whom the Union men had to flee and seek for refuge amid the rough and dreary mountains in order to save their lives; and I came to the conclusion to submit no longer to the insults of these thieving scoundrels without making some efforts to requite them for their monstrous villainies.

I disliked the idea of being called a bushwhacker; and as I was now busy in collecting the men together who desired to go through the lines with me, I concluded to wait until I should make another trip through to the Federal lines, when I intended to lay the deplorable condition of the Union families in Carter County before the commanding general, and ask him to furnish me with a small number of men and some ammunition, to enable me to return and punish the infernal villains who were robbing the houses of the absent Union soldiers, and tyrannizing over their helpless families; and I thought, if this request should be refused, I would procure the requisite amount of arms and ammunition, and return to my native county, and spend the remainder of my days, if need be, in shooting at these reckless villains from behind trees. I could not for a moment entertain the idea of sitting around the camps at Knoxville, or any where else, while the rebels were perpetrating outrages upon the families of the Union soldiers in my native county sufficient, in their enormity, to shock the sensibilities of any person whose heart was not as destitute of human sympathy as the flinty rock itself.

The hills and mountains were now swarming with escaped prisoners and rebel deserters, and also with a number of Federal soldiers who had not yet returned to their regiments, all of whom were now anxious to go through the lines. Many of my friends were entirely unwilling for me to take rebel deserters through with me, as they were afraid that they were only expressing a desire to leave the rebel service in order to mature some plan to secure my destruction. But I was very careful, and was never very hasty in reposing confidence in a rebel deserter until I was thoroughly convinced in regard to his sincerity in wishing to lay aside his rebel uniform. It was a great source of aggravation to the rebel leaders when they found that some of their best soldiers were deserting and going to the Federal army; and they generally attached the blame to me, for they would say that, not being satisfied with taking off the conscripts, I was now taking off many of their best soldiers. This was true; for their worst soldiers were afraid to risk themselves in the hands of stampeders and scouters, and many would have deserted who did not, had it not been for this reason.

CHAPTER XLIII.

On the night of the 14th of February, 1865, I started on another journey to the Federal lines. My company on this occasion consisted of one hundred and twenty-five men, and forty horses. The company presented rather a motley assemblage, for there were Federal officers occupying the rank of both captain and lieutenant, with their marks upon their shoulders; and there were the Federal soldiers, with their gayly-trimmed vests and shining blue pants; and there were the Union citizens, looking sad and dejected enough at the thought of leaving their homes and families; and there were also the rebel soldiers who had deserted the Southern army, some of whom were gentlemen, and were highly respected by the Union men. But it was not so with a number of the hated home-guards, who had become tired of the rebel service, and had ventured to risk themselves into the company, hoping thereby to make a safe retreat from farther oppression. They stood like condemned criminals, with downcast eyes, and listened in mute silence to the ribaldry and abuse which was heaped upon them by the Union citizens and soldiers, who would most assuredly have inflicted upon them severe corporal punishment, had it not been for my interference in their behalf, which relieved them from their threatening destiny. And last of all, in this mixed retinue of stampeders, there were a number of negroes, who were going through the lines to join the Federal army.

As soon as it was dark we started forward, and Duvall

and his gang of thieves, having heard that I had started
with a large company, followed us as far as James Doug-
lass's house, which is situated on the turnpike road leading
on through the Doe River Cove. The rebels stopped at
this point, and made particular inquiry in regard to the
company, and, after being informed of its magnitude, they
very wisely concluded to turn back, and left us to pursue
our journey without interruption. The night was dark, the
whole canopy of the sky being overcast with black and dismal clouds, from which snow frequently descended, and
was whirled along upon the wings of a cold and chilling
wintry wind; but, notwithstanding the dreary gloom of the
night and the severity of the cold temperature of the air,
we pressed on our journey, the footmen wading through
the creeks and branches, and stumbling along over logs,
stumps, and rocks. We hastened on, and by daylight we
were near the Greasy Cove, in Washington County; we
did not stop at this place, but pushed on toward Chucky
River, where we had the good luck of finding a canoe, in
which the footmen crossed, while those who were riding
had to swim their horses through the river. We went on
five miles farther, when we stopped to eat something ourselves, and also to feed our horses. I now considered that
we were beyond the reach of our enemies, and therefore I
felt entirely easy. Some of my readers may wonder why
it was that I preferred to scout secretly through the mountains, when my company was composed of a number of Federal officers and soldiers. The principal reason was, that
we did not have the proper arms to fight with, neither did
we have ammunition sufficient to authorize us to engage in
a fight with the rebels. Besides, it was just about as much
as the men could do to carry enough of provisions on their
backs to last them until they got through the lines, for the

road was very rough, and provisions for so large a company of men could not be obtained along the road.

While we were resting for a short time, we observed several women, who lived in the mountains, going in the direction of Chucky River to hunt for provision for their families; and some of them told us that they had walked fourteen or fifteen miles, and would be compelled to carry upon their shoulders whatever they might be able to procure all the way back to their homes. Some of them said that their children had not had a piece of bread for several days; and I thought, from every indication, they were telling the truth, for they looked pale and haggard, their clothing was thin and very indifferent, and their worn-out shoes were tied upon their feet with strings; in fact, some of them were entirely destitute of shoes, and had rags wrapped around their feet. Some of them said their husbands were in the Federal army, and that they were then living in camps, their houses having been burned and all their property destroyed by the rebels, and that they were now compelled to carry on their backs whatever they could procure for their little children to eat for a distance of fifteen miles through snow, rain, and ice. I divided what money I had among them, which seemed to dry up their tears, and they went on their way rejoicing at the unexpected and timely assistance they had received. I thought it was very inadequate assistance, considering their destitute condition.

It was now the 16th of February, and we started on our journey at daylight, and traveled on steadily all day; crossing knobs, and wading creeks and branches, which a number of the men found to be a serious impediment, for every little stream of water was full to overflowing. Late in the evening we reached Shelton Laurel, and, as we were going down a branch, we overtook a poor woman, who was carry-

ing two bushels of corn-meal on her shoulder, and a pretty-
well-grown child on her hip. This I thought was a tolerably good load; she was not far from her house when we
overtook her, but I got one of the men to take the child before him on his horse and carry it to the house. She said
she had carried her heavy burden about two miles and a
half.

We arrived at an immense pine thicket, where we stopped
to spend the night. After eating supper and feeding our
horses, we laid down to sleep, but it seemed to be altogether impossible for us to court its soothing influence to rest
upon our eyelids, for the ground was wet, and the air was
so extremely cold that we could not rest with any degree
of satisfaction. We all passed a very uncomfortable night,
and when daylight came we were ready to start on our
journey. We made our way toward the road that leads
on from Marshall, North Carolina, to Greenville, Tennessee;
we had all the water-courses to wade, which was a very serious inconvenience, for the weather was very cold. It was
nearly night when we got to Shell's Cove, at which place
there was a company of rebels stationed; consequently, we
waited until dark to cross the cove, which we did with perfect safety. It was a beautiful starlight night, and we traveled on until midnight, when we stopped to rest until morning.

We started on early the next morning, and, after traveling about five miles, we came near a valley which we had
to cross, and stopped until night came on again, when we
started on at a rapid pace, and traveled until three o'clock
the next morning, when we stopped. The men were suffering very much from cold and from their wet clothing, for
all of them who were walking had to wade the streams of
water which occurred in our road, and, consequently, they

had been thoroughly drenched with water. At daylight we started on, and had it not been for the horses we had with us, some of the men would have been left on the road, for they were completely tired down, and some of their feet were in a bad condition, for they were bleeding profusely; their worn-out shoes afforded very indifferent protection from the extremely cold weather. About three o'clock in the evening we arrived at Leaper's Mill, on Chucky River, where we had the good-fortune to find two canoes, in which the men who were walking crossed the river, and those who were riding had to swim their horses. We then went on to Spring Vale, where the Federal forces were stationed. We stopped here long enough to procure something to eat for ourselves, and also feed for our horses, and then pushed on until we found a good situation to locate our encampment for the night; we built up large fires, and passed the night quite comfortably, for we had no fears now of being surprised by the rebels. We started on very early the next morning, and traveled steadily forward all day; we now got provisions from the people, as we passed along, without any difficulty.

When night came on we camped out in the woods. So soon as daylight appeared we started on, and, after a very hard day's march, we arrived at the Strawberry Plains. The men who had horses went on to the 13th Regiment, which was stationed six miles below the Plains, and I went on to Knoxville with the escaped prisoners and deserters.

Colonel Trowbridge, of the 10th Michigan Regiment, was now occupying the position of provost-marshal at Knoxville. He had issued an order that all citizens, escaped prisoners, and deserters from the rebel army who might come through the lines should be arrested and brought before him, so that he might dispose of them as he should think proper.

Therefore, when I arrived at Knoxville, I went with my company to the marshal. All the rebel deserters took the oath, and were sent north of the Ohio River. The escaped prisoners were provided with food and clothing, and sent to their respective posts, and the citizens were permitted to do whatever they thought best for their own personal welfare. Some of them immediately joined the army.

The troubles attendant on this trip were now over, and I returned to my regiment. However, I did not intend to remain very long, for I had not forgotten the situation of the Union people in Carter County, nor what I had suffered from the gang of rebel scoundrels who were now infesting my native mountains. My determination still was, if assistance was denied me to enable me to return and fight the rebels openly, that I would return alone, and bushwhack them on every occasion that I possibly could.

I proceeded to make application for the assistance which I desired, and the authorities at once detailed thirty-two soldiers out of the 13th Regiment to return with me, nearly all of them being originally citizens of Carter and Johnson Counties. We were provided with an abundant supply of arms and ammunition, and with four horses to carry our supplies. The worst of all was, we were compelled to travel on foot, which was a hard task for the soldiers, for they had not been accustomed to traveling in that way. It was expected that we would soon provide ourselves with horses and clothing from the rebels, and also provisions if we desired to eat much, for the Union people had but little to furnish us with, yet I know that what little they still had would be freely given if it should be required.

CHAPTER XLIV.

On the 14th day of March, 1865, we left the regiment, the company consisting of thirty-two regular soldiers, and a few citizens who were returning to their homes. The weather was clear and warm, which made traveling very agreeable, and the men were in fine spirits. We spent the first night six miles south of New Market, where the men made up large fires, and passed off the night in telling "long yarns" about the number of fights they had been engaged in, and how narrowly they had frequently escaped from being killed. They were now on their way home to fight for their families, whom some of them had not seen for eighteen months; they now declared they would have vengeance for the insults and abuse which their families had been subjected to, and they said that no hardship or privation which could come upon them would be too great for them to suffer if they could only be permitted to accomplish their design.

As soon as daylight appeared we started on our journey; some were singing merrily, while others were talking with the utmost cheerfulness. We traveled twenty miles on that day, and staid all night at the residence of Captain Carter. The men were very tired, and their feet were badly blistered. They did not recount so many of their deeds of valor, nor "fight their battles o'er again" on that night, for they went to bed at an early hour, and slept soundly until morning.

We breakfasted early, and started again, and at night we arrived at Leaper's Mill, on Chucky River. We crossed the river in a canoe, and had to swim our horses. We had con-

templated staying with the 4th Tennessee Regiment that
night, but on that evening it had been removed to Morristown. We now had to use some exertions to procure something to eat. The rain poured down all night, and early the
next morning we put on our gum blankets and started.
The mud and water was shoe-mouth deep along the road
and in the fields. After a disagreeable walk of about six
miles, we got into the woods. In the evening the rain ceased
falling, and the air turned very cold. At length we arrived
at a house in the ridges, where we stopped to obtain something to eat. When the occupants of the house saw us approaching they immediately commenced hiding their little
household affairs, and when we went into the house they
seemed to be very much frightened and confused. We told
them we were Yankees, and were on our way home, and had
stopped to see if we could get something to eat. The lady
of the house would not believe us for some time, and, after
we had remained for a while, she said, "Well, I really believe
you are Yankees, for if you were rebels you would have
searched throughout the whole house by this time."

When she became convinced that we were not rebels she
was remarkably kind to us; she showed us where we could
get corn to feed our horses, and soon had a plentiful supper
ready for us. After a while she went into another room,
where she lifted up a plank, and her son came creeping out
from his hiding place. He was a conscript, and the rebels
had been after him. The family were now in fine spirits,
and some of them told us how we had frightened them
when we were approaching the house. Part of the company
remained all night there, and the balance scattered about to
the nearest cabins.

It was now the 18th of March. We assembled early, and
started on our journey. The people among whom we had

staid did not charge us any thing for our night's lodging, but they were very particular in charging us to whip the rebels if we could; and this the men whom I had with me had never doubted their ability to do whenever they could have an opportunity to "break a lance" with their enemies. We traveled all day without any thing of interest happening, and late in the evening we stopped to get supper and to feed our horses. We then went on to Meadow-creek Mountain, where we "took up camps" in a deep hollow, and passed the night there. We were now anxious to keep as much concealed in our movements as possible until we arrived at Shell's Cove, hoping to catch a scout of rebels there who always ran when they saw Yankees approaching, but were constantly watching for the men who were passing through the mountains, in order to murder and rob them of whatever they might have.

Early the next morning we set out along the side of the mountain. After we had traveled some distance, we stopped at a house to get something to eat; but the lady of the house said she had nothing that she could give us to eat, but she furnished us with corn to feed our horses. We now went in search of the rebels, but, as usual, they had just left. The people in that neighborhood would have gladly assisted us in capturing them if they had been there. We now changed our course, and made for Shelton Laurel, which was the best place to procure provisions. It was now ten o'clock, and we yet had thirteen miles to travel. We traveled in a hurry, and just at dark we reached Shelton Laurel. The old men, women, and children had been engaged in log-rolling on that day, and had now assembled to partake of an abundant feast, and also to enjoy themselves for a while in the festive dance. We enjoyed ourselves finely, for we had plenty to eat, and spent the night in dancing. The women were all about as stout and robust as the one I had seen carrying the bag of meal on her shoulder and the child on her hip, to which I have alluded in the previous chapter. I really do believe that every woman who participated in the dance on that night could have shouldered two bushels of corn and carried it to mill. They could chop with an axe, roll logs, and plow equal to men. But they were remarkably kind to strangers, and would willingly have fed us for a week if we had requested it.

Early the next morning we set out for the red banks of Chucky River. The men did not feel much like traveling after their night's frolic. But we traveled on in a steady gait all day, and reached the river just as it was getting dark, and crossed it in a canoe. We had to travel on five miles farther before we could get any thing to eat, and when we got near to the Greasy Cove the men scattered out among the people, and fared tolerably well. We were now inside of the rebel lines, and I told the soldiers that we should all have to be very careful, or, in spite of their boasted valor and achievements, we might all fall into the hands of the enemy. Next morning we traveled eight miles farther, when we halted to wait for night to throw her dark wings o'er the earth, as I thought it advisable to make our entrance into Carter County as secretly as we possibly could, so that we might recruit our exhausted energies for a short time before the rebels could be apprised of our arrival into the county. I thought that I had but a small company to operate against the enemy with, and I therefore determined to make a good beginning. When night came on we pushed forward; and when we arrived at the residence of Elijah Simerley, in Carter County, nine miles south of Elizabethton, we stopped and rested for a day and night, and fared elegantly during the time. My main object now was to find a party of rebel soldiers somewhere, so that I might get their horses and mount my company, as we could not get about fast enough on foot.

I now concluded that we would go and make an attack on my old tormentors, whom I thought were still at Elizabethton, or in its vicinity; but, when we arrived near that place, we learned that the rebels had all left and gone to Bristol. This intelligence, I must confess, gave me no little vexation, for now there was not a rebel soldier to be found. We fared sumptuously among the Union people in the vicinity of Elizabethton for a day and night, and then started for Johnson County up the Watauga River, and by the way of Stony Creek, where some of the soldiers' families resided. We staid one night on Stony Creek, and fared very well; for during the night the news was spread abroad that a company of Yankees had come into the neighborhood, and against morning the place where we were encamped was swarming with men and women, who had brought with them an abundant supply of provisions for us.

When we started on our journey quite a number of people had gathered all along the road to see us, and also to furnish us with something to eat, and it would be impossible for me to say how many pies and fowls we devoured while we remained in this vicinity. The day we left Stony Creek we reached Johnson County, and passed the night in a laurel thicket. We did not fare so well as we did on the previous night, for we were now in a rebel section of country, and, consequently, we remained pretty closely concealed. We started next morning and traveled all day along the side of Stone Mountain, through briers, and through laurel and ivy thickets. In the evening we arrived at a place called "The Laurel," on the road leading on to Abingdon, Virginia. A party of rebels were hauling provisions and forage along this road, and my intention was to go to Providence Gap, which is a narrow pass through the mountain, where I thought we could blockade the road and capture their teams. I knew that this might be easily accomplished by cutting trees across the road, and then wait until they came to the proper place, when we could then take them by surprise.

The men were in fine spirits at the prospect of an immediate encounter with the rebels, and at the thought of getting a good horse to ride, so that they might be enabled to travel about briskly in spite of their bruised feet and tired limbs. But, as before, we were again doomed to disappointment, for the rebel wagon-train had passed on toward Abingdon some three hours before our arrival, and we could hear of no more rebels in that portion of the country. The men were now completely disheartened, at least all of them who yet remained with me, for ten of my men had deserted and gone to their homes after they had sworn to stand to their posts, no matter what misfortunes might betide them. The balance of my company remained with me, and I must say that their conduct throughout the whole of this expedition is worthy of the highest commendation, for I do not think that there was ever any better or braver men. My company now numbered twenty-two soldiers and a small number of citizons.

We went to the cabins in the mountains, and the people gave us something to eat, and we again encamped for the night. The soldiers in the company seemed to be greatly disappointed, and I have no doubt they were as sorely vexed because they could find no rebels to fight, as Alexander was when he sat down and wept because there were no more nations for him to conquer. I must confess that I felt a desire to be actively engaged, for we were now dependent on the Union people for our supplies, and I wished to do every thing in my power to relieve them from the terrible rebel oppression under which they had suffered so long.

While we were discussing the dullness of our prospects, and considering what was best to be done, an old man happened to pass our encampment; he was scouting from the rebels, and came upon us accidentally. I immediately called him, and told him to come into our encampment. He started toward us, looking very distrustfully, indeed, for he was terribly frightened until he found out who we were and what our business was. When I convinced him thoroughly in regard to our political status and the object of our visit to Johnson County, I never saw a man exhibit greater demonstrations of enjoyment in all my life. He told us that a company of rebels was then stationed at Wills's Barn, about five miles distant, and that they had been there for some time, resting and feeding their horses.

We immediataly commenced making arrangements to go in pursuit of the enemy, and taking the old man with us, who I must say was entirely willing to go, we set out for the barn. When we got within two miles of the place, we stopped to wait until daylight before making an attack. We got into a deep hollow, where we built up fires. The men passed away the time in telling big tales until late in the night, and then laid down to sleep, telling one another to remember what they dreamed, for when morning came they would have to fight. After a short time all was still. I did not attempt to sleep, neither did I wish to do so, as I preferred to act as sentinel until it was time to arouse the men to prepare for action. How often I looked at my watch to see how the night was passing away I do not know; but I thought it was a long time before the chick-en-cocks at the neighboring barns began to announce that daylight was approaching. I now proceeded to arouse the men, and soon had them ready to march, as I wished to get to the rebel encampment against daylight. The old man acted as our guide, and, after following him about two miles, we came in sight of the rebel camp-fires. There were two large fires burning, one on the left, and one on the right side of the barn.

CHAPTER XLV.

THE next morning, March 31, 1865, the golden beams of the sun were early visible in the eastern sky, and the men were looking pretty anxious. We found that the rebels were in a log barn, which, of course, gave them the advantage of us in regard to position; and besides, we had no means of ascertaining the number of the rebels, about which there was a great contrariety of opinion, some saying that there were sixty or seventy of them, and others said there were at least a hundred. According to the tale of the old man who had served as our guide, there were at least twice as many rebels as there were men in my company. I encouraged the men by' reminding them that we would take them by surprise; besides, we were well provided with arms and ammunition. From the position we occupied we could see some of the rebels busily engaged in cooking around their fires, while others were feeding their horses. We marched up four deep, and, when we got within about sixty yards of them, we fell in a line to make a charge; and when the men were forming a line they made a noise with their feet, and the rebels discovered us, for some of them immediately exclaimed, "Look yonder at the men!" I now gave orders to fire and charge on them at the same time. We were armed with seven-shooters and Colt's repeaters, and, when we commenced, we kept up an incessant firing until we reached the rebel encampment. I ran up on the left, where most of the rebels were, and hal-

R

looed to my men to charge them on the right and left, and to keep up a brisk fire all the time.

The rebels now began to give way, and I must confess I never saw men run before. At first they did not seem to know what to think of us, and I have no doubt they thought we were bushwhackers, as no Yankee soldiers had ever before made their appearance in that region of country. But they soon found out that they had either to fight or run, and they immediately commenced jumping over the fence which surrounded the barn. There was a pet sheep in the barn-lot, which started off at full speed after the flying rebels, bleating most vehemently at every jump; and it was hard to determine which would win the race, the pet sheep or its rebel companions.

We now turned our attention to those who still remained in the barn, and my men climbed up and began to search for the rebels. The barn was composed of one log pen, and the threshing-floor was nearly four feet from the ground. Some, of the rebels had taken refuge under the floor, and some had concealed themselves in the barn; but we soon made them come out and surrender. When we looked under the floor, we could see the eyes of the rebels shining like those of so many cats in the dark. We called upon them to come out, but none of them made any answer. Some of my men then commenced shooting under the floor, which at once caused the whole party of rebels to come out and surrender.

Fifteen of the rebels fought bravely during the whole engagement; and if the whole company had fought as gallantly as they did, they would, most unquestionably, have given us a severe fight, and probably would have defeated us, for they outnumbered us two to one. We captured thirty-six horses, together with saddles, bridles, and blankets, besides a large number of guns, pistols, shoes, boots, hats, and overcoats; and I do not know how many satchels fell into our hands which were filled with clothing, and which, on examination, we found to be ladies' clothing of every description, which they had taken from the Union women in the country; and last, though not the least of all, we took possession of their breakfast, which was nearly cooked. We also found in their deserted encampment a large lot of bread, meat, and potatoes.

The rebels who were standing out on picket, when they first heard the firing and hallooing, cut their horses loose from where they had tied them, and, mounting on them barebacked, started off in the direction of Taylorsville as if they expected some frightful calamity momentarily to overtake them. Many of those who fled so precipitately from the barn were seen going through Taylorsville mounted on old sore-backed horses that they had come across in their flight, without shoes, hats, or pants, with their hair standing straight up, holding on with both of their hands to old pieces of bridles or strings, telling the astonished people, as they passed along, that all of their companions had been killed or captured by the Yankees, and that they alone were left to tell the tale. The aspect they exhibited, as they passed through Taylorsville, was ludicrous in the highest degree.

We captured one sixteen-shooter and several Spencer rifles, besides a large lot of navy pistols; some of my men had four and five apiece. Our prisoners were all Kentuckians. There were two officers among them—Captain Harris and Lieutenant Gentry—the balance of them were privates. They said they had been in the Southern army for three years, and that they had never been in such a severe encounter on any previous occasion. I at once paroled them and turned them loose, but they would not leave until they persuaded some of the Union citizens to accompany them some distance on their journey. Union men were tolerably hard to find, for we had frightened both the Union men and the rebels away for at least three miles around; and it is no wonder that they were frightened, for the terrible shooting, together with our boisterous shouting and screaming, was enough to make them think that a band of wild Indians had been turned loose to desolate the country.

The last intelligence we received of the fugitives who first fled away from the barn was, that they were still moving rapidly on toward Jefferson, North Carolina, not even stopping to look behind them.

Several of the men in my company had their clothes cut with the rebel bullets, and one of them was wounded in the neck. None of the rebels were killed on the ground, but several of them were wounded so badly that they died shortly after the fight.

We now selected from the arms we had captured such as we desired to retain, and broke the balance of them to pieces; and when we left the rebel encampment we were in a much better condition than when we came to it, for every man now had in his possession a good horse, saddle, bridle, and blanket. The men all seemed to be very much pleased; we had walked one hundred and fifty miles, and I thought when we started that we would be able to mount ourselves much sooner than we did, but this was the first company of rebels we had met with. We removed our wounded man into the mountains among his friends. He was a citizen of Johnson County, and was a brave and good Union man. The poor fellow died from the wound he had received in the fight with the rebels in ten days.

We went on down Little Doe River to the residence of Andrew Wilson, where we got corn for our horses, and also something to eat for ourselves, after which we fell back among the ridges and passed the night. When morning came, we went on up Roan's Creek to the residence of Hog Dave Wagner, who was a wealthy man, and was also one of the leading rebels in Johnson County. He had left home, but had left an abundance of every thing behind him both for man and brute to eat. We were the first Yankees who had visited him; consequently, we and our horses fared most sumptuously during the whole time of our stay on his premises; however, we did not tarry long, for we started on early the next morning toward Taylorsville to hunt for more rebels, but, when we arrived there, we found that all the rebel soldiers had deserted the place. We went back, and stopped at the residence of Samuel E. M'Queen, another bad rebel, where we again ate and fed our horses. Our next stopping-place was at James Brown's, who was a notorious home guard. He was gone from home, and some of the rebel women said he had gone to get the home guards and rebel soldiers to run us out of the county. But he was too slow in his movements, for during his absence we visited his house, where we found ample provisions for ourselves and horses to subsist on for a day and night; and for this I felt no check of conscience, for most of the grain and provisions which the rebels of Johnson County then had in their possession had been taken from the Union people, and they left to starve.

While we were in this section of country, a portion of Stoneman's men marched through the mountains of Carter and Johnson Counties on their way to North Carolina. This was the first Federal force that had ever passed through the mountains of these two counties, and one of my men facetiously remarked, that they could not have passed through on this occasion had it not been for our company, who had run the rebels away before them. I remarked to the men, if that was the case, that we had better go down the country to Elizabethton and Johnson's Dépôt, in order to protect the dispatch-bearers and stragglers, for I thought the rebels might be watching the roads to capture them. We started, and traveled on down the country until we got within three miles of Elizabethton, where we went into camp in a pine thicket, for we had been informed that the rebels were very numerous in the country, and I therefore deemed it advisable to observe all necessary caution to avoid the danger of being surprised. We kept up good fires all night, and the men passed off the time in telling long tales about their adventures in the army. I now received information that a party of rebels were at Elizabethton, in hot pursuit after us; they had been hunting for us all the day before, but had failed to hunt in the right direction. They had captured a little boy, who, of course, was the son of a Union man, had taken him some distance away from his home, and had treated him most shamefully by beating him, to make him tell where we were; but this the little boy was entirely unable to do, for he was altogether ignorant in regard to our movements. These scoundrels then hung him up with a halter rein until he was nearly dead, and then let him down, and rode off and left him.

I at once determined that on the next morning we would find them, although they had been unable to find us, and told my men to prepare for another encounter with the rebels. This intelligence stopped their fun, and they began to inquire how many of the rebels were in pursuit of us, but this I was unable to tell them. I told them that all I had been able to learn in regard to the rebels was, that they were in Elizabethton, and that we must give them a fight at all hazards. The men now laid down to rest, so that they might feel vigorous and active when they were called on to engage in the anticipated conflict; they remarked to one another that they ought to be particular to engage in prayer, for they did not know how much longer they had to live.

We started just at daylight on our road to Elizabethton, which is situated between the Watauga and Doe Rivers. We left the Watauga, and traveled along the Doe River Road, as I thought that the rebel pickets would be most likely to be on the Watauga River. I divided my company into three squads, as there were three streets leading into town in the direction we were going. I placed two of the squads under competent leaders, and I led the other one myself, and after I had designated a point for us all to meet at, I started on up the main street. Not a single rebel knew that we were any where near the town until I was seen with a small body of men coming up the main street, when a citizen suddenly hallooed out to some of the rebel soldiers, "The Yankees are coming," and the rebels, looking down the street, saw us for the first time. They made no attempt to fight, but some of them ran into the Courthouse, while others mounted their horses and started toward Doe River; we pursued them very closely, and before they crossed the river we got so near to them that one of my men shot one of the rebels off of his horse while he was in the water. My horse was uncommonly swift, and I plunged through the river after the fugitives, and very soon got a considerable distance away from my men. I now halted for a moment, and by this time I saw the company of men which I had placed under Treadaway crossing higher up the river. The rebels, who had gone on some distance ahead, were now seen waving their hats and telling us to come on, thinking that we could not again overtake them.

We now started in pursuit of them, and, as before, my horse soon carried me far ahead of the balance of my men, and I found myself in the presence of the rebels entirely alone, without a single load in my pistols, for I had shot them out in the early part of the chase, and consequently I had no time to spare to reload them. I captured two of the rebels with an empty pistol, while both of them had loaded guns, which they threw down, and got down off of their horses and surrendered. Some of the men now came up and took charge of them, while I started on after the others, one of whom turned his course and ran by himself. I followed him some distance, when, seeing his horse fall, I directed two of my men to go forward and capture him, and I started on after three others, who were going in a different direction. Elbert Treadaway was with me, but his horse choked down and fell to the earth, leaving me alone again, for the men had not yet come up, and my swift-footed animal continually left them far behind.

I had not yet taken time to load my pistols; but this the rebels did not know, and when I overtook them I ordered them to surrender; but they rushed onward, and continued shooting at me whenever they had a chance, and also declaring that they would never surrender to one man. They were still on their horses, and the ground was very wet and slippery. We were ascending a steep hill, and their horses tiring down, they dismounted, and one of them presented his gun and burst a cap at me, saying, "I will kill you, you damned scoundrel!" I thought I could see half way down the barrel of his gun, for we were not more than five steps apart, and one of my men getting the gun a minute or so afterward, found the ball smoking in it. I sprang off of my horse and knocked him down with the butt-end of my pistol, striking him in his face, and cutting it very badly. I now turned toward the other two, and caught one of them by the collar, telling him to surrender. The third one threw down his gun, hat, and coat, and away he went. I looked at the man I had knocked down, and saw that he was up and busily engaged in putting a cap on his gun, and, when I saw this, I immediately let the one go that I was holding and knocked him down again, and then grasped hold of the other man a second time. I tried to beat him down to the place where the other man was lying, but I could not do it. Just at this time Treadaway and another one of my men, by the name of William Williams, came up and shot the man whom I had knocked down, and we retained the one which I had caught as a prisoner. The one who threw down his gun succeeded in getting away.

We now started back, and met with the balance of the company. In this engagement we killed three of the rebels, and captured eleven prisoners—Olford Smith, their leader, and one other being all who made their escape out of the whole company. We now set out with our prisoners toward the hills, where we could rest in security; for I knew we were not strong enough to stay where there was much danger of being surprised. We guarded our prisoners for four days in an old house in the mountain, and I then sent them on to Greenville. They were sent on from there to Knoxville, and finally they were sent to a Northern prison. I was convinced that we had captured a very bad set of rebels, and I wished them to suffer for the mischief they had done.

After these prisoners had been sent away, the mother of one of my best soldiers, Mrs. Henry Little, came to our en-

ELLIS ATTACKING.

campment to see her son, for he could not leave the company to visit her, and she told me that she had been broken up by this same gang of rebels that we had succeeded in capturing. She was then with her family, living away from her home. There was a frightful scar upon her head, which had been caused by a rebel soldier striking her with his gun because she presumed to get between him and her husband when he was endeavoring to kill him, and by her timely interference her husband managed to make his escape. She said that the rebels were mad at her because her son was in the Federal-army, and they were also mad at her husband because he had concealed his horses so securely that they had been entirely unable to discover them. The reader will doubtless think that these were very slight offenses to cause them to be the recipients of such brutal rebel malignity.

CHAPTER XLVI.

In the early part of the month of April, 1865, General Tillson was stationed at the mouth of Roan's Creek, near the line between Carter and Johnson Counties, with four regiments of Federal troops. He sent one regiment, under the command of Colonel Kirk, to the town of Boone, in North Carolina, and leaving one regiment at the mouth of Roan's Creek, he marched with the other two regiments to Taylorsville. I was in his service until the return of my men, which was four days, during which time I acted as a guide for him in his movements through the mountains. When General Tillson approached Taylorsville, the rebels all left without making the least resistance. The little damage that was done to the leading rebels of Johnson County by my company amounted comparatively to nothing, when it was compared with the damage that was done by Tillson's army; for the rebels had all left their houses, and had left their property behind them to risk its chances amid the turbulent tide of war which was now deluging the county. There was not a thing left but the bare walls of their houses, and many of the rebel families, who had always lived in affluence and ease, were now compelled to draw their supplies from the army.

On the 13th day of April my men returned, and being of no more service to Tillson, who intended to remain stationary for some time, after a day or two, which my men spent in resting, I started with my little company in search of rebels, for I had heard that a company of them were making regular trips to Carter Station. We went to this place first, but failed to find any of them. After waiting for some time, we went on toward Bristol, but we could not find any trace of them. ·We now returned to the mountains, and staid all night, and on the morning of the 18th of April we started for Sullivan County, where we knew there were some very bad rebels, if we could find them, for all the leading rebel citizens of Carter County, and many of the rebel soldiers, had taken refuge in Sullivan County. The rebel soldiers had been in the habit of robbing the Union citizens of Carter and Johnson Counties, and conveying their ill-gotten plunder to Sullivan County. A gang of them would frequently assemble together, headed by the mean rebel citizens, of whom Isaac L. Nave, Henry C. Nave, and his son, Jacob Nave, were ringleaders, who would never fail to kill, with the utmost cruelty, every man whom they found scouting in the mountains who had the misfortune of accidentally falling into their hands. They would rob Union men's houses of every article, from a yard of Dixie cotton cloth or an infant's clothing, up to a feather bed or a horse. But so far as horses were concerned, at this period of time there was scarcely a Union family in Carter County that could boast of having one. These were the men that we were now in pursuit of.

When we started to Sullivan County, we crossed Watauga River near Elizabethton, and went on to the head of Indian Creek, traveling in an unfrequented road, thinking that we might meet with some renegade rebels. We went on in this road for about ten miles toward Sullivan, when we observed three men running from a house. We called on them to surrender, and galloped on after them, but they continued to run. Some of the men commenced shooting at them, and one of them fell mortally wounded. The other two surrendered, and we immediately turned them loose, al-

though they had been in company with the very man whom
we were so anxious to capture, but they were not quite so
bad.   After pursuing our journey a little farther, we saw
two men run out of a violent old rebel's house.   Some of
the men commenced shooting, and calling on them to halt;
but the more we called on them to stop the faster they run.
When I got up closer I heard one of my men say, "That is
Henry Nave."   I instantly turned my horse, and rode off in
a different direction, for I did not wish to see him killed, and
I knew it would be perfect folly to endeavor to prevent the
men from killing a man who had been such a desperate
enemy to them and their families.   As I rode up toward
the other man that some of my men were pursuing, I heard
the gun fire that killed him.   When I got close to the other
man, to my very great surprise, I found that it was Isaac L.
Nave. He would not surrender, and, being well armed, he
continued to shoot as long as he could; but he was soon
killed.   Both these men were my inveterate enemies, and
had often, in company with the rebel soldiers, searched the
hills around my home, hoping to effect my capture and consequent death, although I had never harmed either one of
them in all my life.   They always talked about me to the
rebel soldiers in the most disparaging manner, which caused
them to rob my house and abuse my family; yet, notwithstanding all this, I did not wish to participate in their destruction.

We went on, and in our onward march we captured many
rebel citizens who had fled from Carter County, but all of
them were released.   When we arrived at Holston River
we met with the rebel soldiers, and, as I expected to have
an immediate engagement with them, I ordered my men to
take a position in a field where we could have a fair chance
with them.   I divided my men, and sent a portion of them

on to flank the rebels on the left, while the river admirably served to flank them on the right. I ordered the flanking-party to charge the flank of the enemy whenever they saw me charging in the centre. We began the charge, and away went the rebels as hard as they could dash, while we started in pursuit of them as rapidly as our horses could carry us along. We should have continued the chase, had we not met with several citizens in whom I put the utmost confidence. They told me that there was a regiment of rebel soldiers stationed at Union, which was but a short distance from the place we were then at, and advised me not to go any farther if I did not wish to have my company captured. I now thought that the rebels were running in order to draw us on to a position where we could be captured by re-enforcements from the regiment which the citizens had spoken of, and I therefore concluded to discontinue any farther pursuit.

We found shortly afterward that what the citizens had told us was entirely false, and, if we had pushed forward, we could have made a "clean sweep" of every rebel soldier from Union to Bristol. We now returned to the mountains of Carter County with the intention of returning to Sullivan County the next day. But, when I arrived in Carter County, I received a dispatch from General Tillson requesting me to go to Jefferson, North Carolina, with a scout. I regretted this considerably, for I was doing a flourishing business with the rebels, and therefore I did not wish to leave them for a while.

On the 19th of April, 1865, I started with my company to Roan's Creek, where I was to meet with General Tillson, and early the next morning I started with a scout for North Carolina. We went to Irving Wilson's, two miles north of Taylorsville, where we staid all night. Food was now very scarce for both man and beast.. Here I fell in with Major Lossing, who belonged to a Kentucky regiment; but he was now commanding a small cavalry force which had been detached from the 8th, 9th, and 13th Regiments. When our men were joined together, our whole force numbered two hundred and fifty. We started for Jefferson, North Carolina, and when we arrived at Taylorsville I was detained for a short time, and the major got on some distance ahead of me. I started on, having fifteen men from Carter and Johnson Counties with me. After we had proceeded on our journey about three miles, we met a detachment of colored· troops, who were guarding as a prisoner Samuel E. M'Queen, of murdering and house-burning notoriety—he who had entered into an agreement to murder Union men, burn their houses, and drive their helpless families through the lines. The men who were along with me seemed to be greatly rejoiced at his capture. He was taken to Taylorsville, and shot by some of the men whose families he had wronged.

We traveled on for two days, and on the night of the second day we overtook Major Lossing, and also found him to be in a considerable agony of trouble; for he had been informed that there were about twelve hundred rebel soldiers some ten miles distant. Neither he nor his men had slept a minute during the whole of the previous night, as they expected every moment that the rebels would pounce upon them and "gobble them up."

Early on the morning after my arrival at the encampment, Major Lossing came to me, and said, "Captain Ellis, I wish you would go and see if there are any rebels on Little Helton Creek, where rumor says they are stationed, and you may have fifty men to accompany you." I told the major I would go, and, after getting my men together, I started on the expedition. Nearly every mile we traveled we captured rebel soldiers, who were straggling about through the country. I was very particular to keep my men in readiness for an engagement, for every person we met with told us that the rebels were just ahead of us. We traveled on until one o'clock in the day, when we came very near to the place where it had been reported there was such a large force of rebels stationed. Here the people told us that we had better go back, for the rebels would be certain to capture us if we continued to move forward. But we moved on, capturing more or less rebel soldiers at every house we came to, and at length we arrived at Little Helton Creek, north of Jefferson, North Carolina, and there was not a rebel soldier to be found; they had all left on the day before our arrival.

There were several buildings at this place, which belonged to a violent rebel by the name of Perkins, but he had gone away with the rebel soldiers. The rebel enrolling-officer, who lived there, had also gone away. A number of rebel deserters came to us, who said that "they were tired of fighting for nothing; that they knew they were already whipped, and now wished to quit the rebel service." We captured twenty rebel soldiers on that day, took their horses from them, and I paroled them and turned them loose, which afforded them quite an agreeable surprise, for they doubtless expected to meet with a much harder fate. We met with a great many Union men, who eloquently related to us their many tales of severe suffering under the terrible rebel oppression.

We started back, and arrived at the encampment a little while after sunset. I at once reported to Major Lossing all that we had seen and done during the day, which seemed to afford him great satisfaction and relief, and that night all the soldiers slept soundly enough, and no terrible visions of armed rebels disturbed their quiet and peaceful repose.

Early the next morning we were all on the alert, getting something to eat and feeding our horses. We started forward, and, after marching about five miles, we observed in the road what we considered to be an infallible sign of rebels, both footmen and cavalry. We now divided the men, the major taking command of one portion of them, and myself of the other portion; the major pursued the infantry, and I started after the cavalry. I followed them on some four or five miles before I overtook them. They had left the little valley they had been traveling in, and had gone up the side of the mountain, and had went on until they had come to an indentation on the side of a ridge, where they had stopped to eat their breakfast and feed their horses. I was in the lead, and was the first one who observed them. I spoke low to my men, who were near me, and directed their attention to the rebels. Their horses were standing between them and ourselves, which prevented them from seeing us until we got within forty steps of them; they were busily engaged in dividing a ham for their breakfast. We went up to them in a gallop, and surrounded them so suddenly that they had no time to scatter. We fired four or five shots over their heads to frighten them; they offered no resistance, and all of them surrendered at once. They were well armed with sharpshooters and pistols, and had good horses. They said they were from Lee's army at Richmond, Virginia, and said that the rebel army at that place were scattering in every direction. They said they were endeavoring to get back to their homes in Georgia.

We took these prisoners on to our head-quarters at Jefferson, North Carolina, and from there they were sent on to the head-quarters of Major Reeve, at Taylorsville, Tennessee. Major Lossing returned to Jefferson that night, but had accomplished nothing, not having captured a single prisoner, and I and my men had a hearty laugh at his expense.

We passed the night at Jefferson, and the next morning we started to the town of Boone, in Watauga County, North Carolina; and when we arrived at that place we received orders to repair immediately to Greenville, Tennessee. Thereupon we started on toward Taylorsville, crossed over Rich Mountain that evening, and camped for the night on the head-waters of Stony Creek, which is in a southeast direction from Taylorsville. We could scarcely procure any thing for ourselves or for our horses to eat at this place. Some of the men succeeded in getting something to eat, while others got nothing.

Early the next morning we started forward. We passed through Taylorsville, and went on through Johnson County, and that night we again camped on Stony Creek, where we fared tolerably well. When morning came we set out on our journey, and on that evening we arrived at Johnson's Dépôt, in Washington County. The next day we went to the residence of Jacob Brown, in Washington County, and on the following day we went on to Greenville, where we arrived on the 30th day of April, 1865. General Tillson was now at Greenville with his regiments, and we were ordered to move on to North Carolina.

The day after our arrival at Greenville we set out for Ashville, North Carolina. All of the men had taken particular care to fill their haversacks with provisions, for they well knew that they were going to march through a barren country, abounding with lofty mountains, where nothing was to be seen but thickets of laurel and ivy bushes, and sharp hills and rocks. The first day we marched to Allen's Stand, on the road which leads on to Madison County, North Carolina, where we remained all night. We started

on early the next morning, but we were delayed a good
deal by the wagon-train, for the road was so narrow, and
the mountains so steep, we could not pass the wagons.
The road ran sometimes for two and three miles where the
mountain sides made it so steep that there was just room
for a wagon to pass.

When night came on we were ten miles from Ashville.
We got a little hay for our horses. There was yet nothing
to be seen but steep mountains, with now and then a little
farm in some of the coves or along the creeks, where the
hills were so steep that nothing but an oxen could stand up
to plow. On the third day after we left Greenville we arrived at Ashville. There had been some rebels there on
that morning, but a portion of the 10th Michigan Regiment
got there before us, and had run them away. We now
went into camps, and found an abundance to eat both for
ourselves and our horses.

My encampment was located on a sharp knob, where
there had been a rebel battery planted, and near the house
of an old Presbyterian minister. He was a violent rebel.
He lived in a very fine house, and owned a considerable
number of negroes. He and his lady came to me on the
evening of my arrival, and gave me a cordial invitation to
spend the night with them. I was very tired, and wished
to stay at my camp, but I could not resist their importunities, and went with them to their mansion; they were afraid
that their property would be destroyed by the soldiers. I
was very sleepy and tired, and was quite anxious for the
hour to arrive when I could retire for the night; but it was
ten o'clock before supper was announced; and, when I went
into the dining-room, I was no longer astonished at the delay which had retarded its preparation, for the table exhibited a most elegant and sumptuous appearance. I was kept

very busily employed in conversing about the Yankees, and my opinion in regard to the confiscation of the lands of the Southern people was particularly requested on several occasions. I answered all their interrogatories as well as I could, and I must confess I was greatly delighted when farther inquiry was suspended in order to make preparations for family prayer. The old gentleman read two or three chapters in the Bible, and then kneeled down to pray. I thought his supplications would extend to, the "crack of doom," for he was certainly blessed with the "gift of continuance" in a higher degree than any other divine I have ever heard address a prayer to the "throne of grace." He prayed for peace to reign once more throughout the land, and for the soldiers to return to their homes; "for," said he, "I have lost twenty negroes by the Yankees coming to North Carolina, and the country will, in all probability, be devastated and ruined; all the corn, hay, oats, and every thing else will be destroyed, for the Southern soldiers are now whipped and scattered to the four winds of the earth!" He at length concluded by reciting the Lord's Prayer, and we all arose from our knees. The family now took an affectionate leave of each other before retiring for the night, just as though they never expected to meet again "beneath the glimpses of the moon," and they proceeded to take each other by the "parting hand" with as much solemnity as if they anticipated that the Yankee soldiers would murder them before morning.

I soon became convinced that all of the rebel citizens entertained the same opinions in regard to the Yankees, and I have no doubt but that it was owing to the fact of their having invariably treated the Union people so badly. The Union men who resided at Nashville told us how the jail had been kept full of Union prisoners; and when the poor

THOMAS'S REBEL INDIANS MURDERING UNION MEN.

women would come to visit their husbands, they would also
be arrested by the rebel soldiers and put into the guard-
house, where they would be kept for two and three weeks,
subjected to the insults and ribaldry of the rebel soldiers,
who would tell them they were Lincolnites, and ought to
have negro husbands; and, after they had retained them in
confinement as long as they desired, would turn them out
and drive them away, without permitting them to see their
husbands and friends, who were languishing within the dismal walls of a filthy prison. And, besides all this, they
would make raids into Tennessee for the purpose of robbing
the people of their horses, cattle, and goods, and would
never fail to murder all the Union men they could find, and
appropriate their property to their own use. It was therefore not much wonder that the rebel citizens of North Carolina were now so greatly alarmed, for many of the men
were now with the Federal forces in that section of country who had been robbed of all their property, their houses
burned to ashes, and their families driven forth to buffet
the dark waves of adversity, while they endeavored to sus-
tain a precarious existence upon the cold charities of an unfeeling world. These vindictive rebels of North Carolina,
while they were sailing along upon the tide of the rebellion
toward the proud citadel of aristocracy, which their hopes
had erected in the dim regions of the dark, uncertain future, entirely forgot to remember that

> "Man's inhumanity to man
> Makes countless thousands mourn."

CHAPTER XLVII.

THE next thing I have to relate is the horrible massacre at Shelton Laurel, North Carolina. The place where this dreadful slaughter occurred is located in Madison County, North Carolina, adjoining Washington and Greene Counties, in Tennessee, and my road, when I was traveling backward and forward to Knoxville, passed directly through it. This settlement lies between two large mountains, one of which is called Sugar-loaf, and the other one is called White-rock Mountain, and it is twenty-five miles from any place of trade; it is situated far out in the recesses of the mountains, and a beautiful valley it was before the dark and dismal cloud of rebellion arose up in our beloved and happy country. It was first settled by several old hunters, whose names were Shelton, Heusley, and Tweede; and in order to enjoy their favorite amusement of hunting to the fullest extent, they sought an abode in this remote and desolate mountainous region of country. The population in this valley had increased very rapidly; and before the rebellion there were between eighty and one hundred voters in the settlement, and all of them being strong Union men, they totally discountenanced the idea of enlisting in the rebel service.

Shortly after the passage of the notorious conscript law by the rebel government, a heartless and blood-thirsty wretch, by the name of James Keith, came into this retired settlement with a small number of rebel soldiers, and told the citizens if they would submit to the authority of the Southern Confederacy and give up their arms they should never be troubled any more, and that they might go forward in the pursuit of their usual avocations without any farther molestation during the continuance of the war. This scoundrel, at the time of his first visit to this settlement, was occupying the position of a rebel colonel, and, consequently, the doomed citizens of this valley were the more easily circumvented by his lying tongue; doubtless thinking that a man who occupied such an elevated position in the rebel service could not possibly be so perfectly destitute of every feeling of humanity as he afterward proved himself to be.

On this occasion Keith succeeded, by his persuasive and false promises, to induce forty of these hard mountaineers to come to his encampment and deliver up their old rifles; these unfortunate men were immediately put into an old house, and a strong guard stationed around them, where they remained until he had enticed all the unsuspecting men to enter his trap that he possibly could, and then started with them to Ashville, North Carolina, where they were confined in a gloomy prison-house until a number of them were released from their miserable bondage by the hand of death, and the balance of them enlisted in the rebel army, from which they afterward deserted and made their way to the Federal lines.

On the 19th of January, 1863, Keith made another visit to this section of country for the purpose of hunting conscripts, accompanied by some four or five hundred rebel soldiers, and Samuel E. Irving, who lives in Washington County, near the red banks of Chucky River, was one of his officers. He now ordered his men to kill all the men and boys they might capture, and his companion in wicked-

S

ness and infamy, Samuel E. Irving, at once sanctioned the terrible order, saying that "it was right to kill all the boys, in order to prevent them from growing up to be Federal soldiers and bushwhackers for the Southern soldiers to have to fight." These reckless fiends soon succeeded in capturing seven men and six boys, and some of these men were far beyond the age which the conscript law had designated for the performance of military service, and, besides all this, they were not captured while scouting in the mountains, but they were arrested while they were engaged in their peaceful domestic employments.

These prisoners were retained in custody for three days, subjected to the insults and foul abuse of their rebel captors, and then Keith informed them that he was going to send them to Knoxville. When they started with their prisoners through the mountains, one of the little boys said to his father, "They are taking us a near way to Knoxville, are they not?" His father replied, "My son, they are going to kill us." The little, trembling captive then said, "Oh, father, surely they are not going to kill us; these men have been raised in a Christian land, and I hope they have better hearts than to murder us without any provocation!" This poor little innocent boy did not know that human feeling and human sympathy had been expelled from the hearts of his oppressors. Ah! little did he think that the young flower of his existence was doomed to be so early blighted by the cold and chilling frost of death!

The rebels marched their prisoners along the main road for a distance of three miles, and then turned up a hollow and went to a sink-hole about three hundred yards from the main road, where they stopped. They now told their prisoners that they might have ten minutes to pray, and, when the time had expired, they at once tied the poor men two and two together, placed them in a line to shoot them, and pulled their hats down over their eyes. They were now ordered to kneel down, and all of them obeyed the order, with the exception of David Shelton, who, when the order was given for him to kneel, indignantly replied, "I would kneel to my God, but I shall not kneel to devils!" The shooting now began, and thirteen men and boys were recklessly and brutally murdered by this inhuman gang of rebel desperadoes.

One of the little boys, when his turn came to be shot, said to the rebel murderers, "Oh, do not shoot me in my forehead, for I do not wish my blood to spoil these little curls, which my dear mother has combed and kissed so often, while she called me her darling boy." One of the fiends now shot him in the breast, but the ball failed to kill him; he crawled toward his murderers, begging them in the most piteous and heart-rending manner to have mercy on him, and to spare his life. Keith now ordered them to fire again, and several of them shot at him, but none of them hit him, for they declared that, when they presented their guns, they became so blind they could not see the little boy. Keith, with his black heart inflated to the utmost extent, with devilish malignity drew out his pistol, stepped toward him, and shot him in the head, holding the pistol so close that the very curls were burned off, which the little boy, in the simplicity of childish innocence, so earnestly desired to save from destruction. Oh, how can the miserable wretch who perpetrated this flagrant outrage expect to escape the frowns of the Almighty in this world, and also in the world to come! If he has succeeded in escaping from the measure of punishment which his monstrous crimes in this world so richly merit, he may rest assured that he will meet with his just reward when death shall have terminated his earthly existence, and transferred his guilty soul into the awful presence of the great Eternal, whose infinite mind can alone comprehend the infinitude of eternity. Truly has it been said by an eminent poet, that

> "Man, proud man, dressed in a little brief authority,
> Plays such fantastic tricks before high heaven's throne
> That make the angels weep."

And the truth of this sentiment is most admirably verified in the conduct of Keith on this occasion; for, during the period of his "brief authority," he perpetrated numerous crimes, sufficient in atrocity not only to excite the tears of pitying angels, but also to cause the whole angelic host to plead with all their eloquence for his vile name to be erased from the everlasting records of heaven, and for his soul to be cast into the dismal lake which burns with fire and brimstone, where there shall forever be "weeping, wailing, and gnashing of teeth."

While several of the men and boys who were murdered on this occasion were struggling in the last agonies of death, one of the rebel demons in human shape, who was armed with a hoe instead of a gun, would chop them on their heads with it, saying, "I never saw men so hard to kill." And, before they had ceased to struggle, the rebel soldiers began to throw them into the sink-hole, where they piled them up in a promiscuous heap, and covered them over with leaves. Some of the poor men who had not yet expired convulsively stretched out their feet from beneath the covering of the leaves, at which time some of the murderers would say, "Lay still, you old Lincolnite!" while others would say, "Where is the man with the hoe?" At this suggestion, the hardened wretch, true to the instincts of his vile nature, coolly walked up and commenced chop-

ping with his hoe on the heads and the legs of the slaughtered victims; and my informant, who was an eye-witness,
and one of the party, told me that, when the unfeeling monster discontinued his bloody work, the hoe was completely
covered with the blood and brains of the murdered men
and boys!

The dead bodies remained in the sink-hole for three weeks,
and they were then taken out for the purpose of being more
decently interred. The hogs had mangled them in a shocking manner, and they would have devoured them entirely,
had not the people in the neighborhood put them up in
order to prevent such a dreadful result. The frightened
citizens were afraid to remove the bodies of the murdered
victims until the rebel Jupiter, in the person of the villain
Keith, gave his permission for them to have the rites of
burial. It was during the season of winter, and the weather
was very cold when this massacre occurred; but notwithstanding, when a few weeping mourners went to remove
the bodies of their murdered relatives and friends, they
found that all their joints and limbs were as flexible and
pliant as if the warm blood of life was still coursing through
their veins. This occasioned a great deal of astonishment;
and it was certainly a very remarkable phenomenon in
natural science to witness the life-like appearance of these
dead bodies after they had been reposing in the cold and
icy arms of death for a period of three weeks.

And now the terrible fate which was meted out to the
wives and mothers of these poor men and boys remains to
be related. They had followed on after the rebel murderers to learn the fate of their sons and husbands, and after
the massacre was accomplished, they were then caught by
the rebels. Some of these poor defenseless women were
then stripped of their clothing, they were tied up, and their

HORRIBLE SCENES DURING THE REBELLION.

naked backs were lashed until the blood trickled down to
their feet, while the balance of them were hung up by the
neck until they were nearly dead. They were then taken
down, and their tormentors then left them tied until their
feet and hands were frozen to such a degree that their nails
all came off.

When the wives and mothers of these murdered men and
boys approached the demon Keith to request him that they
might be permitted to remove the dead bodies, so that they
might bestow upon them the last sad rites of burial, he
spoke to them in a very angry manner, saying, "You may
go and remove the bodies, but you shall not put them in
coffins nor in boxes." They then asked him if they might
wrap them in blankets before they committed them to the
cold embrace of the grave. He answered them in a very
peremptory manner, "No, you shall not take a single blanket
to wrap one of them in, for I want all the blankets I can get
for my soldiers."

The poor women, with their heads bowed down with sorrow and grief, went on to engage in their melancholy task,
followed by two degraded and brutal rebel soldiers, one of
whom called himself Doctor Roberts, and the other villain
passed under the name of Williams. And while the women
were removing the mangled bodies of the murdered men
and boys, these two rebel barbarians employed themselves
in singing indecent and unbecoming songs; they also told
the women that, if they pretended to shed a tear, they would
run their bayonets through them. Some of the women
fainted while they were engaged in this dreadful task.

The following are the names of the men and boys who
were murdered on this occasion by the black-hearted Keith
and his reckless outlaws: James Shelton, David Shelton,
Azariah Shelton, William Chandler, Wade H. Moore (fifty-

four years of age), Roderick Shelton, David Shelton, Jr., James Shelton, Jr., William Shelton, Joseph Woods, Allison King, Halen Moore, and James Metcalfe.

The following are the names of the women who were hung up by their necks until they were nearly dead by these merciless scoundrels: Mrs. Riddle, who was seventy years of age; Mrs. Moore, who was fifty-four years of age; Nancy Hall, and Nancy Shelton.

After Keith and his band of murderers had almost entirely ruined the people of Shelton Laurel, he left the country; and I have been informed by a number of the citizens who reside in that neighborhood that the next rebel destroyer that visited that doomed section of country was the redoubtable General Alfred E. Jackson, or General "Mudwall" Jackson, which is the title under which he was generally known during his military career in the rebellion. In his expedition to this section of country he was accompanied by his son, who passed under the appellation of Captain Jackson. When Jackson arrived, he ordered eight or ten families to be moved into one house, and in this way he had nearly all the houses vacated, with the exception of a few which contained the women and children, and these he had closely guarded. He ordered all the vacant houses to be burned to ashes, and he also gave orders for all the stock in the country to be destroyed. He adopted this method, he said, in order to starve the Union men out of the mountains, so that they would be compelled to come in and join the Confederate army. It was now February, the snow was deep, and the weather was extremely cold.

The rebel soldiers would build up large fires out of fence-rails, and lay around them, while the shivering women and children in the houses were not permitted to have any fire at all. Sometimes the little children would go to the fires where the rebel soldiers were, to warm their aching hands and feet; the rebels would then compel them to stand so close to the burning flames that the little innocent creatures would scream out in severe agony of suffering; and, when their mothers would approach to rescue them, the rebels would present their pistols, and tell them, if they attempted to relieve their children, they would blow a ball through them. The poor women would therefore be compelled to stand and witness the dreadful suffering and the cruel torture of their children without being able to afford them any relief, while the rebel miscreants would laugh loudly, and exhibit the utmost demonstrations of delight at the shocking and savage spectacle which the suffering children presented when the hot flames of fire were burning their tender flesh.

The women and children suffered greatly for something to eat, for the rebels devoured all their provisions. At times, while the rebel soldiers would be cooking and eating, the poor little famished children would softly approach them and beg for a piece of bread; but they would receive an abrupt denial, and the rebel scoundrels would say to them, " You must do without bread, or else you must go to Old Abe for it; we want all that we have for ourselves!" Very frequently it occurred that, for a whole day together, these poor women and children could not obtain any thing at all to eat.

This gang of rebel soldiers remained in this neighborhood for eighteen or twenty days, and then returned to Greenville. After all their active operations, they only succeeded in murdering one man. But before leaving they went to the house of a poor widow by the name of Lucinda Carter, and killed fourteen hogs, and laid them in a pile on the floor of her dwelling-house; they then killed her house-dog, and laid it on the top of the pile of hogs. They ar-

S 2

rested several women, and took them on to Greenville with them, where they were detained for several days, subjected to gross abuse and indignity, while their little children remained at their gloomy and desolate homes, suffering all the terrible afflictions which cold and hunger could produce.

Shelton Laurel having now been thoroughly ravaged and despoiled of all its internal resources, the people who resided there were consequently in a dreadful extremity, for nearly all of their humble habitations were burned to the ground, the grain and stock were all destroyed, and many poor families were left in a perfect state of starvation.

After Jackson left this section of country in the winter of 1863, the notorious Colonel James Keith, Captain William Keith, and Riley Keith, were detailed in the fall of the same year to hunt for conscripts in the mountains of North Carolina, and also in the adjoining counties in the State of Tennessee. These scoundrels visited Shelton Laurel again in the month of September, and burned a number of houses belonging to Union men. They murdered John Metcalfe by shooting him in the head and running their bayonets through him six times. They also murdered Robert Hare by shooting him three times. Their next victim was Marion Franklin. He was plowing in the field, perfectly unconscious of his dreadful doom, when one of the rebel outlaws walked up to the fence and shot him in the hip. When the ball struck him, he ran to a large stump which was surrounded with bushes and laid down; there he remained for a short time, writhing and groaning with severe agony of pain, until his murderers came up, and relieved him from his misery by shooting him in the breast.

These infamous murderers went coolly and calmly along in their horrible work of destruction and death. The next victims who had the misfortune of falling into their hands

were Tilman Landers, Absalom Brucks, and a little boy, all
of whom they caught at Mrs. Ruth Shelton's stable, and
were unceremoniously murdered on the spot.   They caught
David Shelton at his house, and hung him until he was
dead, and then dragged him to a laurel thicket, where they
covered him over with leaves. A few women afterward
removed his body, and gave it a more humane burial.   In
the month of July, 1864, these rebel demons caught five
more men in Shelton Laurel, and murdered all of them in a
most shocking and barbarous manner.   The five men whom
they murdered on this occasion were Isaac Shelton, Hamp-
ton Burget, old David Shelton, William Shelton, Jr., and
William Fillmore, making, in all, forty-seven men and boys
who were brutally murdered by Keith and his vile assassins
at different times during the progress of the iniquitous rebellion.   The reader will doubtless think that this depraved
scoundrel run the conscript law with a vengeance.   Oh,
what a terrible record this will be for him to meet with in
eternity, where he will have to appear before the great Omnipotent Judge of the universe, confronted by forty-seven
immortal souls, who by him, and through his instrumental-
ity, were deprived of their earthly existence, and suddenly
hurled into the eternal world!   The awful groans of his
murdered victims will surely haunt him while he lives in
the world, plant thorns upon his death-bed, and, when he
sinks down into the dismal regions of everlasting despair,
they will forever afford a keen torture to his guilty and
never-dying soul.   When he was engaged in his abomina-
ble work of murdering his fellow-men, he doubtless forgot
to remember that

>   "There's a divinity that shapes our ends,
>   Rough hew them as we may;"

and when he shall have been summoned to appear before

the inflexible bar of the infinite Jehovah, where he will
meet his murdered victims face to face, and when they shall
severally arise and reproach him with the awful crime of
murder, he will then stand, like a convicted criminal, trembling beneath his oppressive load of guilt; and the only re-
sponse which he will then be able to make to the dreadful
accusations of his accusers will be, guilty! guilty!! guilty!!!

CHAPTER XLVIII.

I REMAINED at Ashville four days after the events related in Chapter XLVI., and on the 5th of May I was ordered to take a scout of forty men and go out toward Waynesville, to see if there were any rebels. We traveled the main road for three miles before we saw a single rebel, but now we could see them on the hills before us, apparently watching our movements; and whenever we would get close to them they would instantly leave, and go on to another high point, where they would remain until we again approached them. I was not very well pleased at this mode of operation, and determined at once to change the order of our march. I therefore divided my men, and, after directing a portion of them to travel along the road in order to attract the notice of the rebels, I took the other part of my men and went around the ridge to head them. We went at a double-quick speed through the woods and along the little paths until we got ahead of them, and then we returned to the road again; we now had them between us, and, making a sudden charge, we succeeded in capturing several of the rebels, while many of them got away into the woods, leaving us their horses and their equipage.

We went on with our prisoners about eight miles farther; they told us that there were a number of rebel soldiers stationed on Big Pigeon River, who intended to give us a fight; but this was farther off than we could go, for we had to report at Ashville on that night. We therefore turned our course, and arrived safely back at our camp in the evening with our prisoners and ten head of good horses. I reported to General Tillson, and he paroled the prisoners, and I returned to my quarters. The soldiers who had been with me passed the night in eating and talking about their adventures during the day, and laughing about the terrible excitement of the rebels when they sprang off of their horses and ran so violently through the woods.

On the next morning I was ordered to go to Franklin, North Carolina, which was about sixty or seventy miles distant, to act as picket for the 2d North Carolina Infantry, commanded by Colonel Bartlett, and also to see where the rebels were. We started in advance of the regiment, and, after we had traveled about ten miles, the citizens told us that the rebels would give us a fight at a place called the Narrows, which was a narrow pass between two large ridges. I reported this information to Colonel Bartlett, and he proceeded to furnish me with some men who were well acquainted with the country, and ordered me to leave the main road and cross over the mountain, and come into the main road on the opposite side of the Narrows, and then pass on through and return to the main force again. I told him if he would push up about the time that I should arrive at the opposite side of the Narrows, we would then be sure to capture the rebels without much difficulty. But the colonel would not consent to this proposition. He told me that I and my men must go on over the mountain, and then return to him through the Narrows, so that we might see if there were any rebels there, and that he would remain stationary until we returned.

Finding that it was altogether unnecessary to argue the matter with the colonel any farther, I took my scout of men

and started. It was a severe task for our horses to climb
the steep precipices on the side of the mountain, and when
we got across to Big Pigeon River, some distance above
the point where the rebels had been reported to be stationed, it was quite dark, and the rain was falling rapidly.
We soon began to find scattering gangs of rebels, and
caught some of them at almost every house, where they
were waiting for the rain to cease falling, so that they
might travel with greater comfort. We passed ourselves
off for rebels going to Waynesville; and when we would
get to a house, I would ask if there were any of the boys
who had not gone on yet? · They would at once answer in
the affirmative, and would then come walking out as calmly
as a "summer's morning," entirely unsuspecting of any design on our part to make them prisoners, when we would
at once take possession of them and their horses. We continued to capture them in this way at almost every house,
until we got all of them who were scattered along our road.
Our prisoners told us that there were rebel soldiers at the
ford of Big Pigeon River, but we could not go there on
that night. They said there were three or four hundred
rebel soldiers there, when they were all together, and that
they would be certain to give us a fight if we went there.

We went on through the Narrows that night, and I reported to Colonel Bartlett; I turned over the rebel prisoners to him, and he proceeded to parole them. I also turned
over twenty-one head of horses and six mules, which I and
my men had captured from the rebels during that night.
It was still raining when we returned to the regiment, and
we were all very wet and hungry, but we had to sit under trees until morning. As soon as daylight made its appearance the colonel ordered me to take another scout of
men, and go on back through the Narrows to the ford of

Pigeon River where it was reported the rebels were stationed.

I collected my men together, and started on toward the ford of Pigeon River, which was ten miles distant. We went on until we came in sight of the place of our destination; we went up on a ridge, and when we looked toward the ford of the river we saw that the rebels were leaving, or, rather, it was their rear which we saw, for the last man was just about getting out of our sight when we looked in the direction which the rebel force had started to travel. We went on to the ford of the river, where we waited for the regiment to come up. We foraged among the people, and got something for ourselves and our horses to eat, and then built up fires to dry our clothes.

When the regiment came up we moved six miles farther down the river, to a place where a lot of corn had been stored up for Thomas and his Indians. Our horses fared well that night, and next morning I was ordered to take a scout and go to Waynesville. I gathered all the horses, and started early, for we expected to meet with Thomas and his Indians, for we were now in Haywood County, North Carolina, where they lived. When we got within a mile of Waynesville, I placed my men four deep in the road, and I leading the way, we charged into the town, but, as usual, the rebels were all gone. Some of the citizens told us that they had just left, and we could not doubt what they told us, for the fresh tracks of their horses were quite visible in the road which they traveled when they left the town.

Some of the citizens told us that the rebel force which had just vacated their town never intended to surrender, but were going to fight on to the bitter end for Haywood and Jackson Counties. We did not tarry at this place ten minutes, for we immediately mounted our horses and started in pursuit of them. We had not proceeded more than half a mile until I saw them returning to the town again; I was still leading my men, and I saw that we would meet the rebels at a turn in the road, which was some distance ahead. We were riding in a slow gallop, and I perceived that the rebels were meeting us at the same rate of speed. I never spoke to my men, but I drew out one of my navy pistols, and when we got within about fifty yards of the rebels they saw us for the first time. As soon as I discovered that they had seen us, I fired at the men who were in front, and called loudly on my men to charge them. The rebels quickly wheeled their horses round, and started on the back track in the greatest confusion imaginable; they ran in every direction, and many of them sprang off of their horses and plunged into the dense thickets of laurel and ivy bushes, which at once saved them from any farther pursuit.

We got their horses, guns, hats, blankets, overcoats, and saddle-pockets, which they had scattered all along the road. We captured one captain and one lieutenant. We also charged on Major M'Dowell, and came so near capturing him that he was compelled to leave his horse and take to the bushes to save himself. I captured his horse, coat, and saddle-pockets, and run him through a swamp, where he made the mud and water fly higher than his head as he passed through it; but I could not overtake him. We continued to pursue the flying rebels until we got within about three hundred yards of their fortifications; we then fell back about one mile, and I immediately sent word to Colonel Bartlett to move on up or send me re-enforcements, so that I might go on and disperse or capture the rebels who were stationed in the gap of the mountain. They were now in

Jackson County, having already been forced to evacuate
Haywood County. Our prisoners told us that their companions intended to fight for Jackson County. They cursed
Haywood most vehemently, while they spoke in the highest
terms of Jackson County, saying that the bravest men came
from that county.

Colonel Bartlett ordered me back to the regiment, which
was now at Waynesville; and when he heard that the rebels
were stationed in front of him, and that we had been fighting them, he immediately ordered his men to cut down trees
across the road, and also to make intrenchments to fight in.
When he ordered me back I went to him, and tried to persuade him to march forward and give the rebels a fight; for
he was commanding an infantry regiment, and therefore his
men could get through the bushes and brush in pursuit of
the enemy much better than we could on horses; and I also
told him that my company was entirely too small for me to
presume to go into a regular engagement with them.

I must confess that I was exceedingly anxious to give this
force of rebels a fight; for Thomas and his Indians were
among them, and I desired to kill some of them for the
mischief they had done in the upper counties of East Tennessee when they were engaged in catching conscripts,
murdering white men, plundering houses, and frightening
women and children to death; and, taking all these things
into consideration, I was in favor of killing all the Indians
that might fall into our hands.

But the colonel was inexorable, for he would not consent
to go himself, neither would he agree to furnish me with re-
enforcements. We remained three days at Waynesville,
and during this time Colonel Kirk came in at Franklin;
consequently, all the rebels who were now between the two
Federal forces at once surrendered, and were paroled. Col.

onel Bartlett was now ordered to meet Kirk at Franklin, but he disobeyed the order, and remained where he was for a week. He then received orders to return to Ashville with his regiment, and I was ordered to take my scout and proceed to Franklin, to carry a dispatch to Colonel Kirk.

Early in the night we started to Franklin with the dispatch. We had to travel through Jackson County, and also had to pass through Webster, where it was reported there were a parcel of rebel soldiers who declared they would not surrender; and it was also reported that the mountains were full of bushwhackers. It was a fine country for such business, the sides of the mountains being very steep and rough, and covered all over with large rocks, where bushwhackers could conceal themselves and shoot down at the traveler with perfect safety.

After we had traveled about six miles, we came to the trees which had recently been cut down across the road by the rebels to prevent the onward progress of the Yankees; and at some places, in order to make the blockade of the road more complete, they had rolled down large rocks from the side of the mountain. We had a severe time in getting through this place; and after we had traveled until two o'clock in the night, we came to a stable which had a parcel of fodder stored away in it. Here we stopped and fed our horses for a short time, and then started on again. Just at daylight we arrived at the town of Webster, which we immediately surrounded, as we fully intended to give the rebels a fight if they still remained there. The morning was very foggy, which rendered it impossible for us to see but a very short distance before us after daylight appeared. But after a short time the fog cleared away, and we then searched throughout the whole town, but there was not a rebel soldier to be found. We now instituted a search for something to eat, but we soon became convinced that provisions were equally as hard to find as rebel soldiers, for we entirely failed to procure any thing at all for either ourselves or our horses to eat.

We traveled on eight miles farther, when we obtained enough of provision and forage to supply us until we arrived at Franklin, which was late in the evening. We found Colonel Kirk and part of his regiment here. They had taken the town without a fight, and had captured several rebel officers, together with a good many privates, all of whom the colonel had already paroled. The colonel was glad to see us, for he was under the impression that the road had been too thoroughly blockaded by the rebels to be traveled. After reading the dispatch, he remarked that he was very sorry that he had been ordered to return to Tennessee so soon, as there were more rebels whom he desired to chastise before he returned.

We now found something to eat for ourselves, and also for our horses. We remained here two nights and one day, and then started back toward Ashville. We started early, and went on to Webster, where we again endeavored to get provision; but we were unable to find any thing, with the exception of a small lot of forage for our horses, which we put in our sacks, and went on some four or five miles farther, where we stopped for the night. We found provision and forage very scarce. We started early the next morning, and on that evening we arrived at Waynesville, without having had a single gun fired at us by the rebels. We remained two days at this place, and then went on to Ashville, where we again met with Colonel Bartlett; and, after resting for two days, we set out for Greenville, Tennessee— our own old home.

We were unable to get any forage to take with us, and

consequently we had to travel sixty miles before we succeeded in getting any thing for ourselves or for our horses to eat. There had been so many troops passing the road from Greenville to North Carolina that nearly every thing in the country which man and beast could eat had already been consumed, and the truth is, there never had been any great abundance of provision and forage in this whole section of country; for along the whole distance from Greenville to Ashville the face of the country is exceedingly rough, which at once forbids the idea of successful farming operations. In fact, there is nothing to be seen but lofty mountains on all sides, and at some places there are large rocks hanging over the road at an altitude of from two to three hundred feet. At some places along the road the traveler is unable to see any thing but rocks for the distance of a mile, and the bottoms on the little farms along the rivers are so narrow that a stone could be thrown across them with ease. In passing along the road, I frequently observed where foundations had been dug out in the side of the mountain, for the purpose of building cabins, shops, or still-houses. This is the sort of country through which we now had to pass in our march to Greenville. Surely, if an Attila or a Tamerlane had marched along this road with their desolating armies, they could not have cleared the country more thoroughly of provision and forage.

Even the men that we met in our march displayed the very roughest specimens of the "human form divine," for their faces looked as rough as a walnut, and as tough as a whalebone, and their naked feet appeared to be so rough and hard, that I have no doubt they could have tramped chestnuts out of the burns without feeling the least sensation of pain from the operation. They could run all over these high mountains in pursuit of a bear or a deer; and whenever they succeeded in killing a large buck, any one of the party could take it on his shoulder and carry it for a number of miles to his mountain home.

We passed by the Warm Springs which are located in Buncombe County, North Carolina, immediately on the road leading from Greenville, Tennessee, to Ashville, North Carolina. This place is quite a fashionable resort for many of the wealthy Southern citizens, who prefer going to the mountains to pass away the hot summer months.

We arrived at Greenville, Tennessee, on the 21st day of May, 1865, and on the 23d of May I received orders from General Gillem to proceed forthwith to the counties of Carter, Johnson, Sullivan, and Washington, to arrest all absentees belonging to his command. I accomplished this task to the perfect satisfaction of the general, and returned to his head-quarters at Lenoir's Station on the 8th day of June. General Gillem remained at this place a short time, and then removed his forces to Sweet Water; from thence he moved back to Knoxville, where I received an honorable discharge from the military service of the United States on the 5th day of September, 1865.

THE END.

www.ingramcontent.com/pod-product-compliance
Lightning Source LLC
Chambersburg PA
CBHW021327110726
47900CB00005B/1387